P9-CNI-250

Bestselling author Tess Gerritsen is also a doctor, and she brings to her novels her first-hand knowledge of emergency and autopsy rooms.

But her interests span far more than medical topics. As an anthropology undergraduate at Stanford University, she catalogued centuries-old human remains, and continues to travel the world, driven by her fascination with ancient cultures and bizarre natural phenomena.

Now a full-time novelist, she lives with her husband in Maine.

For more information about Tess Gerritsen and her novels, visit her website at www.tessgerritsen.co.uk

HAVE YOU READ THEM ALL?

The thrillers featuring Jane Rizzoli and Maura Isles are:

THE SURGEON

**Introducing Detective Jane Rizzoli of the
Boston Homicide Unit**
In Boston, there's a killer on the loose. A killer who
targets lone women and performs ritualistic acts of
torture before finishing them off . . .

'If you've never read Gerritsen, figure in the price of electricity
when you buy your first novel by her, 'cause, baby, you are going
to be up all night'
Stephen King

THE APPRENTICE

The surgeon has been locked up for a year, but his chilling legacy
still haunts the city, and especially
Boston homicide detective Jane Rizzoli . . .

'Gerritsen has enough in her locker to seriously worry Michael
Connelly, Harlan Coben and even the great Dennis Lehane.
Brilliant'
Crime Time

THE SINNER

Long-buried secrets are revealed as Dr Maura Isles and detective
Jane Rizzoli find themselves part of an investigation that leads to
the awful truth.

'Gutsy, energetic and shocking'
Manchester Evening News

BODY DOUBLE

Dr Maura Isles has seen more than her share of
corpses. But never has the body on the autopsy table been her
own . . .

'It's scary just how good Tess Gerritsen is. This is crime writing at
its unputdownable, nerve-tingling best'
Harlan Coben

VANISH

When medical examiner Maura Isles looks down at the body of a
beautiful woman she gets the fright of her life. The corpse opens its
eyes . . .

'A horrifying tangle of rape, murder and blackmail'
Guardian

THE MEPHISTO CLUB

Can you really see evil when you look into
someone's eyes? Dr Maura Isles and detective Jane Rizzoli
encounter evil in its purest form.

'Gruesome, seductive and creepily credible'
Peter Millar, *The Times*

THE BONE GARDEN

Boston 1830: A notorious serial killer preys on his victims, flitting
from graveyards and into maternity wards. But no one knows who
he is . . .

'Fascinating . . . gory . . . a fast-paced novel that will leave you
with a real appreciation of just how far medicine has come in the
past century'
Mail on Sunday

**Have you read the thrillers that first made
Tess Gerritsen a crime-writing star?**

HARVEST

How far would you go to save a life? A young
surgical resident is drawn into the deadly world
of organ smuggling.

'Suspense as sharp as a scalpel's edge. A page-turning, hold your
breath read'
Tami Hoag

LIFE SUPPORT

A terrifying and deadly epidemic is about
to be unleashed . . .

'If you like your crime medicine strong, this will
keep you gripped'
Mail on Sunday

KEEPING THE DEAD

TESS GERRITSEN

BANTAM BOOKS

LONDON • TORONTO • SYDNEY • AUCKLAND • JOHANNESBURG

TRANSWORLD PUBLISHERS
61–63 Uxbridge Road, London W5 5SA
A Random House Group Company
www.rbooks.co.uk

KEEPING THE DEAD
A BANTAM BOOK: 9780553818383

First published in Great Britain
in 2008 by Bantam Press
an imprint of Transworld Publishers
Bantam edition published 2009

Copyright © Tess Gerritsen 2008

Tess Gerritsen has asserted her right under the Copyright, Designs and
Patents Act 1988 to be identified as the author of this work.

This book is a work of fiction and, except in the case of historical fact, any
resemblance to actual persons, living or dead, is purely coincidental.

A CIP catalogue record for this book
is available from the British Library.

This book is sold subject to the condition that it shall not,
by way of trade or otherwise, be lent, resold, hired out,
or otherwise circulated without the publisher's prior
consent in any form of binding or cover other than that
in which it is published and without a similar condition,
including this condition, being imposed on the
subsequent purchaser.

Addresses for Random House Group Ltd companies outside the UK
can be found at: www.randomhouse.co.uk
The Random House Group Ltd Reg. No. 954009

The Random House Group Limited supports The Forest Stewardship
Council (FSC), the leading international forest certification organisation. All
our titles that are printed on Greenpeace approved FSC certified paper carry
the FSC logo. Our paper procurement policy can be found at
www.rbooks.co.uk/environment

Typeset in 11/14pt Sabon by
Falcon Oast Graphic Art Ltd.
Printed in the UK by CPI Cox & Wyman, Reading, RG1 8EX.

4 6 8 10 9 7 5 3

To Adam and Joshua,
for whom the sun doth shine

ACKNOWLEDGMENTS

I owe a huge debt of thanks to Dr. Jonathan Elias of the Akhmim Mummy Studies Consortium, and to Joann Potter of the Vassar College Frances Lehman Loeb Art Center, for allowing me to share in the excitement of Shep-en-Min's CT scan. Many thanks as well to Linda Marrow for her brilliant editorial suggestions, to Selina Walker for her keen insights, and to my tireless literary agent, Meg Ruley of the Jane Rotrosen Agency.

Most of all, I thank my husband, Jacob. For everything.

Every mummy is an exploration, an undiscovered continent that you're visiting for the very first time.

—DR. JONATHAN ELIAS, Egyptologist

KEEPING THE DEAD

1

He is coming for me.

I feel it in my bones. I sniff it in the air, as recognizable as the scent of hot sand and savory spices and the sweat of a hundred men toiling in the sun. These are the smells of Egypt's western desert, and they are still vivid to me, although that country is nearly half a globe away from the dark bedroom where I now lie. Fifteen years have passed since I walked that desert, but when I close my eyes, in an instant I am there again, standing at the edge of the tent camp, looking toward the Libyan border, and the sunset. The wind moaned like a woman when it swept down the wadi. I still hear the thuds of pickaxes and the scrape of shovels, can picture the army of Egyptian diggers, busy as ants as they swarmed the excavation site, hauling their gufa baskets filled with soil. It seemed to me then, when I stood in that desert fifteen years ago, as if I were an actress in a film about someone else's adventure. Not mine. Certainly it was not an adventure that a quiet girl from Indio, California, ever expected to live.

The lights of a passing car glimmer through my closed eyelids. When I open my eyes, Egypt vanishes. No longer am I standing in the desert gazing at a sky smeared by sunset the color of bruises. Instead I am once again half a world away, lying in my dark San Diego bedroom.

I climb out of bed and walk barefoot to the window to look out at the street. It is a tired neighborhood of stucco tract homes built in the 1950s, before the American dream meant mini mansions and three-car garages. There is honesty in the modest but sturdy houses, built not to impress but to shelter, and I feel safely anonymous here. Just another single mother struggling to raise a recalcitrant teenage daughter.

Peeking through the curtains at the street, I see a dark-colored sedan slow down half a block away. It pulls over to the curb, and the headlights turn off. I watch, waiting for the driver to step out, but no one does. For a long time the driver sits there. Perhaps he's listening to the radio, or maybe he's had a fight with his wife and is afraid to face her. Perhaps there are lovers in that car with nowhere else to go. I can formulate so many explanations, none of them alarming, yet my skin is prickling with hot dread.

A moment later the sedan's taillights come back on, and the car pulls away and continues down the street.

Even after it vanishes around the corner, I am still

jittery, clutching the curtains in my damp hand. I return to bed and lie sweating on top of the covers, but I cannot sleep. Although it's a warm July night, I keep my bedroom window latched, and insist that my daughter, Tari, keeps hers latched as well. But Tari does not always listen to me.

Every day, she listens to me less.

I close my eyes and, as always, the visions of Egypt come back. It's always to Egypt that my thoughts return. Even before I stood on its soil, I'd dreamed about it. At six years old, I spotted a photograph of the Valley of the Kings on the cover of *National Geographic,* feeling instant recognition, as though I were looking at a familiar, much-beloved face that I had almost forgotten. That was what the land meant to me, a beloved face I longed to see again.

And as the years progressed, I laid the foundations for my return. I worked and studied. A full scholarship brought me to Stanford, and to the attention of a professor who enthusiastically recommended me for a summer job at an excavation in Egypt's western desert.

In June, at the end of my junior year, I boarded a flight to Cairo.

Even now, in the darkness of my California bedroom, I remember how my eyes ached from the sunlight glaring on white-hot sand. I smell the sunscreen on my skin and feel the sting of the wind peppering my face with desert grit. These memories make me happy. With a trowel in my hand and the sun on my shoulders, this was the culmination of a young girl's dreams.

How quickly dreams become nightmares. I'd boarded the plane to Cairo as a happy college student. Three months later, I returned home a changed woman.

I did not come back from the desert alone. A monster followed me.

In the dark, my eyelids spring open. Was that a footfall? A door creaking open? I lie on damp sheets, heart battering itself against my chest. I am afraid to get out of bed, and afraid not to.

Something is not right in this house.

After years of hiding, I know better than to ignore the warning whispers in my head. Those urgent whispers are the only reason I am still alive. I've learned to pay heed to every anomaly, every tremor of disquiet. I notice unfamiliar cars driving up my street. I snap to attention if a co-worker mentions that someone was asking about me. I make elaborate escape plans long before I ever need them. My next move is already planned out. In two hours, my daughter and I can be over the border and in Mexico with new identities. Our passports, with new names, are already tucked away in my suitcase.

We should have left by now. We should not have waited this long.

But how do you convince a fourteen-year-old girl to move away from her friends? Tari is the problem; she does not understand the danger we're in.

I pull open the nightstand drawer and take out the gun. It is not legally registered, and it makes me nervous, keeping a firearm under the same roof with my daughter. But after six weekends at the shooting range, I know how to use it.

My bare feet are silent as I step out of my room and move down the hall, past my daughter's closed door. I conduct the same inspection that I have made a thousand times before, always in the dark. Like any prey, I feel safest in the dark.

In the kitchen, I check the windows and the door. In the living room, I do the same. Everything is secure. I come back up the hall and pause outside my daughter's bedroom. Tari has become fanatical about her privacy, but there is no lock on her door, and I will never allow there to be one. I need to be able to look in, to confirm that she is safe.

The door gives a loud squeak as I open it, but it won't wake her. As with most teenagers, her sleep is akin to a coma. The first thing I notice is the breeze, and I give a sigh. Once again, Tari has ignored my wishes and left her window wide open, as she has so many times before.

It feels like sacrilege, bringing the gun into my daughter's bedroom, but I need to close that window. I step inside and pause beside the bed, watching her sleep, listening to the steady rhythm of her breathing. I remember the first time I laid eyes on her, red-faced and crying in the obstetrician's hands. I had been in labor eighteen hours, and was so exhausted I could barely lift my head from the pillow. But after one glimpse of my baby, I would have risen from bed and fought a legion of attackers to protect her. That was the moment I knew what her name would be. I thought of the words carved into the great temple at Abu Simbel, words chosen by Ramses the Great to proclaim his love for his wife.

NEFERTARI, FOR WHOM THE SUN DOTH SHINE

My daughter, Nefertari, is the one and only treasure that I brought back with me from Egypt. And I am terrified of losing her.

Tari is so much like me. It's as if I am watching myself sleeping. When she was ten years old, she could already read hieroglyphs. At twelve, she could recite all the dynasties down to the Ptolemys. She spends her weekends haunting the Museum of Man. She is a clone of me in every way, and as the years pass there is no obvious trace of her father in her face or her voice or, most important of all, her soul. She is my daughter, mine alone, untainted by the evil that fathered her.

But she is also a normal fourteen-year-old girl, and this has been a source of frustration these past weeks as I've felt darkness closing in around us, as I lie awake every night, listening for a monster's footsteps. My daughter is oblivious to the danger because I have hidden the truth from her. I want her to grow up strong and fearless, a warrior woman who is unafraid of shadows. She does not understand why I pace the house late at night, why I latch the windows and double-check the doors. She thinks I am a worrywart, and it's true: I do all the worrying for both of us, to preserve the illusion that all is right with the world.

That is what Tari believes. She likes San Diego and she looks forward to her first year in high school. She's managed to make friends here, and heaven help the parent who tries to come between a teenager and her friends. She is as strong-willed as I am, and were it not for her resistance, we would have left town weeks ago.

A breeze blows in the window, chilling the sweat on my skin.

I set the gun down on the nightstand and cross to the window to close it. For a moment I linger, breathing in cool air. Outside, the night has fallen silent, except for a mosquito's whine. A prick stings my cheek. The significance of that mosquito bite does not strike me until I reach up to slide the window shut. I feel the icy breath of panic rush up my spine.

There is no screen over the window. *Where is the screen?*

Only then do I sense the malevolent presence. While I stood lovingly watching my daughter, *it* was watching me. It has always been watching, biding its time, waiting for its chance to spring. Now it has found us.

I turn and face the evil.

2

Dr. Maura Isles could not decide whether to stay or to flee.

She lingered in the shadows of the Pilgrim Hospital parking lot, well beyond the glare of the klieg lights, beyond the circle of TV cameras. She had no wish to be spotted, and most local reporters would recognize the striking woman whose pale face and bluntly cut black hair had earned her the nickname Queen of the Dead. As yet no one had noticed Maura's arrival, and not a single camera was turned in her direction. Instead, the dozen reporters were fully focused on a white van that had just pulled up at the hospital's lobby entrance to unload its famous passenger. The van's rear doors swung open and a lightning storm of camera flashes lit up the night as the celebrity patient was gently lifted out of the van and placed onto a hospital gurney. This patient was a media star whose newfound fame far outshone any mere medical examiner's. Tonight Maura was merely part of the awestruck audience, drawn here for the same reason the reporters had converged like frenzied groupies outside the hospital on a warm Sunday night.

All were eager to catch a glimpse of Madam X.

Maura had faced reporters many times before, but the rabid hunger of this mob alarmed her. She knew that if some new prey wandered into their field of vision, their attention could shift in an instant, and tonight she was already feeling emotionally bruised and vulnerable. She considered escaping the scrum by turning around and climbing back into her car. But all that awaited her at home was a silent house and perhaps a few too many glasses of wine to keep her company on a night when Daniel Brophy could not. Lately there were far too many such nights, but that was the bargain she had struck by falling in love with him. The heart makes its choices without weighing the consequences. It doesn't look ahead to the lonely nights that follow.

The gurney carrying Madam X rolled into the hospital, and the wolf pack of reporters chased after it. Through the glass lobby doors, Maura saw bright lights and excited faces, while outside in the parking lot she stood alone.

She followed the entourage into the building.

The gurney rolled through the lobby, past hospital visitors who stared in astonishment, past excited hospital staff waiting with their camera phones to snap photos. The parade moved on, turning down the hall-way and toward Diagnostic Imaging. But at an inner doorway, only the gurney was allowed through. A hospital official in suit and tie stepped forward and blocked the reporters from going any farther.

"I'm afraid we'll have to stop you right here," he said. "I know you all want to watch this, but the room's very small." He raised his hands to silence the dis-appointed grumbles. "My name is Phil Lord. I'm the public relations officer for Pilgrim Hospital, and we're thrilled to be part of this study, since a patient like Madam X comes along only every, well, two thousand years." He smiled at the expected laughter. "The CT scan won't take long, so if you're willing to wait, one of the archaeologists will come out immediately afterward to announce the results." He turned to a pale man of about forty who'd retreated into a corner, as though hoping he would not be noticed. "Dr. Robinson, before we start, would you like to say a few words?"

Addressing this crowd was clearly the last thing the bespectacled man wanted to do, but he gamely took a breath and stepped forward, nudging his drooping glasses back up the bridge of his beakish nose. This archaeologist bore no resemblance at all to Indiana Jones. With his receding hairline and studious squint, he looked more like an accountant caught in the unwelcome glare of the cameras. "I'm Dr. Nicholas Robinson," he said. "I'm curator at—"

"Could you speak up, Doctor?" one of the reporters called out.

"Oh, sorry." Dr. Robinson cleared his throat. "I'm curator at the Crispin Museum here in Boston. We are immensely grateful that Pilgrim Hospital has so generously offered to perform this CT scan of Madam X. It's an extraordinary opportunity to catch an intimate glimpse into the past, and judging by the size of this crowd, you're all as excited as we are. My colleague Dr. Josephine Pulcillo, who is an Egyptologist, will come out to speak to you after the scan is completed. She'll announce the results and answer any questions then."

"When will Madam X go on display for the public?" a reporter called out.

"Within the week, I expect," said Robinson. "The new exhibit's already been built and—"

"Any clues to her identity?"

"Why hasn't she been on display before?"

"Could she be royal?"

"I don't know," said Robinson, blinking rapidly under the assault of so many questions. "We still need to confirm it's a female."

"You found it six months ago, and you still don't know the sex?"

"These analyses take time."

"One glance oughta do it," a reporter said, and the crowd laughed.

"It's not as simple as you think," said Robinson, his

glasses slipping down his nose again. "At two thousand years old, she's extremely fragile and she must be handled with great care. I found it nerve-racking enough just transporting her here tonight, in that van. Our first priority as a museum is preservation. I consider myself her guardian, and it's my duty to protect her. That's why we've taken our time co-ordinating this scan with the hospital. We move slowly, and we move with care."

"What do you hope to learn from this CT scan tonight, Dr. Robinson?"

Robinson's face suddenly lit up with enthusiasm. "Learn? Why, everything! Her age, her health. The method of her preservation. If we're fortunate, we may even discover the cause of her death."

"Is that why the medical examiner's here?"

The whole group turned like a multieyed creature and stared at Maura, who had been standing at the back of the room. She felt the familiar urge to back away as the TV cameras swung her way.

"Dr. Isles," a reporter called out, "are you here to make a diagnosis?"

"Why is the ME's office involved?" another asked.

That last question needed an immediate answer, before the issue got twisted by the press.

Maura said, firmly: "The medical examiner's office is not involved. It's certainly not paying me to be here tonight."

"But you are here," said Channel 5's blond hunk, whom Maura had never liked.

"At the invitation of the Crispin Museum. Dr. Robinson thought it might be helpful to have a medical examiner's perspective on this case. So he called me last week to ask if I wanted to observe the scan. Believe me, any pathologist would jump at this chance. I'm as fascinated by Madam X as you are, and I can't wait to meet her." She looked pointedly at the curator. "Isn't it about time to begin, Dr. Robinson?"

She'd just tossed him an escape line, and he grabbed it. "Yes. Yes, it's time. If you'll come with me, Dr. Isles."

She cut through the crowd and followed him into the Imaging Department. As the door closed behind them, shutting them off from the press, Robinson blew out a long sigh.

"God, I'm terrible at public speaking," he said. "Thank you for ending that ordeal."

"I've had practice. Way too much of it."

They shook hands, and he said: "It's a pleasure to finally meet you, Dr. Isles. Mr. Crispin wanted to meet you as well, but he had hip surgery a few months ago and he still can't stand for long periods of time. He asked me to say hello."

"When you invited me, you didn't warn me I'd have to walk through that mob."

"The press?" Robinson gave a pained look. "They're a necessary evil."

"Necessary for whom?"

"Our survival as a museum. Since the article about Madam X, our ticket sales have gone through the roof. And we haven't even put her on display yet."

Robinson led her into a warren of hallways. On this Sunday night, the Diagnostic Imaging Department was quiet and the rooms they passed were dark and empty.

"It's going to get a little crowded in there," said Robinson. "There's hardly space for even a small group."

"Who else is watching?"

"My colleague Josephine Pulcillo; the radiologist, Dr. Brier; and a CT tech. Oh, and there'll be a camera crew."

"Someone you hired?"

"No. They're from the Discovery Channel."

She gave a startled laugh. "Now I'm *really* impressed."

"It does mean, though, that we have to watch our language." He stopped outside the door labeled CT and said softly: "I think they may be already filming."

They quietly slipped into the CT viewing room, where the camera crew was, indeed, recording as Dr. Brier explained the technology they were about to use.

"*CT* is short for 'computed tomography.' Our machine shoots X-rays at the subject from thousands of different angles. The computer then processes that information and generates a three-dimensional image of the internal anatomy. You'll see it on this monitor. It'll look like a series of cross sections, as if we're actually cutting the body into slices."

As the taping continued, Maura edged her way to the viewing window. There, peering through the glass, she saw Madam X for the first time.

In the rarefied world of museums, Egyptian mummies were the undisputed rock stars. Their display cases were where you'd usually find the schoolchildren gathered, faces up to the glass, every one of them fascinated by a rare glimpse of death. Seldom did modern eyes encounter a human corpse on display, unless it wore the acceptable countenance of a mummy. The public loved mummies, and Maura was no exception. She stared, transfixed, even though what she actually saw was nothing more than a human-shaped bundle resting in an open crate, its flesh concealed beneath ancient strips of linen. Mounted over the face was a cartonnage mask—the painted face of a woman with haunting dark eyes.

But then another woman in the CT room caught Maura's attention. Wearing cotton gloves, the young woman leaned into the crate, removing layers of Ethafoam packing from around the mummy. Ringlets of black hair fell around her face. She straightened and shoved her hair back, revealing eyes as dark and striking as those painted on the mask. Her Mediterranean features could well have appeared on any Egyptian temple painting, but her clothes were thoroughly modern: skinny blue jeans and a Live Aid T-shirt.

"Beautiful, isn't she?" murmured Dr. Robinson. He'd

moved beside Maura, and for a moment she wondered if he was referring to Madam X or to the young woman. "She appears to be in excellent condition. I just hope the body inside is as well preserved as those wrappings."

"How old do you think she is? Do you have an estimate?"

"We sent off a swatch of the outer wrapping for carbon fourteen analysis. It just about killed our budget to do it, but Josephine insisted. The results came back as second century BC."

"That's the Ptolemaic period, isn't it?"

He responded with a pleased smile. "You know your Egyptian dynasties."

"I was an anthropology major in college, but I'm afraid I don't remember much beyond that and the Yanomamo tribe."

"Still, I'm impressed."

She stared at the wrapped body, marveling that what lay in that crate was more than two thousand years old. What a journey it had taken, across an ocean, across millennia, all to end up lying on a CT table in a Boston hospital, gawked at by the curious. "Are you going to leave her in the crate for the scan?" she asked.

"We want to handle her as little as possible. The crate won't get in the way. We'll still get a good look at what lies under that linen."

"So you haven't taken even a little peek?"

"You mean have I *unwrapped* part of her?" His mild

eyes widened in horror. "God, no. Archaeologists would have done that a hundred years ago, maybe, and that's exactly how they ended up damaging so many specimens. There are probably layers of resin under those outer wrappings, so you can't just peel it all away. You might have to chip through it. It's not only destructive, it's disrespectful. I'd never do that." He looked through the window at the dark-haired young woman. "And Josephine would kill me if I did."

"That's your colleague?"

"Yes. Dr. Pulcillo."

"She looks like she's about sixteen."

"Doesn't she? But she's smart as a whip. She's the one who arranged this scan. And when the hospital attorneys tried to put a stop to it, Josephine managed to push it through anyway."

"Why would the attorneys object?"

"Seriously? Because this patient couldn't give the hospital her informed consent."

Maura laughed in disbelief. "They wanted informed consent from a *mummy*?"

"When you're a lawyer, every *i* must be dotted. Even when the patient's been dead for a few thousand years."

Dr. Pulcillo had removed all the packing materials, and she joined them in the viewing room and shut the connecting door. The mummy now lay exposed in its crate, awaiting the first barrage of X-rays.

"Dr. Robinson?" said the CT tech, fingers poised over the computer keyboard. "We need to provide the required patient information before we can start the scan. What shall I use as the birth date?"

The curator frowned. "Oh, gosh. Do you really need a birth date?"

"I can't start the scan until I fill in these blanks. I tried the year zero, and the computer wouldn't take it."

"Why don't we use yesterday's date? Make it one day old."

"Okay. Now the program insists on knowing the sex. Male, female, or other?"

Robinson blinked. "There's a category for *other*?"

The tech grinned. "I've never had the chance to check that particular box."

"Well then, let's use it tonight. There's a woman's face on the mask, but you never know. We can't be sure of the gender until we scan it."

"Okay," said Dr. Brier, the radiologist. "We're ready to go."

Dr. Robinson nodded. "Let's do it."

They gathered around the computer monitor, waiting for the first images to appear. Through the window, they could see the table feed Madam X's head into the doughnut-shaped opening, where she was bombarded by X-rays from multiple angles. Computerized tomography was not new medical technology, but its use as an archaeological tool was relatively recent. No one in that room had ever before watched a live CT scan of a mummy, and as they all crowded in, Maura was aware of the TV camera trained on their faces, ready to capture their reactions. Standing beside her, Nicholas Robinson rocked back and forth on the balls of his feet, radiating enough nervous energy to infect everyone in the room. Maura felt her own pulse quicken as she craned for a better view of the monitor. The first image that appeared drew only impatient sighs.

"It's just the shell of the crate," said Dr. Brier.

Maura glanced at Robinson and saw that his lips were pressed together in thin lines. Would Madam X turn out to be nothing more than an empty bundle of rags? Dr. Pulcillo stood beside him, looking just as tense, gripping the back of the radiologist's chair as she stared over his shoulder, awaiting a glimpse of anything recognizably human, anything to confirm that inside those bandages was a cadaver.

The next image changed everything. It was a startlingly bright disk, and the instant it appeared, the observers all took in a sharply simultaneous breath.

Bone.

Dr. Brier said, "That's the top of the cranium. Congratulations, you've definitely got an occupant in there."

Robinson and Pulcillo gave each other happy claps on the back. "This is what we were waiting for!" he said.

Pulcillo grinned. "Now we can finish building that exhibit."

"Mummies!" Robinson threw his head back and laughed. "Everyone loves mummies!"

New slices appeared on the screen, and their attention snapped back to the monitor as more of the cranium appeared, its cavity filled not with brain matter but with ropy strands that looked like a knot of worms.

"Those are linen strips," Dr. Pulcillo murmured in wonder, as though this was the most beautiful sight she'd ever seen.

"There's no brain matter," said the CT tech.

"No, the brain was usually evacuated."

"Is it true they'd stick a hook up through the nose and yank the brain out that way?" the tech asked.

"Almost true. You can't really yank out the brain, because it's too soft. They probably used an instrument to whisk it around until it was liquefied. Then they'd tilt the body so the brain would drip out the nose."

"Oh man, that's gross," said the tech. But he was hanging on Pulcillo's every word.

"They might leave the cranium empty or they might pack it with linen strips, as you see here. And frankincense."

"What *is* frankincense, anyway? I've always wondered about that."

"A fragrant resin. It comes from a very special tree in Africa. Valued quite highly in the ancient world."

"So that's why one of the three wise men brought it to Bethlehem."

Dr. Pulcillo nodded. "It would have been a treasured gift."

"Okay," Dr. Brier said. "We've moved below the

level of the orbits. There you can see the upper jaw, and . . ." He paused, frowning at an unexpected density.

Robinson murmured, "Oh my goodness."

"It's something metallic," said Dr. Brier. "It's in the oral cavity."

"It could be gold leaf," said Pulcillo. "In the Greco-Roman era, they'd sometimes place gold-leaf tongues inside the mouth."

Robinson turned to the TV camera, which was recording every remark. "There appears to be metal inside the mouth. That would correlate with our presumptive date during the Greco-Roman era—"

"Now what is *this*?" exclaimed Dr. Brier.

Maura's gaze shot back to the computer screen. A bright starburst had appeared within the mummy's lower jaw, an image that stunned Maura because it should not have been present in a corpse that was two thousand years old. She leaned closer, staring at a detail that would scarcely cause comment were this a body that had arrived fresh on the autopsy table. "I know this is impossible," Maura said softly. "But you know what that looks like?"

The radiologist nodded. "It appears to be a dental filling."

Maura turned to Dr. Robinson, who appeared just as startled as everyone else in the room. "Has anything like this ever been described in an Egyptian mummy before?" she asked. "Ancient dental repairs that could be mistaken for modern fillings?"

Wide-eyed, he shook his head. "But it doesn't mean the Egyptians were incapable of it. Their medical care was the most advanced in the ancient world." He looked at his colleague. "Josephine, what can you tell us about this? It's your field."

Dr. Pulcillo struggled for an answer. "There—there are medical papyri from the Old Kingdom," she said. "They describe how to fix loose teeth and make dental bridges. And there was a healer who was famous as a maker of teeth. So we know they were ingenious when it came to dental care. Far ahead of their time."

"But did they ever make repairs like *that*?" said Maura, pointing to the screen.

Dr. Pulcillo's troubled gaze returned to the image. "If they did," she said softly, "I'm not aware of it."

On the monitor, new images appeared in shades of gray, the body viewed in cross section as though sliced through by a bread knife. She could be bombarded by X-rays from every angle, subjected to massive doses of radiation, but this patient was beyond fears of cancer, beyond worries about side effects. As X-rays continued to assault her body, no patient could have been more submissive.

Shaken by the earlier images, Robinson was now arched forward like a tightly strung bow, alert for the next surprise. The first slices of the thorax appeared, the cavity black and vacant.

"It appears that the lungs were removed," the

radiologist said. "All I see is a shriveled bit of mediastinum in the chest."

"That's the heart," said Pulcillo, her voice steadier now. This, at least, was what she'd expected to see. "They always tried to leave it in situ."

"Just the heart?"

She nodded. "It was considered the seat of intelligence, so you never separated it from the body. There are three separate spells contained in the Book of the Dead to ensure that the heart remains in place."

"And the other organs?" asked the CT tech. "I heard those were put in special jars."

"That was before the Twenty-first Dynasty. After around a thousand BC, the organs were wrapped into four bundles and stuffed back into the body."

"So we should be able to see that?"

"In a mummy from the Ptolemaic era, yes."

"I think I can make an educated guess about her age when she died," said the radiologist. "The wisdom teeth were fully erupted, and the cranial sutures are closed. But I don't see any degenerative changes in the spine."

"A young adult," said Maura.

"Probably under thirty-five."

"In the era she lived in, thirty-five was well into middle age," said Robinson.

The scan had moved below the thorax, X-rays slicing through layers of wrappings, through the shell of dried skin and bones, to reveal the abdominal cavity. What Maura saw within was eerily unfamiliar, as strange to her as an alien autopsy. Where she expected to see liver and spleen, stomach and pancreas, instead she saw snake-like coils of linen, an interior landscape that was missing all that should have been recognizable. Only the bright knobs of vertebral bone told her this was indeed a human body, a body that had been hollowed out to a mere shell and stuffed like a rag doll.

Mummy anatomy might be alien to her, but for both Robinson and Pulcillo this was familiar territory. As new images appeared, they both leaned in, pointing out details they recognized.

"There," said Robinson. "Those are the four linen packets containing the organs."

"Okay, we're now in the pelvis," Dr. Brier said. He pointed to two pale arcs. They were the top edges of the iliac crests.

Slice by slice, the pelvis slowly took shape, as the computer compiled and rendered countless X-ray beams. It was a digital striptease as each image revealed a tantalizing new peek.

"Look at the shape of the pelvic inlet," said Dr. Brier.

"It's a female," said Maura.

The radiologist nodded. "I'd say it's pretty conclusive." He turned and grinned at the two archaeologists. "You can now officially call her Madam X. And not *Mister* X."

"And look at the pubic symphysis," said Maura, still focused on the monitor. "There's no separation."

Brier nodded. "I agree."

"What does that mean?" asked Robinson.

Maura explained. "During childbirth, the infant's passage through the pelvic inlet can actually force apart the pubic bones, where they join at the symphysis. It appears this female never had children."

The CT tech laughed. "Your mummy's never been a mommy."

The scan had moved beyond the pelvis, and they could now see cross sections of the two femurs encased in the withered flesh of the upper thighs.

"Nick, we need to call Simon," said Pulcillo. "He's probably waiting by the phone."

"Oh gosh, I completely forgot." Robinson pulled out his cell phone and dialed his boss. "Simon, guess what I'm looking at right now? Yes, she's gorgeous. Plus, we've discovered a few surprises, so the press conference is going to be quite the—" In an instant he fell silent, his gaze frozen on the screen.

"What the hell?" blurted the CT tech.

The image now glowing on the monitor was so unexpected that the room had fallen completely still. Were a living patient lying on the CT table, Maura would have had no difficulty identifying the small metallic object embedded in the calf, an object that had shattered the slender shaft of the fibula. But that bit of metal did not belong in Madam X's leg.

A bullet did not belong in Madam X's millennium.

"Is that what I think it is?" said the CT tech.

Robinson shook his head. "It has to be postmortem damage. What else could it be?"

"Two thousand *years* postmortem?"

"I'll—I'll call you back, Simon." Robinson disconnected his cell phone. Turning to the cameraman, he ordered: "Shut it off. Please shut it off *now*." He took a deep breath. "All right. All right, let's—let's approach this logically." He straightened, gaining confidence as an obvious explanation occurred to him. "Mummies have often been abused or damaged by souvenir hunters. Obviously, someone fired a bullet into the mummy. And a conservator later tried to repair that damage by rewrapping her. That's why we saw no entry hole in the bandages."

"That isn't what happened," said Maura.

Robinson blinked. "What do you mean? That has to be the explanation."

"The damage to that leg wasn't postmortem. It happened while this woman was still alive."

"That's impossible."

"I'm afraid Dr. Isles is right," said the radiologist. He looked at Maura. "You're referring to the early callus formation around the fracture site?"

"What does that mean?" asked Robinson. "Callus formation?"

"It means the broken bone had already started the process of healing when this woman died. She lived at least a few weeks after the injury."

Maura turned to the curator. "Where did this mummy come from?"

Robinson's glasses had slipped down his nose yet again, and he stared over the lenses as though hypnotized by what he saw glowing in the mummy's leg.

It was Dr. Pulcillo who answered the question, her voice barely a whisper. "It was in the museum basement. Nick—Dr. Robinson found it back in January."

"And how did the museum obtain it?"

Pulcillo shook her head. "We don't know."

"There must be records. Something in your files to indicate where she came from."

"There are none for her," said Robinson, at last finding his voice. "The Crispin Museum is a hundred thirty years old, and many records are missing. We have no idea how long she was stored in the basement."

"How did you happen to find her?"

Even in that air-conditioned room, sweat had broken out on Dr. Robinson's pale face. "After I was hired three years ago, I began an inventory of the collection. That's how I came across her. She was in an unlabeled crate."

"And that didn't surprise you? To find something as rare as an Egyptian mummy in an unlabeled crate?"

"But mummies *aren't* all that rare. In the 1800s, you could buy one in Egypt for only five dollars, so American tourists brought them home by the hundreds. They turn up in attics and antiques stores. A freak show in Niagara Falls even claims they had King Ramses the

First in their collection. So it's not all that surprising that we'd find a mummy in our museum."

"Dr. Isles?" said the radiologist. "We've got the scout film. You might want to take a look at it."

Maura turned to the monitor. Displayed on the screen was a conventional X-ray like the films she hung on her own viewing box in the morgue. She did not need a radiologist to interpret what she saw there.

"There's not much doubt about it now," said Dr. Brier.

No. There's no doubt whatsoever. That's a bullet in the leg.

Maura pulled out her cell phone.

"Dr. Isles?" said Robinson. "Whom are you calling?"

"I'm arranging for transport to the morgue," she said. "Madam X is now a medical examiner's case."

3

"Is it just my imagination," said Detective Barry Frost, "or do you and I catch all the weird ones?"

Madam X was definitely one of the weird ones, thought Detective Jane Rizzoli as she drove past TV news vans and turned into the parking lot of the medical examiner's building. It was only eight AM, and already the hyenas were yapping, ravenous for details of the ultimate cold case—a case that Jane had greeted with skeptical laughter when Maura had phoned last night. The sight of the news vans made Jane realize that maybe it was time to get serious, time to consider the possibility that this was not, after all, some elaborate practical joke being played on her by the singularly humorless medical examiner.

She pulled into a parking space and sat eyeing the vans, wondering how many more cameras would be waiting out here when she and Frost came back out of the building.

"At least this one shouldn't smell bad," Jane said.

"But mummies can give you diseases, you know."

Jane turned to her partner, whose pale and boyish face looked genuinely worried. "What diseases?" she asked.

"Since Alice has been away, I've been watching a lot of TV. Last night I saw this show on the Discovery Channel, about mummies that carry these spores."

"Ooh. Scary spores."

"It's no joke," he insisted. "They can make you sick."

"Geez, I hope Alice gets home soon. You're getting overdosed on the Discovery Channel."

They stepped out of the car into cloying humidity that made Jane's already unruly dark hair spring into frizzy waves. During her four years as a homicide detective, she had made this walk into the medical examiner's building many times, slip-sliding across ice in January, dashing through rain in March, and slogging across pavement as hot as ash in August. These few dozen paces were familiar to her, as was the grim destination. She'd believed this walk would become easier over time, that one day she'd feel immune to any horrors the stainless-steel table might serve up. But since her daughter Regina's birth a year ago, death held more terror for her than it ever had before. Motherhood didn't make you stronger; it made you vulnerable and afraid of what death could steal from you.

Today, though, the subject waiting in the morgue inspired fascination, not horror. When Jane stepped into the autopsy suite anteroom, she crossed straight to the window, eager for her first glimpse of the subject on the table.

Madam X was what *The Boston Globe* had called the mummy, a catchy moniker that conjured up a vision of sultry beauty, a Cleopatra with dark eyes. Jane saw a dried-out husk wrapped in rags.

"She looks like a human tamale," said Jane.

"Who's the girl?" asked Frost, staring through the window.

There were two people in the room whom Jane did not recognize. The man was tall and gangly, professorial glasses perched on his nose. The young woman was a petite brunette wearing blue jeans beneath an autopsy gown. "Those must be the museum archaeologists. They were both going to be here."

"*She's* an archaeologist? Wow."

Jane gave him an annoyed jab with her elbow. "Alice leaves town for a few weeks, and you forget you're a married man."

"I just never pictured an archaeologist looking as hot as her."

They pulled on shoe covers and autopsy gowns and pushed into the lab.

"Hey, Doc," said Jane. "Is this really one for us?"

Maura turned from the light box, and her gaze, as usual, was dead serious. While the other pathologists might crack jokes or toss out ironic comments over the autopsy table, it was rare to hear Maura so much as laugh in the presence of the dead. "We're about to find out." She introduced the pair Jane had seen through the window. "This is the curator, Dr. Nicholas Robinson. And his colleague, Dr. Josephine Pulcillo."

"You're both with the Crispin Museum?" asked Jane.

"And they're very unhappy about what I'm planning to do here," said Maura.

"It's destructive," said Robinson. "There has to be some other way to get this information besides cutting her open."

"That's why I wanted you to be here, Dr. Robinson," said Maura. "To help me minimize the damage. The last thing I want to do is destroy an antiquity."

"I thought the CT scan last night clearly showed a bullet," said Jane.

"Those are the X-rays we shot this morning," said Maura, pointing to the light box. "What do you think?"

Jane approached the display and studied the films clipped there. Glowing within the right calf was what certainly looked to her like a bullet. "Yeah, I can see why this might've freaked you out last night."

"I did not *freak out*."

Jane laughed. "You were as close to it as I've ever heard you."

"I admit, I was damn shocked when I saw it. We all were." Maura pointed to the bones of the right lower leg. "Notice how the fibula's been fractured, presumably by this projectile."

"You said it happened while she was still alive?"

"You can see early callus formation. This bone was in the process of healing when she died."

"But her wrappings are two thousand years old," said Dr. Robinson. "We've confirmed it."

Jane stared hard at the X-ray, struggling to come up with a logical explanation for what they were looking at. "Maybe this isn't a bullet. Maybe it's some sort of ancient metal thingie. A spear tip or something."

"That is not a spear tip, Jane," said Maura. "It's a bullet."

"Then dig it out. Prove it to me."

"And if I do?"

"Then we have a hell of a mind bender, don't we? I mean, what are the possible explanations here?"

"You know what Alice said when I called her about it last night?" Frost said. " 'Time travel.' That was the first thing she thought."

Jane laughed. "Since when did Alice go woo-woo on you?"

"It's theoretically possible, you know, to travel back in time," he said. "Bring a gun back to ancient Egypt."

Maura cut in impatiently: "Can we stick to real possibilities here?"

Jane frowned at the bright chunk of metal that looked like so many she had seen before glowing in countless X-rays of lifeless limbs and shattered skulls. "I'm having trouble coming up with any of those," she said. "So why don't you just cut her open and see what that metal thing is? Maybe these archaeologists are right. Maybe you're jumping to conclusions, Doc."

Robinson said, "As curator, it's my duty to protect her and not let her be mindlessly ripped apart. Can you at least limit the damage to the relevant area?"

Maura nodded. "That's a reasonable approach." She moved to the table. "Let's turn her over. If there's an entrance wound, it will be in the right calf."

"It's best if we work together," said Robinson. He went to the head, and Pulcillo moved to the feet. "We need to support the whole body and not put strain on any part of her. So if four of us could pitch in?"

Maura slipped gloved hands beneath the shoulders and said, "Detective Frost, could you support the hips?"

Frost hesitated, eyeing the stained linen wrappings. "Shouldn't we put on masks or something?"

"We're just turning her over," said Maura.

"I've heard they carry diseases. You breathe in these spores and you get pneumonia."

"Oh, for God's sake," said Jane. She snapped on gloves and stepped up to the table. Sliding her hands beneath the mummy's hips, she said: "I'm ready."

"Okay, lift," said Robinson. "Now rotate her. That's it . . ."

"Wow, she hardly weighs anything," said Jane.

"A living human body's mostly water. Remove the organs, dry out the carcass, and you end up with just a fraction of its former weight. She probably weighs only around fifty pounds, wrappings and all."

"Kind of like beef jerky, huh?"

"That's exactly what she is. Human jerky. Now let's ease her down. Gently."

"You know, I wasn't kidding about the spores," said Frost. "I saw this show."

"Are you talking about the King Tut curse?" said Maura.

"Yeah," said Frost. "*That's* what I'm talking about! All those people who died after they went into his tomb. They breathed in some kind of spores and got sick."

"Aspergillus," said Robinson. "When Howard Carter's team disturbed the tomb, they probably breathed in spores that had collected inside over the centuries. Some of them came down with fatal cases of aspergillus pneumonia."

"So Frost isn't just bullshitting?" said Jane. "There really was a mummy's curse?"

Annoyance flashed in Robinson's eyes. "Of course there was no curse. Yes, a few people died, but after what Carter and his team did to poor Tutankhamen, maybe there *should* have been a curse."

"What did they do to him?" asked Jane.

"They brutalized him. They sliced him open, broke his bones, and essentially tore him apart in the search for jewels and amulets. They cut him up in pieces to get him out of the coffin, pulling off his arms and legs. They severed his head. It wasn't science. It was desecration."

He looked down at Madam X, and Jane saw

admiration, even affection in his gaze. "We don't want the same thing to happen to her."

"The last thing I want to do is mangle her," said Maura. "So let's unwrap her just enough to find out what we're dealing with here."

"You probably won't be able to just unwrap her," said Robinson. "If the inner strips were soaked in resin, as per tradition, they'll be stuck together as solid as glue."

Maura turned to the X-ray for one more look, then reached for a scalpel and tweezers. Jane had watched Maura slice other bodies, but never before had she seen her hesitate so long, her blade hovering over the calf as though afraid to make the first cut. What they were about to do would forever damage Madam X, and Drs. Robinson and Pulcillo both were watching with outright disapproval in their eyes.

Maura made the first cut. This was not the usual confident slice into flesh. Instead, she used the tweezers to delicately lift the band of linen so that her blade slit through successive layers of fabric, strip by strip. "It's peeling away quite easily," she said.

Dr. Pulcillo frowned. "This isn't traditional. Normally the bandages would be doused in molten resin. In the 1830s, when they unwrapped mummies, they sometimes had to pry the bandages off."

"What was the point of the resin, anyway?" asked Frost.

"To make the wrappings stick together. It gave them

rigidity, like making a papier-mâché container to protect the contents."

"I'm already through the final layer," Maura said. "There's no resin adhering to any of this."

Jane craned forward to catch a glimpse of what lay under the wrapping. "That's her skin? It looks like old leather."

"Dried skin is precisely what leather is, Detective Rizzoli," said Robinson. "In a way."

Maura reached for the scissors and gingerly snipped away the strips, exposing a larger patch of skin. It looked like brown parchment wrapped around bones. She glanced, once again, at the X-ray, and swung a magnifier over the calf. "I can't find any entry hole in the skin."

"So the wound's not postmortem," said Jane.

"It goes along with what we see on that X-ray. That foreign body was probably introduced while she was still alive. She lived long enough for the fractured bone to start mending. For the wound to close over."

"How long would that take?"

"A few weeks. Perhaps a month."

"Someone would have to care for her during that time, right? She'd have to be fed and sheltered."

Maura nodded. "This makes the manner of death all the more difficult to determine."

Robinson asked, "Manner of death? What do you mean?"

"In other words," said Jane, "we're wondering if she was murdered."

"Let's settle the most pressing issue first." Maura reached for the knife. Mummification had toughened the tissues to the consistency of leather, and the blade did not cut easily into the withered flesh.

Glancing across the table, Jane saw Dr. Pulcillo's lips tighten, as though to stifle a protest. But as much as she might object to the procedure, the woman could not look away. They all leaned in, even spore-phobic Frost, their attention glued to that exposed patch of leg as Maura picked up forceps and plunged the tips into the incision. It took only seconds of digging around in the shriveled flesh before the teeth of the forceps clamped down on the prize. Maura dropped it onto a steel tray, and it gave a metallic clang.

Dr. Pulcillo sucked in a sharp breath. This was no spear tip, no broken bit of knife blade.

Maura finally stated the obvious. "I think we can now safely say that Madam X is not two thousand years old."

4

"I don't understand," Dr. Pulcillo murmured. "The linen was analyzed. The carbon dating confirmed the age."

"But that's a bullet," said Jane, pointing to the tray. "A twenty-two. Your analysis was all screwed up."

"It's a well-respected lab! They were certain about the date."

"You could both be right," said Robinson quietly.

"Yeah?" Jane looked at him. "I'd like to know how."

He took a deep breath and stepped back from the table, as though needing the space to think. "I see it come up for sale from time to time. I don't know how *much* of it is genuine, but I'm sure there are caches of the real thing out there on the antiquities market."

"What?"

"Mummy wrappings. They're easier to find than the bodies themselves. I've seen them on eBay."

Jane gave a startled laugh. "You can go online and buy mummy wrappings?"

"There was once a thriving international trade in mummies. They were ground up and used as medicines. Carted off to England for fertilizer. Wealthy tourists brought them home and held unwrapping parties. You'd invite your friends over to watch while you peeled away the linen. Since amulets and jewels were often among the wrappings, it was sort of like a treasure hunt, uncovering little trinkets for your guests."

"That was entertainment?" said Frost. "Unwrapping a corpse?"

"It was done in some of the finest Victorian homes," Robinson said. "It goes to show you how little regard they had for the dead of Egypt. And when they'd finish unwrapping the corpse, it would be disposed of or burned. But the wrappings were often kept as souvenirs. That's why you still find stashes of them for sale."

"So these wrappings *could* be ancient," said Frost, "even if the body isn't."

"It would explain the carbon fourteen dating. But as for Madam X herself . . ." Robinson shook his head in bewilderment.

"We still can't prove this was homicide," said Frost. "You can't convict someone based on a gunshot wound that was already healing."

"I kind of doubt she volunteered for mummification," said Jane.

"Actually," said Robinson, "it's possible that she did."

Everyone turned to stare at the curator, who looked perfectly serious.

"Volunteer to have her brains and organs ripped out?" said Jane. "No, thanks."

"Some people *have* bequeathed their bodies for precisely that purpose."

"Hey, I saw that show, too," said Frost. "Another one on Discovery Channel. Some archaeologist actually mummified a guy."

Jane stared down at the wrapped cadaver. She imagined being encased in layer after layer of smothering bandages. Being bound in a linen straitjacket for a thousand, two thousand years, until a day when some curious archaeologist would decide to strip away the cloth and reveal her shriveled remains. Not dust to dust, but flesh to leather. She swallowed. "Why would anyone volunteer for that?"

"It's a type of immortality, don't you think?" said Robinson. "An alternative to rotting away. Your body preserved. Those who love you never have to surrender you to decay."

Those who love you. Jane glanced up. "You're saying this could have been an act of affection?"

"It would be a way to hold on to someone you love. To keep them safe from the worms. From rotting."

The way of all flesh, thought Jane, and the temperature in the room suddenly seemed to plummet. "Maybe it's not about love at all. Maybe it's about ownership."

Robinson met her gaze, clearly unsettled by that possibility. He said softly: "I hadn't thought of it that way."

Jane turned to Maura. "Let's get on with the autopsy, Doc. We need more information to work with."

Maura crossed to the light box, removed the leg X-rays, and replaced them with the CT scan films. "Let's turn her onto her back again."

This time, as Maura cut through the linen strips covering the torso, she wasted no effort on preservation. They now knew this was no ancient cadaver she was cutting into; this was a death investigation, and the answers lay not in the linen strips but in the flesh and bone itself. The cloth parted, revealing the torso's brown and shrunken skin through which the outlines of ribs were visible, arching up in a bony vault beneath its parchment tent. Moving toward the head, Maura pried off the painted cartonnage mask and began to snip at the strips covering the face.

Jane looked at the CT films hanging on the light box, then frowned at the exposed torso. "The organs are all taken out during mummification, right?"

Robinson nodded. "Removal of the viscera slows down the process of putrefaction. It's one of the reasons the bodies don't decay."

"But there's only one little wound on the belly." Jane pointed to a small incision on the left, sewn closed by ungainly stitches. "How do you get everything out through that opening?"

"That's exactly how the Egyptians would have removed the viscera. Through a small wound on the left side. Whoever preserved this body was familiar with the ancient methods. And clearly adhered to them."

"What *are* these ancient methods? How, exactly, do you make a mummy?" asked Jane.

Dr. Robinson looked at his associate. "Josephine knows more about it than I do. Maybe she'll explain it."

"Dr. Pulcillo?" said Jane.

The young woman still looked shaken by the discovery of the bullet. She cleared her throat and straightened. "A large part of what we know comes down to us from Herodotus," she said. "I guess you could call him a Greek travel writer. Twenty-five hundred years ago, he roamed the ancient world and recorded what he learned. The problem is, he was known to get details wrong. Or get snookered by the local tour guides." She managed a smile. "It makes him seem human, doesn't it? He was like any tourist in Egypt today. Probably hounded by trinket sellers. Duped by crooked tour guides. Just another innocent abroad."

"What did he say about making mummies?"

"He was told that it all starts with a ritual washing of the corpse in dissolved natron."

"Natron?"

"It's essentially a mixture of salts. You can reproduce it by blending plain old table salt and baking soda."

"Baking soda?" Jane gave an uneasy laugh. "I'll never look at a box of Arm and Hammer the same way again."

"The washed body is then laid out on wooden blocks," Pulcillo continued. "They use a razor-sharp blade of Ethiopian stone—probably obsidian—to slice a small incision like the one you see here. Then, with some sort of hooked instrument, they pull out the organs, dragging them out through the hole. The empty cavity is rinsed, and they pack dry natron inside. Natron is poured over the body as well, to dehydrate it for forty days. Sort of like salting a fish." She paused, staring as Maura's scissors cut through the last strips covering the face.

"And then?" prodded Jane.

Pulcillo swallowed. "By then it's lost about seventy-five percent of its weight. The cavity is stuffed with linen and resin. The mummified internal organs might be returned as well. And . . ." She stopped, her eyes widening as the final wrappings fell away from the head.

For the first time, they saw the face of Madam X.

Long black hair was still affixed to the scalp. The skin was stretched taut over prominent cheekbones. But it was the lips that made Jane recoil. They had been sewn together with crude stitches, as though joined by the tailor of Frankenstein's monster.

Pulcillo shook her head. "That—that's all wrong!"

"The mouth isn't usually sewn shut?" asked Maura.

"No! How would you eat in the afterlife? How would you speak? This is like condemning her to eternal hunger. And eternal silence."

Eternal silence. Jane looked down at the ugly stitches and wondered: Did you say something to offend your killer? Did you speak back to him? Insult him? Testify against him? Is this your punishment, to have your lips bound together for eternity?

The corpse now lay fully revealed, her body stripped of all wrappings, her flesh little more than shriveled skin clinging to bones. Maura sliced into the torso.

Jane had witnessed Y-incisions before, and always before, she'd found herself recoiling from the odors as the blade first cut into the chest cavity. Even the freshest of corpses released a stench of decay, however faint, like the sulfurish scent of bad breath. Except that the subjects weren't breathing. Dead breath was what Jane called it, and just a whiff of it could nauseate her.

But Madam X emitted no such sickening odors as the knife cut into her thorax, as Maura methodically snapped apart ribs, as the chest wall was lifted like an ancient breastplate to reveal the chest cavity. What wafted up was a not-unpleasant scent that reminded her of incense. Instead of backing away, Jane leaned closer and took a deeper whiff. Sandalwood, she thought. Camphor. And something else, something that reminded her of licorice and cloves.

"Now, this is not what I expected," said Maura. She lifted a dried nugget of spice from the cavity.

"It looks like star anise," said Jane.

"Not traditional, I take it?"

"Myrrh would be traditional," said Pulcillo. "Melted resin. It was used to mask the stench and help stiffen the corpse."

"Myrrh's not exactly easy to obtain in large quantities," said Robinson. "It might explain why substitute spices were used."

"Substitute or not, this body looks very well preserved." Maura pulled wads of linen from the abdomen and placed them in a basin for later inspection. Staring into the hollowed-out torso, she said, "It's as dry as leather in here. And there's no odor of decay."

"So how will you figure out the cause of death?" asked Frost. "With no organs?"

"I can't. Not yet."

He looked at the CT scan on the light box. "What about the head? There's no brain, either."

"The cranium's intact. I didn't see any fractures."

Jane stared at the corpse's mouth, at the crude stitches sewing the lips together, and she winced at the thought of a needle piercing tender flesh. *I hope it was done after death and not before. Not when she could feel it.* Shuddering, she turned to look at the CT scan. "What's this bright thing?" she said. "It looks like it's in the mouth."

"There are two metallic densities in her mouth," said Maura. "One appears to be a dental filling. But there's also something in the oral cavity, something much

larger. It may explain why her mouth was sewn shut—
to secure that object in place." She picked up scissors.

The suture material was not mere thread, but dried
leather, the strips rock-hard. Even after she'd cut
through them, the lips adhered together as though permanently frozen in place, the mouth a tight slit that
would have to be pried open.

Maura introduced the tip of a hemostat between the
lips, metal grating against teeth as she gently widened
the opening. The jaw joint suddenly gave a shocking
snap and Jane flinched as the mandible broke off. The
lower jaw sagged open, revealing straight teeth that
were so cosmetically perfect, any modern orthodontist
would be proud to claim the alignment as his work.

"Let's see what this thing is in her mouth," said
Maura. Reaching in with the hemostat, she pulled out
an oblong-shaped gold coin, which she set on the steel
tray, where it landed with a soft clang. They all stared
in astonishment.

Jane suddenly burst out laughing. "Someone," she
said, "has a sick sense of humor."

Stamped on the gold were words in English:

I visited the pyramids
Cairo, Egypt

Maura turned over the object. On the reverse side
were three engraved symbols: an owl, a hand, and a
bent arm.

"It's a cartouche," said Robinson. "A personal seal.

They sell these souvenirs all over Egypt. Tell a jeweler your name, and he'll translate it into hieroglyphs and engrave it right on the spot for you."

"What do these symbols mean?" asked Frost. "I see an owl. Is that like a sign of wisdom or something?"

"No, these glyphs aren't meant to be read as ideograms," said Robinson.

"What's an ideogram?"

"That's a symbol that represents exactly what's illustrated. For instance, a picture of a running man would mean the word *run*. Or two fighting men would mean the word *war*."

"And that's not what these are?"

"No, these symbols are phonograms. They represent sounds, like our own alphabet."

"So what does it say?"

"This isn't my area of expertise. Josephine can read it." He turned to his colleague and suddenly frowned. "Are you feeling all right?"

The young woman had gone as pale as any corpse that had ever been stretched out on the morgue table. She stared at the cartouche as though she saw some undreamed-of horror in those symbols.

"Dr. Pulcillo?" said Frost.

She glanced up sharply, as though startled to hear her name. "I'm fine," she murmured.

"What about these hieroglyphs?" Jane asked. "Can you read them?"

Pulcillo's gaze dropped back to the cartouche. "The

owl—the owl is the equivalent of our *M* sound. And the little hand beneath it, that would sound like a *D.*"

"And the arm?"

Pulcillo swallowed. "It's pronounced like a broad *A.* As in *car.*"

"*M-D-Ah?* What kind of name is that?"

Robinson said, "Something like *Medea,* maybe? That would be my guess."

"*Medea?*" said Frost. "Isn't there some Greek tragedy written about her?"

"It's a tale of vengeance," said Robinson. "According to the myth, Medea falls in love with Jason of the Argonauts, and they have two sons. When Jason leaves her for another woman, Medea retaliates by slaughtering her own sons and murdering her female rival. All to get back at Jason."

"What happens to Medea?" asked Jane.

"There are various versions of the tale, but in them all, she escapes."

"After killing her own kids?" Jane shook her head. "That's a lousy ending, having her go free."

"Perhaps that's the point of the story: that some who commit evil never face justice."

Jane looked down at the cartouche. "So Medea's a murderer."

Robinson nodded. "She's also a survivor."

5

Josephine Pulcillo stepped off the city bus and walked in a daze along busy Washington Street, oblivious to the traffic and the relentless thump of car stereos. At the corner she crossed the road, and even the sharp squeal of tires skidding to a stop a few feet away did not shake her as deeply as what she had seen that morning, in that autopsy suite.

Medea.

Surely it was a coincidence. A startling one, but what else could it be? Most likely the cartouche wasn't even an accurate translation. Trinket sellers in Cairo would tell you any tale in hopes of taking your dollars. Dangle enough money in front of them and they'd brazenly swear that Cleopatra herself had worn some worthless piece of junk. Perhaps the engraver had been asked to write Maddie or Melody or Mabel. It was far less likely that the hieroglyphs were meant to spell out *Medea*, since it was a name rarely heard except in the context of Greek tragedy.

She flinched as a horn blared and turned to see a black pickup truck crawling along the street beside her. The window rolled down, and a young man called out: "Hey gorgeous, want a ride? There's plenty of room on my lap!"

One rude gesture involving her middle finger was all it took to let him know what she thought of his offer. He gave a laugh and the truck roared off, spewing exhaust. Her eyes were still watering from the fumes as she climbed the stairs and stepped into her apartment building. Pausing by the lobby mailboxes, she dug through her purse for her mailbox key and suddenly gave a sigh.

She crossed to Apartment 1A and knocked.

The door swung open and a bug-eyed alien peered out. "You found your keys yet?" the alien asked.

"Mr. Goodwin? That is you, isn't it?"

"What? Oh, sorry. These old eyes aren't what they used to be. Need Robocop glasses just to see the darn screw heads." The building superintendent pulled off his pair of magnifying goggles, and the bug-eyed alien transformed to an utterly ordinary man in his sixties, unruly tufts of gray hair standing up on his head like miniature horns. "So did that key ring ever turn up?"

"I'm sure I just misplaced it at work. I've managed to make copies of my car keys and apartment keys, but—"

"I know. You want the new mailbox key, right?"

"You said you'd have to change the lock."

"I did it this morning. Come on in and I'll give you the new key."

Reluctantly, she followed him into his apartment. Once you stepped into Mr. Goodwin's lair, it could be a good half hour before you escaped. Mr. Goodwrench was what the tenants called him, for reasons that were apparent as she walked into his living room—or what *ought* to be a living room. Instead it was a tinkerer's palace, every horizontal surface covered with old hair dryers and radios and electronic gizmos in various stages of being dismantled or reassembled. *Just a hobby of mine,* he'd once told her. *No need to throw anything away ever again. I can fix it for you!*

You just had to be willing to wait a decade or more for him to get around to it.

"I hope you find that key ring of yours," he said as he led her past dozens of repair projects gathering dust. "Makes me nervous, having loose apartment keys floating around out there. The world is full of creeps, you know. And did you hear what Mr. Lubin's been saying?"

"No." She didn't want to hear what grumpy Mr. Lubin across the hall had to say.

"He's seen a black car casing our building. It drives by real slow every afternoon, and there's a man at the wheel."

"Maybe he's just looking for a parking place. That's the reason I hardly drive my car anywhere. Besides the price of gas, I hate giving up my parking spot."

"Mr. Lubin's got a keen eye for these things. Did you know he used to work as a spy?"

She gave a laugh. "Do you really think that's true?"

"Why wouldn't it be? I mean, he wouldn't lie about something like that."

You have no idea what some people lie about.

Mr. Goodwin opened a drawer, setting off a noisy rattle, and pulled out a key. "Here you go. I'll have to charge you forty-five bucks for changing the lock."

"Can I just add it to my rent check?"

"Sure thing." He grinned. "I trust you."

I'm the last person you should be trusting. She turned to leave.

"Oh, wait. I got your mail here again." He crossed to the cluttered dining room table and gathered up a stack of mail and a package, all bundled together with a rubber band. "The mailman couldn't fit this into your box, so I told him I'd give it to you." He nodded at the package. "I see you ordered something else from L.L. Bean, eh? You must like that company."

"Yes, I do. Thank you for holding my mail."

"So do you buy clothes or camping gear from them?"

"Clothes, mostly."

"And they fit you okay? Even through the mail?"

"They fit me fine." With a tight smile, she turned to leave before he could start asking her where she bought her lingerie. "See you later."

"Me, I'd just as soon try on clothes before I buy 'em," he said. "Never could get a decent fit through mail order."

"I'll give you the rent check tomorrow."

"And you keep looking for those keys, okay? You've got to be careful these days, especially a pretty girl like you, living all alone. Not a good thing if your keys end up in the wrong hands."

She bolted out of his apartment and started up the stairs.

"Hold on!" he called out. "There's one more thing. I almost forgot to ask you. Do you know anyone named Josephine Sommer?"

She froze on the steps, her arms clamped around the bundle of mail, her back rigid as a board. Slowly she turned to look at him. "What did you say?"

"The mailman asked me if that might be you, but I told him no, your name was Pulcillo."

"Why—why did he ask that question?"

"Because there's a letter in there with your apartment number and the last name says Sommer, not Pulcillo. He figured it might be your maiden name or something. I told him you were single, as far as I knew. Still, it *is* your apartment number, and there aren't too many Josephines around, so I figured it must be meant for you. That's why I kept it in with the rest of your mail."

She swallowed. "Thank you," she murmured.

"So *is* it you?"

She didn't respond. She just kept climbing the stairs, even though she knew he was watching her and waiting for an answer. Before he had the chance to lob another question, she ducked into her apartment and shut the door.

She was hugging the bundle of mail so tightly she could feel her heart slamming against it. She yanked off the rubber band and dumped the mail onto her coffee table. Envelopes and glossy catalogs spilled across the surface. Shoving aside the box from L.L. Bean, she sifted through the swirl of mail until she spotted an envelope with the name JOSEPHINE SOMMER written in an unfamiliar hand. It had a Boston postmark, but there was no return address.

Somebody in Boston knows this name. What else do they know about me?

For a long time she sat without opening the envelope, afraid to read its contents. Afraid that, once she opened it, her life would change. For this one last moment, she could still be Josephine Pulcillo, the quiet young woman who never spoke of her past. The underpaid archaeologist who was content to hide away in the Crispin Museum's back room, fussing over bits of papyrus and scraps of linen.

I've been careful, she thought. So careful to keep my head down and my eyes on my work, yet somehow the past has caught up with me.

Taking a deep breath, she finally tore open the envelope. Tucked inside was a note with only six words written in block letters. Words that told her what she already knew.

THE POLICE ARE NOT YOUR FRIENDS.

6

The museum guide at the Crispin Museum appeared ancient enough to be exhibited in a display case herself. The gray-haired little gnome was barely tall enough to peer over the counter of the reception desk as she announced: "I'm sorry, but we don't open until exactly ten AM. If you'd like to come back in seven minutes, I'll sell you the tickets then."

"We're not here to tour the museum," said Jane. "We're with Boston PD. I'm Detective Rizzoli and this is Detective Frost. Mr. Crispin is expecting us."

"I wasn't informed."

"Is he here?"

"Yes. He and Miss Duke are in a meeting upstairs," the woman said, clearly enunciating the title *Miss* and not *Ms.*, as though to emphasize that in this building, old-fashioned rules of etiquette still applied. She came around from behind the counter, revealing a plaid kilt-skirt and enormous orthopedic shoes. Pinned to her

white cotton blouse was a name tag: MRS. WILLE-
BRANDT, MUSEUM GUIDE. "I'll take you to his office. But
first I need to lock up the cash box. We're expecting a
large crowd again today, and I don't want to leave it
unattended."

"Oh, we can find the way to his office," said Frost.
"If you'll tell us where it is."

"I don't want you to get lost."

Frost gave her his best charm-the-old-ladies smile. "I
was a Boy Scout, ma'am. I promise, I won't get lost."

Mrs. Willebrandt refused to be charmed. She eyed
him dubiously through steel-rimmed spectacles. "It's on
the third floor," she finally said. "You can take the
elevator, but it's *very* slow." She pointed to a black grille
cage that looked more like an ancient death trap than
an elevator.

"We'll take the stairs," said Jane.

"They're straight ahead, through the main gallery."

Straight ahead, however, was not a direction that one
could navigate in this building. When Jane and Frost
stepped into the first-floor gallery, they confronted a
maze of display cases. The first case that greeted them
contained a life-sized wax figure of a nineteenth-century
gentleman garbed in a fine woolen suit and waistcoat.
In one hand he held a compass; in the other, he clutched
a yellowed map. Though he faced them through the
glass, his eyes looked elsewhere, focused on some lofty
and distant destination that only he could see.

Frost leaned forward and read the plaque at the

gentleman's feet. " 'Dr. Cornelius M. Crispin, Explorer and Scientist, 1830 through 1912. The treasures he brought home from around the world were the beginnings of the Crispin Museum Collection.' " He straightened. "Wow. Imagine listing that as your occupation. *Explorer.*"

"I think *rich guy* would be more accurate." Jane moved on to the next case, where gold coins glittered under display lights. "Hey, look. This says these are from the kingdom of Croesus."

"Now *there* was a rich guy."

"You mean Croesus was for real? I thought he was just some fairy tale."

They continued to the next case, which was filled with pottery and clay figurines. "Cool," said Frost. "These are Sumerian. You know, this is really old stuff. When Alice gets home, I'm going to bring her here. She'd love this museum. Funny how I never even heard of it before."

"Everyone's heard of it now. Nothing like a murder to put your place on the map."

They wandered deeper into the maze of cases, past marble busts of Greeks and Romans, past rusted swords and glinting jewelry, their footsteps creaking on old wood floors. So many cases were crammed into the gallery that the passages between them were narrow alleys, and every turn brought a fresh surprise, another treasure that demanded their attention.

They emerged at last into an open area near the

stairwell. Frost started up the steps to the second floor, but Jane did not follow him. Instead, she was drawn toward a narrow doorway, framed in faux stone.

"Rizzoli?" said Frost, glancing back.

"Hold on a minute," she said, gazing up at the seductive invitation that beckoned from the doorway lintel: COME. STEP INTO THE LAND OF THE PHARAOHS.

She could not resist.

Moving through the doorway, she found the space beyond so dimly lit that she had to pause as her eyes adjusted to the shadows. Slowly a room filled with wonders revealed itself.

"Wow," whispered Frost, who had followed.

They stood in an Egyptian burial chamber, its walls covered with hieroglyphs and funerary paintings. Displayed in the room were tomb artifacts, illuminated softly by discreetly placed spotlights. She saw a sarcophagus, gaping open as though awaiting its eternal occupant. A carved jackal head leered from atop a stone canopic jar. On the wall hung funerary masks, dark eyes staring eerily from painted faces. Beneath glass, a papyrus scroll lay open to a passage from the Book of the Dead.

Against the far wall was a vacant glass case. It was the size of a coffin.

Peering into it, she saw a photograph of a mummy resting inside a crate, and an index card with the hand-written notice: FUTURE RESTING PLACE OF MADAM X. WATCH FOR HER ARRIVAL!

Madam X would never make an appearance here, yet already she'd served her purpose, and crowds were now turning up at the museum. She'd drawn in the curious, the hordes seeking morbid thrills eager for a glimpse of death. But one thrill seeker had taken it a step further. He had been twisted enough to actually *make* a mummy, to gut a woman, to salt and pack her cavities with spices. To wrap her in linen, binding her naked limbs and torso strip by strip, like a spider spinning silken threads around its helpless prey. Jane stared at that empty case and considered the prospect of eternity inside that glass coffin. Suddenly the room seemed close and airless, and her chest felt as constricted as if she were the one bound head-to-toe, strips of linen strangling her, suffocating her. She fumbled at the top button of her blouse to loosen her collar.

"Hello, Detectives?"

Startled, Jane turned to see a woman silhouetted in the narrow doorway. She was dressed in a formfitting pantsuit that flattered her slender frame, and her short blond hair gleamed in a backlit halo.

"Mrs. Willebrandt told us you'd arrived. We've been waiting upstairs for you. I thought you might have gotten lost."

"This museum is really interesting," said Frost. "We couldn't help taking a look around."

As Jane and Frost stepped out of the tomb exhibit, the woman offered a brisk and businesslike handshake. In the brighter light of the main gallery, Jane saw that she was a handsome blonde in her forties—about a century younger than the museum guide they'd encountered at the front desk. "I'm Debbie Duke, one of the volunteers here."

"Detective Rizzoli," said Jane. "And Detective Frost."

"Simon's waiting in his office, if you'd like to follow me." Debbie turned and led the way up the stairs, her stylish pumps clicking against the well-worn wooden steps. On the second-floor landing, Jane was once again distracted by an eye-catching exhibit: A stuffed and mounted grizzly bear had its claws bared as though about to slash anyone coming up the stairs.

"Did one of Mr. Crispin's ancestors shoot this thing?" asked Jane.

"Oh." Debbie glanced back with a look of distaste. "That's Big Ben. I'll have to check, but I think Simon's father brought that thing home from Alaska. I'm just learning about the collection myself."

"You're new here?"

"Since April. We're trying to recruit new volunteers, if you know anyone who'd like to join us. We're especially looking for younger volunteers, to work with the children."

Jane still couldn't take her eyes off those lethal-looking bear claws. "I thought this was an archaeology museum," she said. "How does this bear fit in?"

"Actually, it's an *everything* museum, and that's what makes it so hard to market ourselves. Most of this was collected by five generations of Crispins, but we also have a number of donated items. On the second floor, we display a lot of animals with fangs and claws. It's strange, but that's where the kids always seem to end up. They like to stare at carnivores. Bunnies bore them."

"Bunnies can't kill you," said Jane.

"Maybe that's what it is. We all like to be scared, don't we?" Debbie turned and continued up the stairs.

"What's up on the third floor?" Frost asked.

"More display space. I'll show you. We use it for our rotating exhibits."

"So you bring in new stuff?"

"Oh, we don't have to bring in anything. There's so much stored down in the basement that we could probably change that exhibit every month for the next twenty years and never repeat ourselves."

"So what have you got up there now?"

"Bones."

"You mean human?"

Debbie gave him a quietly amused look. "Of course. How else do we catch the attention of a hopelessly jaded public? We could show them the most exquisite Ming vase, or a carved ivory screen from Persia, and they'd turn their backs and go straight for the human remains."

"And where do these bones come from?"

"Trust me. *These* are well documented. They were brought back from Turkey a century ago by one of the

Crispins. I can't remember which one, probably Cornelius. Dr. Robinson thought it was time to get them out of storage and back in the public eye. This exhibit's all about ancient burial practices."

"You sound like an archaeologist yourself."

"Me?" Debbie laughed. "I've just got a lot of time on my hands, and I love beautiful things. So I think museums are worth supporting. Did you see the exhibit downstairs? Aside from the mounted carnivores, we have treasures that deserve to be seen. That's what the museum should focus on, not stuffed bears, but you have to give the public what it wants. That's why we had such high hopes for Madam X. She would have brought in enough cash to keep our heat turned on, at least."

They reached the third floor and walked into the Ancient Cemeteries exhibit. Jane saw glass cases containing human bones arranged on sand, as though just uncovered by the archaeologist's trowel. While Debbie walked briskly past them, Jane found herself falling behind, staring at skeletons curled into fetal positions, at a dead mother's bony limbs lovingly embracing the fragmented remains of a child. The child could not have been much older than her own daughter, Regina. A whole village of the dead lies here, thought Jane. What sort of man would so brutally rip these people from their resting places and ship them to be ogled in a foreign land? Did Simon Crispin's ancestor feel any inkling of guilt as he'd wrenched these bones from their

graves? Old coins or marble statues or human bones—
all were treated the same by the Crispin family. They
were items to be collected and displayed like trophies.

"Detective?" said Debbie.

Leaving behind the silent dead, Jane and Frost
followed Debbie into Simon Crispin's office.

The man who sat waiting for them looked far frailer
than she'd expected. His hair had thinned to white
wisps, and brown age spots blotted his hands and scalp.
But his piercing blue eyes were agleam with keen
interest as he shook hands with his two visitors.

"Thank you for seeing us, Mr. Crispin," said
Jane.

"I wish I could have attended the autopsy myself," he
said. "But my hip hasn't quite healed from surgery, and
I'm still hobbling around with a cane. Please, sit down."

Jane glanced around at the room, which was
furnished with a massive oak desk and armchairs
upholstered in frayed green velvet. With its dark wood
paneling and Palladian windows, the room looked like
it belonged in a genteel club from an earlier century, a
place where gentlemen sipped sherry. But like the rest of
the building, the room showed its age. The Persian
carpet was worn almost threadbare, and the yellowing
volumes in the barrister's bookcase appeared to be at
least a hundred years old.

Jane sat in one of the velvet chairs, feeling dwarfed by
the throne-sized furniture, like a child playing queen for
a day. Frost, too, settled into one of the massive chairs,

but instead of looking kingly, he looked vaguely constipated on his velvet throne.

"We'll do all we can to help you with this investigation," said Simon. "Dr. Robinson's the one in charge of daily operations. I'm afraid I'm rather useless since I broke my hip."

"How did it happen?" asked Jane.

"I fell into an excavation pit in Turkey." He saw Jane's raised eyebrow and smiled. "Yes, even at the ripe old age of eighty-two, I was working in the field. I've never been merely an armchair archaeologist. I believe one has to get one's hands dirty or you're nothing but a *hobbyist*." The note of contempt he used for that last word left no doubt what he thought of such dabblers.

Debbie said, "You'll be back in the field before you know it, Simon. At your age, it just takes time to heal."

"I don't *have* time. I left Turkey seven months ago, and I'm worried the excavation's turned into a mess." He gave a sigh. "But it couldn't be as big a mess as we're dealing with here."

"I assume Dr. Robinson told you what we found in the autopsy yesterday," said Jane.

"Yes. And to say that we're shocked is an understatement. This is not the kind of attention any museum wants."

"I doubt it's the kind of attention Madam X wanted, either."

"I wasn't even aware we *had* a mummy in our

collection until Nicholas discovered her during his inventory."

"He said that was back in January."

"Yes. Soon after I had my hip operation."

"How does a museum lose track of something as valuable as a mummy?"

He gave a sheepish smile. "Visit any museum with a large collection, and chances are you'll find basements as disorganized as ours. We're a hundred and thirty years old. In that time, over a dozen curators and hundreds of interns, museum guides, and other volunteers have worked under this roof. Field notes get lost, records go missing, and items get misplaced. So it's not surprising we've lost track of what we own." He sighed. "I'm afraid I must assume the largest burden of blame."

"Why?"

"For too long, I left the operational details entirely in the hands of Dr. William Scott-Kerr, our former curator. I was abroad so much, I didn't know what was happening here at home. But Mrs. Willebrandt saw his deterioration. How he began to misplace papers or affix the wrong labels to displays. Eventually he became so forgetful, he couldn't identify even common implements. The tragedy is, this man was once brilliant, a former field archaeologist who'd worked all over the world. Mrs. Willebrandt wrote me about her concerns, and when I got home, I could see we had a serious problem. I didn't have the heart to immediately dismiss him, and as it turned out, I didn't have to. He was struck by a car and killed, right outside this building. Only seventy-four years old, but it was probably a blessing, considering the grim prognosis had he lived."

"Was it Alzheimer's?" asked Jane.

Simon nodded. "The signs were probably there for a decade, but William managed to cover it up well. The collection was left in complete disarray. We didn't realize how bad things were until I hired Dr. Robinson three years ago, and he discovered that accession ledgers were missing. He couldn't find documentation for a number of crates in the basement. In January, when he opened up the crate containing Madam X, he had no idea what was inside it. Believe me, we were all stunned. We had no inkling there was *ever* a mummy in the collection."

"Miss Duke told us that most of the collection comes down from your family," said Frost.

"Five generations of Crispins have personally wielded trowels and shovels. Collecting is our family passion. Unfortunately, it's also a costly obsession, and this museum has sucked up what was left of my inheritance." He sighed again. "Which leaves it where it is today—short of funds and dependent on volunteers. And donors."

"Could that be how Madam X ended up here?" asked Frost. "From a donor?"

"Donated artifacts do come our way," Simon said. "People want a safe home for some prized antiquity that they can't properly care for. Or they want a nice little plaque with their name on a permanent display for everyone to see. We're willing to take almost anything."

"But you have no record of a donated mummy?"

"Nicholas found no mention of one. And believe me, he searched. He made it his mission. In March we hired Josephine to help us with the Madam X analysis, and she couldn't track down the mummy's origins, either."

"It's possible Madam X was added to the collection when Dr. Scott-Kerr was curator," said Debbie.

"The guy with Alzheimer's," said Jane.

"Right. And he could have misplaced the paperwork. It would explain things."

"It sounds like a reasonable theory," said Jane. "But we have to pursue other theories as well. Who has access to your basement?"

"The keys are kept at the reception desk, so pretty much everyone on staff does."

"Then anyone on your staff could have placed Madam X in the basement?"

There was a moment's silence. Debbie and Simon looked at each other, and his face darkened. "I don't like what you're implying, Detective."

"It's a reasonable question."

"We are a venerable institution, staffed by excellent people, most of them volunteers," said Simon. "Our museum guides, our student interns—they're here because they're dedicated to preservation."

"I wasn't questioning anybody's dedication. I just wondered who had access."

"What you're really asking is, Who could have stashed a dead body down there?"

"It's a possibility we have to consider."

"Trust me, we've had no murderers employed here."

"Can you be absolutely certain of that, Mr. Crispin?" Jane asked quietly, but her gaze left him no easy escape. She could see that her question had disturbed him. She had forced him to confront the awful possibility that someone he knew, now or in the past, could have brought death into this proud bastion of learning.

"I'm sorry, Mr. Crispin," she finally said. "But things may be a little disrupted here for a while."

"What do you mean?"

"Somehow a dead body ended up in your museum. Maybe she was donated to you a decade ago. Maybe she was placed here recently. The problem is, you have no documentation. You don't even know what else is in your collection. We're going to need to take a look at your basement."

Simon shook his head in bewilderment. "And just what are you expecting to find?"

She didn't answer the question; she didn't need to.

7

"Is this absolutely necessary?" said Nicholas Robinson. "Do you have to do it this way?"

"I'm afraid we do," said Jane, and handed him the search warrant. As he read it, Jane stood by with her team of three male detectives. Today she and Frost had brought in Detectives Tripp and Crowe for the search, and they all waited as Robinson took a painfully long time examining the warrant. The ever-impatient Darren Crowe give a loud huff of frustration, and Jane shot him an annoyed look of *Cool it,* a pointed reminder that she was in charge of this team, and he'd better toe the line.

Robinson frowned at the paperwork. "You're searching for human remains?" He looked up at Jane. "Well, of course you'll find them here. This is a *museum.* And I assure you, those bones on the third floor *are* ancient. If you'd like me to point out the relevant dental evidence—"

"It's what you have stored in the basement that

interests us. If you'll unlock the door down there, we can get started."

Robinson glanced at the other detectives who stood nearby and spotted the crowbar in Detective Tripp's hands. "You can't just go breaking open crates! You could damage priceless artifacts."

"You're welcome to observe and advise. But please don't move anything or touch anything."

"Why are you turning this museum into a crime scene?"

"We're concerned that Madam X may not be the only surprise in your collection. Now, please come down with us to the basement."

Robinson swallowed hard and looked at the senior museum guide, who'd been watching the confrontation. "Mrs. Willebrandt, would you call Josephine and tell her to come in right away? I need her."

"It's five minutes to ten, Dr. Robinson. Visitors will be arriving."

"The museum will have to stay closed today," said Jane. "We'd prefer that the media not catch wind of what's going on. So please lock the front doors."

Her order was pointedly ignored by Mrs. Willebrandt, who kept her gaze on the curator. "Dr. Robinson?"

He gave a resigned sigh. "It appears we have no choice in the matter. Please do as the police say." Opening a drawer behind the reception desk, he took out a set of keys, then led the way past the wax statue of Dr. Cornelius Crispin, past the Greek and Roman marble busts, to the stairwell. A dozen creaking steps took them down to the basement level.

There he paused. Turning to Jane, he said: "Do I need an attorney? Am I a suspect?"

"No."

"Then who is? Tell me that much at least."

"This may date back to before your employment here."

"How far back?"

"To the previous curator."

Robinson gave a startled laugh. "That poor man had Alzheimer's. You don't really think old William was storing dead bodies down here, do you?"

"The door, Dr. Robinson."

Shaking his head, he unlocked the door. Cool, dry air spilled out. They stepped into the room, and Jane heard startled murmurs from the other detectives as they glimpsed the vast storage area, filled with row upon row of crates stacked almost to the ceiling.

"Please keep the door closed, if you could," said Robinson. "This is a climate-controlled area."

"Man," said Detective Crowe. "This is going to take us forever to look through all of these. What's in these crates, anyway?"

"We're more than halfway through our inventory," said Robinson. "If you'd only give us another few months to complete it, we'd be able to tell you what every crate contains."

"A few months is a long time to wait."

"It's taken me a year just to inspect those rows there, all the way to the back shelves. I can personally vouch for their contents. But I haven't yet opened the crates at this end. It's a slow process because one needs to be careful and document everything. Some of the items are centuries old and may already be crumbling."

"Even in a climate-controlled room?" asked Tripp.

"The air-conditioning wasn't installed until the 1960s."

Frost pointed to a crate on the bottom of a stack. "Look at the date stamped on that one. '1873. Siam.' "

"You see?" Robinson looked at Jane. "There may be treasures here that haven't been unpacked in a hundred years. My plan was to go through these crates systematically and document everything." He paused. "But then I discovered Madam X and the inventory came to a halt. Otherwise, we'd be further along by now."

"Where did you find her crate?" asked Jane. "Which section?"

"Down this row, back against the wall." He pointed to the far end of the storage area. "She was at the bottom of the stack."

"You looked in the crates that were on top of hers?"

"Yes. They contained items acquired during the 1910s. Artifacts from the Ottoman Empire, plus a few Chinese scrolls and pottery."

"The 1910s?" Jane thought of the mummy's perfect

dentition, the amalgam filling in her tooth. "Madam X was almost certainly more recent than that."

"Then how did she end up underneath older crates?" asked Detective Crowe.

"Obviously someone rearranged things in here," said Jane. "It would have made her less accessible."

As Jane gazed around the cavernous space, she thought of the mausoleum in which her grandmother had been interred, a marble palace where every wall was etched with the names of those who rested within the crypts. *Is this what I'm looking at now? A mausoleum packed with nameless victims?* She walked toward the far end of the basement, where Madam X had been found. Two lightbulbs overhead had burned out in this area, throwing the corner into shadow.

"Let's start our search here," she said.

Together Frost and Crowe pulled the top crate off the stack and lowered it to the floor. On the lid was scrawled: MISCELLANEOUS. CONGO. Frost used a crowbar to pry up the lid, and at his first glimpse of what lay inside, he flinched back, bumping against Jane.

"What is it?" she asked.

Darren Crowe suddenly laughed. Reaching into the crate, he pulled out a wooden mask and held it over his face. "Boo!"

"Be careful with that!" said Robinson. "It's valuable."

"It's also creepy as hell," murmured Frost, staring

at the mask's grotesque features carved into wood.

Crowe set the mask aside and pulled out one of the crumpled newspapers used to cushion the crate's contents. "London *Times,* 1930. I'd say this crate predates our perp."

"I really must protest," said Robinson. "You're touching things—contaminating things. You should all be wearing gloves."

"Maybe you should wait outside, Dr. Robinson," said Jane.

"No, I won't. The safety of this collection is my responsibility."

She turned to confront him. Mild-mannered though he appeared, he stubbornly stood his ground as she advanced, his eyes blinking furiously behind his glasses. Outside this museum, if confronted by a police officer, Nicholas Robinson would probably respond deferentially. But here on his own territory, in defense of his precious collection, he appeared fully prepared to engage in hand-to-hand combat.

"You're rampaging through here like wild cattle," he said. "What makes you think there are more bodies down here? What kind of people do you think work in museums?"

"I don't know, Dr. Robinson. That's what I'm trying to find out."

"Then ask *me.* Talk to *me,* instead of tearing apart crates. I know this museum. I know the people who've worked here."

"You've been curator here for only three years," said Jane.

"I also worked here as a summer intern when I was in college. I knew Dr. Scott-Kerr, and he was utterly harmless." He glared at Crowe, who had just fished a vase out of the open crate. "Hey! That's at least four hundred years old! Treat it with respect!"

"Maybe it's time for you and me to step outside," said Jane. "We need to talk."

He shot a worried glance at the three detectives, who had started opening another crate. He reluctantly followed her out of the basement and up the stairs to the first-floor gallery. They stood by the Egyptian exhibit, its faux tomb entrance looming above them.

"Exactly when were you an intern here, Dr. Robinson?" Jane asked.

"Twenty years ago, during my junior and senior years in college. When William was curator, he tried to bring in one or two college students every summer."

"Why are there no interns now?"

"We no longer have money in our budget to pay their expenses. So we find it almost impossible to attract any students. Besides, when you're young, you'd rather be working out in the field anyway, with other kids your age. Not confined to this dusty old building."

"What do you remember about Dr. Scott-Kerr?"

"I liked him quite a bit," he said. And a smile flickered on his lips at the memory. "He was a little absentminded even then, but he was always pleasant, always generous with his time. He gave me a great deal of responsibility right off the bat, and that made it the best experience I could have had. Even if it did set me up for disappointment."

"Why?"

"It raised my expectations. I thought I'd be able to land a job just like it when I finished my doctorate."

"You didn't?"

He shook his head. "I ended up working as a shovel bum."

"What does that mean?"

"A contract archaeologist. These days, that's pretty much the only kind of job one can get with a fresh archaeology degree. They call it cultural resource management. I worked at construction sites and military bases. I dug test pits, looking for any evidence of historic value before the bulldozers moved in. It's a job only for young people. There are no benefits, you're always living out of a suitcase, and it's damn hard on the knees and back. So when Simon called me three years ago to offer me this job, I was glad to hang up my shovel, even if I'm earning less than I did in the field. Which explains why this position went vacant for so long after Dr. Scott-Kerr died."

"How can a museum operate without a curator?"

"By letting someone like Mrs. Willebrandt run the show, if you can believe it. She left the same displays in the same dusty cases for years." He glanced toward the reception desk, and his voice dropped to a whisper. "And you know what? *She* hasn't changed a whit since I was an intern. That woman was born ancient."

Jane heard footsteps thump on the stairwell and turned to see Frost trudging up the basement steps. "Rizzoli, you'd better come down and see this."

"What did you find?"

"We're not sure."

She and Robinson followed Frost back down to the basement storeroom. Spilled wood shavings littered the floor where the detectives had searched through several more crates.

"We were trying to pull that crate down, and I braced myself against the wall," said Detective Tripp. "It kind of gave way behind me. And then I noticed *that*." He pointed toward the bricks. "Crowe, shine your flashlight this way, so she can see it."

Crowe aimed his beam and Jane frowned at the wall, which was now bowed outward. One of the bricks had fallen away, leaving a gap through which Jane could see only blackness beyond.

"There's a space back there," said Crowe. "When I shine my light through, I can't even see a back wall."

Jane turned to Robinson. "What's behind these bricks?"

"I have no idea," he murmured, staring in bewilderment at the bowed wall. "I always assumed these walls were solid. But it's such an old building."

"How old?"

"At least a hundred and fifty years. That's what the plumber told us when he came to update the restroom. This was once their family residence, you know."

"The Crispins?"

"They lived here in the mid-1800s, then the family moved into a new home out in Brookline. That's when this building was turned into the museum."

"Which direction does this wall face?" asked Frost.

Robinson thought about it. "That would be facing the street, I think."

"So there's no building on the other side of this."

"No, just the road."

"Let's pull some of these bricks out," said Jane, "and see what's on the other side."

Robinson looked alarmed. "If you start removing bricks, it could all collapse."

"But this obviously isn't a weight-bearing wall," said Tripp. "Or it would already have fallen."

"I want you all to stop right now," said Robinson. "Before you go any further, I need to speak to Simon."

"Then why don't you go ahead and call him?" said Jane.

As the curator walked out, the four detectives remained in place, a silent tableau poised for his departure. The instant the door shut behind him, Jane's attention shot back to the wall. "These lower bricks aren't even mortared together. They're just stacked up, loose."

"So what's holding up the top of that wall?" asked Frost.

Gingerly, Jane eased out one of the loose bricks, half expecting the rest of them to come tumbling down. But the wall held. She glanced at Tripp. "What do you think?"

"There's got to be a brace on top supporting the upper third."

"Then it should be safe to pull out these lower ones, right?"

"It should be. I guess."

She gave a nervous laugh. "You fill me with such confidence, Tripp." As the three men stood by and watched, she gently eased out another loose brick, and another. She couldn't help noticing that the other detectives had backed away, leaving her alone at the base of the wall. Despite the gap she'd now opened, the structure continued to hold. Peering through, she confronted only pitch blackness.

"Give me your flashlight, Crowe."

He handed it to her.

Dropping to her knees, she shone the beam through the gap. She could make out the rough surface of a facing wall a few yards away. Slowly she panned across it, and her beam came to a sudden halt on a niche carved into the stone. On a face that stared back at her from the darkness.

She stumbled backward, gasping.

"What?" said Frost. "What did you see in there?"

For a moment, Jane could not speak. Heart thudding, she stared at the gap in the bricks, a dark window into a chamber she had no wish to explore. Not after what she'd just glimpsed in those shadows.

"Rizzoli?"

She swallowed. "I think it's time to call the ME."

8

This was not Maura's first visit to the Crispin Museum.

A few years ago, soon after her move to Boston, she had found the museum listed in a guidebook to area attractions. On one cold Sunday in January, she had stepped through the museum's front door, expecting to compete with the usual weekend sightseers, the usual harried parents tugging along bored children. Instead she'd entered a silent building staffed by a lone museum guide at the reception desk, an elderly woman who had taken Maura's entrance fee and then ignored her. Maura had walked alone through gallery after gloomy gallery, past dusty glass cases filled with curiosities from around the world, past yellowed tags that looked as if they had not been replaced in a century. The struggling furnace could not drive the chill from the building, and Maura had kept on her coat and scarf during the entire tour.

Two hours later, she had walked out, depressed by the experience. Depressed, also, because that solitary visit seemed to symbolize her life at the time. Recently divorced and without friends in a new city, she was a solitary wanderer in a cold and gloomy landscape where no one greeted her or even seemed aware of her existence.

She had not returned to the Crispin Museum. Until today.

She felt a twinge of that same depression as she stepped into the building, as she once again breathed in its scent of age. Though years had passed since she'd last set foot here, the gloom she'd felt on that January day instantly resettled upon her shoulders, a reminder that her life, after all, had not really changed. Although she was now in love, she still wandered alone on Sundays—particularly on Sundays.

But today's official duties demanded her attention as she followed Jane down the stairs to the basement storage area. By now, the detectives had made the hole in the wall large enough for her to squeeze through. She paused at the chamber entrance and frowned at the pile of bricks that had been pulled loose.

"Is it safe to go in there? Are you sure it won't collapse?" Maura asked.

"It's supported by a cross brace at the top," said Jane. "This was meant to look like a solid wall, but I think there may have been a door here at one time, leading to a hidden chamber."

"Hidden? For what purpose?"

"To stash valuables? To hide booze during

Prohibition? Who knows? Even Simon Crispin has no idea what this space was intended for."

"Did he know it existed?"

"He said he'd heard stories when he was a kid about a tunnel connecting this building with one across the street. But this chamber's just a dead end." Jane handed her a flashlight. "You first," she said. "I'll be right behind you."

Maura crouched at the hole. She felt the gazes of the detectives silently watching her, waiting for her reaction. Whatever waited inside that chamber had disturbed them, and their silence made her reluctant to proceed. She could not see into the space, but she knew that something foul waited in the darkness—something that had been shut away so long, the air within seemed rank and chill. She dropped to her knees and squeezed through the opening.

Beyond, she found a space just high enough for her to stand. Reaching out straight in front of her, she felt nothing. She turned on her flashlight.

A disembodied face squinted back at her.

She sucked in a shocked breath and jerked back, colliding with Jane, who had just squeezed into the space behind her.

"I guess you saw them," said Jane.

"Them?"

Jane turned on her flashlight. "There's one right here." The beam landed on the face that had just startled Maura. "And a second one's here." The beam shifted, landing on a second niche, which held another face, grotesquely shriveled. "And finally there's a third one right here." Jane aimed her flashlight at a stone ledge just above Maura. The wizened face was framed by a waterfall of lustrous black hair. Brutal stitches bound the lips together, as though condemning them to eternal silence.

"Tell me these aren't real heads," said Jane softly. "Please."

Maura reached in her pocket for gloves. Her hands felt chilled and clumsy, and she fumbled in the darkness to pull latex over clammy fingers. As Jane aimed her beam up at the ledge, Maura gently pulled the head from its stone shelf. It felt startlingly weightless and was compact enough to rest in her palm. The curtain of hair was unbound, and she flinched as silky strands brushed across her bare arm. Not mere nylon, she thought, but real hair. *Human hair.*

Maura swallowed. "I think this is a *tsantsa*."

"A what?"

"A shrunken head." Maura looked at Jane. "It seems to be real."

"It could also be old, right? Just some antique the museum collected from Africa?"

"South America."

"Whatever. Couldn't these be part of their old collection?"

"They could be." Maura looked at her in the darkness. "Or they could be recent."

*   *   *

The museum staff stared at the three *tsantsas* resting on the museum's lab table. Mercilessly lit by the glare of exam lights, every detail of the heads was illuminated, from their feathery eyelashes and eyebrows to the elaborate braiding of the cotton strings that bound their lips closed. Crowning two of the heads was long, jet-black hair. The hair of the third had been cut in a blunt bob that looked like a woman's wig perched atop a far-too-small doll's head. The heads were so diminutive, in fact, that they could easily be mistaken for mere rubber souvenirs, were it not for the clearly human texture of the brows and lashes.

"I have no idea why these were behind that wall," Simon murmured. "Or how they got there."

"This building is full of mysteries, Dr. Isles," said Debbie Duke. "Whenever we update the wiring or fix the plumbing, our contractors find some new surprise. A bricked-up space or a passage that serves absolutely no purpose." She looked across the table at Dr. Robinson. "You remember that fiasco with the lighting last month, don't you? The electrician had to break down half the third-floor wall just to figure out where the wires tracked. Nicholas? Nicholas?"

The curator was staring so intently at the *tsantsas* that only when he heard his name called again did he glance up. "Yes, this building's something of a puzzle," he said. And he added, softly: "It makes me wonder what else we haven't found behind these walls."

"So these things are real?" asked Jane. "They're actually shrunken human heads?"

"They're definitely real," said Nicholas. "The problem is . . ."

"What?"

"Josephine and I scanned all the inventory records we could locate. According to the accession ledgers, this museum does indeed have *tsantsas* in the collection. They were added in 1898, when they were brought back from the upper Amazon basin by Dr. Stanley Crispin." He looked at Simon. "Your grandfather, I believe."

Simon nodded. "I'd heard we had them in our collection. I never knew what became of them."

"According to the curator who worked here in the 1890s, the items are described as follows." Robinson flipped to the page in the ledger. " 'Ceremonial Jivaro trophy heads, both in excellent condition.' "

Registering the significance of that description, Maura glanced up at him. "Did you say *both*?"

Robinson nodded. "According to these records, there are only two in the collection."

"Could a third have been added later, but never recorded?"

"Certainly. That's one of the issues we've been struggling with, our incomplete records. That's why I began the inventory, so I could finally get a handle on what we have."

Maura frowned at the three shrunken heads. "So

now the question is, which one is the new addition? And how recent is it?"

"I'm betting on her being the new one." Jane pointed to the *tsantsa* with the bobbed hair. "I swear I saw a haircut just like that on my barista this morning."

"First of all," said Robinson, "it's almost impossible to tell, just by appearance, if a *tsantsa* is male or female. Shrinking the head distorts the features and makes the sexes look alike. Second, the hair of some traditional *tsantsas* may be cut short like that one. They're unusual, but the haircut doesn't really tell us anything."

"So how do you tell a traditional shrunken head from a modern copy?" asked Maura.

"You will permit me to handle them?" Robinson asked.

"Yes, of course."

He crossed to the cabinet to get gloves and pulled them on as deliberately as a doctor about to perform delicate surgery. This man would be meticulous no matter what his profession, Maura thought. She could not remember any medical school classmate more exacting than Nicholas Robinson.

"First," he said, "I should explain what constitutes a genuine Jivaro *tsantsa*. It was one of my particular interests, so I know a bit about them. The Jivaro people live along the border between Ecuador and Peru, and they regularly raid each other's tribes. Warriors will take anyone's head—men, women, children."

"Why take the heads?" asked Jane.

"It has to do with their concept of the soul. They believe that people can have up to three different types of souls. There's an ordinary soul, which is what everyone possesses at birth. Then there's an ancient vision soul, and it's something you have to earn through ceremonial efforts. It gives you special powers. If someone earns an ancient vision soul, and then he's murdered, he transforms into the third kind—an avenging soul, who will pursue his killer. The only way to stop an avenging soul from exacting retribution is to cut off the head and turn it into a *tsantsa*."

"How do you make a *tsantsa*?" Jane looked down at the three doll-sized heads. "I just don't see how you can shrink a human head down to something that small."

"Accounts of the process are contradictory, but most reports agree on a few key steps. Because of the tropical environment, the process had to be started immediately after death. You take the severed head and slice open the scalp in a straight line, from the crown all the way to the base of the neck. Then you peel the skin away from the bone. It actually comes off quite easily."

Maura looked at Jane. "You've seen me do almost the same thing at autopsy. I peel the scalp away from the skull. But my incision goes across the crown, ear to ear."

"Yeah, and that's the part that always grosses me out," said Jane. "Especially when you peel it over the face."

"Oh yes. The face," said Robinson. "The Jivaro peel

that off, too. It takes skill, but the face comes off, along with the scalp, all in one piece. What you have, then, is a mask of human skin. They turn it inside out and scrape it clean. Then the eyelids are sewn shut." He lifted one of the *tsantsas* and pointed to the almost invisible stitches. "See how delicately it's been done, leaving the eyelashes looking completely natural? This is *really* skillful work."

Was that a note of admiration in his voice? Maura wondered. Robinson did not seem to notice the uneasy looks that Maura and Jane exchanged; he was focused entirely on the craftsmanship that had turned human skin into an archaeological oddity.

He turned the *tsantsa* over to look at the neck, which was merely a leathery tube. Coarse stitches ran up the back of the neck and the scalp, where they were almost hidden by the thick hair. "After the skin is removed from the skull," he continued, "it's simmered in water and plant juices, to melt away the last of the fat. When every last bit of flesh and fat is scraped away, it all gets turned right-side out again, and the incision in the back of the head is sewn up, as you can see here. The lips are fastened together using three sharpened wooden skewers. The nostrils and ears are plugged with cotton. At this point, it's just a floppy sack of skin, so they stuff hot stones and sand into the cavity to sear the skin. Then it's rubbed with charcoal and hung over smoke, until the skin shrinks down to the consistency of leather. This whole process doesn't take long. Probably not more than a week."

"And what do they do with it?" asked Jane.

"They come home to their tribe with their preserved trophies and celebrate with a feast and ritual dances. They wear their *tsantsas* like necklaces, hung by a cord around the warrior's neck. A year later, there's a second feast, to transfer the power from the victim's spirit. Finally, a month after that, there's a third celebration. That's when the last touches are performed. They take the three wooden skewers out of the lips and thread cotton string through the holes and braid it. And they add the ear ornaments. From then on, the heads are seen as bragging rights. Whenever the warrior wants to display his manhood, he wears his *tsantsa* around his neck."

Jane gave a disbelieving laugh. "Just like guys today, with their gold chains. What is it with macho men and necklaces?"

Maura surveyed the three *tsantsas* on the table. All were of similar size. All had braided lip strings and delicately sutured eyelids. "I'm afraid I can't see any difference among these three heads. They all appear skillfully crafted."

"They are," said Robinson. "But there's one important difference. And I'm not talking about the haircut." He turned and looked at Josephine, who had been standing silently at the foot of the table. "Can you see what I'm talking about?"

The young woman hesitated, loath to step any closer.

Then she pulled on gloves and moved to the table. She picked up the heads one by one and studied each under the light. At last she picked up a head with long hair and beetle-wing ornaments. "This one isn't Jivaro," she said.

Robinson nodded. "I agree."

"Because of the earrings?" asked Maura.

"No. Earrings like those are traditional," said Robinson.

"Then what made you choose that particular one, Dr. Pulcillo?" said Maura. "It looks pretty much like the other two."

Josephine stared down at the head in question, and her black hair spilled over her shoulders, the strands as dark and glossy as the *tsantsa*'s, the colors so eerily similar they could have blended one into the other. Just for an instant, Maura had the unsettling impression that she was staring at the same head, before and after. Josephine alive, Josephine dead. Was that why the young woman was so reluctant to touch it? Did she see herself in those shriveled features?

"It's the lips," said Josephine.

Maura shook her head. "I don't see any difference. All three have their lips sewn shut with cotton thread."

"It has to do with Jivaro ritual. What Nicholas just said."

"Which part?"

"That the wooden pegs are eventually removed from the lips and cotton string is threaded through the holes."

"All three of these have cotton thread."

"Yes, but it doesn't happen until the *third* feast. Over a year after the kill."

"She's absolutely right," said Robinson, looking pleased that his young colleague had picked up on precisely the detail he'd wanted her to notice. "The lip pegs, Dr. Isles! When they're left in for a whole year, they leave gaping holes behind."

Maura studied the heads on the table. Two of the *tsantsas* had large holes punched through the lips. The third did not.

"No pegs were used in this one," said Robinson. "The lips were simply stitched together, right after the head was removed. This one isn't Jivaro. Whoever made it took a few shortcuts. Maybe he didn't know exactly how it should be done. Or this was merely meant to be sold to tourists, or bartered as trade goods. But it's not a ceremonial specimen."

"Then what are its origins?" asked Maura.

Robinson paused. "I really can't tell you. I can only say that it is not authentic Jivaro."

With gloved hands, Maura lifted the *tsantsa* from the table. She had held severed human heads in her palms before, and this one, minus its skull, was startlingly light, a mere husk of dried skin and hair.

"We can't even be certain of its sex," said Robinson. "Although its features, distorted though they are, seem feminine to me. Too delicate to be a man's."

"I agree," said Maura.

"What about the skin color?" asked Jane. "Does that tell us its race?"

"No," said Robinson. "The process of shrinking darkens the skin. This could even be a Caucasian. And without a skull, without any teeth to X-ray, I can't tell you how old this specimen is."

Maura turned the *tsantsa* upside down and stared into the neck opening. It was startling to see merely a hollow space rather than cartilage and muscle, trachea and esophagus. The neck was half collapsed, the dark cavity hidden from view. Suddenly she flashed back to the autopsy she'd performed on Madam X. She remembered the dry cave of a mouth, the glint of metal in the throat. And she remembered the shock she'd felt at her first glimpse of the souvenir cartouche. Had the killer left a similar clue tucked into this victim's remains?

"Could I have more light?" she said.

Josephine swung a magnifying lamp toward her, and Maura aimed the beam into the neck cavity. Through the narrow opening, she could just make out a pale mass balled up within. "It looks like paper," she said.

"That wouldn't be unusual," said Robinson. "Sometimes you find crumpled newspapers stuffed inside, to help maintain the shape of the head for shipping. If it's a South American newspaper, then at least we'll know something about its origins."

"Do you have forceps?"

Josephine retrieved a pair from the workroom drawer and handed them to her. Maura introduced the forceps into the neck opening and grasped what was inside. Gingerly she tugged, and crumpled newspaper emerged. Smoothing out the page, she saw it was printed in neither Spanish nor Portuguese, but English.

"The *Indio Daily News*?" Jane gave a startled laugh. "It's from California."

"And look at the date." Maura pointed to the top of the page. "It's only twenty-six years old."

"Still, the head could be much older," said Robinson. "That newspaper could have been stuffed in there later, just for shipping."

"But it does confirm one thing." Maura looked up. "This head wasn't part of the museum's original collection. She could be another victim, added as recently as . . ." She paused, her gaze suddenly focused on Josephine.

The young woman had gone pale. Maura had seen that sickly color before, on the faces of young cops observing their first autopsies, and she knew that it usually heralded a nauseated dash to the sink or a stagger toward the nearest chair. Josephine did neither; she simply turned and walked out.

"I should check on her." Dr. Robinson stripped off his gloves. "She didn't look well."

"I'll see how she's doing," Frost volunteered, and he followed Josephine out of the room. Even after the door swung shut, Dr. Robinson stood staring after him, as though debating whether he should follow.

"Do you have the records from twenty-six years ago?" asked Maura. "Dr. Robinson?"

Suddenly aware that she'd said his name, he turned to her. "Excuse me?"

"Twenty-six years ago. The date of this newspaper. Do you have documents from that period?"

"Oh. Yes, we have found a ledger from the 1970s and 1980s. But I don't recall any *tsantsa* mentioned in it. If it came in during that time, it wasn't recorded." He looked at Simon. "Do you remember?"

Wearily, Simon shook his head. He appeared drained, as if he'd aged ten years in the last half hour. "I don't know where that head came from," he said. "I don't know who put it behind that wall or why."

Maura stared at the shrunken head, its eyes and lips sewn shut for eternity. And she said softly: "It looks like someone has been compiling a collection all his own."

9

Josephine was desperate to be left alone, but she could think of no graceful way to brush off Detective Frost. He'd followed her upstairs to her office and was now standing in her doorway, watching her with a look of concern. He had mild eyes and a kind face, and his shaggy blond hair made her think of the towheaded twin boys she often saw whooshing down the slide in the neighborhood playground. Nevertheless, he was a policeman, and policemen frightened her. She shouldn't have left the room so abruptly. She shouldn't have called attention to herself. But a glimpse of that newspaper had hit her like a fist, stealing her breath, rocking her off her feet.

Indio, California. Twenty-six years ago.

The town where I was born. The year that I was born.

It was yet another eerie connection to her past, and she didn't understand how it could be possible. She needed time to think about this, to figure out why so many old and secret ties to her own life should be hidden in the base*ment of the obscure museum where she had taken a job. It's as if my own life, my own past, has been preserved in this collection.* Even as she mentally struggled for an explanation, she was forced to smile and keep up the small talk with Detective Frost, who refused to leave her doorway.

"Are you feeling better?" he asked.

"I got a little light-headed in there. Probably low blood sugar." She sank into her chair. "I shouldn't have skipped breakfast this morning."

"Do you need a cup of coffee or something? Can I get one for you?"

"No, thank you." She managed a smile, hoping it would be enough to send him on his way. Instead, he stepped into her office.

"Did that newspaper have some special significance to you?" Frost asked.

"What do you mean?"

"It's just that I noticed you looked really startled when Dr. Isles opened it up and we saw it was from California."

He was watching me. He's still watching me.

Now was not the time to let him see how close she was to panic. As long as she kept her head down, as long as she stayed on the periphery and played the role of the quiet museum employee, the police would have no reason to glance her way.

"It's not just the newspaper," she said. "It's this whole creepy situation. Finding bodies—and body parts—in this building. I think of museums as sanctuaries. Places of study and contemplation. Now I feel like I'm working in a house of horrors and I'm just wondering when the next body part's going to pop up."

He gave a sympathetic smile, and his boyishness made him look like anything but a policeman. She judged him to be in his midthirties, yet there was something about him that made him seem much younger, and even callow. She saw his wedding ring and thought: There's yet another reason to keep this man at arm's length.

"To be honest, I think this place is already pretty creepy," said Frost. "You've got all those bones displayed on the third floor."

"Those bones are two thousand years old."

"Does that make them less disturbing?"

"It makes them historically significant. I know it doesn't seem like much of a difference. But something about the passage of time gives death a sense of distance, doesn't it? As opposed to Madam X, who could be someone we might actually have known." She paused, feeling a chill. And said, softly: "Ancient remains are easier to deal with."

"They're more like pottery and statues, I guess."

"In a way." She smiled. "The dustier the better."

"And that appeals to you?"

"You sound like you can't understand it."

"I'm just wondering what kind of person chooses to spend a lifetime studying old bones and pottery."

"*What's a girl like you doing in a job like this?* Is that the question?"

He laughed. "You're the youngest thing in this whole building."

Now she, too, smiled, because it was true. "It's the connection with the past. I love to pick up a pottery shard and imagine the man who spun the clay on his wheel. And the woman who used that pot to carry water. And the child who one day dropped it and broke it. History's never been dead for me. I've always felt it was alive and pulsing in those objects you see in the museum cases. It's in my blood, something I was born with, because . . ." Her voice trailed off as she realized she'd strayed into hazardous territory. *Don't talk about the past.*

Don't talk about Mom.

To her relief, Detective Frost did not pick up on her sudden wariness. His next question wasn't about her at all. "I know you haven't been here too long," he said, "but did you ever get the feeling things weren't quite right here?"

"How do you mean?"

"You said that you feel as if you've been working in a house of horrors."

"That was a figure of speech. You can understand it, can't you, after what you just found behind the basement wall? After what Madam X turned out to be?" The temperature in her air-conditioned office seemed to keep dropping. Josephine reached back to pull on the sweater she'd hung on her chair. "At least my job isn't nearly as horrifying as yours must be. You wonder why I choose to work with pottery and old bones. And I wonder why someone like you would choose to work with—well, fresh horrors." She looked up and saw a glimmer of discomfort in his eyes because this time, the question was directed at him. For a man accustomed to interrogating others, he did not seem eager to reciprocate with personal details of his own.

"I'm sorry," she said. "I guess I'm not allowed to ask questions. Only answer them."

"No, I'm just wondering what you meant."

"Meant?"

"When you said *someone like you.*"

"Oh." She gave a sheepish laugh. "It's just that you strike me as such a nice person. A kind person."

"And most policemen aren't?"

She flushed. "I keep digging the hole deeper, don't I? Really, I meant it as a compliment. Because I'll admit, most policemen scare me a little." She looked down at her desk. "I don't think I'm the only one who feels that way."

He sighed. "I'm afraid you may be right. Even though I think I'm the least scary person in the world."

But I'm afraid of you anyway, she thought. Because I know what you could do to me if you learned my secret.

"Detective Frost?" Nicholas Robinson had appeared in her doorway. "Your colleague needs you back downstairs."

"Oh. Right." Frost shot a smile at Josephine. "We'll talk more later, Dr. Pulcillo. And get something to eat, why don't you?"

Nicholas waited until Frost had left the room, then he said to her: "What was that all about?"

"We were just chatting, Nick."

"He's a detective. I don't think they *just chat*."

"It's not as if he was interrogating me or anything."

"Is something bothering you, Josie? Something that I should know about?"

Though his question put her on guard, she managed to say calmly: "Why would you think that?"

"You're not yourself. And it's not just because of what happened today. Yesterday, when I came up behind you in the hallway, you almost jumped out of your skin."

She sat with her hands on her lap, grateful that he could not see them tighten into two knots. In the short time they'd worked together, he had become eerily astute at reading her moods, at knowing when she needed a good laugh and when she needed to be left alone. Surely he could see that this was one of the times she wanted to be alone, yet he did not retreat. It was unlike the Nicholas she knew, a man who was unfailingly respectful of her privacy.

"Josie?" he said. "Do you want to talk about anything?"

She gave a rueful laugh. "I guess I'm mortified that I blew it so badly with Madam X. That I didn't realize we were dealing with a fake."

"That carbon fourteen analysis threw us both off. I was just as wrong as you were."

"But your background isn't Egyptology. That's why you hired me, and I screwed up." She leaned forward, massaging her temples. "If you'd hired someone more experienced, this wouldn't have happened."

"You didn't screw up. You're the one who insisted on the CT scan, remember? Because *you* didn't feel completely confident about her. You were the one who led us to the truth. So stop beating yourself up about this."

"I made the museum look bad. I made *you* look bad, for hiring me."

He didn't respond for a moment. Instead he pulled off his glasses and wiped them with a handkerchief. Always carrying linen handkerchiefs was one of those anachronistic little habits of his that she found so endearing. Sometimes Nicholas reminded her of a gentleman bachelor from an earlier, more innocent time. A time when men would stand up if a woman walked into the room.

"Maybe we should look at the bright side of all this," he said. "Think of the publicity we've gotten. Now the whole world knows the Crispin Museum exists."

"But for all the wrong reasons. They know us as the museum with murder victims in our basement." She felt a fresh pulse of cold air blow in through the vent, and shivered in her sweater. "I keep wondering what else we're going to find in this building. Whether there's another shrunken head stuck in that ceiling up there, or another Madam X bricked in behind this wall. How could this happen without the curator knowing about it?" She looked at Robinson. "It had to be him, didn't it? Dr. Scott-Kerr. He was in charge here all those years, so he must have been the one."

"I knew the man. I find it very hard to believe."

"But did you *really* know him?"

He considered this. "Now I have to wonder how well any of us knew William. How well we ever know anyone. He came off as a quiet and utterly ordinary man. Not someone you'd particularly notice."

"Isn't that how they usually describe the psychopath with two dozen bodies buried in his basement? *He was so quiet and ordinary.*"

"That does seem to be the universal description. But then, it could apply to almost anyone, couldn't it?" Nicholas gave a wry shake of the head. "Including me."

Josephine stared out the window as she rode the bus home. Didn't they say that life was full of coincidences? Hadn't she heard startling tales of vacationers abroad spotting their next-door neighbors on the streets of Paris? Strange convergences happened all the time, and this could simply be one of them.

But it wasn't the first coincidence. That had been the name on the cartouche. Medea. Now there's the Indio Daily News.

At her stop, she stepped out of the bus into a syrupy heat thick with humidity. Black clouds threatened, and as she walked toward her building she heard thunder rumble, felt the hairs feather on her arms, as though stirred by the static of lightning-charged air. Rain pelted her head, and by the time she reached her apartment building it had become a tropical downpour. She dashed up the steps and into the foyer, where she stood dripping water as she opened her mailbox.

She'd just pulled out a bundle of envelopes when the door to Apartment 1A swung open and Mr. Goodwin said, "I thought I saw you running in. It's pretty wet out there, isn't it?"

"It's a mess." She shut the mailbox. "I'm glad I'm in for the evening."

"He delivered another one today. Thought you'd want to take care of it."

"Another what?"

"Another letter addressed to Josephine Sommer. The mailman asked me what you said about the last one, and I told him you took it."

She glanced through the mail she'd just collected and spotted the envelope. It was the same handwriting. This one, too, bore a Boston postmark.

"It's kind of confusing for the post office, you know?" said Mr. Goodwin. "You might want to tell the sender to update your name."

"Right. Thanks." She started up the stairs.

"Did you find your old key ring yet?" he yelled.

Without answering, she scurried into her apartment and shut the door. Dropping the rest of the mail on the couch, she quickly ripped open the envelope addressed to Josephine Sommer and pulled out a folded sheet of paper. She stared at the words BLUE HILLS RESERVATION and wondered why anyone would send her a photo-copied map of nearby hiking trails. Then she turned the sheet over and saw what had been handwritten in ink on the other side:

FIND ME.

Beneath that were numbers:

42 13 06.39
71 04 06.48

She sank onto the couch, the two words staring up from her lap. Outside, the rain had intensified to a tor-rent. Thunder rumbled closer, and a slash of lightning lit the window.

FIND ME.

There was no threat implied in that message, nothing that made her think the sender meant any harm.

She thought of the earlier note she had received a few days ago: *The police are not your friends.* Again not a threat, but a sensible whisper of advice. The police were *not* her friends; this was something she already knew, something she'd known since she was fourteen years old.

She focused on the two numbers. It took her only seconds to recognize what they must represent.

With the lightning storm moving closer, it was not a good time to turn on her computer, but she booted it up anyway. She navigated to the site for Google Earth and used the two numbers as latitude and longitude. Magically the screen panned across a map of Massachusetts and zoomed in on an area of forested land near Boston.

It was the Blue Hills Reservation.

She had guessed correctly; the two numbers were coordinates, and they pointed to a precise location within the park. Clearly this was the location she was meant to visit, but for what reason? She saw no time or date given for any rendezvous. Certainly no one would patiently wait in a park for the hours or days it might take until she showed up. No, there was something specific she was supposed to find there. Not a person, but a thing.

She made a quick Internet search for Blue Hills Reservation and learned that it was a seven-thousand-acre park south of Milton. It had 125 miles of trails that traversed forest, swamp, meadows, and bogs, and was home to a diversity of wildlife, including the timber rattlesnake. Now, *there* was an attraction to recommend it. A chance to encounter rattlesnakes. She retrieved a Boston-area map from her bookshelf and spread it open on the coffee table. Gazing at the large area of green that represented the park, she wondered if she'd have to bushwhack her way through trees and swamp in search of . . . what? Something bigger or smaller than a bread box?

And how will I know when I've reached it?

It was time to pay a call on the gadget man.

She went downstairs and knocked on the door to 1A. Mr. Goodwin appeared, his magnifying goggles perched on top of his head like a second pair of eyes.

"I wonder if I could ask you a favor?" she said.

"I'm right in the middle of something. Will it be quick?"

She glanced past him, into the room cluttered with small appliances and electronics waiting to be repaired. "I'm thinking of buying a GPS for my car. You have one, don't you? Is it easy to figure out?"

Instantly his face lit up. Ask him about a gadget, any gadget, and you could make him a happy man. "Oh my, yes! I don't know what I'd do without mine. I have three of them. I took one to Frankfurt last year, when I visited my daughter, and just like that I knew the streets like a native. Didn't have to ask for directions, just plugged in the address and off I went. You should've seen the looks of envy I got. There were guys stopping me on the street just so they could get a closer look at it."

"Is it complicated?"

"You want me to show you? Come in, come in!" He led her into the living room, having forgotten whatever task had been occupying him earlier. From a drawer, he pulled out a sleek little device scarcely larger than a pack of cards. "Here, I'll turn it on and you can give it a spin. You won't need my help at all. It's all intuitive, you see, just a matter of navigating through the menu.

If you know the address, it'll take you right to the door. You can search for restaurants, hotels. You can even make it speak to you in French."

"I like to hike. What if I'm in the woods and I break my leg? How do I know where I am?"

"You mean if you want to call for help? That's easy. You just dial nine one one on your phone and tell them your coordinates." He snatched the device from her and tapped the screen a few times. "See? This is our location. Latitude and longitude. If I were a hiker, I wouldn't go into the wilds without it. It's as essential as a first-aid kit."

"Wow." She gave him an appropriately impressed smile. "I just don't know if I'm ready to shell out the money for one of these things."

"Why don't you borrow it for a day? Play with it. You'll see how easy it is."

"Are you sure? That would be great."

"Like I said, I have two others. Let me know how you like it."

"I'll take good care of it, I promise."

"You want me to come with you? Give you some operating tips?"

"No, I'll figure it out." She gave him a wave and stepped out of his apartment. "I'm just going to take it on a little hike tomorrow."

10

Josephine pulled into the trailhead parking area and turned off the engine. She sat for a moment, studying the entrance to the trail, which was merely a narrow passage carved into the gloom of thick forest. According to Google Earth, this was the closest point she could reach by car to the coordinates written on the map. It was time to get out and walk.

Though the heaviest of the rain had ended last night, gray clouds still hung low in the sky this morning, and the air itself seemed to drip with lingering moisture. She stood at the edge of the woods, staring at a narrow footpath that faded from view into deep shadows. She felt a chill, like a breath of frost on her neck. Suddenly she wanted to climb back into her car and lock the doors. To drive home and forget she'd ever received that map. Apprehensive as she was about venturing into the woods, though, she was even more fearful of the consequences should she ignore the note.

Whoever had sent it could turn out to be her best friend.

Or her worst enemy.

She glanced up at the cold kiss of water dripping from the tree branches overhead. Pulling up the hood of her jacket, she started down the trail.

The dirt path was studded with brightly colored toadstools, their caps glistening with rainwater. The fungi were no doubt poisonous; the pretty ones usually were. As the saying went: *There are bold mushroom hunters and old mushroom hunters, but there are no old, bold mushroom hunters*. The coordinates on the handheld GPS began to change, the numbers readjusting as she hiked deeper into the woods. The device would not be able to give her pinpoint accuracy. The best she could hope for was to be led to within a few dozen yards of what she was supposed to find. If the item she sought was small, how would she locate it among these dense trees?

Thunder crackled in the distance; another storm was coming. Nothing to worry about yet, she thought. If the lightning got closer, she'd stay away from the tallest tree and crouch down in a ditch. That was the theory, anyway. The drip of rain from the leaves became steady, drops clattering onto her jacket. The nylon hood trapped noise, magnifying the sound of her own breathing, her own heartbeat. In tiny fractions of degrees, the GPS coordinates inched slowly toward her goal.

Though it was midmorning, the woods seemed to be falling swiftly darker. Or maybe it was just the thickening rain clouds, threatening to turn this slow and steady drip into a torrent. She quickened her pace, moving at a brisk walk now, her boots splashing through mud and wet leaves. Suddenly she halted, frowning at the GPS.

She'd overshot. She needed to go back.

Retracing her steps, she returned to a bend in the path and stared into the trees. The GPS was telling her to leave the trail. Beyond the tangle of branches, the trees seemed to open up, revealing a tantalizing peek of a clearing.

She clambered off the footway and toward the clearing, twigs snapping beneath her boots, her progress as loud and clumsy as an elephant's. Branches hit her face in wet slaps. She climbed onto a fallen log and was about to drop down on the other side when her gaze froze on the soil, and on the large shoe print stamped into the earth. Rain had worried away the edges, melted the tread marks. Someone else had climbed over this log. Someone else had scrambled through this underbrush. But he had been moving in the other direction, toward the trail, not away from it. The print did not look fresh. Nevertheless, she paused to scan her surroundings. She saw only drooping branches and tree trunks scabby with lichen. Who in his right mind would hang out here all night and all day in the woods, waiting to ambush a woman who might not ever come? A woman who might not even recognize that those numbers on the map were coordinates?

Reassured by her own logic, she hopped off the log and kept walking, her gaze back on the GPS, watching the numbers slowly shift. Closer, she thought. Almost there.

The trees suddenly thinned and she stumbled out of the woods, into a meadow. For a moment she stood blinking at the broad expanse of tall grass and wildflowers, blossoms drooping with moisture. Where now? According to the GPS, this was the spot where she was meant to come, but she saw no markers, no outstanding features of any kind. Just this meadow and, at its center, a lone apple tree, its branches gnarled with age.

She walked into the clearing, her jeans swishing through wet grass, the dampness seeping through her pant legs. Except for the drip, drip of rain, the day was eerily still, with only the distant bark of a dog. She walked to the center of the meadow and slowly turned, taking in the periphery of trees, but saw no movement, not even the flutter of a bird.

What do you want me to find?

A crack of thunder split the air, and she glanced up at the blackening sky. Time to get out of this clearing. It was the height of foolhardiness to stand beside a lone tree during a lightning storm.

Only at that instant did she focus on the apple tree itself. On the object that hung on a nail that had been pounded into the trunk. It was above her eye level, partly hidden by a branch, and she had missed seeing it until now. She stared up at what dangled from the nail.

My missing keys.

She pulled them off the nail and whirled around,

frantically searching the meadow for whoever might have left them hanging on the tree. Thunder cracked. Like the shot of a starter pistol, it sent her running. But it wasn't the storm that made her flee headlong into the trees, that made her tear through the underbrush and back toward the trail, heedless of the branches whipping her face. It was the image of her own keys on that tree trunk, keys that she was now clutching tightly, even though they felt alien. Contaminated.

She was gasping for breath by the time she stumbled from the trailhead. Her car was no longer the only vehicle sitting in the lot; a Volvo was now parked nearby. Her hands cold and numb, she fumbled to open the door. Scrambling in behind the wheel, she clicked the locks shut.

Safe.

For a moment, she sat breathing hard, the windshield fogging up from her breath. She stared down at the keys she'd just plucked from the lone apple tree. They looked exactly the same as always, five keys dangling from a ring made in the shape of an ankh, the ancient Egyptian symbol for life. There were the two keys to her apartment, the keys for her car, and the key to her mailbox. Someone had had them for over a week. While I slept, she thought, someone could have walked into my apartment. Or stolen my mail. Or rifled through . . .

My car.

With a gasp of panic, she jerked around, expecting to see a monster waiting to pounce from the backseat. But all she saw were stray museum files and an empty water bottle. No monsters, no ax murderer. She sank back against her seat, and the laugh that escaped her throat had the faint note of hysteria.

Someone is trying to drive me insane. Just like they drove my mother insane.

She inserted the key in the ignition and was about to start the engine when her gaze fixed on the trunk key, clattering against the others. All last night, she thought, my car was parked on the street near my apartment building. Exposed and unguarded.

She looked out at the parking area. Through the steamed window, she saw the owners of the parked Volvo come up the road. It was a young couple with a boy and a girl of about ten. The boy was walking a black Labrador. Or rather, the Labrador seemed to be walking the boy, dragging him as the boy tried to hold on to the leash.

Reassured that she was not alone, Josephine took the keys and stepped out of the car. Raindrops pelted her bare head, but she scarcely noticed the wetness sliding down her neck and seeping into her shirt collar. She circled to the back of the car and stared at the trunk, trying to remember when she'd last opened it. It had been her weekly visit to the grocery store. She could still picture the bulging plastic bags sitting in the trunk, and remembered lifting them out and carrying them upstairs in a single trip. There should be nothing left behind in the trunk now.

The dog began to bark wildly, and the boy holding the leash yelled, "Sam, come *on*! What's the matter with you?"

Josephine turned and saw the boy was trying to drag his dog toward the family Volvo, but the dog kept barking at Josephine.

"Sorry," the boy's mother called out. "I don't know what's gotten into him." Now she took the leash, and the dog yelped as he was forced toward the Volvo.

Josephine unlocked her trunk. It lifted open.

When she saw what lay inside she stumbled backward, gasping. Rain tap-tapped in a steady tattoo down her cheeks, soaking her hair, trickling like the stroke of icy fingers. The dog broke loose and came tearing toward her, barking hysterically. She heard one of the children start to scream.

Their mother cried out, "Oh my God. Oh my *God*!"

As the father dialed 911, Josephine staggered over to a tree and sank down in shock onto the rain-sodden moss.

11

Whatever the hour, whatever the weather, Maura Isles always managed to arrive looking elegant. Jane stood shivering in damp slacks, her hair dripping with rain, and she felt a twinge of envy as she saw the medical examiner step out of the black Lexus. Maura's hair was sleek and perfect as a helmet, and she managed to make even a rain parka look fashionable. But then, she hadn't spent the last hour as Jane had, standing in this parking lot, rain pelting her hair.

As Maura moved through the police line, cops respectfully stepped aside for her, as though making way for royalty. And like royalty, Maura moved with aloof purpose and headed straight toward the parked Honda where Jane was now waiting.

"Isn't Milton a little out of your jurisdiction?" asked Maura.

"When you see what we've got, you'll understand why they called us."

"This is the car?"

Jane nodded. "It belongs to Josephine Pulcillo. She says that a week ago she lost track of her keys and assumed she'd just misplaced them. Now it looks like they might have been stolen, and whoever had them also had access to her car. Which explains how this thing got into the trunk." Jane turned to the Honda. "Hope you're ready for this. Because this one is definitely going to give me nightmares."

"I've heard you say that before."

"Yeah, well, this time I really mean it." With gloved hands, Jane lifted the hood of the trunk, releasing what smelled like rotting leather. Jane had been subjected before to the odors of a decaying body, but this was different; it did not smell of putrefaction. It did not even smell human. Certainly, she'd never seen any human being look like what now lay curled in the trunk of that Honda.

For a moment, Maura could not seem to muster a sound. She stared in silence at a mass of tangled black hair, at a face darkened to the color of tar. Every skin fold, every fine line of the nude body was perfectly preserved, as though frozen in bronze. Just as preserved was the woman's dying expression, her face twisted and her mouth agape in an eternal shriek.

"At first, I thought it couldn't be real," said Jane. "I thought it was a rubber Halloween gag that you'd hang up to scare the trick-or-treaters. Not flesh, but some kind of fake zombie. I mean, how could you turn a woman into something like *that*?" Jane paused and took a breath. "Then I saw her teeth."

Maura stared into the gaping mouth and said softly: "She has a dental filling."

Jane turned away and looked instead at a TV news van that had just pulled up beyond the police line. "So tell me how a woman gets to look that way, Doc," she said. "Tell me how you transform a body into a Halloween monster."

"I don't know."

That answer surprised Jane. She'd come to think of Maura Isles as the authority on every manner of death, no matter how obscure. "You can't do something like this in a week, right?" asked Jane. "Maybe not even a month. It's gotta take time to turn a woman into that thing." *Or into a mummy.*

Maura looked at her. "Where is Dr. Pulcillo? What does she say about this?"

Jane pointed toward the road, where the lineup of parked cars was steadily growing larger. "She's down there, sitting in the car with Frost. She says she has no idea how the body got into her trunk. The last time she used her car was a few days ago, when she bought groceries. If this body were in the trunk more than a day or two, it would probably smell worse. She would have noticed it inside her car."

"Her keys went missing a week ago?"

"She has no idea how she lost them. All she remembers is getting home from work one day, and they weren't in her purse."

"What was she doing up here?"

"She came out for a hike."

"On a day like this?"

Heavier raindrops began to plop onto their parkas, and Maura closed the trunk, shutting off their view of the monstrous thing lying inside. "Something is not right about this."

Jane laughed. "You think?"

"I'm talking about the weather."

"Well, I'm not happy about the weather, either, but what can you do?"

"Josephine Pulcillo came up here all alone, on a day like today, to take a hike?"

Jane nodded. "That bothered me, too. I asked her about it."

"What did she say?"

"She needed to get outdoors. And she likes to hike alone."

"And apparently during thunderstorms." Maura turned to look at the car where Josephine was now sitting. "She's a very attractive girl, don't you think?"

"Attractive? More like drop-dead gorgeous. I'm going to have to put Frost on a leash, the way he's panting after her."

Maura was still gazing toward Josephine, her frown deepening. "There's been a great deal of publicity about Madam X. That big article in the *Globe* back in March. More news reports these past few weeks, with photos."

"You mean photos of Josephine."

Maura nodded. "Maybe she's picked up an admirer."

One particular admirer, thought Jane. Someone who'd known all along what was hidden in the museum basement. The publicity about Madam X would certainly have drawn his attention. He would have read every article, perused every photo. He would have seen Josephine's face.

She looked down at the trunk, grateful that it was now closed and she did not have to see the wretched occupant, its body twisted as though in the throes of agony. "I think our collector has just sent us a message. He's telling us he's still alive. And hunting for new specimens."

"He's also telling us he's right here in Boston." Once again, Maura turned to look in Josephine's direction. "You said she lost her keys. Which keys?"

"To her car. And her apartment."

Maura's chin lifted in dismay. "That's not good."

"Her locks are being changed as we speak. We've already spoken to her building manager, and we'll see that she gets home safely."

Maura's cell phone rang, and she glanced at the number. "Excuse me," she said, turning away to take the call. Jane noted the furtive dip of Maura's head, the way her shoulders curled forward, as though to block anyone's view of her conversation.

"What about Saturday night, can you make it then? It's been so long . . ."

It was the whispers that gave her away. She was talking to Daniel Brophy, but Jane heard no joy in the murmured conversation, only disappointment. *What else but disappointment can you expect when you fall in love with an unattainable man?*

Maura ended the conversation with a soft, "I'll call you later." She turned to face Jane but didn't meet her gaze. Instead she focused her attention on the Honda. A dead body was a safer topic of conversation. Unlike a lover, a corpse would not break her heart or disappoint her or leave her lonely at night.

"I assume CSU will be examining the trunk?" Maura said, and she was all business now, once again snapping into the role of the coldly logical medical examiner.

"We're impounding the vehicle. When will you do the autopsy?"

"I want to do some preliminary studies first. X-rays, tissue samples. I need to understand exactly what preservation process I'm dealing with before I start cutting her open."

"So you won't do the autopsy today?"

"It won't be until after the weekend. By the looks of the body, she's been dead a long time. A few extra days won't change the postmortem results." Maura glanced toward Josephine. "What about Dr. Pulcillo?"

"We're still talking to her. After we get her home and into some dry clothes, maybe she'll remember a few more details."

Josephine Pulcillo is one odd duck, thought Jane as she and Frost stood in the young woman's apartment, waiting for her to emerge from the bedroom. The living room was furnished in the décor of *starving college student*. The fabric of the sleeper sofa was ratty from the claws of some phantom cat, and the coffee table was stained with drink rings. There were textbooks and technical journals lining the bookshelves, but Jane saw no photographs, no personal mementos, nothing that gave any clues to the occupant's personality. On the computer, screensaver images of Egyptian temples cycled in a continuous loop.

When Josephine at last reappeared, her damp hair was tamed into a ponytail. Though she wore fresh jeans and a cotton pullover, she still looked chilled, her face as rigid as a stone carving. A statue of an Egyptian queen, perhaps, or some mythical beauty; Frost openly stared, as though he were in the presence of a goddess. If his wife, Alice, were here, she'd probably give him a swift and badly needed kick in the shins. *Maybe I should do it on Alice's behalf.*

"Are you feeling better, Dr. Pulcillo?" he asked. "Do you need some more time before we talk about this?"

"I'm ready."

"Maybe a cup of coffee before we start?"

"I'll make some for you." Josephine turned toward the kitchen.

"No, I was thinking of *you*. Whether you needed anything."

"Frost," snapped Jane, "she just said she's ready to talk. So why don't we all sit down and get started?"

"I just want to be sure she's comfortable. That's all."
Frost and Jane settled onto the battered-looking couch. Through the cushion, Jane felt the bite of a broken spring. She slid away from it, leaving a wide gap between her and Frost. They sat at opposite ends of the couch, like an estranged couple at a counseling session.

Josephine sank onto a chair, and her face was as unreadable as onyx. She might be only twenty-six, but she was eerily self-contained, any emotions she might possess kept under tight lock and key. Something is not right here, thought Jane. Was she the only one who felt it? Frost seemed to have lost any sense of objectivity.

"Let's talk about those keys again, Dr. Pulcillo," Jane began. "You said they went missing over a week ago?"

"When I got home last Wednesday, I couldn't find my key ring in my purse. I thought I'd misplaced it at work, but I couldn't find it there, either. You can ask Mr. Goodwin about it. He charged me forty-five dollars to replace the mailbox key."

"And the missing key ring never turned up again?"

Josephine's gaze dropped to her lap. What followed was only a few beats of silence, but it was enough to catch Jane's attention. Why would such a straight-forward question require so much thought?

"No," said Josephine. "I never saw those keys again."

Frost asked, "When you're at work, where do you keep your purse?"

"In my desk." Josephine visibly relaxed, as though

this was a question she had no problem answering.

"Is your office locked?" He leaned forward, as though afraid to miss a single word she said.

"No. I'm in and out of my office all day, so I don't bother to lock it."

"I assume the museum has security tapes? Some record of who might have gone into your office?"

"Theoretically."

"What does that mean?"

"Our security camera system went on the blink three weeks ago and it hasn't been repaired yet." She shrugged. "It's a budget issue. Money's always short, and we thought that just having the cameras in public view would be enough to deter any thieves."

"So any visitor to the museum could have wandered upstairs to your office and taken the keys."

"And after all the publicity about Madam X, we've had droves of visitors. The public's finally discovered the Crispin Museum."

Jane said, "Why would a thief take just your key ring and leave your purse? Was anything else missing from your office?"

"No. At least, I haven't noticed. That's why I didn't worry about it. I just assumed I'd dropped the keys somewhere. I never imagined someone would use them to get into my car. To put that . . . thing in my trunk."

"Your apartment building doesn't have a parking lot," observed Frost.

Josephine shook her head. "It's every man for

himself. I park on the street like all the other tenants. That's why I don't keep anything valuable in my car, because they're always getting broken into. But it's usually to take things." She gave a shudder. "Not put things *in*."

"How is security in this building?" asked Frost.

"We'll get to that issue in a minute," said Jane.

"Someone has her key ring. I think that's the most pressing concern, the fact that he has access to her car and to her apartment. The fact that he seems to be focused on her." He turned to the young woman. "Do you have any idea why?"

Josephine's gaze skittered away. "No, I don't."

"Could it be someone you know? Someone you've recently met?"

"I've only been in Boston for five months."

"Where were you before that?" Jane asked.

"Job hunting in California. I moved to Boston after the museum hired me."

"Any enemies, Dr. Pulcillo? Any ex-boyfriends you don't get along with?"

"No."

"Any archaeologist friends who'd know how to turn a woman into a mummy? Or a shrunken head?"

"That knowledge is available to a lot of people. You don't have to be an archaeologist."

"But your friends *are* archaeologists."

Josephine shrugged. "I don't have all that many friends."

"Why not?"

"As I told you, I'm new to Boston. I only got here in March."

"So you can't think of anyone who might have stalked you? Stolen your keys? Anyone who might try to terrify you by putting a body in your trunk?"

For the first time, Josephine's composure slipped, revealing the frightened soul beneath the mask. She whispered: "No, I don't! I don't know who's doing this. Or why he chose *me*."

Jane studied the young woman, begrudgingly admiring the flawless skin, the coal-dark eyes. What would it be like to be so beautiful? To walk into a room and feel every man's gaze on you? *Including gazes that you don't welcome?*

"You understand, I hope, that you're going to have to be a lot more careful from now on," said Frost.

Josephine swallowed. "I know."

"Is there somewhere else you can stay? Some place you'd like us to take you?" he asked.

"I think . . . I think I may leave town for a while." Josephine straightened, as though heartened by having a plan of action. "My aunt lives in Vermont. I'll stay with her."

"Where in Vermont? We need to be able to check on you."

"Burlington. Her name is Connie Pulcillo. But you can always reach me on my cell phone."

"Good," said Frost. "And I assume you won't do

anything as foolhardy as hiking all alone again."

Josephine managed a weak smile. "I won't be doing that anytime soon."

"You know, that's something I wanted to ask you about," said Jane. "That little hike you took today."

Josephine's smile faded, as though she realized that Jane could not be so easily charmed. "It wasn't a wise thing to do, I know," she admitted.

"A rainy day. Muddy trails. Why on earth would you want to be there?"

"I wasn't the only one in the park. That family was there, too."

"They're out-of-towners and their dog needed a walk."

"So did I."

"Judging by your muddy boots, you did more than take just a stroll."

"Rizzoli," said Frost, "what are you getting at?"

Jane ignored him and kept her focus on Josephine. "Is there something else you want to tell us, Dr. Pulcillo, about why you were up at Blue Hills Reservation? On a Thursday morning, when I assume you're supposed to be at work?"

"I'm not due at work until one."

"The rain didn't discourage you?"

Josephine's face took on the expression of a hunted animal. She's scared of me, thought Jane. What am I not getting about this picture?

"It's been a really hard week," said Josephine. "I

needed to get outside, just to think. I'd heard the park was a pretty place to walk, so I went." She straightened, her voice now stronger. More assured. "That's all it was, Detective. A walk. Is there something illegal about that?"

The two women locked eyes for a moment. A moment that confused Jane because she did not understand what was really going on.

"No, there's nothing illegal about it," said Frost. "And I think we've pressed you hard enough today."

Jane saw the young woman abruptly look away. And she thought: *We haven't pressed hard enough.*

12

"Who appointed you the Good Cop?" said Jane as she and Frost slid into her Subaru.

"What do you mean?"

"You were so busy making goo-goo eyes at Pulcillo, you forced me to play the Bad Cop."

"I don't know what you're talking about."

"*Can I make you a cup of coffee?*" Jane snorted. "Are you a detective or a butler?"

"What's your problem? The poor girl just got the crap scared out of her. Her keys were stolen, a body's in her trunk, and we've impounded her car. Doesn't that sound like someone who needs a little sympathy? You were treating her like a suspect."

"Sympathy? Is that all you were giving her in there? I was waiting for you to ask her out on a date."

In all the time they'd worked together, Jane had never seen Frost truly angry at her. So to witness the fury that suddenly flared up in his eyes was more than unsettling; it was almost scary. "Fuck you, Rizzoli."

"Hey."

"You've got some real issues, you know that? What is it about her that ticks you off? The fact that she's pretty?"

"Something about her doesn't add up. Something doesn't feel right."

"She's scared. Her life's just been turned upside down. That's got to freak a person out."

"And you want to swoop right in and rescue her."

"I'm trying to be a decent human being."

"Tell me you'd be acting this way if she looked like a dog."

"Her looks have nothing to do with this. Why do you keep suggesting I've got other motives?"

Jane sighed. "Look, I'm just trying to keep you out of trouble, okay? I'm Mama Bear, doing her duty and keeping you safe." She thrust the key into the ignition and turned on the engine. "So when's Alice coming home? Hasn't she been visiting her parents long enough?"

He shot her a suspicious look. "Why are you asking about Alice?"

"She's been gone for weeks. Isn't it about time she came home?"

That elicited a snort. "Jane Rizzoli, marriage counselor. I kind of resent it, you know."

"What?"

"That you think I'd ever go off the rails."

Jane pulled away from the curb and merged into traffic. "I just thought I should say something. I'm all for heading off trouble."

"Yeah, that strategy worked *really* well on your dad. Is he talking to you these days, or did you piss him off for good?"

At the mention of her father, her grip on the steering wheel tightened to a stranglehold. After thirty-one years of apparent marital bliss, Frank Rizzoli had suddenly developed a hankering for cheap blondes. Seven months ago, he had walked out on Jane's mother.

"I only told him what I thought about his bimbo."

Frost laughed. "Yeah. Then you tried to beat her up."

"I did not beat her up. We had words."

"You tried to arrest her."

"I should have arrested *him* for acting like a middle-aged moron. It's so frigging embarrassing." She stared grimly at the road. "Now my mom's doing a pretty good job embarrassing me, too."

"Because she's dating?" Frost shook his head. "You see? You're so damn judgmental, you're gonna piss her off as well."

"She's acting like a teenager."

"Your dad dumped her and now she's dating, so what? Korsak's a good guy, so let her have some fun."

"We weren't talking about my parents. We were talking about Josephine."

"*You* were talking about Josephine."

"There's something about her that bothers me. Do you notice how she hardly looks us in the eye? I think she couldn't wait to get us out of her apartment."

"She answered all our questions. What more did you expect?"

"She didn't give us everything. She's holding something back."

"Like what?"

"I don't know." Jane stared ahead at the road. "But it wouldn't hurt to find out a little more about Dr. Pulcillo."

From her window above the street, Josephine watched the two detectives climb into the car and drive away. Only then did she open her purse and pull out her ankh key ring, the one she'd found hanging on the apple tree. She'd said nothing to the police about the return of these keys. If she'd mentioned it, then she would also have had to tell them about the note directing her there, the note addressed to Josephine Sommer. And Sommer was a name they must never know about.

She gathered together the notes and envelopes addressed to Josephine Sommer and ripped them up, wishing that at the same time she could rip away the part of her life she'd been trying all these years to forget. Somehow it had caught up with her, and no matter how hard she tried to outrun it, it would always be part of who she was. She brought the shredded bits of paper into the bathroom and flushed them down the toilet.

She had to leave Boston.

Now was the logical time to get out of town. The police knew she was frightened by what had happened today, so her departure would rouse no suspicions. Perhaps later, they might ask questions, search records, but for now they had no reason to examine her past. They would assume she was who she said she was: Josephine Pulcillo, who lived quietly and modestly, who'd worked her way through college and grad school while waitressing at the Blue Star cocktail lounge. All of that was true. All of that would check out fine. As long as they didn't dig deeper or earlier, as long as she gave them no reason to, she would never trip any alarms. She could slip away from Boston with no one the wiser.

But I don't want to leave Boston.

She stared out the window at a neighborhood she'd grown attached to. Rain clouds had given way to splashes of sunshine, and the sidewalks sparkled, fresh and clean. When she'd arrived to take the job, it had been March and she'd been a stranger to these streets. She'd trudged through the icy wind, thinking that she wouldn't last long here, believing that, like her mother, she was a warm-weather creature, bred for desert heat, not a New England winter. But one April day after the snow had melted, she'd walked through the Boston Common, past budding trees and the golden blush of daffodils, and she'd suddenly realized she belonged here. That in this city where every brick and stone seemed to resonate with the echoes of history, she felt at home. She'd walked the cobblestones of Beacon Hill and could almost hear the clatter of horses' hooves and carriage wheels. She'd stood on the pier at Long Wharf and imagined the call of the fishmongers, the laughter of seamen. Like her mother, she had always been more interested in the past than in the present, and in this city, history still breathed.

Now I'll have to leave it. And leave behind this name, as well.

The apartment buzzer startled her. She crossed to the intercom, pausing to calm her voice before she pressed the speaker button. "Yes?"

"Josie, it's Nicholas. Can I come up?"

She could think of no way to gracefully decline his visit, so she buzzed him in. A moment later he was at her door, his hair sparkling with rain, his gray eyes pinched with worry behind drizzle-fogged glasses.

"Are you all right? We heard what happened."

"How did you find out?"

"We were waiting for you to come into work. Then Detective Crowe told us there'd been some trouble. That someone broke into your car."

"It's a lot worse than that," she said, and sank down wearily on the couch. He stood watching her, and for the first time his gaze made her uneasy; he was studying her far too closely. Suddenly she felt as exposed as Madam X, her protective wrappings stripped away to reveal the ugly reality underneath.

"Someone had my keys, Nick."

"The ones you misplaced?"

"They weren't misplaced. They were stolen."

"You mean—on purpose?"

"Theft usually is." She saw his perplexed expression and thought: Poor Nick. You've been trapped too long with your musty antiquities. You have no idea how ugly the real world is. "It probably happened while I was at work."

"Oh dear."

"The museum keys weren't on the ring, so you don't have to worry about the building. The collection's safe."

"I'm not worried about the collection. I'm worried about *you*." He took in a deep breath, like a swimmer about to plunge deep underwater. "If you don't feel safe here, Josephine, you could always . . ." Suddenly he straightened and boldly announced: "I have a spare bedroom in my house. You're absolutely welcome to stay with me."

She smiled. "Thank you. But I'm going to leave town for a while, so I won't be coming in to work for a few weeks. I'm sorry to leave you in the lurch, especially now."

"Where are you going?"

"It seems like a good time to visit my aunt. I haven't seen her in a year." She went to the window, where she looked out at a view that she would miss. "Thank you for everything, Nicholas," she said. *Thank you for being the closest thing to a friend I've had in years.*

"What's really going on?" he asked. He came up

behind her, close enough to touch her, yet he didn't. He merely stood there, a quiet presence patiently hovering nearby, as he always did. "You can trust me, you know. No matter what."

Suddenly she wanted to tell him the truth, tell him everything about her past. But she did not want to witness his reaction. He had believed in the bland fiction known as Josephine Pulcillo. He had always been kind to her, and the best way for her to repay that kindness was to maintain the illusion and not disappoint him.

"Josephine? What happened today?" he asked.

"You'll probably see it on the news tonight," she said. "Someone used my keys to get into my car. To leave something in my trunk."

"What did they leave?"

She turned and faced him. "Another Madam X."

13

Josephine awakened to the glare of the late-afternoon sun in her eyes. Squinting through the window of the Greyhound bus, she saw rolling green fields cloaked in the golden haze of sunset. Last night she had scarcely slept, and only after boarding the bus that morning had she finally nodded off from sheer exhaustion. Now she had no idea where she was, but judging by the time they must be close to the Massachusetts–New York State border. Had she been driving her own car, the entire journey would take only six hours. By bus, with transfers in Albany and Syracuse and Binghamton, the journey would take all day.

When they finally pulled into her last transfer stop in Binghamton, it was dark. Once again she dragged herself off the bus and made her way to a pay phone. Cell phone calls could be traced, and she'd left hers turned off since leaving Boston. Instead she reached into her pocket for quarters and deposited coins into the hungry phone. The same answering machine message greeted her, delivered in a brisk female voice.

"I'm probably out digging. Leave a number and I'll call you back."

Josephine hung up without saying a word. Then she hauled her two suitcases to the next bus and joined the short line of passengers waiting to board. No one spoke; they all seemed as drained as she was, and resigned to the next stage of their journey.

At eleven PM, the bus pulled into the village of Waverly.

She was the only passenger to step off, and she found herself standing alone in front of a dark mini-mart. Even a village this small had to have a taxi service. She headed toward a phone booth and was about to deposit quarters when she saw the OUT OF SERVICE note taped across the coin slot. It was the final blow at the end of an exhausting day. Staring at that useless pay phone, she suddenly laughed: a raw, desperate sound that echoed across the empty parking lot. If she couldn't get a cab, she faced a five-mile hike in the dark, hauling two suitcases.

She weighed the risks of turning on her cell phone. Use it even once, and she could be tracked here. But I'm so tired, she thought, and I don't know what else to do, or where else to go. I'm stranded in a small town and the only person I know here seems to be unreachable.

Headlights appeared on the road.

The car moved toward her—a patrol car with blue

rack lights. She froze, unsure whether to duck into the shadows or to brazenly maintain her role of stranded passenger.

It was too late to run now; the police cruiser was already turning into the mini-mart parking lot. The window rolled down, and a young patrolman peered out.

"Hello, miss. Do you have someone coming to get you?"

She cleared her throat. "I was about to call a cab."

"That phone's out of order."

"I just noticed."

"Been out of order for six months. These phone companies hardly bother fixing them now that everyone's got a cell."

"I have one, too. I'll just use it."

He eyed her for a moment, no doubt wondering why someone who had a cell phone would fuss with a pay phone.

"I needed to use the directory," she explained and opened the phone book that was hanging in the booth.

"Okay, I'll just sit here till the cab arrives," he said.

As they waited together, he explained that the previous month there'd been an unpleasant incident involving a young lady in this same parking lot. "She got off the eleven PM bus from Binghamton, just like you," he said. Since then, he'd made it a point to drive by just to make sure no other young ladies were accosted. Protect and serve, that was his job, and if she knew about the terrible things that sometimes happened, even in a little village like Waverly, population forty-six hundred, she'd never again be caught standing alone at a dark mini-mart.

When the taxi finally arrived, Officer Friendly had been bending her ear for so long she was afraid he might follow her home, just to continue the conversation. But his cruiser headed in the opposite direction and she sank back with a sigh and considered her next moves. The first order of business was a good night's sleep, in a home where she felt safe. A home where she need not hide who she really was. She'd juggled truth and fiction for so long that she sometimes forgot which details of her life were real and which were fabrications. A few too many drinks, a moment of carelessness, and she might let slip the truth, which could send the whole house of cards tumbling down. In her college dormitory of partying students, she had remained the sober one, adept at meaningless chitchat that revealed absolutely nothing about herself.

I'm tired of this life, she thought. Tired of having to consider the consequences of every word before I say it. Tonight, at last, I can be myself.

The taxi pulled to a stop in front of a large farmhouse and the driver said, "Here we are, miss. Want me to carry those bags to the door?"

"No, I can handle them." She paid him and started up the walkway, wheeling her suitcases toward the front steps. There she paused, as though searching for her keys, until the taxi drove away. The instant it vanished from sight, she turned and headed back to the road.

A five-minute walk brought her to a long gravel driveway that cut through thick woods. The moon had risen, and she could see the path just well enough not to stumble. The sound of the suitcase wheels plowing through the gravel seemed alarmingly loud. In the woods crickets had fallen silent, aware that a trespasser had entered their kingdom.

She climbed the steps to the dark house. A few knocks on the door, a few rings of the bell, told her what she'd already suspected. No one was home.

Not a problem.

She found the key where it was always hidden, wedged under the stack of firewood on the porch, and let herself in. Flipping on the light, she found the living room exactly as she remembered it since she'd last visited two years ago. The same clutter filled every available shelf and niche, the same photos framed in Mexican tin shadow boxes hung on the walls. She saw sunburned faces grinning from beneath broad-brimmed hats, a man leaning on a shovel in front of a crumbling wall, a redheaded woman squinting up from the trench where she knelt with trowel in hand. Most of the faces in those photos she did not recognize; they belonged to another woman's memories, another woman's lifetime.

She left her suitcases in the living room and went into the kitchen. There the same clutter reigned, blackened pots and pans hanging from ceiling racks, the windowsills a depository of everything from sea glass to bits of broken pottery. She filled a teakettle and put it on the stove. As she waited for it to boil, she stood in front of the refrigerator, studying all the snapshots taped to the door. In the midst of that jumbled collage was one face she did recognize. It was her own, taken when she was about three years old, seated in the lap of a raven-haired woman. She reached up and gently stroked the woman's face, remembering the smoothness of that cheek, the scent of her hair. The kettle whistled, but Josephine remained transfixed by the photo, by those hypnotic dark eyes gazing back at her.

The whistle of the kettle abruptly cut off, and a voice said, "It's been years since anyone's asked me about her, you know."

Josephine whirled around to face the lanky middle-aged woman who'd just shut off the burner. "Gemma," she murmured. "You're home after all."

Smiling, the woman strode forward to give her a powerful hug. Gemma Hamerton was built more like a boy than a woman, lean but muscular, her silvery hair cropped in a practical bob. Her arms were ridged with ugly burn scars, but she brazenly showed them off to the world in a sleeveless blouse.

"I recognized your old suitcases in the living room." Gemma stepped back to give Josephine a thorough perusal. "My God, every year you look more and more like her." She shook her head and laughed. "That's some formidable DNA you've inherited, kid."

"I tried to call you. I didn't want to leave a message on your answering machine."

"I've been traveling all day." Gemma reached into her purse and pulled out a newspaper clipping from the *International Herald Tribune*. "I saw that article before I left Lima. Does this have anything to do with why you're here?"

Josephine looked at the headline: CT SCAN OF MUMMY STUNS AUTHORITIES. "So you know about Madam X."

"News gets around, even in Peru. The world's become a small place, Josie."

"Maybe too small," Josephine said softly. "It leaves me no place left to hide."

"After all these years? I'm not sure you need to anymore."

"Someone's found me, Gemma. I'm scared."

Gemma stared at her. Slowly she sat down across from Josephine. "Tell me what happened."

Josephine pointed to the clipping from the *Herald Tribune*. "It all started with her. With Madam X."

"Go on."

At first the words came haltingly; it had been a long time since Josephine had spoken freely, and she was accustomed to catching herself, to weighing the dangers of every revelation. But with Gemma, all secrets were safe, and as she spoke, she found the words spilling faster in a torrent that could no longer be held back. Three cups of tea later, she finally fell silent and slumped back in her chair, exhausted. And relieved, although her situation had scarcely changed. The only difference was that now she no longer felt alone.

The story left Gemma stunned and staring. "A body turns up in your car? And you left out that little detail about the notes you got in the mail? You didn't tell the police?"

"How could I? If they knew about the notes, they'd find out everything else."

"Maybe it's time, Josie," said Gemma quietly. "Time to stop hiding and just tell the truth."

"I can't do that to my mother. I can't pull her into this. I'm just glad she isn't here."

"She'd want to be here. *You're* the one she's always tried to protect."

"Well, she can't protect me now. And she shouldn't have to." Josephine rose and carried her cup to the sink. "This has nothing to do with her."

"Doesn't it?"

"She was never in Boston. She never had anything to do with the Crispin Museum." Josephine turned to Gemma. "Did she?"

Gemma shook her head. "I can't think of any reason why the museum should have those links to her. The cartouche, the newspaper."

"Coincidence, maybe."

"That's *too* much coincidence." Gemma wrapped her hands around her teacup, as though to ward off a sudden chill. "What about the body in your car? What are the police doing about it?"

"What they're supposed to do in a murder case. They'll investigate. They've asked me all the questions you'd expect. Who might be stalking me? Do I have any sick admirers? Is there anyone from the past I'm afraid of? If they keep asking questions, it's only a matter of time before they find out who Josephine Pulcillo really is."

"They may not bother to dig that up. They've got murders to solve, and you're not the one they're interested in."

"I couldn't take that risk. That's why I ran. I packed up and left a job I loved and a city I loved. I was happy there, Gemma. It's an odd little museum, but I liked working there."

"And the people? Is there any chance one of them might be involved?"

"I don't see it."

"Sometimes you *can't* see it."

"They're completely harmless. The curator, the director—they're both such kind men." She gave a sad laugh. "I wonder what they'll think of me now. When they find out who they really hired."

"They hired a brilliant young archaeologist. A woman who deserves a better life."

"Well, this is the life I got." She turned on the faucet to rinse her cup. The kitchen was organized exactly as it had always been, and she found the dish towels in the same cabinet, the spoons in the same drawer. Like any good archaeological dig, Gemma's kitchen stood preserved in a state of domestic eternity. What a luxury to have roots, thought Josephine as she placed the clean cup back on the shelf. What would it be like to own a home, to build a life she would never have to abandon?

"What are you going to do now?" asked Gemma.

"I don't know."

"You could go back to Mexico. She'd want that."

"I'll just have to start over again." The prospect of that suddenly made Josephine sag against the countertop. "God, I've lost twelve years of my life."

"Maybe you haven't. Maybe the police will drop the ball."

"I can't count on that."

"Watch and wait. See what happens. This house will be empty for most of the summer. I need to be back in Peru in two weeks, to oversee the excavation. You're welcome to stay here as long as you need to."

"I don't want to cause you any trouble."

"Trouble?" Gemma shook her head. "You have no idea what kind of trouble your mother saved *me* from. Anyway, I'm not convinced the police are as clever as you think they are. Or as thorough. Think how many cases go unsolved, how many mistakes we hear about in the news."

"You haven't met this detective."

"What about him?"

"It's a her. The way she looks at me, the questions she asks—"

"A woman?" Gemma's eyebrow twitched upward. "Oh, that's too bad."

"Why?"

"Men are so easily distracted by a pretty face."

"If Detective Rizzoli keeps digging, she's eventually going to end up here. Talking to you."

"So let them come. What are they going to find out?" Gemma waved at her kitchen. "Look around! They'll walk in here, get a look at all my herbal teas, and dismiss me as some harmless old hippie who couldn't possibly tell them anything useful. When you're a fifty-year-old woman, no one really bothers to look at you anymore, much less value your opinion. It's hard on the old ego. But damn, it does make it easy to get away with a lot."

Josephine laughed. "So all I have to do is wait till I'm fifty and I'm home free?"

"You may be home free already, as far as the police are concerned."

Josephine said softly: "It's not just the police who scare me. Not after those notes. Not after what was left in my car."

"No," Gemma agreed. "There are worse things to be afraid of." She paused, then looked across the table at Josephine. "So why are you still alive?"

The question startled Josephine. "You think I should be dead."

"Why would some weirdo waste time scaring you with creepy little notes? With grotesque gifts in your car? Why not just kill you?"

"Maybe because the police are involved? Ever since the scan of Madam X, they've been hovering around the museum."

"Another thing puzzles me. Putting a body in your car seems designed to draw attention to you. The police are watching you now. It's a strange move if someone really wants you dead."

The statement was typical for Gemma: factual and brutally blunt. *Someone wants you dead.* But I am dead, she thought. Twelve years ago, the girl I used to be dropped off the face of the earth. And Josephine Pulcillo was born.

"She wouldn't want you dealing with this all alone, Josie. Let's make that phone call."

"No. It's safer for everyone if we don't. If they're watching me, that's just what they're waiting for." She took a breath. "I've managed on my own since college and I can deal with this, too. I just need some time to catch my breath. Throw a dart at the map and decide where to go next." She paused. "And I think I'll need some cash."

"There's still about twenty-five thousand dollars left in the account. It's been sitting there for you. Waiting for a rainy day."

"I think this qualifies." Josephine stood to leave the room. In the kitchen doorway she stopped and looked back. "Thank you for everything you've done. For me. And for my mother."

"I owe it to her, Josie." Gemma looked down at her burn-scarred arms. "It's only because of Medea that I'm still alive."

14

On Saturday night, Daniel finally came to her.

At the last minute, before he arrived, Maura rushed out to the local market where she bought kalamata olives and French cheeses and a far-too-extravagant bottle of wine. This is the way I'll woo a lover, she thought as she handed over her credit card. With smiles and kisses and glasses of Pinot Noir. I will win him over with perfect evenings that he'll never forget, never stop craving. And someday, maybe, he'll make his choice. He'll choose me.

When she got home, he was already waiting for her in her house.

As the garage door rolled open, she saw his car parked inside where the neighbors wouldn't see it, where it would cause no raised eyebrows, no lascivious gossip. She pulled in beside it and quickly closed the garage door again, shutting off any view of the blatant evidence that she was not alone tonight. Keeping secrets so easily becomes second nature, and it was automatic for her now to close the garage door, to draw the curtains and smoothly fend off the innocent queries from colleagues and neighbors. *Are you seeing someone? Would you like to come to dinner? Would you like to meet this nice man I know?* Over the months, she'd declined so many such invitations that few were now offered. Had everyone simply given up on her, or had they guessed the reason for her disinterest, for her unsociability?

That reason was standing in the doorway, waiting for her.

She stepped into the house, into Daniel Brophy's arms. It had been ten days since they'd last been together, ten days of ever-deepening longing that was now so gnawing she could not wait to satisfy it. The groceries were still in the car, and she had dinner to cook, but food was the last thing on her mind as their lips met. Daniel was all she wanted to devour, and she feasted on him as they kissed their way into her bedroom, guilty kisses made all the more delicious because they were illicit. How many new sins will we commit this evening, she wondered as she watched him unbutton his shirt. Tonight he did not wear his clerical collar; tonight he came to her as a lover, not a man of God.

Months ago he had broken the vows that bound him to his church. She was the one responsible; she had caused his fall from grace, a fall that once again brought him into her bed, into her arms. It was a destination so familiar to him now that he knew exactly what she wanted, what would make her clutch him and cry out.

When at last she fell back with a satisfied shudder, they lay together as they always did, with arms and legs wrapped around each other, two lovers who knew each other's bodies well.

"It feels like it's been forever since you were here," she whispered.

"I would have come Thursday, but that workshop went on forever."

"Which workshop?"

"Couples counseling." He gave a sad, ironic laugh. "As if I'm the person who can tell them how to heal their marriages. There's so much anger and pain, Maura. It was an ordeal just sitting in the same room with those people. I wanted to tell them, *It will never work, you'll never be happy with each other. You married the wrong person!*"

"That might be the best advice you could have given them."

"It would have been an act of mercy." Gently he brushed the hair from her face, and his hand lingered on her cheek. "It would have been so much kinder to give them permission to leave. To find someone who *would* make them happy. The way you make me happy."

She smiled. "And *you* make me hungry." She sat up, and the scent of their lovemaking wafted up from the rumpled sheets. The animal smells of warm bodies and desire. "I promised you dinner."

"I feel guilty that you're always feeding me." He, too, sat up and reached for his clothes. "Tell me what I can do."

"I left the wine in the car. Why don't you get the bottle and open it? I'll put the chicken in the oven."

In her kitchen they sipped wine as the chicken roasted, as she sliced the potatoes and he made the salad. Like any married couple, they cooked and they touched and they kissed. But we're not married, she thought, glancing sideways at his striking profile, his graying temples. Every moment together was a stolen one, a furtive one, and although they laughed together, sometimes she heard a desperate note in that laughter, as though they were trying to convince themselves that they were happy, damn it, yes they were, despite the guilt and the deceptions and the many nights apart. But she was beginning to see the emotional toll in his face. In just the past few months, his hair had gone noticeably grayer. When it's completely white, she thought, will we still be meeting with the curtains closed?

And what changes does he see in my face?

It was after midnight when he left her house. She had fallen asleep in his arms and did not hear him rise from the bed. When she awakened he was gone, and the sheet beside her was already cold.

That morning she drank her coffee alone, cooked pancakes alone. Her best memories of her otherwise disastrous and brief marriage to Victor were of Sunday mornings together, rising late from bed to lounge on the couch, where they'd spend half the day reading the newspaper. She would never enjoy such a Sunday with Daniel. While she dozed in her bathrobe with the pages of *The Boston Globe* spread out all around her, Father Daniel Brophy would be ministering to his flock in the church of Our Lady of Divine Light, a flock whose shepherd had himself gone terribly astray.

The sound of her doorbell startled her awake. Groggy from her nap, she sat up on the couch and saw that it was already two in the afternoon. *That could be Daniel at the door.*

Scattered newspapers crackled beneath her bare feet as she hurried across the living room. When she opened the door and saw the man who stood on her porch, she suddenly regretted not combing her hair or changing out of the bathrobe.

"I'm sorry I'm a little late," said Anthony Sansone. "I hope it's not inconvenient."

"Late? I'm sorry, but I wasn't expecting you."

"Didn't you get my message? I left it on your answering machine yesterday afternoon. About coming by to see you today."

"Oh. I guess I forget to check the machine last night." *I was otherwise occupied.* She stepped back. "Come in."

He walked into the living room and stopped, gazing at the scattered newspapers, the empty coffee cup. It had been months since she'd seen him, and she was struck yet again by his stillness, by the way he always seemed to be testing the air, searching for the one detail he'd missed. Unlike Daniel, who was quick to reach out even to strangers, Anthony Sansone was a man surrounded by walls, a man who could stand in a crowded room yet seem coolly apart and self-contained. She wondered what he was thinking as he looked at the clutter of her wasted Sunday. Not all of us have butlers, she thought. Not all of us live the way you do, in a Beacon Hill mansion.

"I'm sorry for bothering you at home," he said. "But I didn't want this to be an official visit to the ME." He turned to look at her. "And I did want to find out how you've been, Maura. I haven't seen you in a while."

"I'm fine. It's been busy."

"The Mephisto Society's resumed our weekly dinners in my house. We could certainly use your perspective, and we'd love to have you join us again some evening."

"To talk about crime? I deal with that subject quite enough at my own job, thank you."

"Not in the way we approach it. You only look at its final effect; we're concerned with the reason for its existence."

She began picking up newspapers and stacking them into a pile. "I don't really fit in with your group. I don't accept your theories."

"Even after what we both experienced? Those murders must have made you wonder. They must have raised the possibility in your mind."

"That there's a unified theory of evil to be found in

the Dead Sea Scrolls?" She shook her head. "I'm a scientist. I read religious texts for historical insights, not for literal truths. Not to explain the unexplainable."

"You *were* trapped with us on the mountain that night. You *saw* the evidence."

On the night he spoke of, a night in January, they had almost lost their lives. That much they could agree on, because the evidence was as real as the blood left in the aftermath. But there was so much about that night that they would never agree on, and their most fundamental disagreement was about the nature of the monster who had trapped them on that mountain.

"What I saw was a serial murderer, like too many others in this world," she said. "I don't need any biblical theories to explain him. Talk to me about *science,* not fables about ancient demonic bloodlines." She set the stack of newspapers on the coffee table. "Evil just *is.* People can be brutal and some of them kill. We'd all like an explanation for it."

"Does science explain why a killer would mummify a woman's body? Why he'd shrink a woman's head and deposit another woman in the trunk of a car?"

Startled, she turned to look at him. "You already know about those cases?"

But of course he would know. Anthony Sansone's ties to law enforcement reached the highest levels, into the office of the police commissioner himself. A case as unusual as that of Madam X would certainly catch his attention. And it would stir interest within the secretive

Mephisto Society, which had its own bizarre theories about crime and how to combat it.

"There are details even you may not be aware of," he said. "Details I think you should be acquainted with."

"Before we talk about this any further," she said, "I'm going to get dressed. If you'll excuse me."

She retreated to her bedroom. There she pulled on jeans and a button-down shirt, casual attire that was perfectly appropriate for a Sunday afternoon, but she felt underdressed for her distinguished visitor. She didn't bother with makeup, but simply washed her face and brushed the tangles from her hair. Staring at herself in the mirror, she saw puffy eyes and new strands of gray that she hadn't noticed before. Well, this is who I am, she thought. A woman who'll never see forty again. I can't hide my age and I won't even try to.

By the time she came out of the bedroom, the smell of brewing coffee was permeating the house. She followed the scent to the kitchen, where Sansone had already pulled two mugs from the cabinet.

"I hope you don't mind that I took the liberty of making a fresh pot."

She watched as he picked up the carafe and poured, his broad back turned to her. He looked perfectly at home in her kitchen, and it annoyed her how effortlessly he had invaded her house. He had the knack of walking into any room, in any house, and just by his presence laying claim to the territory.

He handed her a cup, and to her surprise he'd added

just the right amount of sugar and cream, exactly as she liked it. It was a detail she hadn't expected him to remember.

"It's time to talk about Madam X," he said. "And what you may really be dealing with."

"How much do you know?"

"I know you have three linked deaths."

"We don't know they're linked."

"Three victims, all preserved in grotesque ways? That's a rather unique signature."

"I haven't done the autopsy on the third victim, so I can't tell you anything about her. Not even how she was preserved."

"I'm told it wasn't a classic mummification."

"If by *classic* you mean salted, dried, and wrapped, no, it wasn't."

"Her features are relatively intact?"

"Yes. Remarkably so. But her tissues still retain moisture. I've never autopsied a body like this one. I'm not even sure how to keep her preserved in her current state."

"What about the owner of the car? She's an archaeologist, isn't she? Does she have any idea how the body was preserved?"

"I didn't speak to her. From what Jane told me, the woman was pretty shaken up."

He set down his coffee cup and his gaze was so direct it almost felt like an assault. "What do you know about Dr. Pulcillo?"

"Why are you asking about her?"

"Because she works for them, Maura."

"Them?"

"The Crispin Museum."

"You make it sound like a malevolent institution."

"You agreed to view the CT scan. You were part of that media circus they organized around Madam X. You must have known what you were getting into."

"The curator invited me to observe. He didn't tell me there *would* be a media circus. He just thought I'd be interested in watching the scan, and of course I was."

"And you didn't know anything about the museum when you agreed to participate?"

"I visited the Crispin a few years ago. It's a quirky collection but it's worth seeing. It's not that different from a number of other private museums I've visited, founded by wealthy families who want to show off their collections."

"The Crispins are something of a special family."

"What makes them special?"

He sat down in the chair across from her so their gazes were level. "The fact that no one really knows where they came from."

"Does it matter?"

"It's a bit curious, don't you think? The first Crispin on record was Cornelius, who surfaced in Boston in 1850. He claimed to be a titled Englishman."

"You're implying it wasn't true."

"There's no record of him in England. Or anywhere

else, for that matter. He simply materialized on the scene one day, and was said to be a handsome man of great charm. He married well and proceeded to build his wealth. He and his descendants were collectors and tireless travelers, and they brought home curiosities from every continent. There were the usual items—carvings and burial goods and animal specimens. But what Cornelius and his family seemed especially interested in were weapons. Every variety of weapon used by armies around the world. It was an appropriate interest of theirs, considering how their fortune was made."

"How?"

"Wars, Maura. Ever since Cornelius, they've been profiteers. He became wealthy during the Civil War, running weapons to the South. His descendants continued the tradition, profiting from conflicts all over the world, from Africa to Asia to the Middle East. They made a secret pact with Hitler to provide weapons for his troops, and simultaneously armed the Allied forces. In China, they supplied both the Nationalist and the Communist armies. Their merchandise ended up in Algiers and Lebanon and the Belgian Congo. It didn't matter who was fighting whom. They didn't take sides; they just took the money. As long as blood was being shed somewhere, they stood to make a profit."

"How is this relevant to the investigation?"

"I just want you to understand the background of this institution, and what kind of legacy it carries. The Crispin Museum was paid for with blood. When you walk through that building, every gold coin you see, every piece of pottery, was paid for by a war somewhere. It's a foul place, Maura, built by a family that hid its past. A family whose roots we'll never know."

"I know where you're going with this. You're going to tell me the Crispins have a demonic bloodline. That they're descended from the biblical Nephilim." She shook her head and laughed. "Please. Not the Dead Sea Scrolls again."

"Why do you think Madam X ended up in that museum?"

"I'm sure you have an answer."

"I have a theory. I think she was a form of tribute. So was the shrunken head. They were donated by an admirer who understands exactly what the Crispin family represents."

"The third victim wasn't found in the museum. The body was placed in Dr. Pulcillo's car."

"She works for the museum."

"And she's now terrified. Her keys were stolen and someone sent her one hell of a gruesome gift."

"Because she was an obvious go-between for the intended recipient, Simon Crispin."

"No, I think Dr. Pulcillo *is* the intended recipient. She's a strikingly pretty woman and she's caught a killer's eye. That's what Jane believes as well." She paused. "Why aren't you talking to her about this? She's the investigator. Why come to me?"

"Detective Rizzoli's mind is closed to alternative theories."

"Meaning she's firmly grounded in reality." Maura rose to her feet. "So am I."

"Before you dismiss this out of hand, maybe you should know one more thing about the Crispin collection. The part of the collection that no one ever saw. It was kept hidden away."

"Why?"

"Because it was so grotesque, so upsetting, that the family couldn't afford to let the public know about it."

"How do you know about this?"

"For years, there were rumors about it in the antiquities market. About six years ago, Simon Crispin put it up for private auction. It seems he's been quite the spendthrift and he's managed to go through what was left of his family's fortune. He needed to raise cash. He also needed to dispose of embarrassing and possibly illegal items. The truly disturbing part is, he actually found a buyer, whose name remains anonymous."

"What did Crispin sell?"

"War trophies. I don't mean army medals and rusty bayonets. I'm talking about rattles made with human teeth from Africa and severed ears from Japanese soldiers. A necklace strung with fingers and a jar with women's . . ." He stopped. "It was a horrifying collection. The point is, I'm not the only one who knew about the Crispin family's interest in grotesque souvenirs. Maybe this archaeology killer did, too.

And he thought he'd contribute to their collection."

"You believe they were gifts."

"Tokens of admiration from some collector who donated a few of his own keepsakes to the museum. Where they've been sitting, forgotten."

"Until now."

Sansone nodded. "I think this mysterious donor has decided to resurface. He's letting the world know that he's still alive." He added, quietly: "There may be more such gifts coming, Maura."

Her kitchen telephone rang, shattering the silence. Startled, she felt her pulse give a kick as she rose from the chair. How easily Sansone was able to rattle her belief in a logical world. How quickly he could cast a shadow over a bright summer day. His paranoia was contagious, and she heard an ominous note to that ringing telephone, a warning that this call would bring unwelcome news.

But the voice that greeted her on the line was both familiar and pleasant. "Dr. Isles, this is Carter from the lab. I have some interesting GC-MS results."

"On what?"

"Those tissue samples you sent us on Thursday."

"From the body in the trunk? You've already done the gas chromatography?"

"I got a call to come into the lab for a weekend expedite. I thought you ordered it."

"No, I didn't." She glanced over her shoulder at Sansone, who was watching her so closely that she felt compelled to turn away. "Go on," she said into the phone.

"I did a flash pyrolysis on the tissue sample, and I found ample presence of both collagenous and non-collagenous proteins when we examined it with gas chromatography and mass spectrometry. Whatever its age, this tissue is really well preserved."

"I also requested a screen for tanning agents. Did you find any?"

"There aren't any benzenediols present. That eliminates most known tanning agents. But it did detect a chemical called four-isopropenylphenol."

"I have no idea what that means."

"I had to do some research myself. That chemical turns out to be a characteristic pyrolysis product of sphagnum moss."

"*Moss?*"

"Yeah. Does that help you at all?"

"Yes," she said quietly. "I think it does." *It tells me exactly what I need to know.* She hung up and stood staring at the phone, stunned by the lab results. This was now beyond her sphere of knowledge, beyond anything she'd ever dealt with in the autopsy room, and she did not want to proceed without technical guidance.

"Maura?"

She turned to Sansone. "Can we continue this discussion another time? I need to make some phone calls."

"May I make a suggestion before I leave? I know a

gentleman you might want to contact. A Dr. Pieter Vandenbrink. I can put you in touch with him."

"Why are you telling me about him?"

"You'll find his name well represented on the Internet. Look up his curriculum vitae, and you'll understand why."

15

The TV news vans were back, and this time, there were more of them. Once a killer earns a nickname, he becomes public property, and every news station wanted a piece of the Archaeology Killer investigation.

Jane felt the all-seeing eyes of the cameras following her as she and Frost walked from the parking lot to the ME's building. When she'd first made detective, she'd gotten a thrill seeing herself for the first time on the evening news. That thrill had long since faded, and these days she viewed reporters with irritation. Instead of mugging for the cameras, she walked with her head down and her shoulders rolled forward; on the six o'clock news tonight, she'd probably look like a hunch-backed troll in a blue blazer.

It was a relief to step inside the building and escape the invasive zoom lenses, but the worst ordeal lay ahead. As she and Frost made their way to the autopsy lab, she felt her muscles tensing, her stomach churning in anticipation of what they'd have to confront on the table today.

In the anteroom, Frost was unusually silent as they both donned gowns and shoe covers. Braving a glimpse through the window, she was relieved to see that the body was still covered by a drape, a brief reprieve before the horror. With a grim sense of duty, she pushed into the autopsy room.

Maura had just clipped X-rays onto the morgue viewing box, and the dental films of Jane Doe Number Three glowed against the backlight. She looked at the two detectives. "So what do you think of these?" she quizzed them.

"Those look like pretty good teeth," said Jane.

Maura nodded. "There are two amalgam fillings here, plus one gold crown on the lower left molar. I see no caries, and there's no alveolar bone loss to indicate any periodontal disease. Finally, there's this detail." Maura tapped a finger on the X-ray. "She's missing both pre-molars."

"You think they were pulled?"

"But there are no gaps between the teeth. And the roots of these incisors have been shortened and blunted."

"And that means?"

"She's had orthodontic work. She's worn braces."

"So we're talking a well-to-do victim."

"Certainly middle class, at the very least."

"Hey, I never got braces." Jane bared her teeth,

revealing an irregular bottom row. "These, Doc, are middle-class teeth." She pointed to the X-ray. "My dad couldn't afford to pay for something like that."

"Madam X had good teeth, too," said Frost.

Maura nodded. "Both women had what I'd guess were privileged childhoods. Privileged enough to pay for good dental care and orthodontics." She pulled down the dental film and reached for a new set, which twanged as she shoved them under the clips. The bones of the lower extremities now glowed on the light box.

"And here's what else the two victims had in common."

Jane and Frost simultaneously sucked in startled breaths. They needed no radiologist to interpret the damage they saw on those X-rays.

"It was done to both of her tibias," said Maura. "With a blunt instrument of some kind. A hammer maybe, or a tire iron. We're not talking about mere glancing blows on her shins. These were brutal and purposeful, meant to shatter bone. Both tibias have transverse diaphyseal fractures, with scattered fragments embedded in the soft tissue. The pain would have been excruciating. She certainly couldn't have walked. I can't imagine how she must have suffered over the days that followed. Infection probably set in, spreading from open wounds into soft tissues. Bacteria would have infiltrated bone, and eventually blood."

Jane looked at her. "Did you say *days*?"

"These fractures wouldn't have been fatal. Not immediately."

"Maybe she was killed first. These could be post-mortem mutilations." *Please make them postmortem, and not what I'm imagining.*

"I'm sorry to say that she lived," said Maura. "For at least several weeks." She pointed to a ragged outline, like a puff of white smoke surrounding the fractured bone. "This is callus formation. It's the bone healing itself, and this doesn't happen overnight, or even over a few days. It takes weeks."

Weeks during which this woman had suffered. Weeks when it must have seemed far better to die. Jane thought of an earlier set of X-rays she'd seen hanging on this same light box. Another woman's shattered leg, the fracture lines blurred by a fog of healing bone.

"Just like Madam X," she said.

Maura nodded. "Neither of these victims was killed immediately. Both suffered crippling injuries to their lower extremities. Both lived for a while. Which means someone brought them food and water. Someone was keeping them alive, long enough for the first signs of healing to show up on these films."

"It's the same killer."

"The patterns are too similar. This is part of his signature. First he maims them, maybe to ensure they can't escape. Then as the days go by, he keeps them fed. And alive."

"What the hell is he doing during that time? Enjoying their company?"

"I don't know."

Jane stared at shattered bone and felt a twinge in her own legs, just a shadow of the agony this victim must have endured. "You know," she said softly, "when you first called me that night about Madam X, I thought it would be an old murder. A cold case, with a perp who was long dead. But if he's the one who put this body in Ms. Pulcillo's car . . ."

"He's still alive, Jane. And he's right here in Boston."

The door to the anteroom swung open, and a silver-haired gentleman stepped in, tying on a surgical gown.

"Dr. Vandenbrink?" said Maura. "I'm Dr. Isles. I'm glad you could make it."

"I hope you haven't started yet."

"We were waiting for you."

The man came forward to shake her hand. He was in his sixties, cadaverously thin, but his deeply tanned face and eager stride revealed not sickness but lean good health. As Maura made the introductions, the man gave scarcely a glance at Jane and Frost—his attention was riveted instead on the table where the victim lay, her twisted form mercifully concealed by a drape. Clearly it was the dead, not the living, that most interested him.

"Dr. Vandenbrink is from the Drents Museum in Assen," said Maura. "He flew in last night from the Netherlands, just for this autopsy."

"And this is her?" he said, his gaze still on the draped body. "Let's take a look at her, then."

Maura handed him a pair of gloves, and they both snapped on latex. Maura reached for the drape, and

Jane steeled herself against the view as the sheet was peeled back.

Naked on stainless steel, exposed by bright lights, the contorted body looked like a charred and twisted branch. But it was the face that would forever haunt Jane, the features glossy as black carbon, frozen in a mortal scream.

Far from horrified, Dr. Vandenbrink instead leaned closer with a look of fascination. "She's beautiful," he murmured. "Oh yes, I'm glad you called me. This was certainly worth the trip."

"You call that beautiful?" said Jane.

"I refer to her state of preservation," he said. "For the moment, it's almost perfect. But I'm afraid the flesh may start to decay now that it's exposed to air. This is the most impressive modern example I've encountered. It's rare to find a recent human subject that's undergone this process."

"Then you know how she got this way?"

"Oh yes. She's very much like the others."

"Others?"

He looked at Jane, his eyes so deep-set that she had the disturbing impression a skull was gazing back at her. "Have you ever heard of the Yde Girl, Detective?"

"No. Who is she?"

"Yde is a place. A village in the northern Netherlands. In 1897, two men from Yde were cutting peat, something that was traditionally dried and burned as fuel. And in the bog, they found something that terrified them. It was a female with long blond hair who had clearly been strangled. A long band of fabric was still wrapped three times around her neck. At first, the people of Yde didn't understand what they were dealing with. She was so small and shrunken, they thought she was an old woman. Or perhaps a demon. But over time, as scientists came to look at her, they were able to learn more about the corpse. And they discovered that she was not an old woman when she died, but a girl of only about sixteen. A girl who had suffered from a crooked spine. A girl who was murdered. She was stabbed beneath the collarbone, and a band was tightened around her neck until she strangled. Then she was placed facedown in the bog, where she lay for centuries. Until those two peat cutters found her and revealed her to the world."

"Centuries?"

Vandenbrink nodded. "Carbon fourteen dating tells us she's two thousand years old. When Jesus walked the earth, that poor girl may already have been lying in her grave."

"Even after two centuries, they could tell how she died?" said Frost.

"She was that well preserved, from her hair to the cloth around her neck. Oh, there was damage done to her body, but it had been inflicted far more recently, when she was dredged up with the peat. Enough of her was left intact to form a portrait of who she was. And how she must have suffered. That's the miracle of bogs,

Detective. They give us a window back in time. Hundreds of these bodies have been found in Holland and Denmark, Ireland and England. Each one is a time traveler, an unfortunate ambassador of sorts, sent to us from people who left no written records. Except for the cruelties they carved into their victims."

"But this woman"—Jane nodded at the body on the table—"she's obviously not two thousand years old."

"Yet her state of preservation is every bit as exquisite. Look, you can even see the ridges on her soles and her finger pads. And see how her skin is dark, like leather? Yet her features clearly tell us she's Caucasian." He looked at Maura. "I completely concur with your opinion, Dr. Isles."

Frost said, "So you're telling us this body was preserved in the same way as that girl in the Netherlands?"

Vandenbrink nodded. "What you have here is a modern bog body."

"That's why I called Dr. Vandenbrink," said Maura. "He's been studying bog bodies for decades."

"Unlike Egyptian mummification techniques," said Vandenbrink, "there's no written record of how to make a bog body. This is a completely natural and accidental process that we don't entirely understand."

"Then how would the killer know how to do it?" Jane asked.

"Within the bog body community, there's been quite a bit of discussion about just this topic."

Jane gave a surprised laugh. "You have a community?"

"Of course. We have our own meetings, our own cocktail parties. A great deal of what we discuss is purely speculative. But we do have some hard science to back up the theories. We know, for instance, that there are several characteristics about bogs that contribute to corpse preservation. They're highly acidic, they're oxygen-poor, and they contain layers of sphagnum moss. These factors help arrest decomposition and preserve soft tissues. They darken the skin to the color you see in this body here. If allowed to steep for centuries, eventually this corpse's bones will dissolve, leaving only the preserved flesh, leathery and completely flexible."

"Is it the moss that does it?" asked Frost.

"It's a vital part of the process. There's a chemical reaction between bacteria and the polysaccharides found in sphagnum moss. Sphagnum binds bacterial cells so they can't degrade organic materials. If you bind the bacteria, you can arrest decomposition. The whole process happens in an acidic soup that contains dead moss and tannins and holocellulose. In other words, bog water."

"And that's it? Just stick the body in bog water, and you're done?"

"It's a little more exacting than that. There've been several experiments using piglet cadavers in Ireland and the UK. These were buried in various peat bogs, then exhumed months later for study. Since pigs are biochemically similar to us, we can assume the results would be the same for humans."

"And they turned into bog pigs?"

"If the conditions were just right. First, the pigs had to be completely submerged or they would decompose. Second, they had to be placed into the bog immediately after death. If you let the corpse sit exposed for just a few hours before you submerged it, it would go on to decompose anyway."

Frost and Jane looked at each other. "So our perp couldn't waste any time once he killed her," said Jane.

Vandenbrink nodded. "She had to be submerged soon after death. In the case of European bog bodies, the victims must have been walked into the bog while still alive. And only then, at the water's edge, were they murdered."

Jane turned and looked at the brutally shattered tibias on the X-ray light box. "This victim couldn't have walked anywhere with two broken legs. She'd have to be carried in. If you were the killer, you wouldn't want to do that in the dark. Not if you're walking through a bog."

"So he does it in broad daylight?" said Frost. "Drags her from his car and hauls her to the water? He'd have to have the location picked out ahead of time. A place he knew he wouldn't be seen, and close enough to a road so he wouldn't have to carry her far."

"There are other conditions required," said Vandenbrink.

"What conditions?" asked Jane.

"The water must be deep enough and cold enough.

Temperature matters. And it would have to be remote enough so the body wouldn't be found until he was ready to claim her."

"That's a long list of conditions," said Jane. "Wouldn't it be easier just to fill a bathtub with water and peat moss?"

"How can you be certain you'd properly replicate the conditions? A bog is a complex ecosystem that we don't fully understand, a chemical soup of organic matter that has to steep over centuries. Even if you manage to make that soup in a bathtub, you'd need to initially chill it to four degrees Celsius and hold it there for at least several weeks. Then the body would need to soak for months, perhaps years. How would you keep it concealed that long? Would there be odors? Suspicious neighbors?" He shook his head. "The ideal place is still a bog. A *real* bog."

But those broken legs remained a problem. Whether the victim was alive or dead, she would need to be carried or dragged to the water's edge, over terrain that might be muddy. "How big was she, do you think?" Jane asked.

"Based on skeletal indices," said Maura, "I estimate her height at around five foot six. And you can see she's relatively slender."

"So maybe a hundred twenty, a hundred thirty pounds."

"A reasonable guess."

But even a slender woman would weigh a man down after a short distance. And if she were already dead, time would be of the essence. Delay too long, and the corpse would begin its inevitable journey to decay. If she were still alive, there would be other difficulties to contend with. A struggling and noisy victim. The chance of being heard while you dragged her from the car. *Where did you find this perfect spot, this killing place?*

The intercom buzzed, and Maura's secretary said over the speaker: "Dr. Isles, there's a phone call on line one. It's a Scott Thurlow from NCIC."

"I'll take it," said Maura. She pulled off her gloves as she went to the telephone. "This is Dr. Isles." She paused, listening, then suddenly straightened and shot a look at Jane that said, *This one's important.* "Thank you for letting me know. I'll take a look at that right now. Hold on." She crossed to the lab computer.

"What is it?" said Jane.

Maura opened one of her e-mails and clicked on the attachment. A series of dental X-rays appeared on the screen. Unlike the morgue panograms that showed all the teeth at once, these were spot films from a dentist's office.

"Yes, I'm looking at them now," said Maura, still on the phone. "I see an occlusal amalgam on number thirty. This is absolutely compatible."

"Compatible with what?" said Jane.

Maura held up a hand to keep her silent, her focus still on the phone conversation. "I'm opening the second attachment," she said. A new image filled the screen. It was a young woman with long black hair, her eyes narrowed against the sunlight. She was wearing a denim shirt over a black tank top. The deeply tanned face, devoid of makeup, suggested a woman who lived her life outdoors, who thrived on fresh air and practical clothes. "I'm going to look over these files," Maura said. "I'll call you back." She hung up.

"Who's the woman?" Jane asked.

"Her name is Lorraine Edgerton. She was last seen near Gallup, New Mexico, about twenty-five years ago."

Jane frowned at the face smiling back at her from the computer screen. "Am I supposed to remember that name?"

"You will now. You're looking at the face of Madam X."

16

Forensic psychologist Dr. Lawrence Zucker had a gaze so penetrating that Jane usually avoided sitting straight across from him, but she'd arrived late to the meeting and had been forced to take the last remaining seat, facing Zucker. Slowly he perused the photographs spread out on the table. They were images of a vibrant young Lorraine Edgerton. In some shots she wore shorts and T-shirts; in others, jeans and hiking boots. Clearly she was an outdoorswoman, with the tan to prove it. He turned next to what she looked like now: stiff and dry as cordwood, her face a leathery mask stretched taut across bone. When he looked up, his eerily pale eyes focused on Jane, and she had the uneasy feeling that he could see straight into the dark corners of her brain, into places she allowed no one to see. Though there were four other detectives in the room, she was the only woman; perhaps that was the reason Zucker focused on her. She refused to let him intimidate her, and she stared right back.

"How long ago did you say Ms. Edgerton vanished?" he asked.

"It was twenty-five years ago," said Jane.

"And does that period of time account for the current condition of her body?"

"We know this *is* Lorraine Edgerton, based on the dental records."

"And we also know it doesn't take centuries to mummify a body," added Frost.

"Yes, but could she have been killed far more recently than twenty-five years ago?" said Zucker. "You said she was kept alive long enough for her bullet wound to begin healing. What if she was kept a prisoner for far longer? Could you turn a body into a mummy in, say, five years?"

"You think this perp could have kept her captive for *decades*?"

"I'm merely speculating, Detective Frost. Trying to understand what our unknown subject gets out of this. What could drive him to perform these grotesque postmortem rituals. With each of the three victims, he went to a great deal of trouble to keep her from decaying."

"He wanted them to last," said Lieutenant Marquette, chief of the homicide unit. "He wanted to keep them around."

Zucker nodded. "Eternal companionship. That's one interpretation. He didn't want to let them go, so he turns them into keepsakes that will last forever."

"So why kill them at all?" asked Detective Crowe. "Why not just keep them as prisoners? We know he kept two of them alive long enough for their fractures to start healing."

"Maybe they died natural deaths from their injuries. From what I read in the autopsy reports, there are no definitive answers as to cause of death."

Jane said, "Dr. Isles was unable to make that determination, but we do know that the Bog Lady . . ." She paused. Bog Lady was the new victim's nickname, but no detective would ever say it in public. No one wanted to see it splashed across the newspapers. "We know that the victim in the trunk suffered fractures of both legs, and they may have become infected. That could have caused her death."

"And preservation would be the only way to keep her around," said Marquette. "Permanently."

Zucker looked down, once again, at the photo. "Tell me about this victim, Lorraine Edgerton."

Jane slid a folder across to the psychologist. "That's what we know about her so far. She was a graduate student working in New Mexico when she vanished."

"What was she studying?"

"Archaeology."

Zucker's eyebrow shot up. "Do I sense a theme here?"

"It's hard not to. That summer, Lorraine was working with a group of students at an archaeological dig in Chaco Canyon. On the day she vanished, she told her colleagues that she was going into town. She left on her motorbike in the late afternoon and never came back. Weeks later, the bike was found miles away, near a Navajo reservation. From what I gather about the area, there's not much in the way of population. It's mostly open desert and dirt roads."

"So there are no witnesses."

"None. And now it's twenty-five years later, and the detective who investigated her disappearance is dead. All we have is his report. Which is why Frost and I are flying out to New Mexico to talk to the archaeologist who was director of the dig. He was one of the last people who saw her alive."

Zucker looked at the photos. "She appears to have been an athletic young woman."

"She was. A hiker, a camper. A woman who spent a lot of time with a shovel. Not the kind of gal who'd give up without a fight."

"But there was a bullet in her leg."

"Which may have been the only way this perp could control his victims. The only way he could bring down Lorraine Edgerton."

"Both of Bog Lady's legs were broken," Frost pointed out.

Zucker nodded. "Which certainly makes the case that the same unsub killed both women. What about the bog victim? The one found in the trunk?"

Jane slid him the folder for Bog Lady. "We have no ID on her yet," she said. "So we don't know if she's linked in any way to Lorraine Edgerton. NCIC is running her through their database, and we're just hoping that someone, somewhere reported her missing."

Zucker scanned the autopsy report. "Adult female, age eighteen to thirty-five. Excellent dentition, orthodontic work." He looked up. "I'd be surprised if her disappearance *wasn't* reported. The method of preservation must tell you what part of the country she was killed in. How many states have peat bogs?"

"Actually," Frost said, "a lot of them. So that doesn't narrow it down a great deal."

"Get ready," Jane warned with a laugh. "Detective Frost is now Boston PD's official bog expert."

"I spoke to a Dr. Judith Welsh, a biologist over at University of Massachusetts," said Frost. He pulled out his notebook and flipped it open to the relevant pages. "Here's what she told me. You can find sphagnum wetlands in New England, Canada, the Great Lakes, and Alaska. Anywhere that's both temperate and wet. You can even find peat bogs in Florida." He glanced up. "In fact, they found bog bodies not far from Disney World."

Detective Crowe laughed. "Seriously?"

"Over a hundred of them, and they're probably eight thousand years old. It's called the Windover Burial Site. But their bodies weren't preserved. They're just skeletons, really, not like our Bog Lady at all. It's hot down there so they decomposed, even though they were soaking in peat."

"That means we can eliminate any southern bogs?" said Zucker.

Frost nodded. "Our victim's too well preserved. At the time of her immersion, the water had to be cold, four degrees Celsius or lower. That's the only way she'd come out looking as good as she does."

"Then we're talking about the northern states. Or Canada."

"Canada would present a problem for our perp," Jane pointed out. "You'd have to bring a dead body over the border."

"I think we can eliminate Alaska as well," said Frost. "There's another border crossing. Not to mention a long drive."

"It still leaves a lot of territory," Zucker said. "A lot of states with bogs where he could have stashed her body."

"Actually," said Frost, "we can narrow it down to ombrogenous bogs."

Everyone in the room looked at him. "What?" said Detective Tripp.

"Bogs are really cool things," said Frost, launching enthusiastically into the topic. "The more I find out about them, the more interesting they get. You start off with plant matter soaking in stagnant water. The water's so cold and low in oxygen that the moss just sits there not decaying, piling up year after year till it's at least a couple of feet deep. If the water's stagnant, then the bog's ombrogenous."

Crowe looked at Tripp and said drily, "A little knowledge is a dangerous thing."

"Is any of this really relevant?" asked Tripp.

Frost flushed. "Yeah. And if you'd just listen, maybe you'd learn something."

Jane glanced at her partner in surprise. Rarely did Frost show irritation, and she hadn't expected him to do so over the subject of sphagnum moss.

Zucker said, "Please continue, Detective Frost. I'd like to know exactly what makes a bog ombrogenous."

Frost took a breath and straightened in his chair. "It refers to the source of water. *Ombrogenous* means it doesn't get any water from streams or underground currents. Which means it gets no added oxygen or nutrients. It's entirely rain-fed and stagnant, and that makes it superacidic. All the characteristics that make it a true bog."

"So it isn't just any wet place."

"No. It has to be fed only by rainwater. Otherwise they'd call it a fen or a marsh."

"How is this important?"

"Only real bogs have the conditions you need to preserve bodies. We're talking about a specific kind of wetland."

"And would that limit where this body was preserved?"

Frost nodded. "The Northeast has thousands of acres of wetland, but only a small fraction of them are true bogs. They're found in the Adirondacks, in Vermont, and in northern and coastal Maine."

Detective Tripp shook his head. "I went hunting once, way up in northern Maine. There's nothing there except trees and deer. If our boy has a little hidey-hole up there, good luck finding it."

Frost said, "The biologist, Dr. Welsh, said she might be able to narrow down the location if she had more information. So we sent her some bits of plant material that Dr. Isles picked out of the victim's hair."

"This all helps," said Zucker. "It gives us another data point for our killer's geographic profile. You know the saying among criminal profilers: *You go where you know, and you know where you go.* People tend to stick to areas where they're comfortable, places they're familiar with. Maybe our unsub went to summer camp in the Adirondacks. Or he's a hunter like you, Detective Tripp, and he knows the back roads, the hidden camps of Maine. What he did to the bog victim required advance planning. How did he get familiar with the area? Does he own a cabin there? And is it accessible at just the right time of year, while the water's cold but not frozen, so she could be deposited quickly into the bog?"

"There's something else we know about him," said Jane.

"What would that be?"

"He knew *exactly* how to preserve her. He knew the right conditions, the right water temperature. That's specialized knowledge, not the kind of information that most people would have."

"Unless you're an archaeologist," said Zucker.

Jane nodded. "We get back to the same theme again, don't we?"

Zucker leaned back, eyes narrowing in thought. "A killer who's familiar with ancient funerary practices. Whose victim in New Mexico was a young woman working on a dig site. Now he seems to be fixated on yet another young woman working in a museum. How does he find these women? How does he meet them?" He looked at Jane. "Have you a list of Ms. Pulcillo's friends and associates?"

"It's a pretty short list. Just the museum staff and the people in her apartment building."

"No gentlemen friends? You said she's quite an attractive young woman."

"She says she hasn't had a date since she moved to Boston five months ago." Jane paused. "Actually, she's kind of a strange bird."

"What do you mean?"

Jane hesitated and glanced at Frost, who was steadfastly avoiding her gaze. "There's something . . . off about her. I can't explain it."

"Did you have the same reaction, Detective Frost?"

"No," Frost said, his mouth tightening. "I think Josephine's scared, that's all."

Zucker glanced back and forth between the two partners, and his eyebrows lifted. "A difference of opinion."

"Rizzoli's reading too much into it," said Frost.

"I just get weird signals from her, that's all," said Jane. "As if she's more afraid of *us* than the perp."

"Afraid of you, maybe," said Frost.

Detective Crowe laughed. "Who isn't?"

Zucker was silent for a moment, and Jane did not like the way he was studying her and Frost, as though probing the depths of the breach between them.

Jane said, "The woman's a loner, that's all I'm saying. She goes to work, she goes home. Her whole life seems to be inside that museum."

"What about her colleagues?"

"The curator's a guy named Nicholas Robinson. Forty years old, single, no criminal record."

"Single?"

"Yeah, it raised a red flag for me, too, but I can't find anything that gives me a tingle. Besides, he's the one who found Madam X in the basement. The rest of the staff are all volunteers, and their average age is around a hundred years old. I can't imagine one of those fossils dragging a body out of a bog."

"So you're left with no viable suspects."

"And three victims who probably weren't even killed in the state of Massachusetts, much less in our jurisdiction," said Crowe.

"Well, they're all in our jurisdiction now," Frost pointed out. "We've managed to search all the crates in the museum basement and we haven't found any other victims. But you never know, there might be hidden spaces behind other walls." He glanced down at his ringing cell phone and suddenly stood. "Excuse me, I gotta take this call."

As Frost stepped out of the room, Zucker's gaze turned back to Jane. "I'm curious about something you said earlier, regarding Ms. Pulcillo."

"What about her?"

"You described her as a strange bird. Yet Detective Frost saw nothing of the kind."

"Yeah. Well, we have a difference of opinion."

"How deep a difference?"

Was she supposed to tell him what she really thought? That Frost's judgment had gone haywire because his wife was out of town and he was lonely and Josephine Pulcillo had big brown eyes?

"Is there something about the woman that may bias you against her?"

"What?" Jane gave a laugh of disbelief. "You think *I'm* the one who—"

"Why does she make you uneasy?"

"She doesn't. There's just a caginess about her. Like she's trying to stay one step ahead."

"Of you? Or the killer? From what I heard, the young woman had every right to be afraid. A body was left in her car. It almost sounds like a gift from the killer—an offering, if you will. To his next companion."

His next companion. That phrase raised gooseflesh on Jane's arms.

"I take it she's in a secure location?" said Zucker. When no one immediately answered him, he looked around the table. "I'm sure we all agree she could be in jeopardy. Where is she?"

"That's an issue we're trying to clear up right now," admitted Jane.

"You don't know where she is?"

"She told us she was going to stay with an aunt named Connie Pulcillo in Burlington, Vermont, but we can't find any listing with that name. We've left messages on Josephine's voice mail and she hasn't responded."

Zucker shook his head. "This is not good news. Have you checked her Boston residence?"

"She's not there. A neighbor in her building saw her leave Friday morning with two suitcases."

"Even if she's left Boston, she may not be safe," said Zucker. "This unsub is clearly comfortable operating across state lines. He doesn't seem to have geographic boundaries. He could have followed her."

"If he knows where she is. Even we can't find her."

"But she's *his* only focus. She may have been his only focus for some time. If he's been watching her, following her, then he may know exactly where she is." Zucker leaned back, clearly disturbed. "Why hasn't she answered her phone? Is it because she can't?"

Before Jane could respond, the door opened and Frost came back into the room. She took one look at his face and knew instantly that something was wrong. "What is it?"

"Josephine Pulcillo is dead," he said.

His stark announcement sent a jolt through the room as shocking as the voltage from a stun gun.

"*Dead?*" Jane shot straight up in her chair. "How? What the hell happened?"

"It was a car accident. But—"

"So it wasn't our killer."

"No. It was definitely not our perp," said Frost.

Jane heard anger in his voice, and she saw it as well in his tight mouth, his narrowed eyes.

"She died in San Diego," said Frost. "Twenty-four years ago."

17

They'd been driving for half an hour before Jane finally brought up the painful subject, a subject they'd managed to avoid during the flight from Boston to Albuquerque.

"You had a thing for her. Didn't you?" she asked.

Frost didn't look at her. He stayed focused on his driving, his gaze fixed on the road where the blacktop shimmered, hot as a griddle under the New Mexico sun. In all the time they'd worked together, she'd never felt such a wall between them, an impenetrable barrier that she could not seem to chip through. This wasn't the good-natured Barry Frost that she knew; this was his evil twin, and any minute now he was going to start speaking in tongues and his head would demonically spin around.

"We really need to talk about this, you know," she insisted.

"Give it a rest, why can't you?"

"You can't keep kicking yourself over this. She's a pretty girl and she pulled the wool over your eyes. It can happen to any guy."

"But not to *me*." He looked at her at last, his anger so raw that it silenced her. "I can't believe I didn't see it," he said and focused, once again, on the road. A moment passed, and the only noise was the air conditioner and the sound of their car slicing through the heat.

She had never traveled to New Mexico before. She'd never even seen the desert before. But she scarcely noticed the landscape flying past their windows; what mattered to her now was healing this rift between them, and the only way to do it was to talk it through, whether Frost was willing to or not.

"You aren't the only one who's surprised," said Jane. "Dr. Robinson had no idea. You should have seen his face when I told him she's a fraud. If she lied about something as basic as her own name, what else did she lie about? She took in a lot of people, including her college professors."

"But not you. You saw through it."

"I just got a funny feeling about her, that's all."

"Cop's instinct."

"Yeah. I guess."

"So what the hell happened to *mine*?"

Jane gave a laugh. "A different instinct was operating. She's pretty, she's scared, and wham-o. The Boy Scout wanted to save her."

"Whoever the hell she is."

They still did not know the answer; what they did know was that she was not the real Josephine Pulcillo, who had died twenty-four years ago when she was only two years old. Yet years later, that dead girl managed to attend college and graduate school. She managed to open a bank account, get a driver's license, and land a job in an obscure Boston museum. The child had been resurrected as a different woman, whose true origins remained a mystery.

"I can't believe I was such a moron," he said.

"You want my advice?"

"Not particularly."

"Call Alice. Tell her to come home. That was part of the problem, you know. Your wife's been gone and you got lonely. You got vulnerable. A pretty girl wanders onto the scene and suddenly you're thinking with a different brain."

"I can't just order her to come home."

"She's your wife, isn't she?"

He gave a snort. "I'd like to see Gabriel try telling *you* what to do. That wouldn't be pretty."

"I can be reasoned with and so can Alice. She's been visiting her parents way too long and you need her back. Just call her."

Frost sighed. "It's more complicated than that."

"What do you mean?"

"Alice and I—well, we've been having problems. Ever since she started law school, it's like I can't talk to her. It's like nothing I say is worth listening to. She spends all day with those smart-ass professors and when she comes home, what're we supposed to talk about?"

"What you did at work, maybe?"

"Yeah, I tell her about our latest arrest and she asks me if police brutality was involved."

"Oh, man. She's gone to the dark side?"

"She thinks we *are* the dark side." He glanced at her. "You're lucky, you know? Gabriel's one of us. He gets what we do."

Yes, she was lucky; she was married to a man who understood the challenges of law enforcement. But she knew how quickly even good marriages could fall apart. Last Christmas, she'd watched her parents' marriage collapse over dinner. She'd seen their household destroyed by one stray blonde. And she knew that Barry Frost was now standing on the threshold of marital disaster.

She said, "My mom's annual neighborhood barbecue is coming up soon. Vince Korsak will be there, so it'll be like a team reunion. Why don't you join us?"

"Is this a pity invitation?"

"I was planning to ask you anyway. I've invited you before, but you hardly ever took me up on it."

He sighed. "That was because of Alice."

"What?"

"She hates cop parties."

"Do you go to her law school parties?"

"Yeah."

"So what the hell?"

He shrugged. "I just wanna keep her happy, you know?"

"I really hate to say this."

"Then don't, okay?"

"Alice is kind of a bitch, isn't she?"

"Jesus. Why'd you have to say it?"

"Sorry. But she is."

He shook his head. "Is there anyone who's on my side?"

"I *am* on your side. I'm looking out for you. That's why I told you to stay a million miles away from that Josephine woman. I'm just glad you finally understand why I said it."

His hands tightened on the wheel. "I wonder who she really is. And what the hell she's hiding."

"We should hear back about her fingerprints tomorrow."

"Maybe she's running from an ex-husband. Maybe that's all this is about."

"If she were running from some creep, she would have told us that, don't you think? We're the good guys. Why would she run from the police unless she's guilty of something?"

He stared at the road. The turnoff to Chaco Canyon was still thirty miles ahead. "I can't wait to find out," he said.

After merely ten minutes of standing in the New

Mexico heat, Jane vowed she'd never again complain about summer in Boston. Seconds after she and Frost had stepped out of their air-conditioned rental car, sweat was blooming on her face, and the sand felt hot enough to sear right through her shoe leather. The glare of the desert sun was so painfully bright that she was squinting even behind the new sunglasses that she'd bought at a gas station along the way. Frost had picked up matching sunglasses, and with his suit and tie, he could have passed for Secret Service or maybe one of those Men in Black, were it not for the fact his face was flushed an alarming shade of red. Any minute now he would keel over from heatstroke.

So how does this old guy manage?

Professor Emeritus Alan Quigley was seventy-eight years old, yet he was crouched down at the bottom of the excavation trench, patiently digging through the stony soil with his trowel. His Tilley Hat, battered and filthy, looked nearly as old as he was. Though he worked in the shade of a tarp, the heat alone would have felled a much younger man. In fact, the college students on his team had already broken off work for the afternoon and were napping in the nearby shade while their far older professor just kept chipping away at the rocks and scooping loose soil into a bucket.

"You get into a rhythm," said Quigley. "The Zen of digging, I call it. These young kids, they attack it full-bore, all that nervous energy. They think it's a treasure hunt and they're in a rush to find the gold before anyone else does. Or before the semester ends, whichever comes first. They exhaust themselves, or they find only dirt and rocks and they lose interest. Most of them do, anyway. But the serious ones, the rare ones who stick with it, they understand that a human lifetime is just a blink of the eye. In a single season, you can't dig up what took centuries to accumulate."

Frost pulled off his sunglasses and mopped the sweat from his forehead. "So, uh, what *are* you digging for down there, Professor?"

"Garbage."

"Huh?"

"This is a trash midden. An area where refuse was discarded. We're looking for broken pottery, animal bones. You can learn a lot about a community by examining what they chose to throw away. And this was a most interesting community here." Quigley rose to his feet, grunting with the effort, and swiped a sleeve across his weathered brow. "These old knees are about ready for replacement again. That's what goes first in this profession, the damn knees." He clambered up a ladder and emerged from the trench. "Isn't this a magnificent spot?" he said, gazing around at the valley, where ancient ruins studded the landscape. "This canyon was once a ceremonial site, a place for sacred rituals. Have you toured the park yet?"

"I'm afraid not," said Jane. "We just flew into Albuquerque today."

"You come all the way from Boston, and you aren't

going to take a look at Chaco Canyon? One of the finest archaeological sites in the country?"

"Our time's limited, Professor. We came to see you."

He gave a snort. "Then take a look around you, because this site *is* my life. I've spent forty seasons in this canyon, whenever I wasn't teaching in the classroom. Now that I'm retired from the university, I can devote myself entirely to digging."

"For trash," said Jane.

Quigley laughed. "Yes. I suppose one could look at it that way."

"Is this the same site where Lorraine Edgerton was working?"

"No, we were over there, across the canyon." He pointed to a tumble of stone ruins in the distance. "I had a team of students working with me, both undergraduate and graduate level. It was the usual mix. Some of them were actually interested in archaeology, but some were here just for the credits. Or to have a good time and maybe get laid."

That was not a word she expected out of a seventy-eight-year-old's mouth, but then this was a man who'd lived and worked for most of his career alongside randy college students.

"Do you remember Lorraine Edgerton?" asked Frost.

"Oh, yes. After what happened, I certainly remember her. She was one of my graduate students. Thoroughly dedicated and tough as nails. As much as they wanted to blame me for what happened to Lorraine, she was perfectly capable of taking care of herself."

"Who wanted to blame you?"

"Her parents. She was their only child, and they were devastated. Since I was supervising the dig, of course they thought I should be held responsible. They sued the university, but that didn't bring their daughter back. In the end, it probably caused her father's heart attack. Her mother died a few years after that." He shook his head. "It was the strangest thing, how the desert just swallowed that girl up. She waved goodbye one afternoon, rode off on her motorbike, and vanished." He looked at Jane. "And now you say her body's turned up in Boston?"

"But we believe she was killed here, in New Mexico."

"So many years ago. And now we finally learn the truth."

"Not all of it. That's why we're here."

"There was a detective back then who questioned us. I think his name was McDonald or something. Have you spoken to him?"

"His name was McDowell. He died two years ago, but we have all his notes."

"Oh, dear. And he was younger than me, too. They were all younger than me, and now they're dead. Lorraine. Her parents." He looked at Jane with clear blue eyes. "And here I am, still hale and hearty. You just never know, do you?"

"Professor, I know it's been a long time, but we want you to think back to that summer. Tell us about the day she disappeared. And about the students who were working with you."

"Detective McDowell interviewed everyone who was here at the time. You must have read his notes."

"But you actually knew the students. You must have kept some field notes. A written record of the excavation."

Professor Quigley shot a worried look at Frost, whose face had flushed an even brighter shade of scarlet. "Young man, I can see you're not going to last much longer in this heat. Why don't we talk in my office, at the Park Service building? It's air-conditioned."

Lorraine Edgerton stood in the last row in the photograph, shoulder-to-shoulder with the men. Her black hair was pulled back in a ponytail, emphasizing the square jaw and the prominent cheekbones of a deeply tanned face.

"We called her the Amazon," said Professor Quigley. "Not because she was particularly strong, but because she was fearless. And I don't mean just physically. Lorraine would always speak her mind, whether or not it got her into trouble."

"Did it get her into trouble?" asked Frost.

Quigley smiled as he gazed at the faces of his former students, who would now be well into middle age. If they were still alive. "Not with me, Detective. I found her honesty refreshing."

"Did the others?"

"You know how it is in any group. There are conflicts and alliances. And these were young people in their twenties, so you have to factor in the hormones. An issue I try my best to stay away from."

Jane studied the photograph, which had been taken midway through the dig season. There were two rows of students, the front row crouched on their knees. Everyone looked trim and tanned and healthy in T-shirts and shorts. Standing beside the group was Professor Quigley, his face fuller, his sideburns longer, but already the lanky man he was today.

"There are a lot more women than men in this group," Frost noted.

Quigley nodded. "I find it's usually that way. Women seem drawn to archaeology more than men, and they're more willing to do the tedious work of cleaning and sifting."

"Tell me about these three men in the photo," said Jane. "What do you remember about them?"

"You're wondering if any of them could have killed her."

"The short answer would be yes."

"Detective McDowell interviewed them all. He found nothing to implicate any of my students."

"Nevertheless, I'd like to know what you remember about them."

Quigley thought about it for a moment. He pointed to the Asian man beside Lorraine. "Jeff Chu, pre-med. Very bright but impatient sort of boy. I think he got bored out here. He's a doctor now, in Los Angeles. And this one's Carl something-or-other. As sloppy as they come. The girls always had to pick up after him. And this third fellow here, Adam Stancioff, was a music major. No talent as an archaeologist, but I remember he played the guitar quite well. The girls liked that."

"Lorraine included?" asked Jane.

"Everyone liked Adam."

"I meant, in the romantic sense. Was Lorraine involved with any of these men?"

"Lorraine had no interest in romance. She was single-minded in the pursuit of her career. That's what I admired about her. That's what I wish I saw more of in my students. Instead they come into my class with visions of *Tomb Raider*. Hauling dirt isn't what they have in mind." He paused, reading Jane's face. "You're disappointed."

"So far I haven't learned anything we didn't see in McDowell's notes."

"I doubt I can add anything useful. Whatever I remember can't really be trusted after all these years."

"You told McDowell that you doubted any of your students could be involved in her disappearance. Do you still believe that?"

"Nothing's changed my mind. Look, Detective, these were all good kids. Lazy, some of them. And inclined to drink a bit too much when they went into town."

"And how often was that?"

"Every few days. Not that there's much to do in

Gallup, either. But then look at this canyon. There's nothing here except the Park Service building, the ruins, and a few campsites. Tourists do come through during the day, and that's something of a distraction because they hang around asking us questions. Other than that, the only amusement is a trip into town."

"You mentioned tourists," said Frost.

"Detective McDowell covered that ground. No, I don't recall any psychopathic killers among them. But then, I wouldn't know one if I saw him. I certainly wouldn't remember his face, not after a quarter of a century."

And that was the gist of the problem, thought Jane. After twenty-five years, memories vanish or, even worse, remake themselves. Fantasies become truth. She gazed out the window at the road leading out of the canyon. It was little more than a dirt track, swirling with hot dust. For Lorraine Edgerton, it had been the road to oblivion. What happened to you out in that desert? she wondered. You climbed aboard your motorbike, rolled out of this canyon, and slipped through some wormhole in time, to emerge twenty-five years later, in a crate in Boston. And the desert had long ago erased all traces of that journey.

"Can we keep this photo, Professor?" asked Frost.

"You'll return it, won't you?"

"We'll keep it safe."

"Because it's the only group picture I have from that season. I'd have trouble remembering them all without these photos. When you take on ten students every year, the names start to add up. Especially when you've been doing this as long as I have."

Jane turned from the window. "You take ten students every year?"

"I limit it to ten, just for logistics. We always get more applications than we can accept."

She pointed to the photo. "There are only nine students there."

He frowned at the picture. "Oh, right. There was a tenth, but he left early in the summer. He wasn't here when Lorraine vanished."

That explained why McDowell's case file contained interviews with only eight of Lorraine's fellow students.

"Who was the student? The one who left?" she asked.

"He was one of the undergrads. He'd just finished his sophomore year. A very bright fellow, but extremely quiet and a bit awkward. He didn't really fit in with the others. The only reason I accepted him was because of his father. But he wasn't happy here, so a few weeks into the season he packed up and left the dig. Took an internship elsewhere."

"Do you remember the boy's name?"

"Certainly I remember his last name. Because his father's Kimball Rose."

"Should I know that name?"

"Anyone in the field of archaeology should. He's the modern-day version of Lord Carnarvon."

"What does that mean?"

"He has money," said Frost.

Quigley nodded. "Exactly. Mr. Rose has plenty of it, made in oil and gas. He has no formal training in archaeology, but he's a very talented and enthusiastic amateur, and he funds excavations around the world. We're talking about tens of millions of dollars. If it weren't for people like him, there'd be no grants, no money to pay for turning over even a single rock."

"Tens of millions? And what does he get back for all that money?" asked Jane.

"Get? Why, the thrill, of course! Wouldn't you like to be the first person to step into a newly opened tomb? The first to peek into a sealed sarcophagus? He needs us and we need him. That's how archaeology has always been done. A union between those with the money and those with the skills."

"Do you remember his son's name?"

"I wrote it in here somewhere." He opened his book of field notes and began flipping through the pages. Several snapshots fell out onto the desk, and he pointed to one of the photos. "There, that's him. I remember his name now. Bradley. He's the young man in the middle."

Bradley Rose sat at a table, pottery shards spread out before him. The other two students in the photo were otherwise distracted, but Bradley stared directly at the camera, as though studying some interesting new creature he'd never seen before. In almost every way he appeared ordinary: average build, a forgettable face, a

look of anonymity that would easily be lost in a crowd.
But his eyes were arresting. They reminded Jane of the
day she'd visited the zoo and stared through the fence at
a timber wolf, whose pale eyes had regarded her with
unsettling interest.

"Did the police ever question the man?" asked Jane.

"He left us two weeks before she vanished. They had
no reason to."

"But he knew her. They'd worked together on the
dig."

"Yes."

"Wouldn't that make him someone worth talking
to?"

"There was no point. His parents said he was home
with them in Texas at the time. An airtight alibi, I
should think."

"Do you remember why he left the dig?" asked Frost.
"Did something happen? Did he not get along with the
other students?"

"No, I think it was because he got bored here. That's
why he took that internship out in Boston. That
annoyed me, because I would have taken on a
different student if I'd known Bradley wouldn't stick it
out here."

"Boston?" Jane cut in.

"Yes."

"Where was this internship?"

"Some private museum. I'm sure his father pulled
strings to get him in."

"Was it the Crispin Museum?"

Professor Quigley thought about it. Then he nodded. "That may have been the one."

18

Jane had heard that Texas was big, but as a New England girl, she had no real appreciation of just what *big* really meant. Nor had she imagined how bright the Texas sun was, or how hot the air could be, as hot as dragon's breath. The three-hour drive from the airport took them through miles of scrub brush, through a sun-baked landscape where even the cattle looked different—rangy and mean, unlike the placid Guernseys she saw on pleasant green farms in Massachusetts. This was a foreign country, a thirsty country, and she fully expected the Rose estate to look like the arid ranches they passed along the way, low-slung and spread out, with white corral fences enclosing parched brown acreage.

So she was surprised when the mansion loomed into view.

It was set on a lushly planted hill that looked shockingly green above the endless expanse of scrubland. A lawn swept down from the home like a velvet skirt. In a paddock enclosed by white fences, half a dozen horses were grazing, their coats gleaming. But it was the residence that held Jane's gaze. She'd expected a ranch house, not this stone castle with its crenellated turrets.

They drove to the massive iron gate and stared up in wonder.

"How much, do you think?" she asked.

"I'm guessing thirty million," said Frost.

"That's all? It's got, like, fifty thousand acres."

"Yeah, but it's Texas. Land's gotta be cheaper than at home."

When thirty million dollars sounded cheap, thought Jane, you know you've stepped into an alternative universe.

A voice over the gate intercom said: "Your business?"

"Detectives Rizzoli and Frost. We're from Boston PD. We're here to see Mr. and Mrs. Rose."

"Is Mr. Rose expecting you?"

"I called him this morning. He said he'd speak to us."

There was a long silence, then the gate finally swung open. "Drive through, please."

The curving road took them up the hill, past a colonnade of cypress trees and Roman statues. A circle of broken marble pillars stood mounted on a stone terrace like an ancient temple partially felled by the ages.

"Where do you get the water out here for all these

plantings?" asked Frost. His gaze suddenly whipped around as they passed a fragmented head of a marble colossus, its remaining eye staring up from a resting place on the lawn. "Hey, do you think that thing's real?"

"People this rich don't have to settle for fakes. You can bet that Lord Carnivore guy—"

"You mean Carnarvon?"

"You can bet he decorated his home with real stuff."

"There are rules against that now. You can't just snatch things out of other countries and bring them home."

"Rules are for you and me, Frost. Not for people like *them.*"

"Yeah, well, people like the Roses aren't going to be too happy once they figure out why we're asking these questions. I give them about five minutes before they throw us out."

"Then this will be the nicest damn place we'll ever get thrown out of."

They pulled up beneath a stone portico, where a man already stood waiting for them. This was not one of the hired help, thought Jane; this must be Kimball Rose himself. Though he had to be in his seventies, he stood tall and ramrod-straight, with a handsome mane of silver hair. He was dressed casually, in khaki trousers and a golf shirt, but Jane doubted he'd picked up that deep tan simply whiling away his retirement on the links. The vast collection of statuary and marble columns on the hillside told her this man had far more compelling hobbies than hitting golf balls.

She stepped out of the car into air so dry, she blinked in the parching wind. Kimball didn't seem at all affected by the heat, and the handshake he gave her was cool and crisp.

"Thank you for seeing us on such short notice," said Jane.

"I said yes only 'cause it's a sure way to end these damn fool questions. There's nothing here for you to chase after, Detective."

"Then this shouldn't take long. We only have a few things to ask you and your wife."

"My wife can't talk to you. She's sick and I won't have you upsetting her."

"It's just about your son."

"She can't handle *any* questions about Bradley. She's been fightin' lymphocytic leukemia for more'n ten years now, and the littlest upset could tip her right over."

"Talking about Bradley would upset her that much?"

"He's our only boy, and she's attached to him. Last thing she needs to hear is that the police are treating him like a suspect."

"We never said he was a suspect, sir."

"No?" Kimball met her gaze with a look that was both direct and confrontational. "Then what're you doing here?"

"Bradley was acquainted with Ms. Edgerton. We're just touching all the bases."

"You've come a long way just to touch *this* base." He turned to the front door. "Come in, let's get it over with. But I'll tell you now you're wasting your time."

After the heat outside, Jane welcomed the chance to cool off in an air-conditioned house, but the Rose residence was startlingly frigid and made to seem even less welcoming by the marble tiles and the cavernous entrance hall. Jane looked up at the huge beams that supported the vaulted ceiling. Though a stained-glass window let in squares of multicolored light, wood paneling and hanging tapestries seemed to absorb all brightness, throwing the house into gloom. This was not a home, she thought; this was a museum, meant to show off the acquisitions of a man addicted to collecting treasures. In the entrance hall, suits of armor stood like soldiers at attention. Mounted on the walls were battle-axes and swords, and a decorated banner hung overhead—the Rose family crest, no doubt. Did every man dream of being a nobleman? She wondered which symbols should be displayed on the Rizzoli family crest. A beer can and a TV, maybe.

Kimball led them out of the grand hall, and as they stepped into the next room, it was as if they'd passed from one millennium into another. A fountain trickled in a courtyard tiled with brilliant mosaics. Daylight shone down through a vast skylight, spilling onto marble statues of nymphs and satyrs at play near the fountain's edge. Jane wanted to linger, to take a closer look at the mosaics, but Kimball was already moving on, into yet another room.

It was Kimball's library, and as they stepped in, both Jane and Frost stared up in wonder. Everywhere they looked were books—thousands of them, shelved on three stories of open galleries. Tucked into niches were Egyptian funerary masks with enormous eyes staring from the shadows. On the domed ceiling was a painting of the night sky and its constellations, and arching across the heavens was a royal procession: an Egyptian sailing vessel followed by chariots and courtiers and women bearing platters of food. In a stone hearth, a real wood fire crackled, an extravagant waste of energy on this summer day. So this was why the house was kept so cold, to make a fire all the more cozy.

They sat down in massive leather chairs near the fireplace. Though July heat blazed outside, in this dark study it might be a winter day in December, the snow flying outside, with only the flames in the hearth to ward off the chill.

"The person we'd really like to speak to is Bradley, Mr. Rose," said Jane. "But we can't seem to locate him."

"That boy's never in one place for long," said Kimball. "Right at this moment, I couldn't tell you where he is."

"When was the last time you saw him?"

"It's been a while. I don't remember."

"That long?"

"We stay in touch by e-mail. Every so often, a letter. You know how it is these days with busy families. Last we heard from him, he was in London."

"Do you know where in London, exactly?"

"No. That was a few months ago." Kimball shifted in his chair. "Let's just cut to the chase, Detective. The reason you're here. This is about that girl in Chaco Canyon."

"Lorraine Edgerton."

"Whatever her name was. Bradley had nothing to do with it."

"You seem pretty sure of that."

" 'Cause he was here with us when it happened. Police didn't even bother to talk to him—that's how little they cared about seeing Bradley. Professor Quigley must've told you that?"

"Yes, he did."

"Then why bother us about this now? It was twenty-five years ago."

"You seem to remember the details well."

"Because I took the trouble to find out about you, Detective Rizzoli. About that missing Edgerton girl, and why Boston PD's mixed up in a case that happened in New Mexico."

"You know that Lorraine Edgerton's body recently turned up."

He nodded. "In Boston, I hear."

"Do you know where in Boston?"

"The Crispin Museum. I read the news."

"Your son worked at the Crispin Museum that summer."

"Yes. I fixed that up."

"You got him the job?"

"The Crispin Museum's always short of cash. Simon's a lousy businessman and he's run that place into the ground. I made a donation, and he gave my Bradley a job. I think they were lucky to get him."

"Why did he leave Chaco Canyon?"

"He was unhappy, stuck out there with that bunch of amateurs. Bradley's dead serious about his archaeology. He was wasted out there, working like some common laborer. Days and days of just scraping away at dirt."

"I thought that's what archaeology was all about."

"That's what I *pay* people to do. You think I spend my time digging? I write the checks and I come up with the vision. I guide the project and choose where to excavate. Bradley didn't need to do grunt work in Chaco—he knows damn well how to handle a trowel. He spent time with me in Egypt, on a project with hundreds of diggers, and he had a knack for looking at the terrain and knowing where to excavate. I'm not just saying that because he's my boy."

"So he's been to Egypt," said Jane. Thinking about what had been engraved in that souvenir cartouche: *I visited the pyramids, Cairo, Egypt.*

"He loves it there," said Kimball. "And I hope one of these days he'll go back and find what I couldn't."

"What was that?"

"The lost army of Cambyses."

Jane looked at Frost, and judging by his blank expression he had no idea what Kimball was talking about, either.

Kimball's mouth curled into an unpleasantly superior smile. "I guess I need to explain it to you all," he said. "Twenty-five hundred years ago, this Persian king named Cambyses sent an army into Egypt's western desert, to take the oracle at Siwa Oasis. Fifty thousand men marched in and were never seen again. The sands just swallowed 'em up, and no knows what became of them."

"Fifty thousand soldiers?" said Jane.

Kimball nodded. "It's one of the big mysteries of archaeology. I spent two seasons hunting for the remains of that army. All I turned up were bits of metal and bone, but that was all. So little, in fact, that the Egyptian government didn't even care enough to lay claim to any of it. That dig was one of my biggest disappointments. One of my few failures." He stared at the fire. "Someday I'll go back. I'm gonna find it."

"In the meantime, how about helping us find your son?"

Kimball's gaze returned to Jane, and it was not friendly. "How about we wrap up this conversation? I don't think there's anything more I can help you with." He stood.

"We only want to speak to him. To ask him about Ms. Edgerton."

"Ask him what? *Did you kill her?* That's what this is all about, isn't it? Trying to find someone to blame."

"He knew the victim."

"Lot of folks probably did."

"Your son worked at the Crispin Museum that summer. The same place where her body has just turned up. That's quite a coincidence."

"I'll ask you both to leave." He turned toward the door, but Jane did not move from her chair. If Kimball was not going to cooperate, it was time to move to a different strategy, one that would almost certainly provoke him.

"Then there was that incident on the Stanford University campus," she said. "An incident you know about, Mr. Rose. Since it was your attorney who arranged for your son's release."

He pivoted and strode toward her so quickly that Frost instinctively stood up to intervene. But Kimball halted just inches from Jane. "He was never convicted."

"But he was arrested. Twice. After following a female student around campus. After breaking into her dorm room while she was sleeping. How many times did you have to bail him out of trouble? How many checks did you write to keep him out of jail?"

"It's time for you all to go."

"*Where is your son now?*"

Before Kimball could respond, a door opened. He froze as a soft voice called out: "Kimball? Are they here about Bradley?"

In an instant his expression transformed from rage to dismay. He turned to the woman and said, "Cynthia, you shouldn't be out of bed. Please go back, darling."

"Rosa told me two policemen came to the house. It's about Bradley, isn't it?" The woman shuffled into the room, and her sunken eyes focused on the two visitors. Though her face had been stretched taut by plastic surgery, her age still showed in the rounded back, the drooping shoulders. Most of all it showed in the wispy gray hair that feathered her nearly bald scalp. As wealthy as Kimball Rose might be, he had not traded in his wife for a younger model. All their money, all their privilege, could not change the obvious fact that Cynthia Rose was seriously ill.

Frail as she was, supported by a cane, Cynthia stood her ground and kept her gaze on the two detectives. "Do you know where my Bradley is?" she asked.

"No, ma'am," said Jane. "We were hoping you could tell us."

"I'm going to walk you back to your room," said Kimball, and he took his wife's arm.

Angrily she shook him off, her attention still fixed on Jane. "Why are you looking for him?"

"Cynthia, this has nothing to do with you," said Kimball.

"It has *everything* to do with me," she shot back. "You should have told me they were here. Why do you keep hiding things from me, Kimball? I have a right to know about my own boy!" The outburst seemed to leave her out of breath, and she tottered toward the nearest chair and sank down. There she sat so motionless, she might have been just another artifact in that dark room of funerary objects.

"They came to ask about that girl again," said Kimball. "The one who disappeared in New Mexico. That's all."

"But that was such a long time ago," murmured Cynthia.

"Her body has just been found," said Jane. "In Boston. We need to speak to your son about it, but we don't know where he is."

Cynthia slumped deeper into the chair. "I don't know, either," she whispered.

"Doesn't he write you?"

"Sometimes. A letter here and there, sent from strange places. An e-mail once in a while, just to say he's thinking of me. And that he loves me. But he stays away."

"Why is that, Mrs. Rose?"

The woman raised her head and looked at Kimball. "Maybe you should ask my husband."

"Bradley's never been all that close to us," he said.

"He was until you sent him away."

"That has nothing to do with—"

"He didn't want to go. You forced him."

"Forced him to go where?" asked Jane.

"It's not relevant," said Kimball.

"I blame myself, for not standing up to you," said Cynthia.

"Where did you send him?" asked Jane.

"Tell her," said Cynthia. "Tell her how you drove him away."

Kimball released a deep sigh. "When he was sixteen, we sent him to a boarding school in Maine. He didn't want to go, but it was for his own good."

"A school?" Cynthia gave a bitter laugh. "It was a mental institution!"

Jane looked at Kimball. "Is that what it was, Mr. Rose?"

"No! The place was recommended to us. Best of its kind in the country, and let me tell you, the price tag reflected it. I only did what I thought was best for him. What any good parent would do. They called it a therapeutic residential community. A place where boys could go to deal with . . . issues."

"We never should have done it," said Cynthia. "*You* never should have done it."

"We had no choice. He had to go."

"He would have been better off here, with *me*. Not sent to some boot camp in the middle of the woods."

Kimball snorted. "A camp? More like a country club." He turned to Jane. "It had its own lake. Hiking and cross-country ski trails. Hell, if I ever go off *my* rocker, I'd love to be sent to a place like that."

"Is that what happened to Bradley, Mr. Rose?" asked Frost. "He went off his rocker?"

"Don't make him sound like a lunatic," said Cynthia. "He wasn't."

"Then why did he end up there, Mrs. Rose?"

"Because we thought—Kimball thought—"

"We thought they could teach him better self-control," her husband finished for her. "That's all. Lotta boys need tough love. He stayed there for two years and came out a well-behaved, hardworkin' young man. I was proud to take him to Egypt with me."

"He resented you, Kimball," said his wife. "He told me that."

"Well, parents have to make hard choices. That was *my* choice, to shake him up a little, set him on the right track."

"And now he stays away. I'm the one who's being punished, all because of that *fine choice* you made." Cynthia lowered her head and began to cry. No one spoke. The only noises were the crackling fire and Cynthia's quiet sobbing, a sound of raw and unremitting pain.

The ring of Jane's cell phone was a cruel interruption. At once, she silenced it and moved away from the hearth to answer the call.

It was Detective Crowe on the line. "Got a surprise for you," he said, his cheerful voice a jarring contrast to the grief that hung over that room.

"What is it?" she asked softly.

"FBI has her fingerprints in their system."

"Josephine's?"

"Or whatever her real name is. We lifted the prints from her apartment and ran them through the AFIS database."

"We got a hit?"

"Now we know why our girl ran. Turns out her prints match some latents that were lifted off a crime scene twelve years ago, in San Diego."

"What was the crime?"

"Homicide."

19

"The victim was a thirty-six-year-old white male named Jimmy Otto," said Detective Crowe. "His body was discovered in San Diego, after a dog dug up a tasty little snack: a human finger. The dog's owner saw what Fido brought home, freaked out, and called 911. Dog led the police back to the body, which was buried in a shallow grave in a neighbor's backyard. The victim had been dead for a few days, and wildlife had gotten at the extremities so they couldn't get any usable fingerprints. There was no wallet on the body, either, but whoever stripped his ID missed a hotel key card that was tucked in his jeans pocket. It was for a local Holiday Inn, where the guest was registered under the name James Otto."

"A hotel key card?" said Jane. "So this victim didn't live in San Diego."

"No. His address was here, in Massachusetts, where he lived with his sister. Carrie Otto flew out to San

Diego and ID'd her brother's clothing. And what was left of him."

Jane tore open a packet of Advil, popped two tablets in her mouth, and washed them down with lukewarm coffee. Last night, she and Frost had not arrived home in Boston until two AM, and what little sleep she did get was repeatedly interrupted by one-year-old Regina, who demanded hugs and reassurance that Mommy really was home again. This morning, Jane had awakened with a monster headache. The twists and turns of the investigation were making that headache worse, and the glow of the fluorescent lights in the conference room made even her eyeballs hurt.

"You both with me so far?" said Crowe, glancing up at Jane and Frost, who looked as exhausted as Jane felt.

"Yeah," she muttered. "So what did the autopsy show?"

"Cause of death was a single gunshot wound to the back of the head. The weapon was never recovered."

"And whose backyard was he buried in?"

"It was a rental house," said Crowe. "The tenants were a single mother and her fourteen-year-old daughter, and they'd already packed up and vanished. The police sprayed the house with luminol, and the girl's bedroom lit up like Vegas. Traces of blood were all over the floor and the baseboards. That's where Jimmy Otto was killed. In the girl's bedroom."

"And this was twelve years ago?"

"Josephine would have been about fourteen," said Frost.

Crowe nodded. "Except her name wasn't Josephine back then. It was Susan Cook." He gave a laugh. "And guess what? The real Susan Cook died as an infant. In Syracuse, New York."

"It was *another* co-opted ID?" said Jane.

"Ditto on the mother, who also had a fake name: Lydia Newhouse. According to the San Diego PD report, mother and daughter rented the house for three years, but they kept to themselves. At the time of the killing, the girl had just finished the eighth grade at William Howard Taft Middle School. Very bright, according to her teachers, work way above her grade level."

"And the mother?"

"Lydia Newhouse—or whatever her real name is—worked at the Museum of Man in Balboa Park."

"Doing what?"

"She was a salesclerk in the gift shop. She also volunteered as a museum guide. What impressed everyone at the museum was how much she seemed to know about the field of archaeology. Even though she claimed she had no formal training."

Jane frowned. "We're back to archaeology again."

"Yeah. We keep returning to that theme, don't we?" said Crowe. "Archaeology runs in the family. The mother. The daughter."

"Are we sure they're even involved with Jimmy Otto's murder?" said Frost.

"Well, they sure behaved as if they did it. They left town in a hurry—only after they'd mopped the floor, washed down the walls, and buried the guy behind their house. That sounds pretty damn guilty to me. Their only mistake was not burying him deep enough, because the neighborhood dog sniffed him out pretty quick."

Tripp said, "I say, good for them. The guy got the ending he deserved."

"What do you mean?" Frost asked.

"Because Jimmy Otto was one sick fuck."

Crowe opened his notebook. "Detective Potrero will be sending us the file, but here's what I got from him over the phone. At age thirteen, Jimmy Otto broke into a woman's bedroom, raided her lingerie drawers, and sliced up her underwear with a knife. A few months later, he was found in another girl's house, standing over her bed with a knife as she slept."

"Jesus," said Jane. "Only thirteen? He got an early start as a creep."

"Age fourteen, he was expelled from his school in Connecticut. Detective Potrero couldn't get the school to release all the details, but he gathered there was some sort of sexual assault involving a female classmate. And a broomstick. The girl ended up in the hospital." Crowe looked up. "And those are just the things he got *caught* doing."

"He should have been thrown into juvenile detention after the second incident."

"Should have. But when your daddy's rich, you have a few extra get-out-of-jail cards."

"Even after the broomstick thing?"

"No, that was the wake-up call for his parents. They finally freaked out and realized their darling son needed therapy. Bad. Their high-priced lawyer got the charges reduced, but only on the condition that Jimmy go into specialized residential treatment."

"You mean a psych ward?" asked Frost.

"Not exactly. It was a very expensive private school for boys with his, uh, impulses. A place out in the boonies with round-the-clock supervision. He stayed there for three years. His doting parents bought a house in the area, just so they could be near him. They were killed in a private plane crash flying up to see him. Jimmy and his sister ended up inheriting a fortune."

"Making Jimmy a very sick and very *rich* fuck," said Tripp.

Specialized residential treatment. A place out in the boonies.

Jane suddenly thought about the conversation she'd had just the day before, with Kimball Rose. And she asked: "Did this private facility happen to be in Maine?"

Crowe looked up in surprise. "How the hell did you guess that?"

"Because we know about another rich sicko who ended up in a Maine treatment center. A place for boys with *issues*."

"Who are you talking about?"

"Bradley Rose."

There was a long silence as Crowe and Tripp absorbed that startling news.

"Holy shit," said Tripp. "That *cannot* be a coincidence. If those two boys were there at the same time, they would have known each other."

"Tell us more about this school," said Jane.

Crowe nodded, his expression now grimly focused. "The Hilzbrich Institute was very exclusive, very pricey. And very specialized. It was essentially a locked unit out in the middle of the woods—probably a smart idea, considering what kind of patients they were treating."

"Psychopaths?"

"Sexual predators. Everything from budding pedophiles to rapists. It just goes to show you that rich people have their own share of perverts. But they also have lawyers to keep these kids out of the justice system, and this facility was a rich man's alternative. A place to enjoy fine dining while a team of therapists tries to convince you it's not nice to torture little girls. The trouble was, it didn't seem to work very well. Fifteen years ago, one of their so-called graduates kidnapped and mutilated two girls, and he did it just a few months after the institute declared him safe to return to society. There was a big lawsuit, and the school was forced to shut down. It's been closed ever since."

"What about Jimmy Otto? What happened after he left?"

"At eighteen, he walked out their doors a free man. But it didn't take long for him to revert to form. Within a few years, he was arrested for stalking and threatening a woman in California. Then he was arrested and questioned right here in Brookline, about the disappearance of a young woman. Police didn't have enough to hold him, so he was released. Ditto thirteen years ago, when he was picked up for questioning after another Massachusetts woman disappeared. Before the police could build a case against him, he abruptly vanished. And no one knew where he was. Until a year later, when he turned up buried in that backyard in San Diego."

"You're right, Tripp," said Jane. "He got what he deserved. But what made this mother and daughter run? If they killed him, if they were just defending themselves, why did they pack up and leave town like criminals?"

"Maybe because they are?" suggested Crowe. "They were living under assumed names even then. We don't know who they really are—or what they might be running from."

Jane rested her head in her hands and began to rub her temples, trying to massage away the headache. "This is getting so damn complicated," she muttered. "I can't keep track of all the threads. We've got a murdered man in San Diego. We've got the Archaeology Killer here."

"And the link seems to be this young woman whose name we don't even know."

Jane sighed. "Okay. What else do we know about Jimmy Otto? Any other arrests, any other links to our current investigation?"

Crowe flipped through his notes. "Some minor stuff. Breaking and entering in Brookline, Massachusetts. DUI and speeding in San Diego. Another DUI and reckless speeding in Durango . . ." He paused, suddenly registering the significance of that last detail. "Durango, Colorado. Isn't that close to New Mexico?"

Jane lifted her head. "It's right over the state line. Why?"

"It happened in July. The same year that Lorraine Edgerton vanished."

Jane reeled back in her chair, stunned by this last piece of information. *Both Jimmy and Bradley were near Chaco Canyon at the same time.*

"That's it," she said softly.

"You think they were hunting partners?"

"Until Jimmy got killed in San Diego." She looked at Frost. "This is finally coming together now. We have a connection. Jimmy Otto and Bradley Rose."

He nodded. "And Josephine," he said.

20

Josephine fought her way back to consciousness and came awake with a gasp, her nightgown soaked with sweat, her heart thudding. Thin curtains rippled in a ghostly film over the moonlit window, and in the woods outside Gemma's house, tree branches rattled and fell still. She pushed off the damp bedcovers and stared up at the darkness as her heart slowed, as the sweat cooled on her skin. After only a week at Gemma's place, her bad dream was back. A dream of gunfire and blood-splattered walls. *Always pay attention to your dreams,* her mother had taught her. *They're voices telling you what you already know, whispering advice you haven't yet heeded.* Josephine knew what this dream meant: It was time to move on. Time to run. She had lingered in Gemma's house longer than she should have. She thought of the cell phone call she'd made from the mini-mart. She thought of the young patrolman who'd chatted with her in the parking lot that night, and the taxi driver who'd driven her to this road. There were so many ways she could be tracked here, so many little mistakes she might have made that she wasn't even aware of.

She remembered what her mother once said: *If someone really wants to find you, he only needs to wait for you to make one mistake.*

And lately, she had made so many.

The night had fallen strangely still.

It took her a moment to register just how still it was. She had fallen asleep to the steady chirp of crickets, but now she heard nothing, only a silence so complete that it magnified the sound of her own breathing.

She rose from bed and went to the window. Outside, moonlight silvered the trees and splashed its pale glow onto the garden. Staring out, she saw nothing to alarm her. But as she stood at that open window, she realized that the night was not entirely silent; through the thump of her own heartbeat she heard a faint electronic beeping. Did it come from outside, or from somewhere inside the house? Now that she was completely focused on the sound, it seemed to intensify, and with it her sense of uneasiness.

Did Gemma hear it?

She went to the door and peeked into the dark hallway. The sound was louder out here, more insistent.

In darkness she navigated up the hallway, her bare feet silent on the wood floor. With every step the beeping grew louder. Reaching Gemma's bedroom, she found the door ajar. She gave it a push and silently it swung open. In the moonlit room, she spotted the source of that sound: the fallen telephone receiver, a disconnect signal issuing from the earpiece. But it wasn't the phone that caught her gaze; it was the dark pool, glistening like black oil on the floor. Nearby a figure crouched, and she thought at first it was Gemma. Until it straightened to its full height and stood silhouetted against the window.

A man.

Josephine's startled intake of breath made his head snap around toward her. For an instant they faced each other, features hidden in the shadows, both of them suspended in that timeless moment before predator springs on prey.

She moved first.

She turned and sprinted for the stairs. Footsteps pounded behind her as she scrambled down the steps. She hit the first floor hard, with both feet. Ahead was the front door, gaping open. She ran for it and stumbled out onto the porch, where broken glass pierced her skin. She scarcely noticed its bite; her attention was focused only on the driveway ahead.

And on the footsteps closing in behind her.

She flew down the porch steps, her gown flapping like wings in the warm night air, and ran headlong up the driveway. Under the moonlight, on that exposed gravel, her nightgown was as visible as a white flag, but she did not veer into the woods, did not waste time seeking the cover of trees. Ahead lay the street, and other houses. *If I pound on doors, if I scream, someone will help me.* No longer could she hear her pursuer's footsteps; she heard only the rush of her panicked breaths, the whoosh of the night air.

And then, a sharp crack.

The bullet's impact was like a brutal kick to the back of her leg. It sent her sprawling to the ground, palms scraping across the gravel. She struggled to stand, warm blood streaming down her calf, but her leg gave out beneath her. With a sob of pain, she collapsed to her knees.

The street. The street is so near.

Her breaths reduced to sobs, she began to crawl. A neighbor's porch light glowed ahead, beyond the trees, and that was what she focused on. Not the crunch of footsteps moving closer, not the gravel biting into her palms. Survival had come down to that lone beacon winking through the branches and she kept crawling toward it, dragging her useless leg as blood left its slick trail behind her.

A shadow moved in front of her and blotted out the light.

Slowly, she lifted her gaze. He stood before her, blocking the way. His face was a black oval, his eyes unfathomable. As he leaned toward her, she closed her eyes, waiting for the crack of the gun, the punch of the bullet. Never had she been more aware of her own beating heart, of the air rushing in and out of her lungs, than in the stillness of this last moment. A moment that seemed to stretch on endlessly, as though he wanted to savor his victory and prolong the torment.

Through her closed eyelids, she saw a light flicker.

She opened her eyes. Beyond the trees, a blue light pulsed. A pair of headlights suddenly veered toward her, and she was trapped in the glare, kneeling in her pitifully thin nightgown. Tires skidded to a halt, spitting gravel. A car door swung open and she heard the crackle of a police radio.

"Miss? Are you okay, miss?"

She blinked, trying to make out who was speaking to her. But the voice faded and the headlights dimmed, and the last thing she registered was the slap of the gravel against her cheek as she slumped to the ground.

Frost and Jane stood in Gemma Hamerton's driveway, staring down at the trail of dried blood that Josephine had left behind in her desperate crawl toward the street. Birds chirped overhead and the summer sun shone down through dappling leaves, but a chill seemed to have settled in this shady patch of driveway.

Jane turned and looked at the residence, which she and Frost had not yet set foot in. It was an unremarkable house with white clapboards and a covered porch, like so many others that she'd seen on this rural road. But even from where she stood in the driveway, she could see the jagged reflection of a broken porch window, and that bright shard of light warned: *Something terrible happened here. Something you have yet to see.*

"Here's where she first fell," said Detective Mike Abbott. He pointed to the start of the bloody trail. "She made it pretty far up the driveway when she was shot. Landed here and started crawling. It took a hell of a lot of determination to move as far as she did, but she managed to get all the way to that point." Abbott indicated the end of the bloody trail. "That's where the patrol car spotted her."

"How did that miracle happen?" asked Jane.

"They came in response to a 911 call."

"From Josephine?" asked Frost.

"No, we think it came from the owner of the house, Gemma Hamerton. The phone was in her bedroom. Whoever made the call never got the chance to speak, though, because the receiver was hung up immediately afterward. When the emergency operator tried to call back, the phone had been taken off the hook again. She dispatched a patrol car, and it got here within three minutes."

Frost gazed down at the stained driveway. "There's a lot of blood here."

Abbott nodded. "The young woman spent three hours in emergency surgery. She's now laid up in a cast, which turns out to be lucky for us. Because we didn't find out till last night that Boston PD had put out a bulletin on her. Otherwise, she might have managed to skip town." He turned toward the house. "If you want to see more blood, follow me."

He led the way to the front porch, which was littered with broken glass. There they paused to pull on shoe covers. Abbott's ominous statement warned of horrors to come, and Jane was prepared for the worst.

But when she stepped in the front door, she saw nothing alarming. The living room looked undisturbed. On the walls hung dozens of framed photos, many of them featuring the same woman with cropped blond hair, posing with a variety of companions. A massive bookcase was filled with volumes on history and art, ancient languages and ethnology.

"This is the owner of the house?" asked Frost, pointing to the blond woman in the photos.

Abbott nodded. "Gemma Hamerton. She taught archaeology at one of the local colleges."

"Archaeology?" Frost shot Jane a *Now, that's interesting* look. "What else do you know about her?"

"Law-abiding citizen as far as we know. Never married. Spent every summer abroad doing whatever it is that archaeologists do."

"So why isn't she abroad now?"

"I don't know. She came home a week ago from Peru, where she was working at some excavation. If she'd stayed away, she'd still be alive." Abbott looked up at the stairs, his face suddenly grim. "It's time to show you the second floor." He led the way, pausing to point out the bloody tread marks on the wood steps.

"Athletic sole. Size nine or ten," he said. "We know these are the killer's, since Ms. Pulcillo was barefoot."

"Looks like he was moving fast," added Jane, noting the smeared imprints.

"Yeah. But she was faster."

Jane stared down at the descending tread marks. Though the blood was dry and sunlight slanted in through a stairwell window, the terror of that chase still lingered on these stairs. She shook off a chill and looked up toward the second floor, where far worse images awaited them. "It happened upstairs?"

"In Ms. Hamerton's bedroom," said Abbott. He took his time climbing the final steps, as though reluctant to revisit what he'd seen two nights before. The marks were darker up here, left by shoes still wet with fresh blood. The prints emerged from the room at the far end of the hall. Abbott pointed into the first doorway they came to. Inside was an unmade bed. "This is the guest room, where Ms. Pulcillo was sleeping."

Jane frowned. "But it's closer to the stairs."

"Yeah. I found that strange, too. The killer walks right past Ms. Pulcillo's room and heads straight up the hall to Ms. Hamerton's. Maybe he didn't know there was a guest in the house."

"Or maybe this door was locked," said Frost.

"No, that's not it. This door doesn't have a lock. For some reason, he bypassed it and went to Ms. Hamerton's room first." Abbott took a breath and continued to the master bedroom. There he paused on the threshold, hesitant to step inside.

When Jane looked past him, through the doorway, she understood why.

Though the body of Gemma Hamerton had been removed, her last moments on earth were recorded in vivid splatters of red on the walls, the bedsheets, the furniture. Stepping into that room, Jane felt a cold breath whisper against her skin, as though a ghost had just brushed past. Violence leaves its imprint, she thought. Not just in bloodstains, but on the air itself.

"Her body was found crumpled in that far corner," said Abbott. "But you can see, from the blood splatters, that the initial wound was made somewhere near the bed. Arterial splashes there, on the headboard." He pointed to the wall on the right. "And over there, I think those are cast-off drops."

Jane tore her gaze from the soaked mattress and stared at the arc of angular droplets thrown off by centrifugal force as the bloody knife had swung away from the body. "He's right-handed," she said.

Abbott nodded. "Judging by the wound, the ME says there was no hesitation, no tentative slices. He did it with one clean stroke, severing major vessels in the neck. The ME estimates she had maybe a minute or two of consciousness. Long enough for her to grab the phone. Crawl to that corner over there. The receiver had her bloody fingerprints on it, so we know she was wounded when she dialed."

"So the killer hung up the phone?" asked Frost.

"I assume so."

"But you said the operator tried calling back and got a busy signal."

Abbott paused, thinking about it. "I guess that is a little weird, isn't it? First he hangs up, then he takes the receiver off the hook again. I wonder why he'd do that."

Jane said. "He didn't want it to ring."

"The noise?" said Frost.

Jane nodded. "It would also explain why he didn't use his gun on this victim. Because he knew someone else was in the house, and he didn't want to wake her."

"But she did wake up," said Abbott. "Maybe she heard the body fall. Maybe Ms. Hamerton managed to cry out. Whatever the reason, something woke up Ms. Pulcillo, because she came into this room. She saw the intruder. And she ran."

Jane stared at the corner where Gemma Hamerton had died, curled up in a lake of her own blood.

She walked out of the bedroom and headed back up the hall. At the doorway to Josephine's room she stopped, gazing at the bed. The killer walked right past this room, she thought. A young woman is sleeping in there and her door is unlocked. Yet he bypassed her and continued to the master bedroom. Did he not know a guest was here? Did he not realize there was another woman in the house?

No. No, he knew. That's why he took the phone off

the hook. That's why he used a knife and not his gun. He wanted the first kill to be silent.

Because he was planning to move to Josephine's room next.

She went down the stairs and stepped outside. The afternoon was sunny, the insects humming in the windless heat, but the chill of the house was still with her. She descended the porch steps.

You pursued her here, down the stairs. On a moonlit night, she would have been easy to follow. Just a lone girl in her nightgown.

She walked slowly up the driveway, following the route along which Josephine had fled, her bare feet cut by glass. The main road was ahead, beyond the trees, and all the fleeing girl had to do was reach a neighbor's house. Scream and pound on a door.

Jane paused, her gaze on the bloodstained gravel.

But here the bullet struck her leg, and she fell.

Slowly she followed the trail of blood that Josephine had smeared along the road as she'd struggled forward on hands and knees. Every inch of the way she must have known he was moving toward her, closing in for the kill. The trail of blood seemed to stretch on and on, until it came to a halt, a dozen yards short of the road. It had been a long and desperate crawl to this spot— long enough for the killer to catch up with her. Certainly long enough for him to pull the trigger one last time and make his escape.

Yet he didn't fire the fatal shot.

Jane halted, staring down at the spot where Josephine had been kneeling when the officers spotted her. When they'd arrived, they had seen no one else, only the injured woman. A woman who should have been dead.

Only then did Jane understand. *The killer wanted her alive.*

21

Everybody lies, thought Jane. But few people managed to inhabit their lies as completely and successfully as had Josephine Pulcillo.

As she and Frost drove to the hospital, she wondered what confabulations Josephine would tell them today, what new tales she'd invent to explain away the undeniable facts that they'd uncovered about her. She wondered if Frost would let himself be seduced once again by those lies.

"I think that maybe you should let me do the talking when we get there," she said.

"Why?"

"I'd just like to handle this myself."

He looked at her. "Any particular reason you feel the need to do it this way?"

She took her time responding because she couldn't truthfully answer the question without widening the breach between them, a breach caused by Josephine. "I just think I should deal with her. Since my instincts about her have been pretty spot-on."

"Instincts? Is that what you call it?"

"You trusted her. I didn't. I was right about her, wasn't I?"

He turned toward the window. "Or jealous of her."

"What?" She turned into the hospital parking lot and shut off the engine. "Is that what you think?"

He sighed. "Never mind."

"No, tell me. What did you mean by that?"

"Nothing." He shoved open the car door. "Let's go," he said.

She stepped out of the car and slammed her door shut, wondering if there was even a thin vein of truth in what Frost had just said. Wondering if the fact that she herself was not beautiful made her resentful of how easily attractive women navigated the world. Men worshiped pretty women, catered to them, and, most important, listened to them. *While the rest of us plug on as best we can.* But even if she were jealous, it didn't change the essential fact that her instincts had been right.

Josephine Pulcillo was a fraud.

She and Frost were silent as they walked into the hospital, as they rode the elevator to the surgical wing. Never before had she felt such a gulf between them. Though they were side by side, there was now a continent separating them, and she didn't even glance at him as they headed up the hall. Grimly, Jane pushed open the door to room 216 and stepped inside.

The young woman they'd known as Josephine stared at them from the bed. In her flimsy hospital gown, she looked fetchingly vulnerable, a doe-eyed maiden in need of rescue. How the hell did she do it? Even with her unwashed hair and her leg in a clunky cast, she managed to look beautiful.

Jane didn't waste time. She crossed straight to the bed and said, "Do you want to tell us about San Diego?"

At once, Josephine's gaze dropped to the sheets, avoiding Jane's. "I don't know what you're talking about."

"You would've been about fourteen years old then. Old enough to remember what took place that night."

Josephine shook her head. "You must have me mistaken for someone else."

"Your name was Susan Cook at the time. You were a student at William Howard Taft Middle School and you lived with your mother, who called herself Lydia Newhouse. One morning, you both packed up and abruptly left town. That was the last time anyone heard of Susan and her mother."

"And I suppose that's illegal, to suddenly leave town?" Josephine retorted, her gaze at last snapping up to meet Jane's in an act of sheer nerve.

"No. That isn't."

"So why are you asking me about it?"

"Because it's very illegal to shoot a man in the back of the head."

Josephine's expression went as smooth as glass. "What man?" she said calmly.

"The man who died in your bedroom."

"I don't know what you're talking about."

The two women stared at each other for a moment. And Jane thought: Maybe Frost can't see through you, but I sure as hell can.

"Have you ever heard of a chemical called luminol?" Jane asked.

Josephine shrugged. "Should I have?"

"It reacts with the iron in old blood. When you spray it on a surface, any blood residue lights up in the dark like neon. No matter how hard you clean up after someone bleeds, you can't wash away all the traces. Even after you and your mother wiped down the walls, mopped the floors, the blood was still there, hiding in the cracks. In the baseboards."

This time Josephine stayed silent.

"When the San Diego police searched your old house, they sprayed luminol. One bedroom lit up like crazy. It was *your* bedroom. So don't tell me you know nothing about it. You must have been there. You know exactly what happened."

Josephine had paled. "I was fourteen," she said softly. "That was a long time ago."

"There's no statute of limitations for murder."

"*Murder?* Is that what you think it was?"

"What happened that night?"

"It wasn't murder."

"Then what was it?"

"It was self-defense!"

Jane nodded in satisfaction. They'd made progress. At last she'd admitted that a man *had* died in her bedroom. "How did it happen?" she asked.

Josephine glanced at Detective Frost, as though seeking his support. He had been standing near the door, his expression cool and unreadable, and clearly she could expect no favors from him, no sympathy.

"It's time to come clean," said Jane. "Do it for Gemma Hamerton. She deserves justice, don't you think? I'm assuming she *was* a friend?"

At the mention of Gemma's name, Josephine's eyes glazed over with tears. "Yes," she whispered. "More than a friend."

"You do know she's dead?"

"Detective Abbott told me. But I already knew," Josephine whispered. "I saw her lying on the floor . . ."

"I'm guessing these two events are connected. Ms. Hamerton's death, and that shooting in San Diego. If you want justice for your friend, you'll answer my questions, Josephine. Or maybe you'd rather be called Susan Cook? Since that was the name you went by in San Diego."

"My name is Josephine now." She gave a weary sigh, all pretenses gone. "It's the name I've had the longest. The one I'm used to now."

"How many names have there been?"

"Four. No, five." She shook her head. "I don't even

remember anymore. There was a new one every time we moved. I thought Josephine would be the last."

"What's your real name?"

"Does it matter?"

"Yes, it does. What name were you born with? You might as well tell us the truth, because I promise you, we'll find out eventually."

Josephine's head drooped in surrender. "My last name was Sommer," she said softly.

"And your first name?"

"Nefertari."

"That's an unusual name."

Josephine gave a tired laugh. "My mother never made conventional choices."

"Wasn't that the name of some Egyptian queen?"

"Yes. The wife of Ramses the Great. *Nefertari, for whom the sun doth shine.*"

"What?"

"It's something my mother used to say to me. She loved Egypt. All she talked about was going back."

"And where is your mother now?"

"She's dead," Josephine said softly. "It was three years ago, in Mexico. She was hit by a car. When it happened, I was in graduate school in California, so I can't tell you much more than that . . ."

Jane pulled over a chair and sat down by the bed. "But you can tell us about San Diego. What happened that night?"

Josephine sat with shoulders slumped. They had her

cornered, and she knew it. "It was summertime," she said. "A warm night. My mother always insisted we close the windows, but that night I left mine open. That's how he broke into the house."

"Through your bedroom window?"

"My mother heard a noise, and she came into my room. He attacked her, and she defended herself. She defended *me*." She looked at Jane. "She had no choice."

"Did you see it happen?"

"I was asleep. The gunshot woke me."

"Do you remember where your mother was standing when it happened?"

"I didn't see it. I told you, I was asleep."

"Then how do you know it was self-defense?"

"He was in our house, in my room. That makes it justified, doesn't it? When someone breaks into your house, don't you have a right to shoot him?"

"In the back of the head?"

"He turned! He knocked her down and turned. And she shot him."

"I thought you didn't see it."

"That's what she told me."

Jane leaned back in her chair but her gaze remained fixed on the young woman. She let the minutes pass, let the silence have its effect. A silence that emphasized the fact Jane was examining every pore, every twitch in Josephine's face.

"So now you and your mother have a dead body in your bedroom," said Jane. "What happened next?"

Josephine took a breath. "My mother took care of everything."

"Meaning she cleaned up the blood?"

"Yes."

"And buried the body?"

"Yes."

"Did she call the police?"

Josephine's hands tightened into knots. "No," she whispered.

"And the next morning, you left town."

"Yes."

"Now, that's the part I don't understand," said Jane. "It seems to me your mother made a strange choice. You claim she killed that man in self-defense."

"He broke into our house. He was in my bedroom."

"Let's think about that. If a man breaks into your house and attacks you, you have a right to use deadly force and defend yourself. A cop might even give you a pat on the back for it. But your mother didn't call the police. Instead, she dragged the body out into the back-yard and buried it. Cleaned up the blood, packed up her daughter, and left town. Does that make sense to you? Because it sure as hell doesn't make any sense to me." Jane leaned in close, an aggressive move meant to invade the young woman's personal space. "She was your mother. She must have told you why she did it."

"I was scared. I didn't ask questions."

"And she never gave you answers?"

"We ran, that's all. I know it doesn't make sense now,

but that's what we did. We left town in a panic. And after you do that, you can't go to the police. You look guilty just because you ran."

"You're right, Josephine. Your mother does look pretty damn guilty. The man she killed was shot in the back of the head. It didn't look like self-defense to the San Diego police. It looked like a cold-blooded murder."

"She did it to protect *me*."

"Then why didn't she call the police? What was she running from?" Jane leaned in even closer, getting right into the woman's face. "I want the *truth*, Josephine!"

The breath seemed to whoosh out of Josephine's lungs. Shoulders sagging, she hung her head in defeat. "Prison," she whispered. "My mother was running from prison."

This was what they'd been waiting for. This was the explanation. Jane could see it in the young woman's posture, could hear it in the conquered voice. Josephine knew the battle was lost, and she was finally handing over the spoils: the truth.

"What crime did she commit?" asked Jane.

"I don't know the details. She said I was just a baby when it happened."

"Did she steal something? Kill someone?"

"She wouldn't talk about it. I didn't even find out about it until that night in San Diego. When she told me why we couldn't call the police."

"And you just packed up and left town with her because she told you to be a good little girl?"

"What would you *expect* me to do?" Josephine's head lifted, defiance in her eyes. "She was my mother and I loved her."

"Yet she told you she committed a crime."

"Some crimes are justified. Sometimes you have no choice. Whatever she did, she had a reason for it. My mother was a good person."

"Who was running from the law."

"Then the law is *wrong*." She stared at Jane, refusing to concede an inch. Refusing to accept that her mother was capable of evil. Could a parent ask for a more loyal child? It might be misguided loyalty, blind loyalty, but there was something to admire here, something that Jane herself would want from her own daughter.

"So your mother dragged you from town to town, from name to name," said Jane. "And where was your father in all this?"

"My father died in Egypt, before I was born."

"Egypt?" Jane arched forward, her attention riveted on the young woman. "Tell me more."

"He was from France. One of the archaeologists at the dig." Josephine's lips turned up in a wistful smile. "She said he was brilliant and funny. And most of all, kind. That's what she liked most about him, his kindness. They planned to get married, but there was an awful accident. A fire." She swallowed. "Gemma was burned as well."

"Gemma Hamerton was with her in Egypt?"

"Yes." At the mention of Gemma, Josephine blinked away a sudden flash of tears. "It's my fault, isn't it? My fault she's dead."

Jane looked at Frost, who appeared just as startled by this information as she was. Though he had been silent so far through the interview, now he could not resist asking a question.

"This excavation you mentioned, where your parents met. Where was it in Egypt?"

"Near Siwa Oasis. It's in the western desert."

"What were they looking for?"

Josephine shrugged. "They never found it."

"It?"

"The lost army of Cambyses."

In the silence that followed, Jane could almost hear the puzzle pieces click into place. *Egypt. Cambyses. Bradley Rose.* She turned to Frost. "Show her his photo."

Frost pulled the snapshot from the file folder that he'd brought into the room and handed it to Josephine. It was the image that Professor Quigley had lent them, the photo taken at Chaco Canyon of a young Bradley staring at the camera lens, his eyes pale as a wolf's.

"Do you recognize this man?" asked Frost. "It's an old picture. He'd be about forty-five now."

Josephine shook her head. "Who is he?"

"His name is Bradley Rose. Twenty-seven years ago he was in Egypt, too. At the same archaeological dig where your mother worked. She would have known him."

Josephine frowned at the photo, as though struggling to see something about that face that she could recognize. "I've never heard that name. She never mentioned him."

"Josephine," said Frost, "we think this is the man who's been stalking you. The man who attacked you two nights ago. And we have reason to believe this is the Archaeology Killer."

She looked up, startled. "He knew my mother?"

"They were at the same excavation. They must have known each other. It could explain why he's now fixated on you. Your photo appeared twice in *The Boston Globe*, remember? Back in March, soon after you were hired by the museum. And then a few weeks ago, just before the CT scan of Madam X. Maybe Bradley saw the resemblance. Maybe he looked at your photo and saw your mother's face. Do you look like her?"

Josephine nodded. "Gemma said I look exactly like my mother."

"What was your mother's name?" asked Jane.

For a moment, Josephine didn't respond, as though that particular secret had been buried so long, she could not even remember it. When she finally did answer, it came out so softly that Jane had to lean forward to hear it.

"Medea. Her name was Medea."

"The name on the cartouche," said Frost.

Josephine stared down at the photo. "Why didn't she tell me about him? Why have I never heard his name?"

"Your mother seems to be the key to everything," said Jane. "The key to what drives this man to kill. Even if you don't know about him, he certainly knows about you, and he's probably been in your life for some time, right on the periphery of your vision. Maybe he drove past your building every day. Or sat on the bus you rode to work. You just haven't noticed him. When we get you back to Boston, we're going to need a list of every place you frequent. Every café, every bookstore."

"But I'm not going back to Boston."

"You have to come back. We can't protect you otherwise."

Josephine shook her head. "I'm better off somewhere else. Anywhere else."

"This man tracked you all the way here. You think he can't repeat that trick?" Jane's voice was quiet and relentless. "Let me tell you what Bradley Rose does to his victims. He cripples them first, so they can't escape. The way he's crippled you. The way he crippled Madam X. For a while, he kept her alive. He kept her someplace where no one could hear her. He held her captive for weeks, and God knows what he did to her during that time." Jane's voice was softer, almost intimate. "And even when she died, she remained his possession. He preserved her as a keepsake. She became part of his harem, Josephine, a harem of dead souls." She added, softly: "You're his next victim."

"Why are you doing this?" Josephine cried. "You think I'm not already scared *enough*?"

"We can keep you safe," said Frost. "Your locks have already been replaced, and every time you leave your building, we'll arrange an escort. Someone will go with you, anywhere you need to go."

"I don't know." Josephine hugged herself, but it was not enough to still her shaking. "I don't know what to do."

"We know who the killer is," said Jane. "We know how he operates, so the advantage is all ours."

Josephine was silent as she considered her choices. Run or fight. There were no in-betweens, no half measures.

"Come back to Boston," said Jane. "Help us put an end to it."

"If you were me, is that *really* what you would do?" Josephine asked softly. She looked up.

Jane stared straight back at her. "It's exactly what I would do."

22

A row of shiny new locks now decorated her apartment door.

Josephine fastened the chain, turned the dead bolt, and slid the latch shut. Then, just for good measure, she wedged a chair beneath the knob—not much of a barrier, but at least it would serve as a warning device.

Clumsy in her cast, she maneuvered on crutches to the window and looked down at the street. She saw Detective Frost emerge from her building and climb into his car. Once, he might have looked up and given her a smile, a friendly wave, but not anymore. He was all business with her now, as cool and detached as his colleague Rizzoli. This is the consequence of telling lies, she thought. I wasn't honest, and now he doesn't trust me. He's right not to trust me.

I haven't told them the biggest secret of all.

Frost had already checked her apartment when they'd arrived, but she now felt compelled to make her own inspection through her bedroom, her bathroom, and then into the kitchen. It was such a modest little kingdom, but at least it was hers. Everything was as she'd left it a week ago; everything comfortingly familiar. Everything once again back to normal.

But later that evening, as she stood at the stove stirring onions and tomatoes into a simmering pot of chili, she suddenly thought about Gemma, who would never again enjoy a meal, never again smell spices or taste wine or feel the heat wafting up from a stove.

When she finally sat down to eat, she could stomach only a few spoonfuls, and then her appetite vanished. She sat staring at the wall, at the only adornment she'd hung there: a calendar. It was a sign of how uncertain she'd been that she'd actually make a home in Boston. She'd never gotten around to properly decorating her apartment. But now I will, she thought. Detective Rizzoli was right: It's time to take control and claim this city as my own. I'm going to stop running. I owe it to Gemma, who sacrificed everything for me, who died so that I could live. So now I *will* live. I'll have a home, and I'll make friends, and maybe I'll even fall in love.

It starts now.

Outside, the afternoon faded to a warm summer dusk.

With her leg in a cast, she could not take her usual evening walk, could not even pace the floor. Instead she opened a bottle of wine and carried it to the couch, where she sat surfing through TV channels, more channels than she ever knew existed, and all of them the same. Pretty faces. Men with guns. More pretty faces. Men with golf clubs.

Suddenly a new image appeared on the TV, one that made her hand freeze on the remote. It was the evening news, and on the screen was a photo of a young woman, dark-haired and pretty.

". . . the woman whose mummified body was found in the Crispin Museum has been identified. Lorraine Edgerton vanished from a remote New Mexico park twenty-five years ago . . ."

It was Madam X. *She looks like my mother. She looks like me.*

She shut off the TV. The apartment seemed more like a cage than a home, and she was a bird beating itself insane against the bars. *I want my life back.*

After three glasses of wine, she finally fell asleep.

It was barely light when she woke up. Sitting at the window, she watched the sun rise and wondered how many days she'd be trapped within these walls. This, too, was a kind of death, waiting for the next attack, the next threatening note. She had told Rizzoli and Frost about the mailings addressed to Josephine Sommer— evidence that, unfortunately, she had ripped up and flushed down the toilet. Now the police were monitoring both her apartment and her mail.

The next move was Bradley Rose's.

Outside, the morning brightened. Buses rumbled past and joggers began their circuit around the block and people headed off to work. She watched as the day progressed and saw the playground fill with children and the afternoon traffic began to build.

By evening, she could stand it no longer. Everyone is getting on with their lives, she thought. *Everyone except me.*

She picked up the phone and called Nick Robinson. "I want to come back to work," she said.

Jane was looking at the face of Victim Zero, the woman who got away.

The photo of Medea Sommer was from the yearbook of Stanford University, where Medea had been a student twenty-seven years earlier. She'd been a dark-haired, dark-eyed beauty with finely sculpted cheekbones and a haunting resemblance to her daughter, Josephine. You were the one Bradley Rose really wanted, thought Jane. The woman he and his partner Jimmy Otto could never catch. So they collected substitutes, women who looked like Medea. But none of their victims *was* Medea; none could match the original. They kept hunting, kept searching, but Medea and her daughter managed to stay one step ahead of them.

Until San Diego.

A warm hand settled onto her shoulder, and she snapped straight in her chair.

"Wow." Her husband, Gabriel, laughed. "A good thing you aren't armed, or you might have just shot me." He set Regina down on the kitchen floor, and she toddled off to play with her favorite pot lids.

"I didn't hear you come in," said Jane. "That was a short trip to the playground."

"The weather doesn't look so good out there. It's going to start raining any minute." He leaned over her shoulder and saw the photo of Medea. "That's her? The mother?"

"I tell you, this woman is a *real* Madam X. There's not much I can dig up on her except her college records."

Gabriel sat down and scanned the few documents that Boston PD had been able to gather so far about Medea, and they provided only the barest sketch of a young woman who seemed more shadow than substance. Gabriel slipped on his glasses and sat back to read Medea's Stanford University records. His horn-rimmed spectacles were new, and they made him look more like a banker than an FBI agent who knew his way around a gun. Even after a year and a half of marriage, Jane had not grown tired of watching him—and admiring him, the way she did now. Despite the thunder rumbling outside, despite the racket in the kitchen where Regina banged pot lids, he focused like a laser on the pages.

Jane went into the kitchen and scooped up Regina, who squirmed, impatient to escape. Won't you ever be content just to rest quietly in my arms? Jane wondered as she hugged her wriggling daughter, as she breathed in the scents of shampoo and warm baby skin, the sweetest smells in the world. Every day, Jane saw more of herself in Regina, in the girl's dark eyes and exuberantly curly hair, and in her fierce independence as well. Her daughter was a fighter, and there would be battles between them to come. But as she looked into Regina's eyes, Jane also knew that theirs was a bond that could never be broken. To keep her daughter safe, Jane would risk anything, endure anything.

Just as Josephine did for her mother.

"This is a puzzling life story," said Gabriel.

Jane set her daughter down on the floor and looked up at her husband. "Medea's, you mean?"

"Born and raised in Indio, California. Stellar grades at Stanford University. Then she abruptly drops out in her senior year to have a baby."

"And soon afterward, they both vanish from the record."

"And become other people."

"Repeatedly," said Jane. She sat down at the table again. "Five name changes, as far as Josephine remembers."

He pointed to a police report. "This is interesting. In Indio, she filed complaints against both Bradley Rose and Jimmy Otto. They were already engaged in co-operative stalking. Like a wolf pack, moving in on their kill."

"What's even more interesting is that Medea abruptly dropped all charges against Bradley Rose and left Indio. And since she didn't stay to testify against Jimmy

Otto, the charges against him never went anywhere."

"Why would she drop the charges against Bradley?" he asked.

"We'll never know."

Gabriel set down the report. "Being the target of stalkers could explain why she'd run and hide. It would make her keep changing her name, just to stay safe."

"But her own daughter doesn't remember it that way. Josephine claims Medea was running from the law." Jane sighed. "And that leads to another mystery."

"What?"

"There are no outstanding warrants for Medea Sommer. If she committed any crime, no one seems to know about it."

The annual neighborhood cookout at the Rizzoli house was a tradition going back nearly twenty years, and neither black clouds nor approaching thunderstorms could derail the event. Every summer, Jane's father, Frank, would proudly fire up his outdoor grill, slap on steaks and chicken, and assume the role of chef for a day—the only day all year that he wielded a cooking utensil of any kind.

Today, though, it wasn't Frank but retired detective Vince Korsak who'd assumed the role of barbecue chef, in carnivore nirvana as he flipped steaks, splashing grease on the extra-large apron draped over his generous belly. This was the first time Jane had seen any man but her father in charge of the backyard grill, a reminder that nothing lasted forever, not even her parents' marriage. A month after Frank Rizzoli had walked out on his wife, Vince Korsak had waltzed in. By the way he assumed control of the grill, he was making it clear to the neighborhood that he was the new man in Angela Rizzoli's life.

And the new master of the barbecue tongs was not about to abandon his post.

As thunder rumbled and clouds darkened overhead, guests scrambled to bring all the dishes inside before an imminent lightning strike. But Korsak stayed by the grill.

"No way am I gonna let nice little filets like these get ruined," he said.

Jane looked up as the first raindrops began to fall. "Everyone's going inside. We could finish those steaks under the broiler."

"Are you kidding? When you go to all the trouble of buying aged beef and wrapping it in bacon, you gotta cook it right."

"Even if it means getting hit by lightning?"

"Like I'm scared of lightning?" He laughed. "Hey, I already died once. Another jolt to the chest can't hurt the ol' ticker."

"But that bacon sure will," she said, watching the grease drip onto the flames. Two years ago, a heart attack had forced Korsak into retirement, but it hadn't scared him off his butter and beef. And Mom hasn't helped matters any, thought Jane, glancing at the patio picnic table, where Angela was retrieving the mayonnaise-cloaked potato salad.

Korsak waved as Angela headed inside through the screen door. "Your ma changed my life, you know," he said. "I was starving to death on that stupid fish-and-salad diet. Then she taught me just to go for the gusto in life."

"Isn't that a beer commercial?"

"She's a real firecracker. Man, ever since we started going out, I can't believe the things she talks me into! Last night, she got me to try octopus for the first time. Then there was that night we went skinny-dipping—"

"Hold on. I don't need to hear this."

"It's like I've been born again. I never thought I'd meet a woman like your ma." He picked up a steak and flipped it over. Fragrant smoke sizzled up from the grill, and she remembered all the earlier summer meals her father had cooked on that same barbecue. But now it was Korsak who'd proudly carry in the platter of steaks, who'd be uncorking the wine bottles. *This is what you gave up, Dad. Is the new girlfriend worth it? Or do you wake up every morning and wonder why the hell you left Mom?*

"I tell ya," said Korsak, "your dad was a moron, letting her go. But it was the best thing that ever happened to me." He suddenly stopped. "Oh. That was not a sensitive thing to say, was it? I just can't help myself. I'm so friggin' *happy*."

Angela came out of the house with a clean platter for

the meat. "What are you so happy about, Vince?" she asked.

"Steak," said Jane.

Her mother laughed. "Oh, does this one have an appetite!" She gave him a provocative bump with her hip. "In more ways than one."

Jane resisted the urge to clap her hands over her ears. "I think I'll go inside. Gabriel's probably ready to hand over Regina."

"Wait," said Korsak, and he dropped his voice. "While we're out here, why don't you tell us the latest about your weirdo case. I hear you know the name of this Archaeology Killer. Son of some rich Texas guy, right?"

"How did you hear that? We haven't released that detail."

"I got my sources." He winked at Angela. "Once a cop, always a cop."

And Korsak had indeed been a canny investigator whose skills Jane had once relied on.

"I hear this guy's a real loony tune," Korsak said. "Whacks ladies and then preserves 'em as souvenirs. Is that about right?"

Jane glanced at her mother, who was eagerly listening in. "Maybe we should talk about this another time. I don't want Mom to get upset."

"Oh, go ahead," said Angela. "I love it when Vince talks about his old job. He's taught me so much about police work. In fact, I'm going to buy one of those police radios." She smiled at Korsak. "And he's going to teach me how to shoot a gun."

"Am I the only one who thinks this is a bad idea?" said Jane. "Guns are dangerous, Ma."

"Well, you have one."

"I know how to use it."

"I will, too." Angela leaned closer. "Now what about this perp? How does he choose these women?"

Had her mom just used the word *perp*?

"There must be something these ladies all have in common," said Angela. She looked at Korsak. "What was that word you used, about studying victims?"

"Victimology."

"That's what it was. What does the victimology show?"

"Same hair color," said Korsak. "That's what I hear. All three victims had black hair."

"Then you need to be extra careful, Janie," said Angela. "If he likes dark-haired girls."

"The world is full of dark-haired girls, Ma."

"But you're right in his face. If he's paying any attention to the news—"

"Then he knows enough to stay out of Jane's way," said Korsak. "If he knows what's good for him." Korsak started pulling the finished steaks off the grill and plopping them onto the platter. "It's been a week since you brought that girl home, right? And nothing's happened."

"There've been no sightings."

"Then he's probably left town. Moved on to easier hunting grounds."

"Or he's just waiting for things to quiet down," said Jane.

"Yeah, that's the problem, isn't it? It takes resources to keep up surveillance. How do you know when to pull back your protection? When's that girl going to be safe?"

Never, thought Jane. Josephine will always be looking over her shoulder.

"Do you think he'll kill again?" said Angela.

"Of course he will," said Korsak. "Maybe not in Boston. But I guarantee you, right at this moment he's out there hunting somewhere."

"How do you know?"

Korsak loaded the last steak onto the platter and shut off the flame. "Because that's what hunters do."

23

All Sunday afternoon, the storm had been building, and now they were caught in the worst of it. As Josephine sat in her windowless office, she could hear the crash of thunder. The reverberations shook the walls with such violence that she did not notice Nicholas approach her doorway. Only when he spoke did she realize he had been standing nearby.

"Is someone driving you home this afternoon?" he asked.

He hesitated in the doorway, as though afraid to step into her space, afraid that approaching any closer might be forbidden. Days before, Detective Frost had briefed the museum staff on security, and had shown them the photo of Bradley Rose, digitally aged to replicate the passage of two decades. Since Josephine's return, the staff had been treating her like fragile goods, politely keeping their distance. No one was comfortable working around a victim.

And I'm not comfortable being one.

"I just wanted to make sure you've got a ride home," said Robinson. "Because if you don't, I'd be happy to drive you."

"Detective Frost is coming to get me at six."

"Oh. Of course." He lingered in the doorway as though he had something else to say, but did not have the nerve to speak. "I'm glad you're back" was all he managed before he turned to leave.

"Nicholas?"

"Yes?"

"I owe you an explanation. About a number of things."

Although he stood only a few feet away, she found it hard to meet his gaze. Never before had he made her feel so uncomfortable. He was one of the few people with whom she usually felt at ease, because they inhabited the same esoteric little corner of the universe and shared the same unlikely passion for obscure facts and amusing oddities. Of all the people she'd deceived, she felt the most guilty about Nicholas, because he, more than anyone, had tried the hardest to be a friend.

"I haven't been honest with you," she said, and gave a sad shake of the head. "In fact, most of what you know about me is a lie. Starting with—"

"Your name isn't really Josephine," he said softly.

Startled, she looked up at him. Before, when their gazes met, he would often look away, flustered. This time, his gaze was absolutely steady.

"When did you find out?" she asked.

"After you left town and I couldn't reach you, I got worried. I called Detective Rizzoli, and that's when I learned the truth." He flushed. "I'm ashamed to admit it, but I called your university. I wondered if maybe . . ."

"If you'd hired a complete fraud."

"It was wrong of me to invade your privacy, I know."

"No, it was *exactly* what you should have done, Nicholas. You had every reason to check my credentials." She sighed. "That's the only thing I *have* been honest about. I'm surprised you let me come back to work. You never said a thing about it."

"I was waiting for the right moment. Waiting until you felt ready to talk. Are you?"

"It sounds like you already know everything you need to."

"How could I, Josephine? I feel as if I'm just getting to know you *now*. All the things you told me about your childhood—your parents—"

"I lied, okay?" Her response was more curt than she'd intended, and she saw him flush. "I had no choice," she added quietly.

He came into her office and sat down. So many times before he had settled into that same chair, with his morning cup of coffee, and they would happily chat about the latest artifact they'd dug out of the basement or the obscure little detail that one of them had managed to track down. This was not to be one of those pleasant chats.

"I can only imagine how betrayed you feel," she said.

"No. It's not that so much."

"Disappointed at the very least."

His nod was painful to see, because it confirmed the gulf between them. As if to emphasize the breach, a crack of thunder split the silence.

She blinked away tears. "I'm sorry," she said.

"What disappoints me most," he said, "is that you didn't trust me. You could have told me the truth, Josie. And I would have stood up for you."

"How can you say that, when you don't know everything about me?"

"But I know *you*. I don't mean the superficial things like what name you call yourself or which towns you've lived in. I know what you care about and what matters to you. And that gets more to the heart of a person than whether or not your name is really Josephine. That's what I came to say." He took a deep breath. "And . . . something else, too."

"Yes?"

He looked down at his suddenly tense hands. "I was wondering if, um . . . do you like movies?"

"Yes, I—of course."

"Oh, that's good. That's really—that's splendid! I'm afraid I don't keep track of what's playing, but this week there must be something that's suitable. Or maybe next week." He cleared his throat. "I can be counted on to get you home safely, and at a reasonable—"

"Nicholas, *there* you are," said Debbie Duke,

appearing in the doorway. "We have to leave now, or the shipping office will close."

He glanced up at her. "What?"

"You promised you'd help me bring that crate over to the shipping office in Revere. It's going to London and I need to deal with the customs forms. I'd do it myself but it weighs over fifty pounds."

"Detective Frost hasn't come for Josephine yet. I hate to leave."

"Simon and Mrs. Willebrandt are here and all the doors are locked."

He looked at Josephine. "You said he's coming to get you at six? That's not for another hour."

"I'll be fine," said Josephine.

"Come on, Nick," said Debbie. "This thunderstorm's going to slow down traffic. We need to leave now."

He stood and followed Debbie out of the office. As their descending footsteps echoed in the stairwell, Josephine sat at her desk, still startled by what had just happened.

Did Nicholas Robinson just try to ask me out on a date?

Thunder rocked the building and the lights briefly dimmed, as if the heavens had just answered her question. *Yes, he did.*

She gave an amazed shake of her head and looked down at the stack of old accession ledgers. They contained the handwritten lists of antiquities that the museum had acquired through the decades, and she had been slowly making her way down that list, locating each item and assessing its condition. Once again, she tried to focus on the task, but her mind drifted back to Nicholas.

Do you like movies?

She smiled. *Yes. And I like you, too. I always have.*

She opened a book from decades before and recognized Dr. William Scott-Kerr's microscopic handwriting. These ledgers were a lasting record of each curator's tenure, and she'd noted the changing handwriting as old curators left and new ones arrived. Some, like Dr. Scott-Kerr, had been with the museum for decades, and she imagined them growing old along with the collection, walking the creaky floors past specimens that over time would have seemed as familiar as old friends. Here was the record of Scott-Kerr's reign, recorded in his sometimes cryptic notations.

—Megaladon tooth, details of collection unk. Donated by Mr. Gerald DeWitt.
—Clay jar handles, stamped with winged sun disks. Iron Age. Collected at Nebi Samwil by Dr. C. Andrews.
—Silver coin, probably 3rd C BC, *stamped with Parthenope and man-headed bull on reverse. Naples. Purchased from private collection Dr. M. Elgar.*

The silver coin was currently on display in the first-floor gallery, but she had no idea where the clay jar handles were located. She made a note to herself to hunt them down, and turned the page, to find the next three items listed as a group.

> *—Various bones, some human, some equine.*
> *—Metallic fragments, possibly remnants of pack animal harness.*
> *—Fragment of dagger blade, possibly Persian. 3rd C. BC.*
> *Collected by S. Crispin near Siwa Oasis, Egypt.*

She looked at the date and froze at her desk. Though thunder crackled outside, she was more aware of the thudding of her own heart. Siwa Oasis. Simon was in the western desert, she thought. *The same year my mother was there.*

She reached for her crutches and started up the hall to Simon's office.

His door was open, but he had turned off the lights. Peering into the gloom, she saw him sitting near the window. The weather had taken a violent turn, and he was gazing out at the lightning. Fierce gusts rattled the window and sheets of rain splattered the glass as though tossed by angry gods.

"Simon?" she said.

He turned. "Ah, Josephine. Come and watch. Mother Nature is providing us with quite a spectacle today."

"May I ask you something? It's about an entry in this ledger."

"Let me see it."

She thumped across the room on her crutches and handed the book to him. Squinting in the gray light, he murmured: "Various bones. Fragment of a dagger." He looked up. "What was your question?"

"Your name is listed as the collector. Do you remember bringing home these items?"

"Yes, but I haven't taken a look at them in years."

"Simon, these were collected from the western desert. The blade's described as possibly Persian, third century BC."

"Ah, of course. You want to examine it for yourself." He grabbed his cane and pushed himself to his feet. "Well then, let's take a look and see if you agree with my assessment."

"You know where these items are stored?"

"I know where they should be. Unless someone's moved them elsewhere since I last saw them."

She followed him up the hall, toward the ancient elevator. She had never trusted the contraption and usually avoided taking it, but now that she was on crutches she had no choice but to step in. As Simon closed the black grille cage, she felt as if the jaws of a trap had suddenly snapped shut. The elevator gave an alarming shudder and slowly creaked down to the basement level, where she was relieved to step out safely.

He unlocked the storage area. "If I recall correctly," he said, "these items were quite compact, so they'd be stored on the back shelves." He led her into the maze of crates. The Boston police had completed their survey, and the floor was still littered with wood shavings and stray Styrofoam peanuts. She followed Simon down a narrow passage into the older section of the storage area, past crates stamped with the names of enticingly exotic locales. JAVA. MANCHURIA. INDIA. At last they arrived at a towering set of shelves, on which dozens of boxes were stored.

"Oh, good," said Simon, pointing to a modest-sized box with the matching date and accession number. "It's right within reach." He pulled it off the shelf and set it on a nearby crate. "It feels a bit like Christmas, doesn't it? Peeking at something that no one's looked at in a quarter century. Ah, look what we have!"

He reached inside and pulled out a container of bones.

Most were merely fragments, but she recognized a few dense nuggets that had endured intact while other parts of the skeleton had cracked and worn away over the centuries. She picked up one of the nuggets and felt a whisper of a chill on her neck.

"Wrist bones," she murmured. *Human.*

"My guess is, these are all from a single individual. Yes, this does bring back the memories. The heat and the dust. The thrill of being right in the thick of it, when you think that at any instant, your trowel might collide with history. Before these old joints gave out. Before I somehow became old, something I never expected to be. I used to think I was immortal." He gave a sad laugh, a sound of bewilderment that the decades could have fled by so quickly, leaving him trapped in a broken-down body. He looked down at the container of bones and said, "This unfortunate man no doubt thought that he, too, was immortal. Until he watched his comrades go insane with thirst. Until his army crumbled around him. I'm sure he never imagined that this would be their end. This is what the passage of centuries does to even the most glorious of empires. Wears them down to mere sand."

Josephine gently set the wrist bone back in the container. It was nothing more than a deposit of calcium and phosphate. Bones served their purpose, and their owners died and abandoned them, much as one abandoned a walking stick. These fragments were all that remained of a Persian soldier doomed to perish in a foreign desert.

"He's part of the lost army," she said.

"I'm almost certain of it. One of the doomed soldiers of Cambyses."

She looked at him. "You were there with Kimball Rose."

"Oh, it was his excavation, and he paid a pretty penny for it. You should have seen the team he assembled! Dozens of archaeologists. Hundreds of diggers. We were there to find one of the holy grails of archaeology, as elusive as the lost Ark of the Covenant or the tomb of Alexander. Fifty thousand Persian soldiers simply vanished in the desert, and I wanted to be there when they were uncovered."

"But they weren't."

Simon shook his head. "We dug for two seasons, and all we found were bits of bone and metal. The remains of stragglers, no doubt. They were such meager spoils that neither Kimball nor the Egyptian government had any interest in keeping any of it. So it came to us."

"I didn't know that you worked with Kimball Rose. You never even mentioned that you knew him."

"He's a fine archaeologist. An exceedingly generous man."

"And his son?" she asked quietly. "How well did you know Bradley?"

"Ah, Bradley." He set the box back on the shelf. "Everyone wants to know about Bradley. The police. You. But the truth is, I scarcely remember the boy. I can't believe that any son of Kimball's would be a threat to you. This investigation has been quite unfair to his family." He turned to her, and the sudden intensity of his gaze made her uneasy. "He has only your best interests in mind."

"What do you mean?"

"Of all the applicants I could have hired, I chose you. Because he said I should. He's been looking out for you."

She backed away.

"You really had no idea?" he said, moving toward her. "All along, he's been your secret friend. He asked me not to say a word, but I thought it was time you should know. It's always good to know who our friends are, especially when they're so generous."

"Friends don't try to kill you." She turned and hobbled away, back through the canyon of crates.

"What are you talking about?" he called out.

She continued through the maze, intent only on reaching the exit. She could hear him following her, his cane tapping against the concrete.

"Josephine, the police are completely wrong about him!"

She rounded a bend in the maze and saw the door ahead, hanging ajar. *Didn't we close it? I'm sure we closed it.*

Simon's cane tapped closer. "Now I'm sorry I told you," he said. "But you really ought to know how generous Kimball has been to you."

Kimball?

Josephine turned. "How does he even know about me?" she asked.

Just as the basement lights went black.

24

Night had already fallen when Jane stepped out of her Subaru and dashed through the pounding rain to the Crispin Museum entrance. The front door was unlocked and she pushed into the building, letting in a whoosh of wet wind that sent museum brochures flying off the reception desk and scattering across the damp floor.

"Time to start building an ark yet?" asked the patrolman standing guard near the desk.

"Yeah, it's wet out there." Grimly, Jane shrugged out of her dripping slicker and hung it on a coat hook.

"Never seen so much rainfall in a single summer, and I've lived here all my life. I hear it's all because of global warming."

"Where is everyone?" Jane said, cutting off the conversation so brusquely that his face tightened. After what had happened tonight, she was in no mood to talk about the weather.

Taking her cue, he responded just as brusquely: "Detective Young's down in the basement. His partner's upstairs, talking to the curator."

"I'll start in the basement."

She pulled on gloves and paper shoe covers and headed for the stairwell. With every step, she girded herself for what she was about to confront. When she reached the basement level, she saw a stark warning of what lay ahead. Bloody shoe prints, a man's size nine or ten, had tracked across the hall from the storage area to the elevator. Alongside the shoe prints was an alarming smear left by something that had been dragged across that floor.

"Rizzoli?" said Detective Young. He had just emerged from the storage room.

"Did you find her?" asked Jane.

"I'm afraid she's nowhere in this building."

"Shit." Jane looked down again, at the smear. "He took her."

"I'd say it looks that way. Pulled her across this hall and brought her up in the elevator to the first floor."

"And then what?"

"Took her out a rear door that leads to their loading dock. There's an alley behind the building where he could have backed up his vehicle. No one would've seen a thing, especially tonight, with all the rain. He just had to load her in and drive away."

"How the hell did he get into the building? Weren't the doors locked?"

"The senior museum guide—her name's Mrs. Willebrandt—said she left around five fifteen and she swears she locked the doors. But she looks like she's about a thousand years old, so who knows what her memory's like?"

"What about everyone else? Where was Dr. Robinson?"

"He and Ms. Duke drove out to Revere to ship a crate. He says he came back to the building around seven to catch up on some work and he didn't see anyone here. He assumed Dr. Pulcillo had left for the day, so he wasn't concerned at first. Until he glanced in her office and noticed her purse was still there. That's when he called 911."

"Detective Frost was supposed to drive her home today."

Young nodded. "So he told us."

"Then where is he?"

"He arrived just after we got here. He's upstairs now." Young paused, and said quietly: "Go easy on him, huh?"

"For screwing up?"

"I'll let him tell you what happened. But first . . ." He turned toward the door. "I have to show you this."

She followed him into the storage area.

The footprints were more vivid here, the killer's soles so wet with blood that they left splash marks. Young moved into the maze of storage items and pointed down a narrow aisle. The object of his attention sat wedged between crates.

"There's not much left of the face," he said.

But there was still enough of it for Jane to recognize Simon Crispin. The blow had slammed into his left temple, shattering bone and cartilage, leaving a crater of gore. Blood had streamed from the wound into the aisle, where the lake had spread across the concrete and soaked into scattered wood shavings. For a short time after the blow, Simon had lived, long enough for his heart to keep beating and keep pumping blood that had spilled from the ruined head and streamed across this floor.

"Somehow this killer managed to time it just right," said Young. "He must have been watching the building. He must have seen Mrs. Willebrandt leave, so he knew that only two people were still here. Dr. Pulcillo and an eighty-two-year-old man." Young looked at Jane. "I hear her leg was in a cast, so she couldn't have run away. And she wouldn't be able to put up much of a fight."

Jane looked down at the drag mark left by Josephine's body. *We told her she'd be safe. That's why she came back to Boston. She trusted us.*

"There's one more thing you need to see," said Young.

She looked up. "What?"

"I'll show you." He led her back toward the exit. They emerged from the maze of crates. "That," said

Young, and he pointed at the closed door. At the two words that had been written in blood:

FIND ME

Jane climbed the stairs to the third floor. By now the medical examiner and the CSU team had arrived, carrying all their paraphernalia, and the building echoed with the voices and the creaking footsteps of an invading army, the sounds spiraling up the central stairwell. She paused at the top, suddenly weary and sick of blood and death and failure.

Most of all, failure.

The perfectly grilled steak that she had eaten at her mother's house just hours before now felt like an undigested brick in her stomach. From one minute to the next, she thought; that's how quickly a pleasant summer Sunday can turn into tragedy.

She walked through the gallery of human bones, past the skeletal mother cradling the fragments of her child, and headed up the hallway toward the administrative offices. Through an open doorway, she spotted Barry Frost sitting alone in one of the offices, his shoulders slumped, his head in his hands.

"Frost?" she said.

Reluctantly he straightened, and she was startled to see that his eyes were red-rimmed and swollen. He turned away, as though embarrassed that she'd glimpsed his anguish, and he quickly swiped a sleeve across his face.

"Jesus," she said. "What happened to you?"

He shook his head. "I can't do this. I need to be taken off the case."

"You want to tell me what went wrong?"

"I fucked up. That's what went wrong."

Seldom did she hear him use profanity, and hearing that word from his lips surprised her even more than his confession. She entered the room and shut the door. Then she pulled over a chair and sat down facing him directly so that he would be forced to look at her.

"You were supposed to escort her home tonight. Weren't you?"

He nodded. "It was my turn."

"So why didn't you get here?"

"It slipped my mind," he said softly.

"You *forgot*?"

He released a tortured sigh. "Yes, I *forgot*. I should have been here at six, but I got sidetracked. That's why I can't work this case anymore. I need to take a leave of absence."

"Okay, you screwed up. But we've got a missing woman here, and I need all hands on deck."

"I'm worthless to you right now. I'll just fuck up again."

"What the hell is wrong with you? You're falling apart right when I need you the most."

"Alice wants a divorce," he said.

She stared at him, unable to come up with an adequate response. If ever there were a time to give her partner a hug, this would be it. But she'd never hugged him before, and it felt fake to start doing it now. So she just said, "Oh man, I'm sorry."

"She flew home this afternoon," he said. "That's why I didn't make it to your barbecue. She came home to break the news in person. At least she was nice enough to say it to my face. And not over the phone." Again, he wiped a sleeve across his face. "I knew something had to be wrong. I could feel it building, ever since she started law school. After that, nothing I did or said seemed to interest her anymore. It was like I'm just this dumb cop she happened to marry, and now she regrets it."

"Did she actually say that to you?"

"She didn't have to. I heard it in her voice." He gave a bitter laugh. "Nine years we're together, and suddenly I'm not good enough for her."

Jane couldn't help but ask the obvious question. "So who's the other guy?"

"What difference does it make if there's another guy? The point is, she doesn't want to be married. Not to me, anyway." His face crumpled and he shook from the effort not to cry. But the tears came anyway and he rocked forward, his head in his hands. Jane had never seen him so broken, so vulnerable, and it almost frightened her. She didn't know how to comfort him. At that moment, she would rather have been anywhere else, even at the bloodiest of crime scenes, instead of trapped in this room with a sobbing man. It occurred to her that she should take his weapon. Guns and depressed men did not mix well. Would he be insulted if she did? Would he resist? All these practical considerations ran through her head as she patted him on the shoulder and murmured useless sounds of commiseration. *Screw Alice. I never liked her anyway. Now the bitch has gone and made my life miserable as well.*

Frost suddenly rose from the chair and started toward the door. "I need to get out of here."

"Where are you going?"

"I don't know. Home."

"Look, I'm going to call Gabriel. You come and stay with us tonight. You can sleep on the couch."

He shook his head. "Forget it. I need to be by myself."

"I think that's a bad idea."

"I don't want to be with anyone, okay? Just leave me alone."

She studied him, trying to gauge how hard she could push him on this point. And realized that if she were in his shoes, she, too, would want to crawl into a cave and talk to no one. "Are you sure?"

"Yeah." He straightened, as though steeling himself for the walk out of the building, past colleagues who'd see his face and wonder what had happened.

"She's not worth crying over," said Jane. "That's my opinion."

"Maybe," he said softly. "But I love her." He walked out of the room.

She followed him to the stairwell and stood there on

the third-floor landing, listening to his footsteps as he descended the stairs. And she wondered if she should have taken his gun.

25

The relentless pings of dripping water were like hammer blows to her aching head. Josephine groaned and her voice seemed to echo back, as though she were in some vast cave that smelled of mold and dank earth. Opening her eyes, she saw a blackness so solid that when she reached out, she half expected to feel it. Though her hand was right in front of her face, she could not see even a hint of movement, not the faintest silhouette. Just the effort to focus in the darkness made her stomach rebel.

Fighting nausea, she closed her eyes and rolled onto her side, where she lay with her cheek pressed against damp fabric. She struggled to make sense of where she was. Little by little she registered the details. Dripping water. Cold. A mattress that smelled of mildew.

Why can't I remember how I got here?

Her last memory was of Simon Crispin. The sound of his alarmed voice, his shouting in the darkness of the museum basement. But that was a different darkness, not this one.

Her eyes shot open again, and this time it wasn't nausea but fear that gripped her stomach. Fighting dizziness, she sat up. She heard her own heartbeat and the whoosh of blood in her ears. Reaching beyond the edge of the mattress, she felt a frigid concrete floor. Her hands swept the perimeter and she discovered, within reach, a jug of water. A waste bucket. And something soft, covered in crackling plastic. She squeezed it and smelled the yeasty fragrance of bread.

Farther and farther she explored, her dark universe expanding as she gradually ventured off the safe island of the mattress. On hands and knees she crawled, her leg cast scraping across the floor. Leaving the mattress behind in the dark, she suddenly panicked that she would not be able to find it again, that she'd be eternally wandering on the cold floor in search of that pitiful bit of comfort. But the wilderness was not such a large place after all; after only a short crawl, she came up against a rough concrete wall.

Propping herself against it, she rose to her feet. The effort left her unsteady and she leaned back, eyes closed, waiting for her head to clear. She became aware of other sounds now. The chirping of insects. The skittering of some unseen creature moving across the floor. And through it all, that relentless dripping of water.

She limped alongside the wall, tracing the boundaries of her prison. A few paces took her to the first corner, and she found it oddly comforting to discover that this blackness was not infinite, that her blind wanderings would not lead her to drop off the edge of the universe. She hobbled on, her hand tracing the next wall. A dozen paces took her to a second corner.

The features of her prison were slowly taking shape in her head.

She moved along the third wall until she reached another corner. Twelve paces by eight paces, she thought. Twenty-four feet by thirty-six feet. Concrete walls and a floor. *A basement.*

She started along the next wall, and her foot bumped up against something that clattered away. Reaching down, her fingers closed around the object. She felt curved leather, the bumpy surface of rhinestones. A spike heel.

A woman's shoe.

Another prisoner has been in this place, she thought. Another woman has slept on that mattress and gulped from that water jug. She cradled the shoe, her fingers exploring every curve, hungrily seeking clues to its owner. *My sister in despair.* It was a small shoe, size five or six, and with the rhinestones, surely it had been a party shoe, meant to be worn with a pretty dress and earrings, for an evening out with a special man.

Or the wrong man.

Suddenly she was shaking from both cold and despair. She hugged the shoe to her chest. The shoe of a dead woman; of this she had no doubt. How many others had been kept here? How many would come after her? She took in a shaky breath and imagined she could smell their scents, the fear and despair of every woman who had trembled in this darkness, a darkness that had sharpened all her other senses.

She heard blood pumping through her arteries and felt cool air swirl into her lungs. And she smelled the damp leather of the shoe she was cradling. When you lose your eyes, she thought, you notice all the invisible details you once would have missed, the way you really only notice the moon after the sun finally sets.

Clutching the shoe like a talisman, she forced herself to continue the survey of her prison, wondering if the darkness hid other clues to past inmates. She imagined a floor littered with the scattered possessions of dead women. A watch here, a lipstick there. And what will they someday find of mine? she wondered. Will there be any trace of me left, or will I be just another vanished woman, whose last hours will never be known?

The concrete wall abruptly dipped and changed to wood. She halted.

I found the door.

Though the knob turned easily, she could not budge the door itself; it was bolted shut on the other side. She screamed and banged on it with her fists, but it was solid wood and her puny efforts succeeded only in bruising her hands. Exhausted, she slumped back against the door and through the thumping of her own heart, she heard a new sound, one that made her snap taut in fear.

The growl was low-pitched and menacing, and in the darkness she could not locate it. She pictured sharp teeth and claws, imagined the creature advancing toward her even now, poised to spring on her. Then she heard a chain rattle and a scratching sound that came from somewhere overhead.

She looked up. For the first time, she spied a crack of light, so faint that at first she didn't trust her own eyes. But as she watched, the crack slowly brightened. It was the first light of dawn, shining through a tiny boarded-up ventilation window.

Claws scraped at the boards as the dog outside tried to tear its way in. It was a large animal by the sound of its growl. I know he's out there, and he knows I'm in here, she thought. He smells my fear and he wants a taste of it as well. She'd never owned a dog, and had imagined one day having a beagle or perhaps a Shetland sheepdog, some sweet and gentle breed. Not the beast that now stood guard outside that window. A beast that, judging by the sound of it, could rip out her throat.

The dog barked. She heard car tires and the sound of an engine shutting off.

She went rigid, her heart slamming against her chest, as the barking grew frenzied. Her gaze shot upward to the ceiling as footsteps creaked overhead.

Dropping the shoe, she retreated as far as she could from the door, until her back pressed up against the concrete wall. She heard a bolt slide. The door squealed open. A flashlight shone in, and as the man approached, she turned away, as blinded as though it were the sun itself burning her retinas.

He merely stood over her, saying nothing. The concrete chamber magnified every sound, and she heard his breathing, slow and steady, as he examined his captive.

"Let me go," she whispered. "Please."

He did not say a word, and it was his silence that frightened her the most. Until she saw what he held in his hand, and she knew that there was far worse in store for her than mere silence.

It was a knife.

26

"You still have time to find her," said forensic psychologist Dr. Zucker. "Assuming this killer repeats his past practices, he will do to her what he did to Lorraine Edgerton and to the bog victim. He's already crippled her, so she can't easily escape or fight back. The chances are he'll keep her alive for days, perhaps weeks. Long enough to satisfy whatever rituals he requires, before he moves on to the next phase."

"The next phase?" said Detective Tripp.

"Preservation." Zucker pointed to the victims' photos displayed on the conference table. "I think she's meant for his collection. As his newest keepsake. The only question is . . ." He looked up at Jane. "Which method will he use on Ms. Pulcillo?"

Jane looked at the images of the three victims and considered the gruesome options. To be gutted, salted, and wrapped in bandages like Lorraine Edgerton? To be beheaded, your face and scalp peeled from your skull, your features shrunken to the size of a doll's? Or to be steeped in the black water of a bog, your death agonies preserved for all time in the leathery mask of your face?

Or did the killer have a special plan reserved for Josephine, some new technique that they hadn't yet encountered?

The conference room had fallen quiet, and as Jane looked around the table at the team of detectives, she saw grim expressions, everyone silently acknowledging the unsettling truth: that this victim's time was quickly running out. Where Barry Frost usually sat, there was only an empty chair. Without him, the team felt incomplete, and she couldn't help glancing at the door, hoping that he'd suddenly walk in and take his usual seat at the table.

"Finding her may come down to one thing: how deeply we can get into the mind of her abductor," said Zucker. "We need more information on Bradley Rose."

Jane nodded. "We're tracking it down. Trying to find out where he's worked, where he's lived, who his friends are. Hell, if he has a pimple on his butt, we'd like to know about it."

"His parents would be the best source of information."

"We've had no luck with them. The mother's too sick to talk to us. And as for the father, he's been stonewalling."

"Even with a woman's life in danger? He won't cooperate?"

"Kimball Rose isn't your ordinary guy. To start off with, he's as rich as Midas and he's protected by an army of lawyers. The rules don't apply to him. Or to his creep of a son."

"He needs to be pressed harder."

"Crowe and Tripp just got back from Texas," said Jane. "I sent them out there thinking that a little macho intimidation might work." She glanced at Crowe, who had the bulky shoulders of the college linebacker he'd once been. If anyone could pull off a macho act, it would have been Crowe.

"We couldn't even get close to him," said Crowe. "We were stopped at the gate by some asshole attorney and five security guards. Never even got in the door. The Roses have circled the wagons around their son, and we're not going to get a thing out of them."

"Well, what *do* we know about Bradley's whereabouts?"

Tripp said, "He's managed to stay under the radar for quite some time. We can't locate any recent credit card charges, and nothing's been deposited in his Social Security account for years, so he hasn't been employed. At least, not a legitimate job."

"In how long?" asked Zucker.

"Thirteen years. Not that he needs to work when he's got Daddy Warbucks as a father."

Zucker thought about this for a moment. "How do you know the man's even alive?"

"Because his parents told me they get letters and

e-mails from him," Jane said. "According to the father, Bradley's been living abroad. Which may explain why we're having so much trouble tracking his movements."

Zucker frowned. "Would any father go this far? Protecting and financially supporting a dangerously sociopathic son?"

"I think he's protecting *himself,* Dr. Zucker. His own name, his own reputation. He doesn't want the world to know his son is a monster."

"I still find it hard to believe that any parent would go to such lengths for a child."

"You never know," said Tripp. "Maybe he actually loves the creep."

"I think Kimball is protecting his wife as well," said Jane. "He told me she has leukemia, and she did look seriously ill. She doesn't seem to think her son is anything but a sweet little boy."

Zucker shook his head in disbelief. "This is a deeply pathological family."

I don't have a fancy psychology degree, but I could've told you that.

"The cash flow may be the key here," said Zucker. "How is Kimball getting money to his son?"

"Tracking that presents a problem," said Tripp. "The family has multiple accounts, some of them offshore. And he has all those lawyers protecting him. Even with a friendly judge on our side, it will take us time to sort through it."

"We're focused only on New England," said Jane.

"Whether there've been financial transactions in the Boston area."

"And friends? Contacts?"

"We know that twenty-five years ago, Bradley worked at the Crispin Museum. Mrs. Willebrandt, one of the museum guides, recalls that he chose to spend most of his time working after hours, when the museum was closed. So no one remembers much about him. He left no impressions, made no lasting friends. He was like a ghost."

And he's still a ghost, she thought. A killer who slips into locked buildings, whose face eludes security cameras. Who stalks his victims without ever being noticed.

"There is one rich source of information," said Zucker. "It would give us the most in-depth psychological profile you could hope for. If the Hilzbrich Institute will release his records."

Crowe gave a disgusted laugh. "Oh yeah. That school for perverts."

"I've called the former director three times," said Jane. "Dr. Hilzbrich refuses to release the records because of patient confidentiality."

"There's a woman's life at stake. He can't refuse."

"But he has refused. I'm driving up to Maine tomorrow to put the squeeze on. And see if I can get something else out of him."

"That would be?"

"Jimmy Otto's file. He was a student there, too. Since Jimmy's dead, maybe the doctor will hand over that record."

"How will that help us?"

"It seems pretty clear to us now that Jimmy and Bradley were longtime hunting partners. They were both in the Chaco Canyon area. They were both in Palo Alto at the same time. And they seemed to share a fixation with the same woman, Medea Sommer."

"Whose daughter is now missing."

Jane nodded. "Maybe that's why Bradley chose her. For revenge. Because her mother killed Jimmy."

Zucker leaned back in his chair, his face troubled. "You know, that particular detail really bothers me."

"Which detail?"

"The coincidence, Detective Rizzoli. Don't you find it remarkable? Twelve years ago, Medea Sommer shot and killed Jimmy Otto in San Diego. Then Medea's daughter, Josephine, ends up working at the Crispin Museum—the same place where Bradley Rose once worked. The same place where the bodies of two of his victims were stashed. How did that happen?"

"It's bothered me, too," Jane admitted.

"Do you know how Josephine got that job?"

"I asked her that question. She said the position was advertised on an employment website for Egyptologists. She applied, and a few weeks later, she received a call offering her the job. She admits that she was surprised that he chose her."

"Who made that call?"

"Simon Crispin."

Zucker's eyebrow lifted at that detail. "Who now happens to be dead," he said softly.

There was a knock on the door, and a detective stuck his head into the conference room. "Rizzoli, we've got a situation. You'd better come out and deal with it."

"What is it?" she asked.

"A certain Texas tycoon just blew into town."

Jane swiveled around in surprise. "Kimball Rose is here?"

"He's in Marquette's office. You need to get over there."

"Maybe he decided to cooperate after all."

"I don't think so. He's out for your head, and he's letting everyone know it."

"Oh, man," muttered Tripp. "Better you than me."

"Rizzoli, you want us to come?" said Crowe, conspicuously cracking his knuckles. "Little psychological backup?"

"No." Tight-lipped, she gathered up her files and stood. "I'll deal with him." *He may want my head. But I'm damn well going to have his son's.*

She walked through the homicide unit and knocked on Lieutenant Marquette's door. Stepping inside, she found Marquette at his desk, his face unreadable. The same could not be said for his visitor, who stared at Jane with unmistakable contempt. By merely performing her job, she had dared to defy him, and in the eyes of a man as powerful as Kimball Rose, that was clearly an unforgivable offense.

"I believe you two have met," said Marquette.

"We have," said Jane. "I'm surprised Mr. Rose is here. Since he's refused to take any of my phone calls."

"You have no right," said Kimball. "Telling lies about my boy when he isn't here to defend himself."

"I'm sorry, Mr. Rose," said Jane. "I'm not sure what you mean by *telling lies*."

"Do you think I'm an imbecile? I didn't get where I am by just being lucky. I ask questions. I got my sources. I know what your investigation's all about. This nutty case you're trying to build against Bradley."

"I admit, the case is certainly bizarre. But let's be clear about one thing: I don't *make* a case. I follow the evidence where it leads me. At the moment, it's pointing straight at your son."

"Oh, I've learned all about you, Detective Rizzoli. You have a history of making snap judgments. Like shooting to death an unarmed man on that rooftop a few years ago."

At the mention of that painful incident, Jane stiffened. Kimball saw it and drove the knife deeper.

"Did you give that man a chance to defend himself? Or did you play judge and jury and just pull the trigger, the way you're doing to Bradley?"

Marquette said, "Mr. Rose, that shooting isn't relevant to this situation."

"Isn't it? It's all about this woman, who's some kind of loose cannon. My son is innocent. He had nothing to do with this kidnapping."

"How can you be so certain of that?" asked Marquette. "You can't even tell us where your son is."

"Bradley's not capable of violence. If anything, violence is more likely to be done against *him*. I know my boy."

"Do you?" asked Jane. She opened the file she'd brought into the room and pulled out a photo, which she slapped down in front of him. He stared at the grotesque image of the *tsantsa*, its eyelids stitched shut, its lips pierced by braided threads.

"You do know what this thing is called, don't you, Mr. Rose?" she asked.

He said nothing. Through the closed door they could hear phones ringing and detectives' voices in the homicide unit, but in Marquette's office, the silence stretched on.

"I'm sure you've seen one of these before," said Jane. "A well-traveled archaeology buff like you has certainly been to South America."

"It's a *tsantsa*," he finally said.

"Very good. Your son would know that, too, wouldn't he? Since I assume he's traveled all over the world with you."

"And that's all you got against him? That my son is an archaeologist?" He snorted. "You'll have to do better than that in a courtroom."

"What about the woman he stalked? Medea Sommer filed a complaint against him in Indio."

"So what? She dropped those charges."

"And tell us about that private treatment program he attended in Maine. The Hilzbrich Institute. I understand they specialize in a certain class of troubled young men."

He stared at her. "How the hell did you—"

"I'm not an imbecile, either. I ask questions, too. I hear the institute was very exclusive, very specialized. Very discreet. I guess it had to be, considering the clientele. So tell me, did the program work for Bradley? Or did it just introduce him to some equally perverted friends?"

He looked at Marquette. "I want her off this case or you're gonna hear from my lawyers."

"Friends like Jimmy Otto," continued Jane. "You do remember the name Jimmy Otto?"

Kimball ignored her and kept his attention on Marquette. "Do I have to go to your police commissioner? 'Cause I'll do that. I'll do whatever it takes, bring in everyone I know. Lieutenant?"

Marquette was silent for a moment. A long moment during which Jane came to appreciate just how overwhelming Kimball Rose could be—not just his physical presence, but his unstated power. She understood the pressure Marquette was under, and she braced herself for the outcome.

But Marquette did not disappoint her. "I'm sorry, Mr. Rose," he said. "Detective Rizzoli is the lead investigator and she calls the shots."

Kimball glared at him, as though unable to believe

that two mere public servants would defy him. Flushing dangerously red, he turned to Jane. "Because of *your* investigation, my wife is in the hospital. Three days after you came asking about Bradley, she collapsed. I had her flown here yesterday, to Dana-Farber hospital. She may not survive this, and I blame you. I will be watching you, Detective. You won't be able to turn over a single rock without my knowing about it."

"That's probably where I'll find Bradley," said Jane. "Under a rock."

He walked out, slamming the door behind him.

"That," said Marquette, "was not a smart thing to say."

She sighed and picked up the photo from his desk. "I know," she admitted.

"How certain are you that Bradley Rose is our man?"

"Ninety-nine percent."

"You'd better be ninety-nine point nine percent certain. Because you just saw who we're dealing with. Now his wife's in the hospital and he's gone ballistic. He has the money—and the connections—to permanently make our lives miserable."

"Then let him make our lives miserable. It doesn't change the fact that his son is guilty."

"We can't afford any more screwups, Rizzoli. Your team's already made one huge mistake, and that young woman paid for it."

If he'd intended to wound her, he couldn't have done a better job. She felt her stomach clench as she stood gripping the file, as though that bundle of papers could salve her guilty conscience about Josephine's abduction.

"But you know that," he said quietly.

"Yes. I know that," she said. *And that mistake will haunt me until the day I die.*

27

The house where Nicholas Robinson lived was in Chelsea, not far from the blue-collar Revere neighborhood, where Jane had grown up. Like Jane's childhood home, Robinson's was a modest house with a covered front porch and a tiny patch of a yard. In the front garden grew the biggest tomato plants that Jane had ever seen, but the recent heavy rains had cracked the fruit, and a number of overripe globes hung rotting on the vines. The neglected plants should have warned her about Robinson's state of mind. When he opened the door, she was startled by how drained and haggard he looked, his hair uncombed, his shirt wrinkled as though he'd been sleeping in it for days.

"Is there any news?" he asked, anxiously searching her face.

"I'm sorry, but there isn't. May I come in, Dr. Robinson?"

He gave a weary nod. "Of course."

In her parents' Revere home, the TV was the center-piece of the living room, and the coffee table was littered with various remotes that had cloned themselves over the years. But in Robinson's living room she saw no television at all, no entertainment center, and not a remote device in sight. Instead there were shelves filled with books and figurines and bits of pottery, and on the wall hung framed maps of the ancient world. It was every inch an impoverished academic's house, but there was an orderliness to the clutter, as though every knick-knack was precisely where it should be.

He glanced around the room as though uncertain what to do next, then helplessly waved his hands. "I'm sorry. I should offer you something to drink, shouldn't I? I'm afraid I'm not a very good host."

"I'm fine, thank you. Why don't we just sit down and talk?"

They sank onto comfortable but well-worn chairs. Outside a motorcycle roared past, but inside the house, with its shell-shocked owner, there was silence. He said softly: "I don't know what I should do."

"I've heard the museum may be closed permanently."

"I wasn't talking about the museum. I meant Josephine. I'd do anything to help you find her, but what can I do?" He gestured to his books, his maps. "*This* is what I'm good at. Collecting and cataloging! Interpreting useless details from the past. What purpose does it serve her, I ask you? It doesn't help Josephine." He looked down in defeat. "It didn't save Simon."

"Maybe you *can* help us."

He looked at her with exhaustion-hollowed eyes. "Ask me. Tell me what you need."

"I'll start with this question. What was your relationship with Josephine?"

He frowned. "Relationship?"

"She was more than a colleague, I think." A lot more, judging by what she saw in his face.

He shook his head. "Look at me, Detective. I'm fourteen years older than she is. I'm hopelessly myopic, I barely make a living, and I'm starting to go bald. Why would someone like her want someone like me?"

"So she wasn't interested in a romantic relationship."

"I can't imagine she would be."

"You mean you don't actually know? You never asked?"

He gave an embarrassed laugh. "I didn't have the nerve to actually get the words out. And I didn't want to make her uncomfortable. It might have ruined what we *did* have."

"What was that?"

He smiled. "She's like me—she's *so* much like me. Hand us an old bone fragment or a rusted blade, and we can both feel the heat of history in it. That's what we had in common, a passion for what came before us. That would have been enough, just being able to share that much." His head drooped and he admitted: "I was afraid to ask for more than that."

"Why?"

"Because of how beautiful she is," he said, his words soft as a prayer.

"Was that one of the reasons you hired her?"

She could see that her question instantly offended him. His face tightened and he straightened. "I would never hire on the basis of physical appearance. My only standards are competence and experience."

"Yet Josephine had almost no experience on her résumé. She was fresh from a doctoral program. You took her on as consultant, yet she was far less qualified than you are."

"But I'm not an Egyptologist. That's why Simon told me he was bringing in a consultant. I suppose I should have felt a bit insulted, but to be honest, I knew I wasn't qualified to evaluate Madam X. I do acknowledge my own limits."

"There must have been Egyptologists more qualified than Josephine to choose from."

"I'm sure there were."

"You don't know?"

"Simon made the decision. After I advertised the job opening, we received dozens of résumés. I was in the process of narrowing down the choices when Simon told me he'd already made the decision. Josephine wouldn't have made even my first cut, but he insisted she had to be the one. And somehow, he found the extra funds to hire her full-time."

"What do you mean, he found the extra funds?"

"A substantial donation came in. Mummies have that

effect, you know. They get donors excited, make them more willing to open their wallets. When you've worked in archaeological circles as long as Simon did, you learn who has the deep pockets. You know whom to ask for money."

"But why did he choose Josephine? That's the question I keep coming back to. Of all the Egyptologists he could have hired, all the freshly minted PhDs who must have applied, why was *she* hired?"

"I don't know. I wasn't enthusiastic about the choice, but I saw no point in arguing because I had the impression that he'd already made up his mind, and there was nothing I could do to change it." Robinson sighed and looked out the window. "And then I met her," he said softly. "And I realized there was no one else I'd rather work with. No one else I'd rather . . ." He fell silent.

On that street of modest homes, the sound of traffic was constant, yet this living room seemed to be a trapped in a different and more genteel era, a time when a rumpled eccentric like Nicholas Robinson might contentedly grow old while surrounded by his books and maps. But he had fallen in love, and there was no contentment in his face, only anguish.

"She's alive," he said. "I need to believe that." He looked at Jane. "*You* believe it, don't you?"

"Yes, I do," she said. She looked away before he could read the rest of the answer in her eyes. *But I don't know if we can save her.*

28

That evening, Maura dined alone.

She had planned a romantic dinner for two, and a day earlier she had cruised the grocery store aisles gathering Meyer lemons and parsley, veal shanks and garlic, all the ingredients she needed to make Daniel's favorite, osso buco. But the best-laid plans of illicit lovers can crumble in an instant with a single phone call. Only hours ago, Daniel had apologetically delivered the news that he was expected to dine that night with visiting bishops from New York. The call had ended as it so often did. *I'm sorry, Maura. I love you, Maura. I wish I could get out of this.*

But he never could.

Now those veal shanks were stored in her freezer, and instead of osso buco, she was resigned to dining alone on a grilled cheese sandwich and a stiff gin and tonic.

She imagined where Daniel was at that moment. She pictured a table with men dressed in somber black, the preliminary bowing of heads, the murmured blessing over the food. The subdued clink of silverware and china as they discussed matters of importance to the church: declining seminary enrollments, the graying of the priesthood. Every profession conducted its own business dinners, yet when theirs was finished, these men would not go home to wives and families, but to their lonely beds. She wondered: As you sip your wine, as you look around the table at your colleagues, are you troubled at all by the absence of women's faces, women's voices?

Are you thinking at all of me?

She pressed the cheese sandwich onto the hot skillet and watched as butter sizzled, as the bread crisped. Like scrambled eggs, a grilled cheese sandwich was one of her meals of last resort, and the scent of browning butter brought back all the exhausted nights she'd known as a medical student. It was also the scent of those wounded evenings after her divorce, when planning a meal took more effort than she could muster. The smell of a grilled cheese sandwich was the scent of defeat.

Outside, darkness was falling, mercifully cloaking the neglected vegetable garden that she had planted so optimistically in the spring. Now it was a jungle of weeds and bolting lettuce and unpicked peapods that hung dry and leathery on tangled vines. Someday, she thought, I'll follow through. I'll keep it weeded and neat. But this summer's garden was a waste, yet another victim of too many demands and too many distractions.

Daniel, most of all.

In the window, she saw herself reflected in the glass, her lips downturned, her eyes tired and pinched. That unhappy image was as startling as a stranger's face. In ten years, twenty years, would the same woman still be staring back at her?

The pan was smoking, the bread starting to burn black. She turned off the burner and opened the window to air out the smoke, then carried her sandwich to the kitchen table. Gin and cheese, she thought as she refilled her drink. All the necessary food groups for a melancholy woman. As she sipped, she sorted through the mail she'd brought in that evening, setting aside unwanted catalogs for the recycling bin and stacking together the bills that she'd pay this weekend.

She paused at an envelope with her typewritten name and address. It had no return address. She slit it open and pulled out a folded sheet of paper. Instantly she dropped the page as though scalded.

Printed in ink were the same two words she had seen painted in blood on the door in the Crispin Museum.

FIND ME

She shot to her feet, knocking over the glass of gin and tonic. Ice cubes clattered onto the floor but she ignored them and crossed straight to the phone.

Within three rings, her call was answered by a brisk voice. "Rizzoli."

"Jane, I think he wrote me!"

"What?"

"It just came in my mail. It's a single sheet of paper—"

"Slow down. I'm having trouble hearing you in this traffic."

Maura paused to collect her nerves and managed to say, more calmly: "The envelope is addressed to me. Inside there's a sheet of paper with only two words: *Find me.*" She drew a breath and said, quietly: "It has to be him."

"Is there anything else written on that page? Anything at all?"

Maura turned the page over and frowned. "There are two numbers on the other side."

Over the phone, she heard a car honk, and Jane muttered an oath. "Look, I'm stuck on Columbus Avenue right now. You're at home?"

"Yes."

"I'm heading right there. Is your computer on?"

"No. Why?"

"Turn it on. I need you to check something for me. I think I know what those numbers are."

"Hold on." Carrying the phone and the note, Maura hurried down the hall to her office. "I'm booting up right now," she said as the monitor flickered on and the hard drive hummed to life. "Tell me about these numbers," she said. "What are they?"

"I'm guessing they're geographic coordinates."

"How do you know that?"

"Because Josephine told us she got a note just like yours with numbers that turned out to be the co-ordinates for Blue Hills Reservation."

"That's why she went hiking there that day?"

"The killer sent her there."

The hard drive had stopped spinning. "Okay. I'm booted up. What do you want me to do?"

"Go to Google Earth. Type in those numbers for latitude and longitude."

Maura looked at the note again, suddenly struck by the significance of the words *Find me*. "Oh God," she murmured. "He's telling us where to find her body."

"I hope to hell you're wrong. Have you typed in those numbers?"

"I'll do it now." Maura set down the receiver and began tapping on the keyboard, entering the numbers for latitude and longitude. On the screen, the global map began to shift, moving toward the coordinates she'd specified. She picked up the receiver and said, "It's starting to zoom in."

"What's it showing?"

"Northeastern U.S. It's Massachusetts . . ."

"Boston?"

"It looks like—no, wait . . ." Maura stared as the details sharpened. Her throat suddenly went dry. "It's in Newton," she said softly.

"Where in Newton?"

Maura reached for the mouse. With each new click the image was magnified. She saw streets, trees. Individual rooftops. Suddenly she realized which neighborhood she was looking at, and a chill raised every hair on the back of her neck. "It's my house," she whispered.

"What?"

"These coordinates are for *my house*."

"Jesus. Listen to me! I'm going to get a cruiser right over there. Is your house secure? I want you to check all your doors. Go, go!"

Maura sprang from her chair and ran to the front door. It was locked. She ran to the garage door—also locked. She turned toward the kitchen and suddenly froze.

I left the window open.

Slowly she moved up the hall, her palms slick, her heart hammering. Stepping into the kitchen, she saw that the window screen was intact, the room unviolated. Melted ice cubes had left a puddle of water glistening under the table. She went to the door and confirmed that it was secured. Of course it would be. Two years ago, an intruder had broken into her home, and ever since then, she'd been careful to lock her doors, to arm her security system. She closed and latched the kitchen window and took calming breaths as her pulse gradually slowed. It was just a piece of mail, she thought. A taunt delivered through the U.S. Postal Service. Turning, she looked at the envelope that the note had arrived in.

Only then did she notice that it had no postmark, that the stamp was pristine.

He delivered it himself. He came to my street and slipped it in my mailbox.

What else did he leave for me?

Looking through the window, she wondered what secrets the darkness concealed. Her hands were clammy again as she crossed to the switch for the outside lamps. She was almost afraid of what the light might reveal, afraid that Bradley Rose himself would be standing right outside her window, staring back at her. But when she flipped the switch, the glare revealed no monsters. She saw the gas barbecue grill and the teak patio furniture that she'd bought only last month, but had yet to enjoy. And beyond the patio, at the periphery of the light, she could just make out the shadowy edge of her garden. Nothing alarming, nothing amiss.

Then a pale ripple caught her eye, a faint white fluttering in the darkness. She strained to make out what it was, but it refused to take shape, refused to reveal itself. She pulled the flashlight from her kitchen drawer and shone it into the night. The beam landed on the Japanese pear tree that she'd planted two summers ago at the far corner of the yard. Suspended from one of its branches was something white and pendulous, something that was now swaying languorously in the wind.

Her doorbell rang.

She spun around, lungs heaving in fright. Hurrying

into the hallway, she saw the electric blue of a cruiser's rack lights pulsing through her living room window. She opened the front door to see two Newton patrolmen.

"Everything okay, Dr. Isles?" one of the officers asked. "We got a report of a possible intruder at this address."

"I'm fine." She released a deep breath. "But I need you to come with me. To check something."

"What?"

"It's in my backyard."

The patrolmen followed her up the hall and into her kitchen. There she paused, suddenly wondering if she was about to make herself look ridiculous. The hysterical single woman, imagining ghosts dangling from pear trees. Now that she had two cops standing beside her, her fear had faded and more practical concerns came to mind. If the killer really had left something in her backyard, she had to approach the object as a professional.

"Wait here just a minute," she said, and ran back to the hall closet, where she kept the box of latex gloves.

"Do you mind telling us what's going on?" the officer called out.

She returned to the kitchen carrying the box of gloves and handed gloves to both of them. "Just in case," she said.

"What are these for?"

"Evidence." She grabbed the flashlight and opened the kitchen door. Outside, the summer night was fragrant with the scent of pine bark mulch and damp grass. Slowly, she walked across the yard, her flashlight beam sweeping the patio, the vegetable plot, the lawn, searching for any other surprises she'd been meant to find. The only thing that did not belong was what now hung fluttering in the shadows ahead. She came to a halt in front of the pear tree and aimed her flashlight at the object dangling from the branch.

"This thing?" said the cop. "It's just a grocery sack."

With something inside it. She thought of all the horrors that might fit inside that plastic sack, all the gruesome keepsakes that a killer might harvest from a victim, and suddenly she did not want to look inside it. Leave it for Jane, she thought. Let someone else be the first to see it.

"Is that what's bothering you?" the cop said.

"He left it here. He came into my yard and hung it on that tree."

The cop pulled on the gloves. "Well geez, let's just see what it is."

"No. Wait—"

But he'd already pulled the sack off the branch. He shone his flashlight at the contents, and even in the darkness she saw him grimace.

"What?" she asked.

"Looks like some kind of animal." He held the sack open for her to look inside.

At first glimpse, what she saw did indeed appear to be a mass of dark fur. But when she realized what it really was, her hands chilled to ice inside the latex gloves.

She looked up at the cop. "It's hair," she said softly. "I think it's human."

29

"It's Josephine's," said Jane.

Maura sat at her kitchen table, staring down at the evidence bag containing a thick mass of black hair. "We don't know that," she said.

"It's the right color. The right length." Jane pointed to the envelope that had contained the note. "He practically tells us he's the one who sent it."

Through the kitchen window, Maura saw the flashlights of the CSU team that had spent the last hour combing her backyard. And on the street three police cruisers were parked, rack lights flashing, and her neighbors were probably peering out their windows at the spectacle. I'm the woman you don't want in your neighborhood, she thought. My house is where police cruisers and crime scene units and news vans regularly turn up. Her privacy had been stripped away, her home exposed to those TV cameras, and she wanted to fling open the front door and scream at the reporters to get off her street and leave her alone. She imagined how that would play out on the late-night news, the enraged medical examiner shrieking like a madwoman.

The true object of her fury was not those cameras, however, but the man who had drawn them here. The man who had written the note and had left that souvenir hanging on her pear tree. She looked up at Jane. "Why the hell did he send this to me? I'm just a medical examiner. I'm peripheral to your investigation."

"You've also been present at almost every death scene. In fact, you were the very first person on this case, starting with the CT scan of Madam X. Your face has been on the news."

"So has yours, Jane. He could have mailed that souvenir to Boston PD. Why come to *my* house? Why leave it in *my* backyard?"

Jane sat down and faced her across the table. "If that hair had been mailed to Boston PD, we would have handled it internally and quietly. Instead cruisers were dispatched and now you've got criminalists tramping around your property. Our boy has turned this into a public spectacle." She paused. "Which may be the point."

"He likes the attention," said Maura.

"And he's certainly getting that attention."

Outside, the CSU team had wrapped up their search. Maura heard the closing thud of van doors, the fading growl of departing vehicles.

"You asked a question earlier," said Jane. "You

asked, *Why me?* Why would the killer leave the souvenir at your house, instead of sending it to Boston PD?"

"We just agreed it's because he wants attention."

"You know, there's another reason I can think of. And you're not going to like this one." Jane turned on the laptop computer that she'd brought in from her car, and navigated to the *Boston Globe* website. "You remember reading this story about Madam X?"

On the monitor was an archived *Globe* article: MYSTERY MUMMY'S SECRETS SOON TO BE REVEALED. Accompanying the article was a color photo of Nicholas Robinson and Josephine Pulcillo, flanking Madam X in her crate.

"Yes, I read it," said Maura.

"This piece was picked up by the wire services. It ran in a lot of newspapers. If our killer spotted this story, then he'd know Lorraine Edgerton's body had just been found. And that there'd be excitement to come after the CT scan. Now look at this."

Jane clicked on a saved file on her computer, and an image appeared on the screen. It was a head shot of a young woman with long black hair and delicately arching brows. This was not a candid shot but a formal pose in front of a professional backdrop, a photo that might have been taken for a college yearbook.

"Who is she?" asked Maura.

"Her name was Kelsey Thacker. She was a college student who was last seen twenty-six years ago, walking home from a neighborhood bar. In Indio, California."

"Indio?" said Maura. And she thought of the crumpled newspaper that she had pulled from the head of the *tsantsa*—a newspaper that had been printed twenty-six years ago.

"We reviewed the missing persons reports for every woman who vanished from the Indio area that year. Kelsey Thacker's name popped front and center. And when I saw her photo, I was sure of it." She pointed to the image. "I think this is what Kelsey looked like before a killer cut off her head. Before he peeled off her face and scalp. Before he shrank it down and hung it on a string like a fucking Christmas ornament." Jane took an agitated breath. "Without a skull, we have no way of matching her dental records. But I'm positive this is her."

Maura's gaze was still fixed on the woman's face. Softly she said, "She looks like Lorraine Edgerton."

"And like Josephine, too. Dark-haired, pretty. I think it's clear what kind of woman attracts this killer. We also know that he watches the news. He hears that Madam X has been found in the Crispin Museum, and maybe all the publicity thrills him. Or maybe it just annoys him. The important thing is, it's all about *him*. And he spots Josephine's photo in that article about the mummy. Pretty face, black hair. Identical to his dream girl. The kind of girl he seems to kill again and again."

"And that draws him to Boston."

"No doubt he saw this article, too." Jane pulled up

yet another news article from the *Boston Globe* archive, this one about Bog Lady: BODY DISCOVERED IN WOMAN'S CAR. Accompanying the story was a file photo of Maura, with the caption: "Medical examiner says cause of death still undetermined."

"It's a photo of another pretty woman with black hair," said Jane. She looked at Maura. "Maybe you never noticed the resemblance, Doc, but I did. The first time I saw you and Josephine in the same room, I thought you could be her older sister. That's why I've asked Newton PD to keep an eye on your house. It might not be a bad idea for you to leave home for a few days. Maybe it's also a good time to think about getting a dog. A great big dog."

"I have an alarm system, Jane."

"A dog has teeth. Plus, he'd keep you company." Jane stood to leave. "I know you like your privacy. But sometimes, a woman just doesn't want to be alone."

But I am alone, thought Maura later as she watched Jane's car drive away and vanish into the night. Alone in a silent house without even a dog for company.

She armed her security system and paced the living room, as restless as a caged animal, her gaze returning again and again to the telephone. At last she could resist the temptation no longer. She felt like a junkie in withdrawal as she picked up the receiver, her hand trembling with need as she punched in Daniel's cell phone number. *Please answer. Please be there for me.*

His voice mail picked up.

She hung up without leaving a message and stared down at the phone, feeling betrayed by its silence. Tonight I need you, she thought, but you're beyond my reach. You've always been beyond my reach, because God is the one who owns you.

The glare of headlights drew her to the window. Outside a Newton PD cruiser crawled slowly past her house. She waved, acknowledging the faceless patrolman who watched over her on a night when the man she loved did not and could not. And what did that patrolman see as he passed her house? A woman with a comfortable home and all the trappings of success who stood alone at her window, isolated and vulnerable.

Her phone rang.

Daniel was her first thought, and by the time she'd snatched up the receiver, her heart was pounding as hard as a sprinter's.

"Are you all right, Maura?" said Anthony Sansone.

Disappointed, she gave a response that sounded more curt than she intended. "Why wouldn't I be?"

"I understand there was some excitement at your house tonight."

She was not surprised that he already knew about it. Sansone always managed to sense every disturbing tremor, every shift in the wind.

"It's all over now," she said. "The police have left."

"You shouldn't be alone tonight. Why don't you pack a bag and I'll come get you? You can stay here on Beacon Hill, as long as you need to."

She looked out the window, at the deserted street and considered the night ahead. She could spend it lying awake, listening anxiously to every creak, every rattle in the house. Or she could retreat to the safety of his mansion, which he'd made secure against a universe of threats that he was convinced stood arrayed against him. In his velvet-cloaked fortress, furnished with antiques and medieval portraits, she would be protected and safe, but it would be a refuge in a dark and paranoid world, with a man who saw conspiracies everywhere. Sansone had always unsettled her; even now, months after she'd made his acquaintance, he seemed unknowable, a man isolated by his wealth and by his disquieting belief in humanity's enduring dark side. She might be safe in his house, but she would not feel at ease.

Outside, the street was still deserted, the police cruiser long gone. There's only one person I want here with me tonight, she thought. And he's the one person I can't have.

"Maura, shall I come and get you?" he asked

"There's no need to fetch me," she said. "I'll come in my own car."

The last time Maura had set foot in Sansone's Beacon Hill mansion, it had been January and there'd been a fire blazing in the hearth to ward off the winter chill. Though it was now a warm summer night, a chill still seemed to cling to the house, as though winter had permanently settled into these dark-paneled rooms, where somber faces gazed from the portraits on the walls.

"Have you had supper yet?" Sansone asked, handing her overnight bag to his manservant, who discreetly withdrew. "I can ask the cook to prepare a meal."

She thought of her grilled cheese sandwich, of which she'd taken only a few bites. It hardly counted as supper, but she had no appetite, so she accepted only a glass of wine. It was a rich Amarone, so dark it appeared almost black in the parlor's firelight. She sipped it under the cool gaze of his sixteenth-century ancestor, whose piercing eyes stared down from the portrait hanging over the hearth.

"It's been far too long since you've visited," he said, settling into the Empire armchair facing hers. "I keep hoping you'll accept the invitations to our monthly suppers."

"I've been too busy to make your meetings."

"Is that the only reason? That you're busy?"

She stared into her glass of wine. "No," she admitted.

"I know you don't believe in our mission. But do you still think we're a group of crackpots?"

She looked up and saw that his mouth was tilted into an ironic smile. "I think the Mephisto Society has a frightening view of the world."

"And you don't have the same view? You stand in that autopsy room and watch the homicide victims roll in. You see the evidence carved into their bodies. Tell me that doesn't shake your faith in humanity."

"All it tells me is that there are certain people who don't belong in civilized society."

"People who can hardly be classified as human."

"But they *are* human. You can call them whatever you want. Predators, hunters, even demons. Their DNA is still the same as ours."

"Then what makes them different? What makes them kill?" He set down his wineglass and leaned toward her, his gaze as disturbing as that of the portrait over the hearth. "What makes a privileged child warp into a monster like Bradley Rose?"

"I don't know."

"That's the problem. We try to blame it on traumatic childhoods or abusive parents or environmental lead. And yes, some criminal behaviors can probably be explained that way. Then there are the exceptional examples, the killers who stand apart for their cruelties. No one knows where these creatures come from. Yet every generation, every society, produces a Bradley Rose and a Jimmy Otto and a host of predators just like them. They're always among us, and we have to acknowledge they exist. And protect ourselves."

She frowned at him. "How did you learn so much about this case?"

"There's been a great deal of publicity."

"Jimmy Otto's name was never released. It's not public knowledge."

"The public doesn't ask the questions I ask." He reached for the wine bottle and refilled her glass. "My sources in law enforcement trust me to be discreet, and I trust them to be accurate. We share the same concerns and the same goals." He set down the bottle and looked at her. "Just as you and I do, Maura."

"I'm not always certain of that."

"We both want that young woman to survive. We want Boston PD to find her. That means we have to understand exactly why this killer took her."

"The police have a forensic psychologist consulting on the case. They're already covering that territory."

"And they're using the conventional approach. *He behaved this way before, so that's the way he'll behave again.* But this abduction is completely different from the earlier ones, the ones we know about."

"Different how? He started by crippling this woman, and that's precisely his pattern."

"But then he deviated from that pattern."

"What do you mean?"

"Both Lorraine Edgerton and Kelsey Thacker vanished without a trace. Neither abductions were followed by taunts of *find me*. There were no notes or souvenirs sent to law enforcement. Those women simply disappeared. This victim is different. With Ms. Pulcillo, the killer seems to be begging for your attention."

"Maybe he's asking to be caught. Maybe it's a plea for someone to finally stop him."

"Or he has another reason to want all this publicity. You have to admit, courting publicity is exactly what he's done by staging high-profile incidents. Putting the bog body in the trunk. Committing the murder and abduction in the museum. And now the latest—leaving a souvenir in your backyard. Did you notice how quickly the press showed up in your neighborhood?"

"Reporters often monitor police radios."

"They were tipped off, Maura. Someone called them."

She stared at him. "You think this killer's that desperate for attention?"

"He's certainly getting it. Now the question is, whose attention is he seeking?" He paused. "I'm concerned it's yours he wants."

She shook her head. "He already has mine, and he knows it. If this is attention-seeking behavior, it's directed at a far larger audience. He's telling the whole world, *Look at me. Look at what I've done.*"

"Or he's aiming it at one person in particular. Someone who's meant to see these news stories and react to them. I think he's communicating with someone, Maura. Maybe it's another killer. Or maybe it's a future victim."

"It's his current victim we need to worry about."

Sansone shook his head. "He's had her for three days now. That's not a good milestone."

"He kept his other victims alive far longer than this."

"But he didn't cut off *their* hair. He didn't play games with the police and the press. This abduction is moving along its own unique time line." The look he gave her was chillingly matter-of-fact. "This time, things are different. The killer's pattern has changed."

31

The Cape Elizabeth neighborhood where Dr. Gavin Hilzbrich lived was a prosperous suburb outside Portland, Maine, but unlike the well-kept properties on the street, Hilzbrich's house was set back on a lot overgrown with trees, and the patchy lawn was slowly dying for want of sunlight. Standing in the driveway of the large Colonial-style house, Jane noticed peeling paint and the green sheen of moss on the shake roof, clues to the ailing health of the doctor's finances. His house, like his bank account, had almost certainly seen better days.

At first glance, the silver-haired man who answered the door had the appearance of prosperity. Though he was in his late sixties, he stood unbowed by either age or economic travails. Despite the warm day he wore a tweed jacket, as though on his way out to teach a university class. Only when she looked more closely did Jane notice that the collar tips were frayed and the jacket hung several sizes too large on his bony shoulders. Nevertheless he regarded her with disdain, as though nothing his visitor might say could possibly interest him.

"Dr. Hilzbrich?" she said. "I'm Detective Rizzoli. We spoke on the phone."

"I have nothing more to tell you."

"We don't have a lot of time to save this woman."

"I can't discuss my former patients."

"Last night, your former patient sent us a souvenir."

He frowned. "What do you mean, what souvenir?"

"The victim's hair. He hacked it off her head, stuffed it into a grocery bag, and hung it on a tree, like a trophy. Now, I don't know how a psychiatrist like you would interpret that. I'm just a cop. But I hate to think of what he might cut off next. And if the next thing we find is a piece of her flesh, I fucking promise you I will be back on this doorstep. And I'll invite a few TV cameras to come along with me." She let that sink in for a moment. "So now do you want to talk?"

He stared at her, his lips pressed together in two tight lines. Without a word, he stepped aside to let her come in.

Inside, it smelled of cigarettes—an unhealthy habit made more so in that house, where she saw stuffed file boxes lining the hallway. Glancing through a doorway into a cluttered office, she spotted overflowing ashtrays and a desk covered with papers and even more boxes.

She followed him into the living room, which was oppressively dark and cheerless because thick trees outside blocked the sunlight. Here some semblance of order had been maintained, but the leather couch she sat down on was stained, and the finely crafted coffee table bore the rings of countless cups set carelessly on unprotected wood. Both had probably been expensive purchases, evidence of their owner's more affluent past. Clearly Hilzbrich's circumstances had gone terribly wrong, leaving him with a house he could not afford to maintain. But the man who sat across from her betrayed no hint of defeat, and certainly no humility. He was still every inch *Doctor* Hilzbrich, facing the minor annoyance of a police investigation.

"How do you know that my former patient is responsible for this young woman's abduction?" he asked.

"We have a number of reasons to suspect Bradley Rose."

"And those reasons are?"

"I'm not at liberty to reveal the details."

"Yet you expect me to open up his psychiatric files to you?"

"When a woman's life is at stake? Yes, I do. And you know very well what your obligations are." She paused. "Since you've been through this situation before."

The sudden rigidity in his face told her he knew exactly what she was talking about.

"You've already had one of your patients go off the rails," she said. "The parents of *his* victim weren't too happy with that whole patient-confidentiality thing, were they? Having their daughter sliced and diced can do that to a family. They grieve, they get angry, and finally they sue. And it all shows up in the newspapers." She glanced around the shabby room. "Are you still treating patients, by the way?"

"You know I'm not."

"I guess it's hard to practice psychiatry when you lose your license."

"It was a witch hunt. The parents needed someone to blame."

"They knew exactly who to blame—your sicko former patient. You were the one who pronounced him cured."

"Psychiatry is an inexact science."

"You had to know it was your patient who did it. When that girl was killed, you must have recognized his handiwork."

"I had no proof it was him."

"You just wanted the problem to go away. So you did nothing, said nothing to the police. Are you going to let that happen again with Bradley Rose? When you can help us stop him?"

"I don't see how I *can* help you."

"Release his records to us."

"You don't understand. If I give them to you, he'll—" He stopped.

"He?" Her gaze was fixed so intently on his face that he drew back, as though physically pressed against the chair. "You're talking about Bradley's father. Aren't you?"

Dr. Hilzbrich swallowed. "Kimball Rose warned me

you'd be calling. He reminded me that psychiatric records are confidential."

"Even when a woman's life is in danger?"

"He said he'd sue me if I released the records." He gave a sheepish laugh and looked around at his living room. "As if there's anything left to take! The bank owns this house. The institute's been shuttered for years and the state's about to foreclose on it. I can't even pay the damn property taxes."

"When did Kimball speak to you?"

He shrugged. "He called me about a week ago, maybe more. I can't remember the date."

That would have been soon after her visit to Texas. From the beginning, Kimball Rose had put up barriers to the investigation, all to protect his son.

Hilzbrich sighed. "I can't give you that file anyway. I don't have it anymore."

"Who does have it?"

"No one. It's been destroyed."

She stared at him in disbelief. "How much did he pay you to do it? Were you a cheap lay?"

Flushing, he rose to his feet. "I have nothing more to say to you."

"But I have plenty to say to you. First, I'm going to show you what Bradley's been up to." She reached into her briefcase and pulled out a bundle of evidence photos. One by one, she slapped the images down on the coffee table, revealing a grotesque gallery of victims. "This is your patient's handiwork."

"I'll ask you to leave now."

"Take a look at what he's done."

He turned toward the door. "I don't need to see those."

"Take a *fucking look*."

He stopped and slowly turned toward the coffee table. As his gaze landed on the photos, his eyes widened in horror. While the doctor stood frozen, she rose from the chair and steadily advanced on him.

"He's collecting women, Dr. Hilzbrich. He's about to add Josephine Pulcillo to that collection. We have only a limited time before he kills her. Before he turns her into something like *that*." She pointed to the photo of Lorraine Edgerton's mummified body. "And if he does, her blood is on your hands."

Hilzbrich had not stopped staring at the images. His legs suddenly seemed to give way, and he stumbled to a chair where he sat with his shoulders slumped.

"You knew Bradley was capable of this. Didn't you?" Jane said.

He shook his head. "I didn't know."

"You were his psychiatrist."

"That was over thirty years ago! He was only sixteen. And he was quiet and well behaved."

"So you remember him."

A pause. "Yes," he admitted. "I remember Bradley. But I don't see how anything I could tell you would be useful. I have no idea where he is now. I certainly never thought he was capable of . . ." He glanced at the photos. *"That."*

"Because he was quiet and well behaved?" She couldn't help a cynical laugh. "You, of all people, must know that it's the quiet ones you have to watch out for. You must have seen the signs, even when he was sixteen. Something that warned you he'd someday be doing *that* to a woman."

Unwillingly, Hilzbrich focused again on the photo of the mummified body. "Yes, he would have the knowledge. And probably the skills to do it," he admitted. "He was fascinated by archaeology. His father sent him a box of Egyptology textbooks, and Bradley read them again and again. Obsessively. So yes, he'd know *how* to mummify a body, but to actually attack and abduct a woman?" He shook his head. "Bradley never took the initiative in anything and had trouble standing up to anyone. He was a follower, not a leader. For that, I blame his father." He looked at Jane. "You've met Kimball?"

"Yes."

"Then you know how he takes command of everyone. In that family, Kimball makes all the decisions. He chooses what's right for his wife, for his son. Whenever Bradley had to make a choice, even for something as simple as what to eat for dinner, he'd have to mull it over in great detail. He'd have trouble making a split-second choice, and that's what abducting a victim requires, isn't it? You spot her, you want her, you take her. You don't have time to dither over whether you'll do it or not."

"But if he had a chance to plan, couldn't he manage it?"

"He might fantasize about it. But the boy I knew would've been afraid to actually *confront* a girl."

"Then how did he end up at the institute? Isn't that what you specialized in, boys with criminal sexual behaviors?"

"Sexual deviances come in a variety of forms."

"Which form did Bradley's take?"

"Stalking. Obsession. Voyeurism."

"You're telling me he was just a Peeping Tom?"

"It had gone some ways beyond that, which was why his father sent him to the institute."

"How far beyond?"

"First he was caught several times peering into a teenage neighbor's window. Then he progressed to following her at school, and when she very publicly rejected him, he broke into her house while it was empty and set fire to her bed. That's when the judge gave Bradley's parents an ultimatum: Either the boy went for treatment, or he faced incarceration. The Roses chose to send him out of state so the gossip wouldn't find its way into their exclusive circle of friends. Bradley came to the institute and stayed for two years."

"That seems like a pretty long stay."

"It was his father's request. Kimball wanted the boy

fully straightened out so the family wouldn't be embarrassed by him again. The mother wanted him back home, but Kimball prevailed. And Bradley seemed contented enough with us. At the institute, we had woods and hiking trails, even a pond for fishing. He enjoyed the outdoors and he managed to make some friends."

"Friends like Jimmy Otto?"

Hilzbrich grimaced at the mention of that name.

"I see you remember Jimmy, too," said Jane.

"Yes," he said softly. "Jimmy was . . . memorable."

"You've heard that he's dead? He was shot to death twelve years ago, in San Diego. When he broke into a woman's house."

He nodded. "A detective called me from San Diego. He wanted background information. Whether I thought Jimmy might have been committing a criminal act when he was killed."

"I'm assuming you told him yes."

"I've treated hundreds of sociopathic boys, Detective. Boys who've set fires, tortured animals, assaulted classmates. But only a few have really scared me." He met her gaze. "Jimmy Otto was one of them. He was the consummate predator."

"And it must have rubbed off on Bradley."

Hilzbrich blinked. "What?"

"You don't know about their partnership? They hunted together, Bradley and Jimmy. And they met at your institute. You didn't notice?"

"We had only thirty inpatients, so of course they'd

know each other. They would have participated in group therapy together. But these boys were completely different personalities."

"Maybe that's why they worked so well together. They would have complemented each other. One the leader, the other the follower. We don't know who chose the victims, or who did the actual killing, but it's clear they *were* partners. They were compiling a collection together. Until the night Jimmy was killed." She fixed him with a hard gaze. "Now Bradley's carried on without him."

"Then he's turned into a different person than I remember. Look, I knew that *Jimmy* was dangerous. Even as a fifteen-year-old, he scared me. He scared everyone, including his own parents. But Bradley?" He shook his head. "Yes, he's amoral. Yes, you could persuade him to do anything, maybe even kill. But he's a follower, not a leader. He needs someone to direct him, someone to make the decisions."

"Another partner like Jimmy, you mean."

Hilzbrich gave a shudder. "Thank God there aren't a lot of monsters like Jimmy Otto around. I hate to think about what Bradley might have learned from him."

Her gaze dropped to the photos on the table. *He learned enough to carry on alone. Enough to become every bit as monstrous as Jimmy.*

She looked at Hilzbrich. "You say you can't give me Bradley's records."

"I told you. They've been destroyed."

"Then give me Jimmy Otto's."

He hesitated, puzzled by her request. "Why?"

"Jimmy's dead, so he can't complain about patient confidentiality."

"What good will the files do you?"

"He was Bradley's partner. They traveled together, killed together. If I can understand Jimmy, it may give me a window into the man Bradley has become."

He considered her request for a moment, then nodded and stood up. "I'll have to find the file. It may take me a while."

"You keep it here?"

"You think I can afford to pay for storage? All the institute's files are here in my house. If you wait, I'll get it," he said, and walked out of the room.

The grotesque photos on the coffee table had served their purpose, and she couldn't bear looking at them any longer. As she gathered them together, she had a disturbing image of a fourth victim, another dark-haired beauty salted down to jerky, and she wondered if at that very moment Josephine was being ushered into the afterworld.

Her cell phone rang. She dropped the photos to answer it.

"It's me," said Barry Frost.

She hadn't expected a call from him. Steeling herself for an update on his marital woes, she asked gently: "How are you doing?"

"I just spoke to Dr. Welsh."

She had no idea who Dr. Welsh was. "Is that the marriage counselor you were planning to visit? I think it's a great idea. You and Alice talk this out and figure what you need to do."

"No, we haven't seen a counselor yet. I'm not calling about that."

"Then who's Dr. Welsh?"

"She's that biologist from UMass, the one who told me all about bogs and fens. She called me back today, and I thought you'd want to hear this."

Talking about bogs and fens was a big improvement, she thought. At least he wasn't sobbing about Alice. She glanced at her watch, wondering how long it would take Dr. Hilzbrich to find Jimmy Otto's file.

". . . and it's really rare. That's why it took her days to identify it. She had to bring it to some botanist at Harvard, and he just confirmed it."

"I'm sorry," she said. "What are you talking about?"

"Those bits of plant matter we picked out of Bog Lady's hair. There were leaves and some kind of seedpod. Dr. Welsh said it's from a plant called . . ." There was a pause, and Jane heard shuffling pages as he searched his notes. "*Carex oronensis*. That's the scientific name. It's also known as Orono sedge."

"This plant grows in bogs?"

"And in fields. It also likes highly disturbed sites like clearings and roadsides. The specimen looked fresh, so she thinks it got picked up in the corpse's hair when the body was moved. Orono sedge doesn't produce seed-pods until July."

Jane was now paying full attention to what he was saying. "You said this plant is rare. How rare?"

"There's only one area in the world where it grows. The Penobscot River Valley."

"Where's that?"

"Maine. Up around the Bangor area."

She stared out the window at the dense curtain of trees surrounding Dr. Hilzbrich's house. *Maine. Bradley Rose spent two years of his life here.*

"Rizzoli," said Frost. "I want to come back."

"What?"

"I shouldn't have bailed out on you. I want to be on the team again."

"Are you sure you're ready?"

"I need to do this. I need to help."

"You already have," she said. "Welcome back."

As she hung up, Dr. Hilzbrich came into the room, carrying three thick folders. "Here are Jimmy's files," he said, handing them to her.

"I need to know one more thing, Doctor."

"Yes?"

"You said the institute's been shut down. What happened to the property?"

He shook his head. "It was on the market for years but it never sold. Too damn remote to interest any developers. I couldn't keep up with the taxes, so now I'm about to lose it."

"It's currently unoccupied?"

"It's been shuttered for years."

Once again, she glanced at her watch, and considered how many hours of daylight she had. She looked up at Hilzbrich. "Tell me how to get there."

31

Lying awake on the mildewed mattress, Josephine stared into the darkness of her prison and thought of the day, twelve years ago, when she and her mother had fled San Diego. It was the morning after Medea had mopped up the blood and washed the walls and disposed of the man who had invaded their home, forever changing their lives.

They had crossed the border into Mexico, and as their car barreled through the arid scrubland of Baja, Josephine was still shaking with fear. But Medea had been eerily calm and focused, her hands perfectly steady on the steering wheel. Josephine had not understood how her mother could be so composed. She had not understood so many things. That was the day she saw her mother for who she really was.

That was the day she learned she was the daughter of a lioness.

"Everything I've done has been for you," Medea told

her as their car hurtled along blacktop that shimmered with heat. "I did it to keep us together. We are a family, darling, and a family has to stick together." She looked at her terrified daughter, who sat huddled beside her like an injured animal. "Do you remember what I told you about the nuclear family? How anthropologists define it?"

A man had just bled to death in their house. They had just disposed of his body and fled the country. And her mother was calmly lecturing her about anthropological theory?

Despite the incredulity in her daughter's eyes, Medea had continued. "Anthropologists will tell you that a nuclear family is not mother, father, and child. No, it's mother and child. Fathers come and go. They sail off to sea or they march off to war, and often they don't come home. But mother and child are linked forever. Mother and child are the primordial unit. *We* are that unit, and I'll do whatever it takes to protect it, to protect *us*. That's why we have to run."

And so they had run. They'd left a city they'd both loved, a city that had been home to them for three years—long enough for friendships to be made, for bonds to be forged.

In one night, with a single gunshot, all those bonds were snapped forever.

"Look in the glove compartment," Medea had said. "There's an envelope."

The daughter, still dazed, found the envelope and

opened it. Inside were two birth certificates, two passports, and a driver's license. "What is this?"

"Your new name."

The girl opened the passport and saw her own photo—a photo that she vaguely remembered posing for months before, at her mother's insistence. She had not realized it was for a passport.

"What do you think?" Medea asked.

The daughter stared at the name. *Josephine.*

"It's beautiful, isn't it?" said Medea. "It's your new name."

"Why do I need it? Why are we doing this again?" The girl's voice rose to a hysterical shriek. *"Why?"*

Medea pulled over to the side of the road and stopped the car. She grasped her daughter's face in her hands and forced her to meet her gaze. "We're doing this because we have no choice. If we don't run, they'll put me in jail. They'll take you from me."

"But you didn't do anything! You're not the one who killed him! *I did!*"

Medea grabbed her daughter's shoulders and gave her a hard shake. "Don't ever tell that to anyone, do you understand? Not *ever.* If we're ever caught, if the police ever find us, you have to tell them that I shot him. Tell them I killed that man, not you."

"Why do you want me to lie?"

"Because I love you and I don't want you to suffer for

what happened. You shot him to protect me. Now I'm protecting you. So promise me you'll keep this secret. *Promise me.*"

And her daughter had promised, even though the events of that night were still vivid: Her mother sprawled on the bedroom floor, the man standing over her. The alien gleam of a gun on the nightstand. How heavy it had felt when she'd picked it up. How her hands had trembled when she'd pulled the trigger. She, and not her mother, had killed the intruder. That was the secret between them, the secret that they alone shared.

"No one ever has to know you killed him," Medea had said. "This is my problem, not yours. It will never be yours. You're going to grow up and go on with your life. You're going to be happy. And this will stay buried in the past."

But it hasn't stayed buried, thought Josephine as she lay in her prison. *What happened that night has come back to haunt me.*

Cracks of light slowly brightened in the window boards as dawn progressed to midday. It was just enough light for her to barely see the outline of her own hand when she held it in front of her face. A few more days in this place, she thought, and I'll be like a bat, able to navigate in the dark.

She sat up, shaking off the morning chill. She heard the chain rattling outside as the dog lapped up water. She followed suit and sipped from her water jug. Two nights ago, when her captor had cut off her hair, he'd also left behind a fresh bag of bread, and she was enraged to discover there were newly chewed holes in the plastic. The mice had been at it. Find your own damn food, she thought as she greedily wolfed down two slices. I need the energy; I need to find a way to get out of here.

I'll do it for us, Mom. For the primordial unit. You taught me how to survive so I will. Because I am your daughter.

As the hours passed, she flexed her muscles, rehearsed her moves. *I am my mother's daughter.* That was her mantra. Again and again, Josephine hobbled around the cell with her eyes closed, memorizing how many steps it took to travel between the mattress and the wall, the wall and the door. The darkness would be her friend, if she knew how to use it.

Outside, the dog began to bark.

She looked up, her heart suddenly banging hard, as footsteps creaked across the ceiling.

He's back. This is it, this is my chance.

She dropped down onto the mattress and curled into a fetal position, assuming the universal pose of the scared and the defeated. He would see a woman who had given up, a woman who was prepared to die. A woman who would give him no trouble.

The bolt squealed. The door opened.

She saw the glow of his flashlight beaming from the doorway. He came into the room and set down a fresh jug of water, another bag of bread. She remained perfectly still. *Let him wonder if I'm dead.*

His footsteps came closer, and she heard him breathing in the dark above her. "Time is running out, Josephine," he said.

She did not move, even as he bent down and stroked her shorn scalp.

"Doesn't she love you? Doesn't she want to save you? Why doesn't she come?"

Don't say a word. Don't move a muscle. Make him lean closer.

"All these years she's managed to hide from me. Now if she doesn't come out, then she's a coward. Only a coward would let her daughter die."

She felt the mattress sag as he knelt beside her.

"Where is she?" he asked. "Where is Medea?"

Her silence frustrated him. He grasped her wrist and said, "Maybe the hair wasn't enough. Maybe it's time to send them another souvenir. Do you think a finger would do?"

No. God, no. Panic was screaming at her to wrench her hand away, to kick and shriek, anything to escape the ordeal to come. But she remained frozen, still playing the victim paralyzed by despair. He shone the flashlight directly in her face and, blinded by the light, she could not read his expression, could not see anything in the black hollows of his eyes. He was so focused on provoking a response from her that he did not notice what she held in her free hand. He did not notice her muscles snap as tense as a bowstring.

"Maybe if I start cutting," he said, "you'll start talking." He pulled out a knife.

She thrust her hand upward and blindly drove the spike of the high-heeled shoe into his face. She heard the heel thud into flesh and he fell backward, shrieking.

She snatched up the flashlight and slammed it against the floor, smashing the bulb. The room went black. *Darkness is my friend.* She rolled away and scrambled to her feet. She could hear him a few feet away, groveling on the floor, but she could not see him, and he could not see her. They were equally blind.

Only I know how to find the door in the dark.

All the rehearsals, all the preparation, had seared the next moves into her brain. From the edge of the mattress, it was three paces to the wall. Follow the wall seven more steps and she'd reach the door. Though the cast on her leg slowed her down, she wasted no time navigating through the darkness. She paced out seven steps. Eight steps. Nine . . .

Where is the damn door?

She could hear him breathing hard, grunting in frustration as he struggled to get his bearings, to locate her in that pitch-black room.

Don't make a sound. Don't let him know where you are.

She backed up slowly, scarcely daring to breathe, each step placed with delicate care so she would not give away her position. Her hand slid across smooth concrete, then her fingers brushed across wood.

The door.

She turned the knob and pushed. The sudden squeal of hinges seemed deafening.

Move!

Already she heard him lunging toward her, noisy as a bull. She stumbled through and swung the door shut. Just as he slammed against it, she slid the bolt home.

"You can't escape, Josephine!" he yelled.

She laughed and it sounded like a stranger's, a wild and reckless bark of triumph. "Well I just did, asshole!" she shouted back.

"You'll be sorry! We were going to let you live, but not now! *Not now!*"

He began screaming, battering the door in impotent fury as she slowly felt her way up a dark stairway. Her cast set off thuds on the wooden steps. She did not know where the stairs led, and it was almost as dark in here as it had been in her concrete bunker. But with each step she climbed, the stairway seemed to brighten. With each step, she repeated the mantra: *I am my mother's daughter. I am my mother's daughter.*

Halfway up the stairs, she saw cracks of light shining around a closed door at the top of the steps. Only as she neared that door did she suddenly focus on what he'd said only a moment before.

We were going to let you live.

We.

The door ahead suddenly swung open and the glare

of light was painful. She blinked as her eyes adjusted, as she tried to focus on the figure that loomed in the bright rectangle of the doorway.

A figure that she recognized.

32

Twenty years of neglect and hard winters and frost heaves had reduced the Hilzbrich Institute's private road to broken blacktop rippling with invading tree roots. Jane paused at the PROPERTY FOR SALE sign, her Subaru idling as she debated whether to drive down that ruined road. No chain blocked the entrance; anyone could enter the property.

Anyone could be waiting there.

She pulled out her cell phone and saw that she still had reception. She considered calling for a little local backup, then decided it would be a humiliatingly bad idea. She didn't want the town cops laughing about the big-city detective who needed an escort just to deal with the scary Maine woods. *Yeah, Detective, those skunks and porcupines can be deadly.*

She started down the road.

Her Subaru slowly bumped along the fractured pavement, and encroaching shrubs clawed at her doors.

Rolling down her window, she smelled the scent of decomposing leaves and damp earth. The road grew even rougher, and as she steered around potholes, she worried about broken axles and being stranded alone in the woods. That thought made her more uneasy than the far more dangerous prospect of walking down the street of any major city. The city she understood, and she could deal with its dangers.

The woods were alien territory.

At last the trees gave way to a clearing, and she pulled to a stop in an overgrown parking area. Jane stepped out of her car and stared at the abandoned Hilzbrich Institute, which loomed ahead. It looked exactly like the institutional facility it once was, made of stern concrete softened only by landscape shrubbery now surrendering to weedy invaders. She imagined the effect this fortress-like building would have on any family arriving here with a troublesome son. This looked like just the place where a boy would get straightened out once and for all, where there'd be no kid gloves, no half measures. This building promised tough love and firm limits. Desperate parents looking up at that unyielding façade would have seen hope.

But now the building revealed just how hollow those hopes had been. Boards covered most of the windows. Piles of dead leaves had drifted up against the front entrance, and brown stains streaked the walls where rusty water had dripped from clogged roof gutters. It was no wonder that Dr. Hilzbrich had been unable to sell this property: The building was a monstrosity.

Standing in the parking lot, she listened to the wind in the trees, the hum of insects. She heard nothing out of the ordinary, just the sounds of a summer afternoon in the woods. She took out the keys that Dr. Hilzbrich had lent her and walked to the front entrance. But when she saw the door, she abruptly halted.

The lock was broken.

She reached for her weapon and gave the door a gentle nudge with her foot. It swung open, admitting a wedge of light into the darkness beyond. Aiming the beam of her pocket Maglite into the room, she saw empty beer cans and cigarette butts littering the floor. Flies buzzed in the darkness. Her pulse kicked into a fast gallop and her hands were suddenly chilled. She smelled the ripe stench of something dead, something already decaying.

Let it not be Josephine.

She stepped into the building and her shoes crunched across broken glass. Slowly she swept her flashlight around the room and glimpsed graffiti scrawled on the walls. GREG AND ME 4EVAH! KARI SUCKS COCK! It was just typical high school crap, and she moved past it, turning her flashlight toward the far corner. There, her beam froze.

Something dark lay huddled on the floor.

As she crossed toward it, the stench of decaying flesh became overpowering. Staring down at the dead raccoon, she saw maggots wriggling, and she thought of rabies. Wondered if bats lurked in the building.

Gagging on the smell, she fled back outside to the parking lot and desperately washed out her lungs with deep breaths of air. Only then, as she stood facing the trees, did she notice the tire tracks. They led from the paved parking lot into the woods, where twin ruts cut across the soft forest floor. Crushed twigs and broken branches told her the damage to the vegetation was recent.

Following the ruts, she walked a short distance into the woods, where the tracks stopped at the beginning of a hiking path that was too narrow for any car. The trailhead sign was still posted, nailed to a tree.

THE CIRCLE TRAIL

It was one of the institute's old hiking paths. Bradley loved the outdoors, Dr. Hilzbrich had told her. Years ago, the boy had probably walked this trail. The prospect of walking into those woods made her pulse quicken. She glanced down at the tire tracks. Whoever had been here was now gone, but he could return at any time. She could feel the weight of the gun on her hip, but she patted the holster anyway, a reflexive check to reassure herself that her weapon was there.

She started down the path, which was so overgrown in spots that occasionally she found she'd veered off and had to backtrack to find the trail again. The canopy of trees thickened, cutting off the sunlight. She glanced at her cell phone and was dismayed to find that she'd lost the signal. Glancing back, she found that the trees had closed in behind her. But ahead, the woods seemed to open up, and she saw sunlight streaming in.

She started toward the clearing, past trees that were dying or already dead, their trunks reduced to hollow stumps. Suddenly the ground gave way and she sank ankle-deep into muck. Pulling her foot out, she almost lost her shoe. In disgust she looked down at her muddied pant cuffs and thought: I hate the woods. I hate the outdoors. I'm a cop, not a forest ranger.

Then she spotted the shoe print: a man's, size nine or ten.

Every rustle, every whine of a bug, seemed magnified. She saw other prints leading away from the trail, and she followed them, past a clump of cattails. No longer did it matter that her shoes were soaked, her pant legs soiled with mud. All she focused on were those footprints, leading her deeper into the bog. By now she'd completely lost track of where she'd left the main trail. Overhead, the sun told her it was now well past noon, and the woods had gone strangely silent. No birdsong, no wind, only the buzz of mosquitoes around her face.

The footprints turned and veered up the bank, toward dry land.

She paused, bewildered by the change in direction, until she noticed the tree. Encircling its trunk was a loop of nylon rope. The other end of the rope trailed into the bog and vanished beneath the surface of the tea-colored water.

She tested the rope and felt resistance as she tugged. Slowly the length began to emerge from the muck. She was pulling hard now, leaning back with all her weight as more and more rope emerged, tangled with vegetation. Abruptly something broke the surface, something that made her scream and stumble backward in shock. She caught a glimpse of a hollow-eyed face peering at her like a grotesque water nymph.

Then it slowly sank back into the bog.

33

It was dusk by the time the Maine State Police divers finished their search of the bog. The water had been only chest-deep; standing on the dry bank, Jane had watched the divers' heads frequently popping up as they surfaced to get their bearings or to bring up some new object for closer inspection. The water was too murky for a visual search, so they had been forced to rake through the slime and decaying vegetation with their hands, a repulsive task that Jane was grateful she did not have to perform.

Especially when she saw what they finally dredged up.

The woman's body now lay exposed on a plastic tarp, her moss-flecked hair dripping black water. So stained was her skin with tannins, it was impossible to distinguish her race or an obvious cause of death. What they did know was that her death was not accidental; her torso had been weighed down with a bag full of heavy stones. Jane stared at the tormented expression preserved in the woman's blackened face and thought: I hope you were dead when he tied that bag of stones around your waist. When he rolled you over the bank and watched you sink into dark water.

"This is clearly not your missing woman," said Dr. Daljeet Singh.

She looked up at the Maine medical examiner who stood beside her on the bank. Dr. Singh's white Sikh headdress stood out in the fading light, making him easy to spot among the more conventionally garbed investigators gathered at the scene. When he'd arrived, she'd been startled to see the exotic figure step out of the truck, not at all what she expected to encounter in the North Woods. But judging by his well-worn L.L. Bean boots and the hiking gear he packed in the back of his truck, Dr. Singh was well acquainted with Maine's rough terrain. Certainly he'd come better prepared than she had, in her city pantsuit.

"The young woman you're looking for was abducted four days ago?" asked Dr. Singh.

"This isn't her," said Jane.

"No, this woman has been submerged for some time. So have those other specimens." Dr. Singh pointed to the animal remains that had also been pulled up from the bog. There were two well-preserved cats and a dog, plus the skeletal remnants of unidentifiable creatures. The stone-filled sacks tied around all the bodies left no doubt that these unfortunate victims had not simply wandered into the mire and drowned.

"This killer has been experimenting with animals," said Dr. Singh. He turned to the woman's corpse. "And it appears he's perfected his preservation technique."

Jane shuddered and looked across the bog at the fading sunset. Frost had told her that bogs were magical places, home to a wondrous variety of orchids and mosses and dragonflies. She didn't see the magic that evening as she stared across the undulating surface of waterlogged peat. What she saw was a cold stew of corpses.

"I'll do the autopsy tomorrow," said Dr. Singh. "If you'd like to observe, you're certainly welcome."

What she really wanted to do was drive home to Boston. Take a hot shower, kiss her daughter good night, and climb into bed with Gabriel. But her work here was not yet finished.

"The autopsy will be in Augusta?" she asked.

"Yes, around eight o'clock. Can I expect you?"

"I'll be there." She took a deep breath and straightened. "I guess I'd better find a place to stay for the night."

"The Hawthorn Motel's a few miles down the road. It serves a good breakfast. Not that awful continental stuff, but lovely omelets and pancakes."

"Thanks for the tip," she said. *Only a pathologist could stand over a dripping corpse and talk so enthusiastically about pancakes.*

She walked back up the trail by flashlight, the path now well marked by little flags of police tape. Emerging from the trees, she found that the parking lot was starting to empty out; only a few official vehicles remained. The state police had already searched the building, but all they'd found was trash and the putrefying remains of that raccoon she had spotted earlier. They had not found Josephine or Bradley Rose.

But he's been here, she thought, gazing toward the woods. He parked near these trees. He walked the trail to the bog. There he tugged on a rope and hauled one of his keepsakes from the water, the way a fisherman hauls in his catch.

She climbed into her car and drove back along that crumbling road, her poor Subaru jouncing across potholes that seemed even more treacherous in the dark. Moments after she turned onto the main road, her cell phone rang.

"I've been trying to reach you for at least two hours," said Frost.

"There was no reception at the bog. They finished searching and found only the one body. I'm wondering if he has another stash—"

"Where are you now?" Frost cut in.

"I'm staying here for the night. I want to watch the autopsy tomorrow."

"I mean right *now*, where are you?"

"I'm going to check into a motel. Why?"

"What's the name of the motel?"

"I think it's called the Hawthorn. It's around here somewhere."

"Okay, I'll see you there in a few hours."

"You're coming up to Maine?"

"I'm already on my way. And someone's joining us."

"Who?"

"We'll talk about it when we get there."

Jane stopped first at a local drugstore for new underwear and socks and then to pick up a take-out
pepperoni pizza. While her hand-washed pants hung
drying in the bathroom, she sat in her room at the
Hawthorn Motel, eating pizza as she read Jimmy Otto's
file. There were three volumes, one for each year he had
been a student at the Hilzbrich Institute. No, not a
student—an inmate, she thought, remembering the ugly
concrete building, the remote location. A place to
securely segregate from society the sort of boys you
didn't want anywhere near your daughters.

Jimmy Otto, most of all.

She paused at the transcript of what Jimmy had said
during a private therapy session. He'd been only sixteen
years old.

When I was thirteen, I saw this picture in a history
book. It was in a concentration camp where all these
women were killed in the gas chambers. Their bodies
were naked, lying in a row. I think about that picture a
lot, about all those women. Dozens and dozens of them,
just lying there like they're waiting for me to do whatever I want with them. Fuck them in any hole. Poke

sticks in their eyes. Slice off their nipples. I want there
to be a bunch of women at one time, a whole row of
them. Or it's not a party, is it?

But how do you collect more than one at a time? Is
there some way to keep a corpse from rotting, a way to
keep it fresh? I'd like to find out, because it's no fun if a
woman just rots away and leaves me . . .

A knock on her motel room door made Jane snap
straight. She dropped the half-eaten slice of pizza in the
box and called out, in a none-too-steady voice: "Yes?
Who is it?"

"It's me," Barry Frost answered.

"Just a second." She went into the bathroom and
pulled on her still-damp slacks. By the time she got to
the door, her nerves were steady again, her heart no
longer racing. She opened the door and found a surprise
awaiting her.

Frost was not alone.

The woman standing beside him was in her forties,
dark-haired and strikingly beautiful. She wore faded
blue jeans and a black pullover, but on her lean, athletic
frame even that casual garb looked elegant. She said not
a word to Jane but slipped right past her into the room
and ordered: "Lock the door."

Even after Frost had turned the dead bolt, the woman
did not relax. She crossed immediately to the window and
yanked the drapes more tightly shut, as though the
narrowest chink might admit the gaze of unfriendly eyes.

"Who are you?" Jane asked.

The woman turned to face her. And in that instant, even before Jane heard the answer, she saw it in the woman's face, in the arched brows, the chiseled cheekbones. A face you'd see painted on a Greek urn, she thought. Or on the wall of an Egyptian tomb.

"My name is Medea Sommer," the woman said. "I'm Josephine's mother."

34

"But . . . you're supposed to be dead," Jane said, stunned.

The woman gave a tired laugh. "That's the story, anyway."

"Josephine thinks you are."

"That's what I told her to say. Unfortunately, not everyone believes her." Medea crossed to the lamp and turned it off, plunging the room into darkness. Then she went to the window and peered out through the slit in the curtains.

Jane glanced at Frost, who was barely a silhouette standing beside her in the shadows. "How did you find her?" she whispered.

"I didn't," he said. "She found me. You were the one she really wanted to speak to. When she found out you'd left for Maine, she tracked down my phone number instead."

"Why didn't you tell me this on the phone?"

"I wouldn't let him," said Medea, her back still turned to them, her gaze still on the street. "What I'm going to tell you now has to stay in this room. It can't be shared with your colleagues. It can't be whispered anywhere. It's the only way I can stay dead. The only way Tari—Josephine—has any chance of a normal life." Even in the dark, Jane could see the taut outline of the curtain she was clutching. "My daughter is all that matters to me," she said softly.

"Then why did you abandon her?" asked Jane.

Medea spun around to face her. "I never abandoned her! I would have been here weeks ago, if only I'd known what was happening."

"*If only you'd known?* From what I understand, she's been fending for herself for years. And you were nowhere around."

"I had to stay away from her."

"Why?"

"Because being around me could mean her death." Once again, Medea turned toward the street. "This has nothing to do with Josephine. She's just a pawn for them. A way to draw me out into the open. The one he really wants is *me*."

"You care to explain that?"

With a sigh, Medea sank into a chair by the window. She was just a faceless shadow sitting there, a soft voice in the darkness. "Let me tell you a story," she said. "About a girl who got involved with the wrong boy. A girl so naïve that she couldn't recognize the difference between sweet infatuation and . . ." She paused. "Fatal obsession."

"You're talking about yourself."

"Yes."

"And who was the boy?"

"Bradley Rose." Medea released a shuddering breath, and her dark form seemed to shrink in the chair, as though folding in on itself for protection. "I was only twenty. What does any girl know at twenty? It was my first time out of the country, my first excavation. In the desert, everything looked different. The sky was bluer, the colors were brighter. And when a shy boy smiles at you, when he starts to leave you little gifts, you think you're in love."

"You were in Egypt with Kimball Rose."

Medea nodded. "The Cambyses dig. When I was offered the chance to go, I jumped at it. So did dozens of other students. There we were in the western desert, living our dreams! Digging by day, sleeping in tents at night. I've never seen so many stars, so many beautiful stars." She paused. "It was a place where anyone could have fallen in love. I was just a girl from Indio, ready to finally start living. And there was Bradley, the son of Kimball Rose himself. He was brilliant and quiet and shy. There's something about a shy man that makes you think he's harmless."

"But he wasn't."

"I didn't know what he really was. I didn't know a lot of things until it was too late."

"What was he?"

"A monster." Medea's head lifted in the darkness. "I didn't see it at first. What I saw was a boy who looked at me with adoring eyes. Who talked with me about the one subject we both loved most. Who started bringing me little gifts. We worked in the trench together. We ate every meal together. Eventually we slept together." She paused. "That's when things began to change."

"How?"

"It was as if he no longer considered me a separate person. I'd become part of him. As if he'd devoured me, absorbed me. If I walked to the other side of the camp, he followed me. If I spoke to anyone else, he insisted on knowing what we'd talked about. If I even looked at another man, he became upset. He was always watching, always spying."

It was such an old story, thought Jane, the same story that had played out so many times between other lovers. A story that too often ended with homicide detectives standing at a bloody crime scene. Medea was one of the lucky ones; she had managed to stay alive.

Yet she had never really escaped.

"It was Gemma who took me aside and pointed out the obvious," said Medea.

"Gemma Hamerton?"

Medea nodded. "She was one of the grad students at the site. A few years older than me, and a hundred years wiser. She saw what was happening, and she told me I needed to assert myself. And if he didn't back off, then

I should tell him to go to hell. Oh, Gemma was good at that, standing up for herself. But I wasn't strong enough then. I wasn't able to break away."

"What happened?"

"Gemma went to Kimball. She told him to get his son under control. Bradley must have learned about the conversation, because the next thing he said to me was that I must never talk to Gemma again."

"I hope you told him where to go."

"I should have," Medea said softly. "But I didn't have the backbone. It seems impossible to believe now. When I think back to what sort of girl I was, I don't recognize myself. I don't know that person. That utterly pitiful victim who couldn't even save herself."

"How did you finally break away from him?"

"It was what he did to Gemma. One night, while she was sleeping, her tent flap was sewn shut. Then the tent was doused with gasoline and set on fire. I was the one who managed to slice the tent open and pull her out."

"Bradley actually tried to kill her?"

"No one could prove it, but I knew. That's when I finally understood what he was capable of. I got on a plane and came home."

"But it wasn't over."

"No, it wasn't." Medea stood and went back to the window. "It was just the beginning." By now, Jane's eyes had adjusted to the darkness and she could see the woman's pale hand clutching the curtain. Could see her shoulders momentarily tense as a car's headlights slowly passed by on the street and then moved on.

"I was pregnant," Medea said softly.

Jane stared at her in astonishment. "Josephine is *Bradley's* daughter?"

"Yes." She turned and faced Jane. "But she can't *ever* know that."

"She told us her father was a French archaeologist."

"All her life I've lied to her. I told her that her father was a good man who died before she was born. I don't know if she actually believes me, but it's the story I've stuck to."

"And what about the other story you told her? Why you kept moving and changing your names? She thinks you were running from the police."

Medea shrugged. "It did explain things, didn't it?"

"But it's not true."

"I had to give her *some* reason, a reason that wouldn't terrify her. Better to be running from the police than from a monster."

Especially when that monster is your own father.

"If you were being stalked, why run? Why not just go to the police?"

"You think I didn't try that? A few months after I came home, Bradley turned up at my college campus. He told me we were soul mates. He told me I belonged to him. I told him I never wanted to see him again. He started following me, sending me flowers every fucking day. I threw them away and called the police and even managed to get him arrested. But then his father sent his attorneys to take care of the problem. When your father's Kimball Rose, you're untouchable." She paused. "Then it got worse. Much worse."

"How?"

"Bradley showed up one day with an old friend. Someone who scared me even more than Bradley ever did."

"Jimmy Otto."

Medea seemed to shudder at the mention of that name. "Bradley could pass for normal—just another quiet man. But with Jimmy, you only had to look in his eyes to know he was different. They were black as a shark's. When he stared at you, you just knew he was thinking about what he'd like to do to you. And he became obsessed with me, too.

"So they both followed me. I'd catch a glimpse of Jimmy staring at me in the library. Or Bradley peeking in my window. They were playing a psychological game of tag team, trying to break me down. Trying to make me look crazy."

Jane looked at Frost. "Even then," she said, "they were already hunting together."

"Finally, I left the university," said Medea. "By then I was eight months pregnant, and my grandmother was dying. I went back to Indio and had the baby. Within a few weeks, Bradley and Jimmy showed up in town. I filed a restraining order and got them both arrested. This time, I was going to put them away. I had a baby to protect and it had to end there."

"But it didn't. You chickened out and dropped the charges against Bradley."

"Not exactly."

"What do you mean, not exactly? You did drop the charges."

"I made a deal with the Devil. Kimball Rose. He wanted his son free of prosecution. I wanted my daughter to be safe. So I dropped the charges, and Kimball wrote me a big check. Enough money to buy my daughter and me a new life, with new names."

Jane shook her head. "You took the money and ran? It must have been a hell of a check."

"It wasn't the money. Kimball used my daughter against me. He threatened to take her from me if I didn't accept his offer. He's her grandfather, and he had an army of lawyers to fight me. I had no choice, so I took the money and dropped the charges. *She's* the reason I did it, the reason I've never stopped running. To keep her away from that family, away from anyone who might hurt her. You understand that, don't you? That a mother will do anything to protect her child?"

Jane nodded. She understood completely.

Medea returned to the chair and sank down with a sigh. "I thought if I kept my daughter safe, she'd never know what it's like to be hunted. She'd grow up fearless and smart. A warrior woman—that's what I wanted her to be. What I always told her to strive for. And she *was* growing up smart. And fearless. She didn't know enough to be afraid." Medea paused. "Until San Diego."

"The shooting in her bedroom."

Medea nodded. "That's the night she learned she could never be fearless again. We packed up the next day and drove to Mexico. Ended up in Cabo San Lucas, where we lived for four years. We were fine there and we were hidden." She sighed. "But girls grow up. They turn eighteen and insist on making their own choices. She wanted to go to college and study archaeology. Like mother, like daughter." She gave a sad laugh.

"You let her go?"

"Gemma promised to keep an eye on her, so I thought it would be safe. She had a new name, a new identity. I didn't think that Jimmy would ever be able to find her."

There was a long silence as Jane took in what Medea had just said. "*Jimmy?* But Jimmy Otto's dead."

Medea's head lifted. "What?"

"You should know that. You shot him in San Diego."

"No."

"You shot him in the back of the head. Dragged his body outside and buried him."

"That's not true. That wasn't Jimmy."

"Then who was buried in the backyard?"

"It was Bradley Rose."

35

"Bradley Rose?" said Jane. "That's not what the police in San Diego told us."

"You think I couldn't recognize the father of my own child?" said Medea. "It wasn't Jimmy who broke into my daughter's bedroom that night. It was *Bradley*. Oh, I'm sure that Jimmy was lurking around nearby, and the gunshot probably scared him off. But I knew he would be back. I knew we had to move fast. So we packed up and left the next morning."

"The body was identified as Jimmy's," said Frost.

"Who identified him?"

"His sister."

"Then she made a mistake. Because I know it *wasn't* Jimmy."

Jane switched on the lamp and Medea shrank from the light, as though the glow from a mere sixty-watt bulb was radioactive. "This is not making sense. How could Jimmy Otto's own sister make a mistake like that?" She snatched up his psychiatric file from the bed and scanned Dr. Hilzbrich's notes. She quickly spotted what she was looking for.

"His sister's name was Carrie." Jane looked at Frost. "Get Crowe on the line. Ask him to find out where Carrie Otto lives."

He pulled out his cell phone.

"I don't understand," said Medea. "What does Jimmy's sister have to do with this?"

Jane flipped through the notes in Jimmy's Hilzbrich Institute chart, searching for any and all references to Carrie Otto. Only now that she was specifically searching for them did she realize how many times Carrie had been mentioned.

> *Sister is visiting again, second time today.*
> *Carrie stayed past visiting hours; reminded she must adhere to rules.*
> *Carrie has been asked not to call so often.*
> *Carrie caught smuggling in cigarettes. Visiting privileges suspended for two weeks.*
> *Sister visiting . . . Sister visiting . . . Carrie here again.*

And finally she came to an entry that stopped her cold:

> *Far more extensive family counseling is indicated. Carrie has been referred to Bangor child psychiatrist to deal with issue of abnormal sibling attachment.*

Frost hung up his cell phone. "Carrie Otto lives in Framingham."

"Tell Crowe to get a team there now. With backup."

"He's already moving on it."

"What's happening?" Medea cut in. "Why are you so focused on the sister?"

"Because Carrie Otto told the police that the body you buried was her brother's," said Jane.

"But I know it wasn't. Why did she say that?"

"There was a warrant out for his arrest," explained Frost. "In connection with a woman's disappearance in Massachusetts. If the authorities believed he was dead, they'd stop looking for him. He could become invisible. She must have lied to protect him."

"Carrie is the key," said Jane. "And we know where she lives."

"You think my daughter is there," said Medea.

"If she isn't, I'm betting that Carrie knows where he's keeping her." Jane was pacing the room now, checking her watch. Mentally calculating how long it would take for Crowe and his team to reach Framingham. She wanted to be there with him, knocking on that door, pushing into that house. Searching those rooms for Josephine. *I should be the one to find her.* It was after midnight, but she was wide awake, energy fizzing like carbonation through her bloodstream. All this time, she thought, we've been chasing a dead man when we should have focused on Jimmy Otto. The invisible man.

The only patient who really scared me, Dr. Hilzbrich

had said about Jimmy. *He scared everyone. Even his own parents.*

Jane stopped and turned to Frost. "Do you remember what Crowe said about Jimmy's parents? About how they were killed?"

"It was an accident, wasn't it? A plane crash."

"Didn't it happen in Maine? They bought a house in Maine, to be close to Jimmy."

Once again, Jane picked up the psychiatric file and flipped to the front page where the patient info was typed. Jimmy's parents were Howard and Anita Otto, and they had two addresses. The first was their primary residence in Massachusetts. The second address, in Maine, had been added later; it was handwritten in ink.

Frost was already dialing Boston PD on his cell phone. "I need you to check a property tax record for me," he said, looking over Jane's shoulder at the address. "State of Maine, a town called Saponac. One Sixty-five Valley Way." A moment later, he hung up and looked at Jane. "It's owned by the Evergreen Trust, whatever that is. She'll call us back with more information."

Once again Jane was in motion, frustrated and impatient. "It can't be that far from here. We could just drive by and take a look."

"It's been decades since they died. That house has probably changed hands several times."

"Or maybe it's still in the family."

"If you just hang on, we'll get that information on Evergreen."

But Jane was in no mood to wait. She was a racehorse at the starting gate, ready to move. "I'm going," she said, and glanced toward the dresser where she'd left her keys.

"Let's take my car," said Frost, already at the door. "We'll need the GPS."

"I'm coming, too," said Medea.

"No," said Jane.

"She's *my* daughter."

"That's why you need to stay out of the way. So we won't be distracted." Jane holstered her weapon and the sight of that gun should have said it all. *This is serious business. This is not for civilians.*

"I want to do something," Medea insisted. "I *need* to do something."

Jane turned and saw a woman as determined as any she had ever met, a woman primed for battle. But this battle was not Medea's; it could not be.

"The best thing you can do tonight is stay right here," said Jane. "And lock the door."

Valley Way was a lonely rural road lined by woods so thick that they could not make out the residences through the trees. The number posted on the roadside mailbox told them they were at the right address, but all they could see in the dark was the beginning of a gravel driveway that trailed off into woods. Jane pulled open the mailbox and found a damp accumulation of advertising circulars. All were addressed to OCCUPANT.

"If anyone lives here," she said, "they haven't cleaned out their mailbox lately. I don't think anyone's home."

"Then no one should object if we take a closer look," said Frost.

Their car slowly rolled down the driveway, gravel crackling under the tires. The trees were so dense that they did not see the house until they rounded a bend and it suddenly stood before them. Once it might have been a handsome vacation cottage, with a gabled roof and a broad front porch, but weeds had sprung up and engulfed the foundation and hungry vines had clambered up and over the porch railings, as though determined to smother the house and any unfortunate occupants.

"Looks abandoned," said Frost.

"I'm going to get out and take a look around." Jane reached for the handle and was about to open the door when she heard the warning clank of a chain, a sound as ominous as a snake's rattle.

Something black bounded out of the darkness.

She gasped and jerked back as the pit bull slammed against her door, as claws scrabbled at glass and white teeth gleamed in the window.

"Jesus!" she cried. "Where the hell did he come from?"

The dog's barking was frantic now, claws scraping as though to tear through metal.

"I don't like this," said Frost.

She laughed, a wildly unhinged sound in the closeness of that car. "I'm not loving this too much myself."

"No, I mean I don't like the fact he's tied up on that chain. This house looks abandoned, so who's feeding the dog?"

She stared at the house, at dark windows that seemed to gaze back at her like malevolent eyes. "You're right," she said softly. "This is all wrong."

"It's time to call for backup," said Frost and he reached for his cell phone. He never got the chance to dial.

The first gunshot shattered the window.

Fragments of stinging glass peppered Jane's face. She dove beneath the dashboard as a second explosion rocked the night, as another bullet slammed into the car. Frost, too, had ducked for cover, and she saw his face was tight with panic as he crouched only inches away from her, both fumbling for their weapons.

A third bullet pinged into metal.

An ominous odor seeped into the car. The fumes stung Jane's eyes and seared her throat. In that instant she and Frost stared at each other, and she saw that he, too, had registered the smell.

Gasoline.

Almost simultaneously, they each kicked open their doors. Jane flung herself out of the car and tumbled away just as the first flames whooshed to life. She could not see if Frost had made it out the other side; she could only hope that he had scrambled away safely, because an instant later the gas tank exploded. Windows shattered and a brilliant inferno spouted flames skyward.

As glass pelted the ground, Jane scrambled for cover. Thorny underbrush ripped through her sleeves, clawed at her arms. She rolled behind a tree and gripped crumbling bark as she frantically tried to catch a glimpse of their assailant, but all she saw were flames consuming what remained of Frost's car. The dog, excited to a frenzy by the fire, ran howling back and forth across the yard, chain clattering behind it.

Another gunshot exploded. She heard a cry of pain, the crash of snapping underbrush.

Frost is down!

Through the obscuring veil of smoke and fire, she saw the shooter emerge from the house and step onto the porch. The woman's blond hair reflected the glow of the flames. Rifle raised, she moved into the light. Only then could Jane see the face of Debbie Duke.

No, not Debbie. Carrie Otto.

Carrie started down the porch steps, her rifle poised to finish off Frost.

Jane fired first. Even as she squeezed the trigger, she wanted it to be a killing shot. She felt no fear, no hesitation, only cold, controlled rage that took possession of her body and guided her aim. In quick succession she fired off *one, two, three* shots. They slammed into her target like repeated punches to the chest. Carrie jerked backward, dropping the rifle, and collapsed onto the porch steps.

Lungs heaving, Jane eased forward. Still clutching her weapon, her gaze stayed on her target. Carrie lay sprawled against the steps, still alive and moaning, her half-open eyes reflecting the satanic glow of the flames. Jane glanced toward Frost, and saw him lying at the edge of the woods.

Be alive. Please be alive.

She managed to take only a few steps toward him when the pit bull slammed into her back.

She had thought she was beyond the reach of the dog's chain, and did not see it hurtling at her, did not have time to brace herself against the impact. His attack sent her sprawling forward. She put out her hands to break the fall, and as she landed, she heard a bone snap and her wrist collapsed beneath her. The pain was so excruciating that even the grip of the dog's jaws on her shoulder seemed merely troublesome, a nuisance to be shaken off before dealing with this true agony. Twisting, she rolled onto her back, her weight landing on top of the dog, but it would not release her. The gun had fallen out of reach. Her right hand was useless. She could not beat the animal away, could not reach back and grip his throat. So she rammed her elbow into his belly, again and again, and heard ribs crack.

Yelping in pain, the dog released its grip. She rolled away and scrambled to her knees. Only then, as she stared down at the whimpering dog, did she see that the chain was no longer attached to the collar. How had he gotten free? Who had released him?

The answer emerged from the shadows.

Jimmy Otto moved into the firelight, pushing Josephine before him as a shield. Jane lunged for her fallen weapon, but a gunshot made her flinch back as the bullet kicked up dirt only inches from her hand. Even if she could reach her gun she did not dare return fire, not with Josephine standing in the way. Jane knelt helpless in the dirt as Jimmy Otto came to a halt beside the burning car, his face aglow in the light of the crackling flames, his temple blackened by an ugly bruise. Josephine tottered against him, unsteady in her leg cast, her head shorn of all hair. Jimmy pressed his gun to her temple, and Josephine's eyes snapped wide with fear.

"Move away from the gun," he ordered Jane. *"Do it!"*

Supporting her broken wrist with her left hand, Jane struggled to her feet. The fracture was so painful that nausea clenched her stomach, shutting down her brain just when she needed it most. She stood swaying as black spots danced before her eyes and a cold sweat bloomed on her skin.

Jimmy looked down at his wounded sister, who was still slumped back against the porch steps, moaning. In one ruthless glance, he seemed to decide that Carrie was beyond saving and no longer worth his attention.

He refocused on Jane. "I'm tired of waiting around," he said. "Tell me where she is."

Jane shook her head. The black spots swirled. "I have no idea what you want, Jimmy."

"*Where the fuck is she?*"

"Who?"

Her answer enraged him. Without warning he fired his gun just above Josephine's head. "Medea," he said. "I know she's back. And you're the one she'd contact, so where is she?"

That shocking explosion swept her brain clear. Despite her pain and nausea, Jane was fully focused now, her attention only on Jimmy. "Medea's dead," she said.

"No, she's not. She's alive. I know damn well she is. And it's time for payback."

"For killing Bradley? She did what she had to do."

"So will I." He pressed the gun to Josephine's head, and in that instant Jane realized that he was fully prepared to pull the trigger. "If Medea won't come back to save her daughter, maybe she will for the funeral."

From the darkness, a voice called out: "Here I am, Jimmy. I'm right here."

He froze, staring toward the trees. "Medea?"

She followed us here.

Medea strode out of the woods, moving without hesitation, without any sign of fear. The mother lion had arrived to save her cub, and she moved with grim purpose toward the battle, coming to a halt only a few yards from Jimmy. They faced each other in the circle of firelight. "I'm the one you want. Let my daughter go."

"You haven't changed," he murmured in wonder. "All these years and you're exactly the same."

"So are you, Jimmy," Medea answered without a note of irony.

"You were the only one he ever wanted. The one he couldn't have."

"But Bradley's not here now. So why are you doing this?"

"This is for me. This is to make you pay." He pressed his gun against Josephine's temple, and for the first time Jane glimpsed terror in Medea's face. If the woman felt any fear at all, it was not for herself but for her daughter. The key to destroying Medea had always been Josephine.

"You don't want my daughter, Jimmy. You have me." Medea was in control now, her fear disguised by a cool glaze of contempt. "I'm the reason you took her, the reason you've been playing these games with the police. Well, here I am. Let her go and I'm all yours."

"Are you?" He gave Josephine a shove, and she stumbled away to safety. He turned his gun instead on Medea. Even with that barrel pointed at her, she managed to look utterly calm. She cast a glance at Jane, a look that said: *I have his attention. The rest is up to you.* She took a step toward Jimmy, toward the gun aimed at her chest. Her voice turned silky, even seductive. "You wanted me just as much as Bradley did. Didn't you? The first time I met you, I saw it in your eyes. What you wanted to do to me. The same thing you did to all those other women. Did you fuck them while they were still alive, Jimmy? Or did you wait until they were dead? Because that's how you like them, isn't it? Cold. Dead. Yours for eternity."

He said nothing, just kept staring as she moved closer. As she enticed him with the possibilities. For years he and Bradley had pursued her, and here she finally was, within his reach. His and his alone.

Jane's weapon lay on the ground only a few feet away. She inched toward it, mentally rehearsing her moves. Drop to the ground, snatch up the gun. Fire. She'd have to do all this with only the use of her left hand. She might be able to get off one shot, two at the most, before Jimmy returned fire. No matter how fast I am, she thought, I won't be able to bring him down in time. Either Medea or I could die tonight.

Medea kept moving toward Jimmy. "All these years, you've been hunting me," said Medea softly. "Now here I am and you don't really want to end it right here and now, do you? You don't really want the hunt to be over."

"But it is over." He raised the gun and Medea went stock-still. This was the ending she'd been running from all these years, an ending she could not alter with pleading or seduction. If she had walked into this thinking she could control the monster, she now saw her mistake.

"This isn't about what I want," said Jimmy. "I was told to finish it. And that's what I'm going to do." The muscles in his forearms snapped taut as he prepared to fire.

Jane lunged for her weapon. But as her left hand closed around the grip, there was a blast of gunfire. She pivoted and the night swirled by in slow motion, a dozen details assaulting her senses at once. She saw Medea drop to her knees, arms crossed protectively over her head. She felt the crackling heat from the flames and the strange heaviness of the weapon in her left hand as she brought it up and her fingers tightened into a firing grip.

But even as Jane squeezed off the first round, she realized that Jimmy Otto had already staggered back, that her bullet was punching into a target that was already bloodied by an earlier gunshot.

Silhouetted by the flames behind him, he tumbled backward like a doomed Icarus, his arms flung out at his sides, his torso in free fall. He slumped back across the hood of the burning car and his hair caught fire, wreathing his head in flames. With a shriek he lurched away from the car. His shirt ignited. He staggered around the yard in an agonized death dance and collapsed.

"No!" Carrie Otto's anguished moan was not a human sound at all, but the guttural cry of a dying animal. She crawled slowly, painfully toward her brother, trailing a black smear of blood across the gravel.

"Don't leave me, baby. Don't leave me."

She rolled on top of his body, heedless of the flames, desperate to smother the fire.

"Jimmy. *Jimmy!*"

Even as her hair and clothes ignited, even as the fire seared her skin, she clung to her brother in an agonized embrace. They remained locked together, their flesh melding into one, and the flames consumed them.

Medea rose unhurt to her feet. But her gaze was not focused on the burning bodies of Jimmy and Carrie Otto; she stared instead toward the woods.

Toward Barry Frost, who had sagged backward against a tree, his weapon still clutched in his hands.

36

The label of hero did not sit comfortably on Barry Frost's shoulders.

He looked embarrassed rather than heroic, sitting in his hospital bed, wearing only the flimsy johnny gown. He'd been transferred to Boston Medical Center two days earlier, and since then a steady stream of well-wishers, everyone from the police commissioner to the Boston PD cafeteria staff, had made the pilgrimage to his hospital room. That afternoon, when Jane arrived, she found three visitors still lingering amid the jungle of flower arrangements and Mylar GET WELL balloons. From kids to old ladies, everybody liked Frost, she thought as she watched from the doorway. And she understood why. He was the Boy Scout who'd cheerfully shovel your sidewalk and jump-start your car and climb a tree to rescue your cat.

He'd even save your life.

She waited for the other visitors to leave before she

finally stepped into his room. "Can you stand one more?" she asked.

He gave her a wan smile. "Hey. I was hoping you'd stick around."

"This seems to be the happening place. I have to fight off all your groupies just to get in." With her right arm now in a cast, Jane felt clumsy as she dragged a chair over to the bed and sat down. "Geez, will you look at us two," she said. "What a pathetic pair of wounded war buddies."

Frost started to laugh, but caught himself as the motion set off fresh pain from his laparotomy incision. He hunched forward, grimacing in discomfort.

"I'll get the nurse," she said.

"No." Frost held up his hand. "I can handle this. I don't want any more morphine."

"Screw the macho stuff. I say take the drugs."

"I don't want to be doped up. Tonight I need to have my head clear."

"What for?"

"Alice is coming to see me."

It was painful to hear the hopeful note in his voice, and she looked away so he could not read the pity in her eyes. Alice didn't deserve this man. He was one of the good guys, one of the decent guys, and that was why he was going to get his heart broken.

"Maybe I should leave," she said.

"No. Not yet. Please." Carefully he settled back against the pillows and released a cautious breath.

Trying to look cheerful, he said: "Tell me the latest news."

"It's been confirmed. Debbie Duke was really Carrie Otto. According to Mrs. Willebrandt, Carrie showed up at the museum back in April and offered to help out as a volunteer."

"April? That's soon after Josephine was hired."

Jane nodded. "It took only a few months for Carrie to become indispensable to the museum. She must have stolen Josephine's keys. Maybe she was the one who left that bag of hair in Dr. Isles's backyard. She gave Jimmy complete access to the building. In every way, brother and sister were a team."

"Why would any sister go along with a brother like Jimmy?"

"We caught a glimpse of it that night. *Inappropriate sibling attachment* was what the therapist wrote in Jimmy's psychiatric file. I spoke to Dr. Hilzbrich yesterday, and he said Carrie was every bit as pathological as her brother. She'd do anything for him, maybe even maintain his dungeon. The crime scene unit found multiple hairs and fibers in that Maine cellar. The mattress had bloodstains from more than one victim. Neighbors on the road said they'd sometimes see both Jimmy and Carrie in the area at the same time. They'd stay in the house for several weeks, then they'd disappear for months."

"I've heard of husband-and-wife serial killer teams. But a brother and sister?"

"The same dynamic applies. A weak personality coupled with a powerful one. Jimmy was the dominator, so overwhelming that he could exert total control over people like his sister. And Bradley Rose. While Bradley was alive, he helped Jimmy in the hunt. He preserved the victims and found places to store their bodies."

"So he was just Jimmy's follower."

"No, they both got something out of the relationship. That's Dr. Hilzbrich's theory. Jimmy fulfilled his teenage fantasies of collecting dead women while Bradley acted out his obsession with Medea Sommer. *She* was what they had in common, the one prey they both wanted, but could never catch. Even after Bradley died, Jimmy never stopped looking for her."

"But instead he found her daughter."

"He probably spotted Josephine's photo in the newspaper. She's the spitting image of Medea, and she's the right age to be her daughter. She's even in the same profession. It wouldn't take much digging to learn that Josephine wasn't who she claimed to be. So he watched her, waiting to see if her mother would turn up."

Frost shook his head. "That was some crazy obsession he had with Medea. After all these years, you'd think he'd move on."

"Remember Cleopatra? Helen of Troy? Men were obsessed with them, too."

"Helen of Troy?" He laughed. "Man, this archaeology thing is rubbing off on you. You sound like Dr. Robinson."

"The point is, men get obsessed. A guy will cling to a particular woman for years." She added, quietly: "Even a woman who doesn't love him."

His face reddened and he looked away.

"Some people just can't move on," she said, "and they waste their lives waiting for someone they can't have." She thought of Maura Isles, another person who wanted someone she couldn't have, who was trapped by her own desires, her own poor choice of a lover. On the night Maura had needed him, Father Daniel Brophy was not there for her. Instead, it was Anthony Sansone who had taken her into his house. It was Sansone who had called Jane to confirm it was safe to let Maura return home. Sometimes, thought Jane, the person who could make you happiest is the one you overlook, the one who waits patiently in the wings.

They heard a knock on the door, and Alice stepped in. Dressed in a sleek skirt suit, she looked blonder and more stunning than Jane remembered, but her beauty had no warmth. She held herself like marble, perfectly chiseled, meant only for looking but not touching. The women exchanged tense but polite greetings, like two rivals for the same man's attention. For years they had shared Frost, Jane as his partner, Alice as his wife, yet Jane felt no connection with this woman.

She stood to leave, but as she reached the door, she couldn't resist a parting remark. "Be nice to him. He's a hero."

*   *   *

Frost saved me, now I'm going to have to save him, Jane thought as she walked out of the hospital and climbed into her car. Alice was going to shatter his heart, the way you shatter flesh with liquid nitrogen and a sharp whack with a hammer. Jane had seen it in Alice's eyes, the grim resolve of a wife who's already left the marriage and was only there to wrap up the final details.

He'd need a friend tonight. She would come back later, to pick up the pieces.

She started her car and her cell phone rang. The number was unfamiliar.

So was the voice of the man who greeted her on the line. "I think you've made a big mistake, Detective," he said.

"Excuse me? Who am I speaking to?"

"Detective Potrero, San Diego PD. I just got off the phone with Detective Crowe, and I heard how it all went down there. You claim you took out Jimmy Otto."

"I didn't. My partner did."

"Yeah, well, whoever you shot, it wasn't Jimmy Otto. Because he died here twelve years ago. I ran that investigation, so I know. And I need to question the woman who killed him. Is she in custody?"

"Medea Sommer isn't going anywhere. She'll be right here in Boston, anytime you want to come out and talk to her. I can assure you, the shooting in San Diego was absolutely justified. It was self-defense. And the man she shot wasn't Jimmy Otto. It was a guy named Bradley Rose."

"No, it wasn't. Jimmy's own sister ID'd him."

"Carrie Otto lied to you. That wasn't her brother."

"We have DNA to prove it."

Jane paused. "What DNA?"

"The report wasn't included in that file we sent you, because the test was completed months after we closed our case. You see, Jimmy was a murder suspect in another jurisdiction. They contacted us because they wanted to be absolutely sure their suspect was dead. They asked Jimmy's sister to provide a DNA sample."

"Carrie's DNA?"

Potrero gave an impatient sigh, as though speaking to a moron. "Yes, Detective Rizzoli. Her DNA. They wanted to prove the dead man really was her brother. Carrie Otto mailed in a cheek swab, and we ran it against the victim's. It was a family match."

"That can't be right."

"Hey, you know what they say about DNA. It doesn't lie. According to our lab, Carrie Otto was definitely a female relative of the man we dug up from that backyard. Either Carrie had *another* brother who got killed here in San Diego, or Medea Sommer lied to you. And she didn't shoot the man she claims she shot."

"Carrie Otto didn't have another brother."

"Exactly. Ergo, Medea Sommer lied to you. So is she in custody?"

Jane didn't answer. A dozen frantic thoughts were

fluttering in her head like moths and she couldn't catch and hold a single one.

"Jesus," said Detective Potrero. "Don't tell me she's free."

"I'll call you back," said Jane, and disconnected. She sat in her car, staring out the windshield. She saw a pair of doctors walk out of the hospital, moving with princely strides, white coats flapping. Sure of themselves, that was the way they walked, like two men with no doubts while she herself was trapped in them. Jimmy Otto or Bradley Rose? Which man had Medea shot and killed in her home twelve years ago, and why would she lie about it?

Who did Frost really kill?

She thought of what she had witnessed in Maine that night. The death of Carrie Otto. The shooting of a man she'd assumed was Carrie's brother. Medea had called him *Jimmy,* and he had answered to that name. So he *must* have been Jimmy Otto, just as Medea claimed.

But the DNA was the obstacle she kept banging into, the bulletproof piece of evidence that contradicted everything. According to the DNA, it wasn't Bradley who'd died in San Diego. It was a male relative of Carrie Otto.

There was only one conclusion. *Medea lied to us*.

And if they let Medea slip free, they were going to look like total incompetents. Hell, she thought, we *are* incompetents, and the proof is in the DNA. Because, as Detective Potrero had said, DNA doesn't lie.

She punched in Crowe's number on her cell phone, and suddenly went still.

Or does it?

37

Her daughter slept. Josephine's hair would grow in again, and her bruises had already faded, but as Medea gazed down at her daughter in the soft light of the bedroom, she thought that Josephine looked as young and as vulnerable as a child. In some ways she had become a child again. She insisted that a light stay on all night in her room. She did not like to be left alone for more than a few hours. Medea knew this fear was temporary, that in time Josephine would once again find her courage. For now, the warrior woman inside her was in hibernation and healing, but she would be back. Medea knew her daughter, just as she knew herself, and inside that fragile-looking shell beat the heart of a lioness.

Medea turned to look at Nicholas Robinson, who stood watching them from the bedroom doorway. He had welcomed Josephine into his house, and Medea knew her daughter would be safe there. In the past week, she'd come to know this man and to trust him.

He was unexciting, perhaps, and a touch too exacting and cerebral, yet in so many ways he was a good match for Josephine. And he was devoted. That's all Medea asked of a man. She'd trusted few people over the years, and she saw in his eyes the same steadfast loyalty that she once saw in Gemma Hamerton's eyes. Gemma died for Josephine.

She believed that Nicholas would, too.

As she walked out of his house, she heard him close the dead bolt behind her, and she felt assured that no matter what happened to her, Josephine would be in good hands. That was the one thing she could count on, and it gave her the courage to climb into her car and drive south, toward the town of Milton.

She had rented a house there, and it stood isolated on a large and weedy lot. It was infested with mice and she heard them at night as she lay in bed, listening for sounds far more ominous than rodent invaders. She didn't relish returning there tonight, but she drove on anyway, and in her rearview mirror, she glimpsed a car's headlights tailing her.

The lights followed her all the way to Milton.

When she let herself in the front door, she smelled the old-house smells of dust and tired carpets, with maybe a few mold spores thrown in. She'd read that mold could make you sick. It could cripple your lungs, turn your immune system against you, and eventually kill you. The last tenant who'd lived here was an eighty-seven-year-old woman who'd died in this house; maybe the mold had finished her off. She felt herself inhaling lethal specks of it as she walked through the house, checking, as she always did, that the windows were closed and locked, and she found some irony in the thought that her obsession with security sealed her inside with air that could poison her.

In the kitchen, she brewed strong coffee, the real stuff. What she truly wanted was a stiff vodka and tonic, and her craving was as ferocious as a junkie's. Just a sip of alcohol would calm her nerves and dispel the sense of dread that seemed to pervade every corner of the house. But tonight was not the night for vodka, so she resisted the urge. Instead she drank the cup of coffee, just enough to sharpen her mind yet not make her jittery. She needed her nerves to be steady.

Before going to bed, she took a last peek out the front window. The street was quiet, so perhaps tonight was not the night. Perhaps she had been granted another reprieve. If so, it was only a temporary one, much like waking up every morning in a death row cell, not knowing if today was the day they would walk you to the scaffold. The uncertainty of one's appointment with doom is what can drive a condemned prisoner insane.

She headed down the hallway to her bedroom, feeling like that condemned prisoner, wondering if tonight would pass as uneventfully as had the last ten nights before. Hoping that it would, yet knowing it would only postpone the inevitable. At the end of the hall, she looked back toward the foyer, one last glance before she switched off the hallway light. As the foyer fell into shadow, she glimpsed the flicker of passing headlights through the front window. The car moved slowly, as though the driver was taking a long, close look at the house.

She knew it, then. She felt the chill, like ice crystallizing in her veins. *It will happen tonight.*

Suddenly she was shaking. She did not feel ready for this, and she was tempted to once again turn to the strategy that had kept her alive for nearly three decades: running. But she had made a promise to herself that this time she would stand and fight. This time it was not her daughter's life on the line, only hers. She was willing to gamble her own life, if it meant she'd finally be free.

She walked into the darkness of the bedroom, where the curtains were far too filmy. If she turned on the lights, her silhouette could easily be seen in the window. If she couldn't be seen, she couldn't be hunted, so she kept the room dark. There was only a flimsy button-lock on the knob, and an intruder could get past it within a minute, but that was one precious minute she might need. She locked the door and turned toward the bed.

And heard a soft exhalation from the shadows.

The sound made every hair stand up on the back of her neck. While she'd been busy locking the doors, checking every window, the invader was already waiting inside her house. Inside her bedroom.

He said, calmly: "Move away from the door."

She could barely make out his faceless form in the corner, sitting in a chair. She didn't have to see it; she knew he was holding a gun. She obeyed.

"You've made a big mistake," she said.

"You're the one who made the mistake, Medea. Twelve years ago. How did it feel to shoot a defenseless boy in the back of the head? A boy who never hurt you."

"He was in my house. He was in my daughter's bedroom."

"He didn't hurt her."

"He could have."

"Bradley wasn't violent. He was harmless."

"The company he kept wasn't harmless, and you knew it. You knew what kind of creature Jimmy was."

"Jimmy didn't kill my son. *You* did. At least Jimmy had the decency to call me the night it happened. To tell me Bradley was gone."

"You call that *decency*? Jimmy used you, Kimball."

"And I used him."

"To find my daughter?"

"No, I found your daughter. I paid Simon to hire her, to keep her where I could watch her."

"And you didn't care what Jimmy did to her?" Despite the gun pointed at her, Medea's voice rose in anger. "She's your own *granddaughter*!"

"He would have let her live. That was my agreement

with Jimmy. He was supposed to let her go after this was over. I only wanted *you* to die."

"This doesn't bring back Bradley."

"But it closes the circle. You killed my son. You have to pay for it. I'm only sorry Jimmy couldn't take care of it for me."

"The police will know it's you. You'd give up everything, just to have your revenge?"

"Yes. Because no one fucks with my family."

"Your wife's the one who'll suffer."

"My wife is dead," he said, and his words dropped like cold stones in the darkness. "Cynthia died last night. All she wanted, all she dreamed about, was seeing our son again. You stole that possibility from her. Thank God she never knew the truth. That's the one thing I could protect her from—knowing that our boy was murdered." He took a deep breath and exhaled with calm inevitability. "Now this is all that's left for me to do."

Through the darkness she saw his arm come up, and she knew that his gun was pointed at her. She knew that what happened next was always meant to happen, that it was set in motion on a night twelve years before, the night Bradley died. This gunshot tonight would be only an echo of that earlier one, an echo twelve years delayed. It was a bizarre form of justice all its own, and she understood why this was about to happen, because she was a mother, and if anyone hurt her child she, too, would demand her revenge.

She did not blame Kimball Rose for what he was about to do.

She felt strangely prepared as he pulled the trigger, and the bullet slammed into her chest.

38

This is where it could all end, I think, as I lie on the floor. My chest is on fire with pain, and I am scarcely able to breathe. All Kimball has to do is take a few steps closer to me and fire the killing shot into my head. But footsteps are pounding up the hallway, and I know he hears them, too. He is trapped in this bedroom, with the woman he has just shot. They are kicking at the door— the door I so stupidly locked, thinking it would keep me safe from an intruder. I never anticipated that it would be my rescuers I was locking out, the police who have followed me home, who have watched over me this past week, waiting for this attack. We have all made mistakes tonight, perhaps fatal mistakes. We did not expect Kimball to slip into my house while I was gone; we did not expect he would already be waiting for me in my bedroom.

But Kimball has made the biggest mistake of all.

Wood splinters and the door crashes open. The police

are like charging bulls. They rush in with shouts and pounding feet and the sharp smells of sweat and aggression. It sounds like a rampaging multitude, but then someone flicks on the light switch and I see that there are only four male detectives, their weapons all trained on Kimball.

"Drop it!" one of the detectives orders.

Kimball looks too stunned to respond. His eyes are grief-stricken hollows, his face lax with disbelief. He is a man accustomed to giving orders, not taking them, and he stands helplessly clutching his gun, as though it has grafted itself to his hand and he's unable to release it even if he wants to.

"Just set the gun down, Mr. Rose," says Jane Rizzoli. "And we can talk."

I did not see her enter. The male detectives, so much bulkier than she is, blocked my view of her. But now she steps past them into the room, a small and fearless woman who moves with formidable confidence despite the cast on her right arm. She looks in my direction, but it's only a quick glance, to confirm that my eyes are open and that I am *not* bleeding. Then she focuses again on Kimball.

"It will go easier if you just put the gun down." Detective Rizzoli says it quietly, like a mother trying to soothe an agitated child. The other detectives radiate violence and testosterone, but Rizzoli appears utterly calm, even though she is the only one not holding a weapon.

"Too many people have already died," she says. "Let's end it right here."

He shakes his head, not a gesture of resistance but of futility. "It doesn't matter now," he murmured. "Cynthia's gone. She won't have to suffer through this, too."

"You kept Bradley's death from her all these years?"

"When it happened, she was sick. So sick that I didn't think she'd survive the month. I thought, Let her die without ever hearing the news."

"But she lived."

He gave a weary laugh. "She went into remission. It was one of those unexpected miracles that lasted twelve years. So I had to keep up the lie. I had to help Jimmy cover up the truth."

"It was your wife's cheek swab they used to identify the body. Your wife's DNA, not Carrie Otto's."

"The police had to be convinced the body was Jimmy's."

"Jimmy Otto belonged in prison. You protected a murderer."

"I was protecting *Cynthia*!"

He was sparing her from the harm he believes I caused their family twelve years ago. While I refuse to feel guilty of any sin except self-preservation, I do acknowledge that Bradley's death destroyed more than one life. I see the destruction in Kimball's tormented face. It's not surprising that he wants vengeance, not surprising that he has continued to search for me these past twelve years, pursuing me as obsessively as Jimmy Otto did.

He has still not surrendered his gun despite the firing squad of detectives now facing him with their weapons aimed. What happens next cannot possibly surprise anyone in that room. I can see it in Kimball's eyes as surely as Jane Rizzoli can. The acceptance. The resignation. Without any preamble, any hesitation, he shoves the gun barrel into his own mouth and pulls the trigger.

The explosion sends a scarlet spray of blood onto the wall. His legs buckle and his body drops like a sack of stones.

It is not the first time I've seen death. I should be immune to the view by now. But as I stare at his destroyed head, at blood that seeps from his shattered skull and pools on the bedroom floor, I suddenly feel as if I am choking. I tear open my blouse and claw at the Kevlar vest that Jane Rizzoli had insisted I wear. Though the vest stopped the bullet, I still smart from the impact. The bullet will almost certainly leave a bruise. I pull off the vest and toss it aside. I don't care that the four men in the room can see my bra. I rip away the microphone and wires that are taped to my skin, a device that has saved my life tonight. Had I not been wired, had the police not been listening, they would not have heard my conversation with Kimball. They would not have known that he was already inside my house.

Outside, sirens are screaming closer.

I rebutton my blouse, rise to my feet, and try not to look at the body of Kimball Rose as I walk out of the room.

Outside, the warm night is alive with radio chatter and the flashing rack lights of police vehicles. I am clearly visible in that kaleidoscopic glare, but I do not shrink from the light. For the first time in a quarter of a century, I do not have to hide in the shadows.

"Are you okay?"

I turn and see Detective Rizzoli standing beside me. "I'm fine," I say.

"I'm sorry about what happened in there. He should never have gotten so close to you."

"But it's over now." I take a sweet breath of freedom. "That's all that matters. It's finally over."

"You still face a number of questions from the San Diego PD. About Bradley's death. About what happened that night."

"I can deal with it."

There's a pause. "Yeah, you can," she says. "I'm sure you can deal with anything." I hear a quiet note of respect in her voice, the same respect I've learned to feel toward her.

"May I leave now?" I ask.

"As long as we always know where you are."

"You know where to find me." *It will be wherever my daughter is.* I sketch a small salute of farewell in the darkness and walk to my car.

Over the years I have fantasized about this moment,

about a day when I would not have to look over my shoulder, when I can finally answer to my real name without fear of consequences. In my dreams, it is a moment of incandescent joy, when the clouds would part, the champagne would flow, and I would shout out my happiness to the sky. But this reality is not what I expected. What I feel instead of delirious, foot-stomping joy is more subdued. I feel relieved and weary and a little lost. All these years, fear has been my constant companion; now I must learn to live without it.

As I drive north, I feel the fear peel away like layers of timeworn linen that flutter away in streams and float off into the night. I let it go. I leave it all behind and drive north, toward a little house in Chelsea.

Toward my daughter.

Tess Gerritsen
reveals the haunting truth
behind why she became a crime writer.

CHINESE WHISPERS

In 1972, on the evening of October 31, a young Chinese immigrant named Janet Bokey Hee was found dead in the bathroom of the home in San Diego that she shared with her husband Wallace and her in-laws. Her head was stuffed in the lavatory bowl and her face was beaten and swollen. Savage blows had left bruises, some of them old, some of them new, on her chest, abdomen, and extremities. At autopsy, her lungs were found to be filled with fluid.

One pathologist testified that the 35-year-old victim had died of drowning from immersion in the lavatory; two other pathologists disagreed and attributed her death to trauma from multiple blows. The victim had second- and third-degree burns on her torso, most likely from scalding water. X-rays showed calcium deposits in her wrists, and she had bedsores, evidence that she had been immobilized for long periods of time. This was more than murder, the prosecutors declared.

Over a period of days, perhaps weeks, Janet Hee had been tortured.

Suspicion for the murder fell upon her husband's younger brother, Michael, who was at home when she died. But the person accused of directing the torture, of instigating the violence, was Janet's 62-year-old mother-in-law, Ida Loo Hee, the frail but iron-willed matriarch of the household. Ida was one of my mother's best friends.

In the Chinese community where I grew up the crime is a shameful secret, reflecting badly on all Chinese. We seldom discuss it with outsiders – still, we all remember it. My mother is certain that the murder happened 40 years ago on Hallowe'en, when my brother and I were still children. My uncle agreed that 40 years sounded about right, but his friend insisted that it's been closer to 50 years. One woman claimed she went to school with Janet's daughter, even though Janet had no daughters, only sons.

Everyone I've spoken to has been wrong about some aspect of the case. The murder has acquired the patina of legend, and like all legends, the facts have mutated through the years, altered by endlessly reworked gossip and by the fallibility of human memory. Only recently have I located the archived news articles about the trial, and I am stunned to discover that the decades have twisted my own recollection of the case as well. I can't trust my own memory because I've learned that memories deceive us. Details I swore were true have turned out to be false. But certain memories stand out so starkly in my mind that I think they must be true.

I remember the fragrance of orange peel and incense that perfumed the home where Janet lived with Wallace and his parents. I remember her ivory white skin and pale legs and the shapeless maternity dresses she wore over what seemed like her eternally pregnant belly. Most of all, I remember her expression, numb and life-less, as though she was already dead long before she drew her last breath. I don't recall ever hearing her speak; perhaps she did not know English. To those who saw her, she was little more than a silent wraith lurking in the shadows of Ida's home, which my family often visited.

According to the news accounts, she was born in Hong Kong and emigrated to the US with her parents when she was 13. When she was 29, a go-between introduced her to Wallace Hee, a 36-year-old medical doctor. They were married, and during the next six years, Janet fulfilled her primary duty as a Chinese wife by producing three sons. Though Wallace claimed it was a love match, their marriage could not have happened without the approval of his fiercely dominating mother Ida, who expected an obedient, hardworking daughter-in-law.

At the murder trial, the district attorney introduced a two-page typewritten document found in the Hees' home. It was a daily work schedule for Janet, listing all the household chores she was supposed to perform from 8 a.m. until 10.30 p.m. At the top was written, 'Janet, this is a tentative schedule for you to follow to care for the two boys. You should have sufficient time to do your work.' And it exhorted her, 'At all times use your ingenuity, initiative, industry, determination and brain to do the right thing.'

Janet did not meet Ida's expectations. One evening, when our family visited their home, I watched Janet listlessly rock her crying baby. One of her stockings had come loose from its garter and had slithered down to her ankle, but she did not seem to notice. She stared into space as though drugged. If she understood what was being said about her, her expression did not reveal it, although Ida's comments were loud enough for her to hear.

'Look at her. She's useless,' Ida said. 'And she's stupid, too.'

Ida had a whole litany of complaints about her daughter-in-law. Janet was sloppy. Janet couldn't keep her children neat. She was dimwitted and disorganized. She let the baby cry too long. Ida said all these cruel things in Janet's presence while the men in their family remained silent, even Wallace, who was too cowed by his mother to stand up for his own wife.

But then, we were all intimidated by Ida, who ruled over one of the most prosperous Chinese families in San Diego. Her husband Robert was a herbalist and importer. Their son Wallace was a doctor and their younger son Michael was a pharmacologist. In the 1970s San Diego had only a small Chinese population, and everyone knew Ida, who owned two mink coats and the latest model of luxury car, and who took her younger son Michael to Europe on holidays. Whatever Ida wanted, Ida got.

The murder could not have been committed without her consent. But everyone also agreed that, at 62 years old and less than seven stone, Ida was too frail to have overpowered and killed a 35-year-old woman. Someone else must have battered Janet and pushed her head into the lavatory. Someone else had shoved her face in the water. Ida may have instigated the abuse, but it took strong arms to carry out the final killing.

'Of course,' my mother says, 'it had to be Michael.'

On the day Janet died, there were three other adults in the house: Ida, her 73-year-old husband Robert, and their son Michael. Wallace Hee later testified that he was attending a medical meeting that day and did not get home until that evening. He said he found his wife slumped with her head in the toilet, and immediately tried to resuscitate her, to no avail. At 7 p.m. he called the coroner, who found the victim lying on the bathroom floor, covered with a blanket. The coroner took one look at the body and called homicide officers.

That night, both Michael and Wallace were arrested. Ida was taken into custody weeks later. All three were indicted for the murder of Janet.

'Michael was the killer,' my mother now acknowledges. But at the time it happened, she could not believe he was guilty. None of us could. Certainly I did not believe it, for one simple reason: I adored Michael Hee.

He was 35 years old, slight and bespectacled, and he lived in the apartment next door to his parents. Never married, he doted on his mother and she in turn pampered him. During the trial, lawyers suggested that the killing resulted from a failed love affair between Michael and Janet, but we scoffed at the idea. After all, Michael loved the theatre and gourmet restaurants and women's fashions. He owned a sewing machine and a flamboyant fur coat.

In those days, especially in the Chinese community, homosexuality was never discussed; we simply acknowledged the fact that Michael was 'different' in ways that endeared him to us. Whenever he turned up at our front door for a visit, the happy announcement that 'Uncle Michael's here!' would bring my brother and me running for hugs. He'd linger with us through the afternoon, giggling and gossiping over tea and cookies. He approved my haircuts and applauded the stories I wrote and helped me repair my latest disastrous sewing project.

He was the only man who truly paid attention to me, in ways that my work-obsessed father never did. Not once did I see him lose his temper. Not once did I glimpse the murderer that the news reports would later portray him as. Michael was indeed different from other men. He was kinder.

My mother remembers that on the day Janet was murdered, Michael came to our house, bringing biscuits and sweets for Hallowe'en. He showed up late in the afternoon; by then, according to the autopsy report, Janet was already dead. My mother has told this story many times over the years: that my brother Tim and I were dressed in our Hallowe'en costumes. That it was a short visit, during which Michael rambled on about a broken washing machine he'd struggled to fix. My mother, busy cooking dinner, only half-listened to him, but she recalls that he was as cheerful as always.

'You were here, remember?' she says to me. 'You and Timmy were getting ready to go out trick-or-treating. You do remember, don't you?'

She has told this story so often, in exactly the same way, that of course I remember it as she describes it: Michael in the kitchen, talking about his broken washing machine. Michael hugging us as he says goodbye. For decades, that was the way I remembered it. It became the creation myth of my crime-writing career: that I did not recognize the killer in my mother's kitchen. That I hugged a man who had just slain his sister-in-law. This, I told people, must be the reason I feel compelled to write about violent crime: I need to explain what happened that day. I want to understand how someone so charming, so seemingly harmless, could do something so terrible.

I have lived with this version of the story for so many years that it became reality; right down to the final hugs, the trick-or-treat costumes. But when I eventually went in search of the archived articles, I was stunned to see the date of Janet's death. It was indeed a Hallowe'en, as my mother has always claimed. But it did not happen in the 1960s, as she believed. It happened in 1972. That year, I was 19 years old and my brother was 15.

Both of us would have been too old to dress in Hallowe'en costumes. And in October, I would have been away at university, so I could not have been at home in San Diego the day that Michael came for his final visit. Yet I remember every detail of that visit. I believed in something that could not have happened, because my mother convinced me of the impossible.

It's not the first time she has done so.

My mother has seen dead people.

The dead were everywhere, of course, during the turbulent war years in China, when the Japanese repeatedly bombed her native province of Yunan. She saw not only the corpses, but their spirits as well, because ghosts haunted the countryside where my mother's family had fled to escape the carnage. One night she saw a man staring through the window, his white and bloodless face pressed against the glass. Her screams sent her father out into the night in search of the creature, but he found no trace, not a single footprint, even though the ground was muddy.

'It was a ghost,' my mother said.

All her immigrant friends agreed, because they too had seen ghosts. The Chinese aunties told their own ghost stories as they smoked cigarettes and played mahjong, their twanging voices shouting over the clatter of the game tiles. Once, in a lonely monastery, Auntie Jackie watched a weeping woman dressed in white vanish into a stone wall. Auntie Helen talked of the headless man who walked past her window.

They told these tales matter-of-factly, as they might describe a new living-room carpet, pausing now and then to place bets on the table or crack open roasted watermelon seeds. In their world, the dead never really leave us, but linger to gaze in at windows and walk through walls. As a child, I longed to see a ghost myself, but I never did.

'If you really want to see a ghost,' my mother said, 'you have to believe in them.'

So I did believe. In those days, I believed everything my mother said.

The years have since turned me into a sceptic. I've learnt that I cannot trust even my own memories, much less my mother's, so it's the news archives I turn to for the true details of Janet Hee's death. And the details are damning.

On the night Michael was arrested, police noticed that

he had scratches and abrasions on his hands. That same evening, he tried to confess to the murder but was quickly hushed by his mother. Criminalists testified that the lower walls of the bathroom where Janet died had been scrubbed clean, but tiny spatters of her blood were found higher on the walls – and on Michael's clothes. During the trial, all three defendants maintained their innocence, and in the tradition of a close-knit Chinese family, they stubbornly refused to testify against each other.

The trial of Michael and Wallace Hee lasted 29 days and produced 4,000 pages of testimony. The Hees hired a famous Los Angeles attorney named Grant Cooper, who was also the defence lawyer for Sirhan Sirhan, the man convicted of murdering Robert Kennedy. Despite Cooper's best efforts, both Michael and Wallace were convicted of second-degree murder and sentenced to a minimum of five years' imprisonment. Ida Hee, tried separately, was found guilty of being an accessory to murder. Because of her frailty and age, she was freed within months.

The archives don't answer the one question that has haunted me these 34 years: how could a man who was always so kind to me, a man I loved, have brutally beaten a woman to death?

If this was one of my mystery novels, I could give you a satisfying answer. I could explain why he did it and how he did it. I could tell you that Michael was born a sociopath, or that he was driven by violent sexual fantasies, or that he secretly tortured animals when he was a boy. But this is not a novel, and I don't believe that any of those things are true.

I have come to accept that, unlike in fiction, this question will never have a satisfying answer.

Michael and Wallace were eventually released from prison. Neither they nor their mother Ida ever spoke of the murder. Despite her scandalous reputation, Ida managed to ease her way back into our social circle, partly because my mother felt sorry for her. So once again Ida joined us at restaurants and at dinner parties. She even attended my wedding. Though everyone whispered about the murder, no one dared confront Ida about Janet's death. Instead, we carried on as though the incident had never happened. The Chinese community reacted as it always does when its reputation is threatened. It saved face by suppressing the secret and hiding its shame.

Ida Loo Hee died in 1989. Her son Wallace died in 1998, at the age of 67. Michael gradually retreated from all social contact, and no one I've spoken to has seen him in years.

My mother believes he is dead. Even if he is still alive, I don't have the heart to seek him out and ask him about what happened that day in October, 34 years ago.

The evidence against him speaks for itself. I know that he is guilty. I know that he beat and tortured a woman to death, a truly monstrous act. Yet to this day, I cannot bring myself to view him as a monster.

Janet's death also taught me that we can never truly know the heart of another human being – a lesson that echoes through every crime novel I have written. Decades later, her murder haunts me still.

Tess Gerritsen
2008

We believe **TESS GERRITSEN'S**

Keeping the Dead

has all the pulse-quickening

excitement and breathtaking detail

of a Kathy Reichs thriller.

If you disagree, we'll happily

refund your money.

Simply return this copy (to reach us before 01/12/09)
along with your till receipt and tell us why you didn't enjoy it.

Include your name and address and post to:

Keeping the Dead Guarantee
Marketing Department
Transworld Publishers
61-63 Uxbridge Road
London, W5 5SA

Refunds will be given to the value of the price paid as shown on the till receipt.
Offer applies to UK and Eire only. Offer ends 1st December 2009.

TESS GERRITSEN'S
UNPUTDOWNABLE FIRST CRIME NOVEL

GIRL MISSING

Assistant coroner Kat Novak knows her way around an autopsy room better than most.

But she's at a loss to explain what it means when an unknown woman is brought in dead, clutching a matchbook with a phone number in it. A few days later two more women are carried into her morgue, and Kat quickly establishes that their deaths are related.

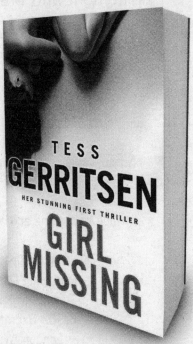

Soon she is racing to expose both a deadly conspiracy and a brutal killer who will stalk her from the dangerous streets of the inner city to the corridors of power.

Because he's closer than she ever dreamt. And every move she makes could be her last.

'You are going to be up all night' Stephen King

NOW AVAILABLE